TROUBLE'S LAST CALL

A Cassidy Adventure Novel

by
Kelly Rysten

CCB Publishing
British Columbia, Canada

Trouble's Last Call: A Cassidy Adventure Novel

Copyright ©2020 by Kelly Rysten
ISBN-13   978-1-77143-421-8
First Edition

Library and Archives Canada Cataloguing in Publication
Title: Trouble's last call : a Cassidy adventure novel / by Kelly Rysten.
Names: Rysten, Kelly, 1960-, author
Identifiers: Canadiana (print) 20200236148 | Canadiana (ebook) 20200236180 |
ISBN 9781771434218 (softcover) | ISBN 9781771434225 (PDF)
Classification: LCC PS3618.Y78 T76 2020 | DDC 813/.6—dc23

Cover artwork credit: by Kelly Rysten: www.kellyrysten.com

Author photo on back cover by Erica Stephens Photography:
https://www.ericastephensphoto.com

This is a work of fiction. Names, places, and characters are a product of the author's imagination or are used fictitiously and are not to be considered as real. Resemblance to any events or persons, living or dead, past or present, is purely coincidental.

Extreme care has been taken by the author to ensure that all information presented in this book is accurate and up to date at the time of publishing. Neither the author nor the publisher can be held responsible for any errors or omissions. Additionally, neither is any liability assumed for damages resulting from the use of the information contained herein.

Publisher: CCB Publishing
              British Columbia, Canada
              www.ccbpublishing.com

Dedicated to the memory of my father
Henry Daniel Saastamoinen
who always believed in me and encouraged me
to share Cassidy with others.

Other books by Kelly Rysten

Kelly Rysten is the author of the Cassidy Callahan Adventure Novels. Cassidy Callahan is a young woman who grew up on a quarter horse ranch. Given free run of the local hills she developed an eye for tracking, and with the help of Detective Rusty Michaels, she joined the local search and rescue team to track lost hikers. Unfortunately she is also a terrible trouble magnet, and her job brings her into contact with more trouble than the police can keep her out of. One adventure follows another as Cassidy tracks her way from one mishap to the next.

The books are:

Triple Trouble - Published 2009 – ISBN 978-1-926585-41-3

Car Trouble - Published 2010 – ISBN 978-1-926918-03-7

A Cache of Trouble - Published 2011 – ISBN 978-1-926918-87-7

A Double Dose of Trouble - Published 2012 – ISBN 978-1-77143-025-8

A Shot of Trouble - Published 2013 – ISBN 978-1-77143-107-1

Looking for Trouble - Published 2015 – ISBN 978-1-77143-249-8

Trouble in Hollywood - Published 2016 – ISBN 978-1-77143-294-8

A Little Trouble - Published 2017 – ISBN 978-1-77143-337-2

Trouble Grande - Published 2018 – ISBN 978-1-77143-366-2

Kelly is also the author of an action adventure romance novel that incorporates the hobby of geocaching. College student Gwendolyn Brody agrees to enter a geocaching contest to help her friend Tony win a trip to the Caribbean. Follow their hilarious cross country trip as they accidentally grow ever closer to each other.

Geogirl - Published 2014 – ISBN 978-1-77143-150-7

Chapter 1

Rusty's Story

Rusty here. I don't know why I feel compelled to sit here and write this. Maybe if I write it out something will jump out at me and set me on the right track. I guess putting the last few weeks into words could be a therapy of sorts. I don't know if I'll finish. Right now it serves a purpose. If it quits being a help I'll just delete it. A lot depends on what happens next. I have a man to find and when I find him one of us isn't going to make it. What he's put me through… I don't know if I can bear it. One thing for sure, though, if he takes me down, it's not going to be without a fight. I've got a lot of rage built up against this guy. It'll either be my downfall or my salvation. I won't know which until I face him. But face him I will. If I don't, I can't live with myself. I barely can anyway. One moment without Cassidy feels like an eon. I live moment to moment and each one feels emptier than the last.

Another reason I am writing about this is that Cassidy started something and she never was a quitter. If this is her last story I want it recorded.

I asked her for minutes, just minutes. If she was only destined to have minutes, I wanted those minutes with her. We could never know how many we had left. Cassidy led a somewhat uncertain life. Somehow the minutes did turn into days and then the days turned into weeks and now she had given me years. Years I treasured beyond anything I had imagined before we met. Sometimes we lived life like it was the last day we had. Sometimes, just like normal folks, life dragged us down into the mundane daily grind. The daily grind in the law enforcement business could be wretched. Some days we barely made it through. Other days, the days when we were free of trouble, were the best I'd ever had.

For the most part, life was unfair to Cass. She was such a delight, a quick wit, a dogged determination; she could have fun like nobody I ever met before. She almost drowned me the first really successful day she had surfing. There she was, treading water next to the bright yellow surfboard I'd bought her years ago. Her eyes sparkled, proud of her accomplishment, and she wrapped herself around me giving me a kiss I'll never forget, not even noticing the big wave bearing down on us. It swamped us, driving us to the ocean bottom. At first I clung to her, worried she would be swept away but we both needed our arms to swim. Even after being swamped she eventually bobbed to the surface, eyes laughing. She pulled her swimsuit back in place and called for a rest. We lay on the beach, the sun slowly drying us, talking about everything and nothing. She analyzed her foot placement on the board, which seemed to her to take forever to figure out. She was very aware of feet, being a tracker. She understood the nuances that translated into balance on the board; she just had trouble, for a long time, making them work.

I'd grown up on a surfboard. I probably couldn't surf now if I had to but at one time it was just a way to pass a summer day. I gave up surfing when I moved to the desert. The ocean was too far away and the job took too much of my time. I was a cop back then when I moved from San Diego to little Joshua Hills, California. Later I became a detective. The hours were long, the pay not great, but I didn't need a lot. I had a condo that I barely visited. It was a place to keep my clothes. A place to sleep. I ate on the job. I lived on the job. I was the job, until I met Cassidy.

Cassidy was… different. I'd never met a girl like her and it took me a long time to discover the girl she really was. She unfolded slowly, oh so slowly, like the rarest flower. When I met her she lied to me. I knew she was lying but I knew she had a reason and intuition told me she wasn't a crook.

I was following leads in a bank robbery. Typically, the first leads don't pan out. They are nervous witnesses spilling out information. Some of it conflicted with other information, but one woman swore she saw a Hispanic man with a bag of money jump into a tan Jeep. She wrote down the plate number and I looked it up, got the address of the woman who owned it and knocked on her door.

Cassidy answered my knock. At first I thought I had the wrong person. I was going to ask for the girl's mother. She looked like a kid and I mentally scratched her off my list. This kid did not drive a getaway car. This kid couldn't even drive. I was wrong. Not only could she drive, she had her situation well in hand. While she told me she had never seen Manuel Silva, she slipped me a note that told me to come back that evening. And something in her attitude told me I'd found my man. And so had she. And she had a plan. And I was to trust her. And she needed my help… And turning my back on that door was the hardest thing I'd ever done. My feet were leaden. I broke out into a cold sweat. I'd seen firsthand the things that could happen behind closed doors in the span of an afternoon. How could I leave her to face that?

I locked myself in my office and planned the evening and kicked myself black and blue. I called my dad and ranted at him. Dad would understand my dilemma. He was a cop. He was a husband, a father. And he did understand, but there was nothing he could do either. We both knew the usual procedure for a hostage situation. But it all came back to the fact that Cassidy knew the circumstances on her side of the door. Dad encouraged me to follow the plan, and keep the hostage procedure as backup.

Quietly, so as not to arouse suspicion, I lined her street with unmarked cars and hid half the force behind them. The neighbors were evacuated. An upper story room was borrowed in the house across the street in case the situation turned ugly and we needed a sniper.

I knew when I went back to Cassidy's door I needed a story. I was supposed to be a neighbor with a question that took some time to answer. She needed time to spot her chance. When she answered the door again I could tell she'd been roughed up. Her eye was blackened and she had a knot on her head. I wanted to grab her out of there, go in, and kill the guy who would do that to her. But I trusted her. I went on with my story, physically and mentally withholding my real desires. I told her I had to cook dinner for my girlfriend and I wanted to know how to make meatloaf. She laughed at me. Even in her situation and the state she was in, she laughed at me. I don't know about her but *I* like meatloaf. I liked anything that wasn't stuck through a car window. She told me meatloaf was not going to impress a girl, that I had to cook something that would be like something she'd order in a restaurant. She explained how to cook a simple chicken dish. And she watched. I couldn't see into the house. I didn't know if there was a man standing there with a gun to her head, like I suspect there had been the first time. There was a moment she knew was right, she caught my eye, indicated a blue BMW Roadster parked at the curb and suddenly we were dashing to the car. She fumbled with the keys as Silva went berserk inside her house and we laid rubber as she hit the gas. She drove to the blockade and screeched to a halt. She was shaken then, the tension of the past few days tumbling over her. I wanted to hold her, tell her everything would be okay, but I was a stranger to her. I couldn't do that. I was a detective. I belonged inside that house. I wanted to slam Manuel Silva up against a wall and… and I didn't know what. Somehow I didn't think Cassidy would want me to act on my anger. She wouldn't have. Now I know that if she had acted against Silva in anger, the guy wouldn't have lived until I came back in the evening.

Cassidy didn't believe in senseless violence. She was as good a shot as any man on the force, and she proved it a time or two, but she wouldn't act against another person unless she was forced. Even a beating wasn't enough to push Cassidy to that point. Over the years how I wished her trigger finger was just a bit freer. Some of the creeps who hurt her didn't deserve to live but somehow she saw something worth preserving and she held back.

Now I laugh when I think of our meeting. Cassidy had to hand Silva over to us not once, but twice.

I'll not relate all the stories she's already written. I didn't even know they were here until one night, determined to get some work done despite the emptiness I felt, I logged into my computer. I ran into computer trouble and decided to weed out some old, useless files. I'd written notes to myself on cases years ago. I'd saved old letters, even some I'd written to Cass but never sent, never admitted they were there. I was deleting files left and right, when I stumbled on one TripleTrouble.doc. Now what was that? I didn't remember any file by that name.

I clicked on it to read it so I could decide whether to keep it or not, and I was stunned. Cassidy had written it. A hundred and ninety pages. Ninety thousand plus words. About… us.

I couldn't read far that first time. I got a big lump in my throat and I sat there, stunned. I pushed back the tears. My girl, she'd left her life on my computer. When I looked closer there was a dozen files, some with titles and some without that detailed her major catastrophes and victories over the years, written in plain English, Cassidy style, no beating around the bush.

Every time I tried to read her files I felt like I was drowning. It took me several days to come to terms with the fact they waited there, a testimony of her life. But as I let them work on me I started wondering… I wanted to know… if I'd made a difference to her. For most of our marriage I knew she loved life. I knew she was kind hearted and gave to me everything she had. She said she loved me. She showed me she loved me. But I always had doubts. I felt selfish leading her life away from the woods she loved. I wondered if I was being fair to her. I finally came to the conclusion that, if she really loved me, the story of her life would tell me. So, finally, I began reading.

The stories started, not as I supposed they would, with her childhood and her first marriage. They started with Manuel Silva. I found out exactly what had happened. Though I wrote up the police report, brought Silva down, and she'd told me in short, shaky sentences what had happened; I'd never had it described to me. As I read I was embarrassed by the way she thought of me. I found I'd been overly cautious. Though she had needed time to come to terms with her past, she wasn't as fragile as I imagined.

I never laughed and cried so much in my life as when I read the story of her life. The times she was beaten to an all-time low, that I thought I'd lost her, she was there, some small part of her fighting for a better life. I remembered sitting by her bed in the hospital willing some strength into her. Wondering how she could hang on through all that befell her. And she was fighting, not so much to live, but to comfort me. To comfort me! To show me things would be all right again. Even in her most desperate hours.

I left the computer.

How could something that precious be taken from me? What cruel person could snuff out the lovely woman who had been my wife? The anger would burn when I thought like that and I felt drawn to the computer to find a glimpse of one of those times that made me laugh. If there was one thing Cassidy had it was a sense of humor. Situations that made me cringe and sent fear lacing through me, she managed to write about with humor, like the time she was cornered in a shack by an angry rattlesnake. She told me to shoot it, but I couldn't because she was behind the snake. She grabbed the rafter of the shack and pulled herself up out of the line of fire but the snake struck at her and latched onto her shoe. She grabbed the snake by the neck directly behind its jaws and pulled it off her shoe, then ran out of the shack and flung it out into the desert. My girl had guts. She faced what came at her. I wish I could say she always won. But now I'm afraid she hasn't.

Chapter 2

One of the hardest things I've ever done was call Cass' family. I'd had to call them before but it was when I had her with me. Things were predictable if difficult. If I knew something, anything, it would have been easier. I decided I needed to call Big Wayne Gordon directly.

"Mister Gordon? This is Rusty."

"Rusty! It's good to hear from you, boy. What can I do for you?"

"Nothing. I have news and it isn't good."

"What did that crazy daughter of mine get herself into this time?"

"Sir, I dearly wish I knew. She hasn't turned up there, has she?"

"Here? No."

"I didn't think so. If she contacts the ranch for any reason, find out where she is and call me."

"Certainly… you're not telling me everything."

"No sir, but that's because I don't know much."

"How about you tell me what you do know."

When I was done I could picture him in his big leather desk chair, arms folded, frowning all the way up to his hairline, not at me, not at Cass, but at circumstances.

"What can I do?" he asked.

"If she contacts you get as much information as you can. She has tried to call me but she only got out half a sentence before something stopped her."

"You'll let me know if you find out anything."

"Yes, sir."

"We're counting on you. I know you'll find her, because you two belong together. She's out there. You can count on that."

I sure wished I could.

The guys on the force tried the best they could to help me through this. They loved Cassidy nearly as much as I did. This guy we were looking for had no chance. Someone was going to find him. I just hoped it was me, because if someone else did we'd go by the book and I had no intention of…

I'm sorry, Babe. I know. You wouldn't think like that. But I can't help it. I hate him. I hate him and I won't quit hating him until I confront him.

The doorbell rang. I answered it, not caring who it was. As angry as I was I was ready for anything.

It was Kelly. Like many, he wouldn't accept Cassidy's loss as permanent. She had rescued him when everybody had given up on finding him. It wasn't in him to give up on her. We'd both do anything to get her back, but after a month had gone by and we were still searching, I didn't have much hope left. I'd seen too many cases. The odds were a million to one.

She'd disappeared on me before. She'd hiked miles of waterless wasteland with no water to get back to me. She'd fought back from near death, groping her way through the murky depths of a coma, so beaten she could barely move, to get back to me.

She had tried. Tried to contact me. But something stopped her. That was the one thing that gave me hope. She had tried. If she tried, and she was able, she'd still be trying.

"How are you holding up?" Kelly asked.

"I'm not. I'm just existing, wishing I didn't have to."

"Is that the life Cassidy would want for you?"

"It's the life she left me to." I guess I was a bit bitter.

"You need to do something."

"Then help me find this guy. All I know is he drove a black four-door sedan. Cass knew the guy from somewhere. No romantic connections. At least none on her side of the equation that I could tell. She could have met him anywhere. The gym, the station, the mountains, search and rescue. Some of her worst experiences were from people she barely met. Teague Stern. He offered to help her change a flat tire. She said she could do it herself. Next thing she knew the guy was stalking her. It didn't take much to get Cass in trouble."

Cassidy gave me a beautiful baby girl. Kaitlyn Elizabeth Michaels. The other light of my life. She missed Cass, too. Even after a month she crawled around the house calling for Mommy. The only reason she wasn't walking was because I was determined Cassidy would see it.

"Rusty... hello?"

"Sorry," I said, "this happens a lot."

"Come on. You can't sit here all day."

"Let me show you something I found."

I led him to the computer and opened the first file. He began reading and a big grin spread across his face.

"You're in that one," I told him. "It covers our meeting through the end of Mario Peccati. It's all there. And that's just one. She must have spent days upon days in here. Probably because I was so hardheaded, I thought I could keep her safe by keeping her home."

"Can I read it?" Kelly asked.

"You sure you want to?"

"Yeah, I can email it to myself. Do you mind?"

"You know you're likely to come up in many of the stories."

"Nobody's written a book about me before."

"A book?"

"What else do you think she had in mind? Look, each file is about the same size. About the size of a typical paperback."

"I sit down and read them. Sometimes I laugh, sometimes I cry. All Cass' memories are in here. Why would she do this?"

Kelly hit *control F* and searched the document for his name. Sure enough, there it was. He read Cassidy's version of his rescue.

"That's really how it was. I could have wrung your neck sending her out there alone."

"You should have. I thought of it like a long camping trip and maybe I'd get a friend back in the process. I never imagined she'd take on a bunch of drug dealers in the process."

"That's Cassidy for you. You should let other people read these. Let the guys at work read about themselves. It'll get you talking instead of dwelling."

"I don't know what Cass had in mind for them."

"She'd want whatever would help you. Go on. Let other people see Cassidy for who she is."

"They've heard all the stories."

"But these are from her point of view. The guys need to see that she didn't get into trouble for fun. She was a thinker. You can see the Cassidy logic in the stories. It all makes sense if you read it."

"She, umm, she really tells it like it was, though."

"What? Everything?"

"Well, no, not everything, just when it really mattered to her. When it fits in the story."

"Oh yeah? How often did it really matter to her?"

"Kel... okay, a time or two a book."

"Detailed?"

"No, well not like in porn books or anything. But... well..."

He grinned at my embarrassment.

"There's not much in the first one, since we were still getting to know each other. A couple of memorable times are a little too detailed for me to, well, to spread around the station."

"Who was it who wanted to share their honeymoon pictures with all his friends? Now you don't want a simple love scene to be read?"

I grinned, "The honeymoon pictures are in there somewhere, too. Read the last chapter or two of book eleven. That's probably the most graphic one. You'll think it's funny."

"Eleven? How many are there?"

"What can I say? Cass had a lot of adventures."

He opened book eleven did a *control end* and scanned up until he hit a chapter break. He read and burst into a fit of laughter.

"That really happened?" he asked.

"It really happened. If I hadn't looked up when I did Cass would have died that night. As it was, we did get to take that second limo ride."

"Was it good?"

"Yeah," I said with a lump in my throat. "It was the best."

"See? This is good for you. You should let other people read these. It'll bring healing."

And so, gradually, a book here and a book there, as I figured out who was in the different ones, I shared the story of Cass' life and gradually, since I had now read most of them, I could talk about them when people came up to me. And Cassidy felt a little more solid to me again. And I did know that she had loved me very much. It also caused a new determination in the force. The officers wore a hard expression, watched the streets with a keener eye. I did, too, but I didn't have much to work with.

One person surprised me, though. It was Schroeder. Schroeder thought of Cass like a daughter. Hmmm, more like a daughter he wouldn't claim as his own. No, that's not right either. She was like Dennis the Menace showing up at Mister Wilson's door. I always thought, deep down that Mister Wilson liked Dennis. I thought that Mister Wilson had a little bit of Dennis in him and could identify with the boy. So it was with Schroeder and Cass. She always seemed to bring trouble, or cookies.

Cassidy always wondered what Schroeder's first name was. When she went to his house, which we sometimes did for dinner, she would watch for mail or hints as to what his real first name was. When he read the book that mentioned that little fact he came to my office and knocked on the door. He stood there, hands in pockets, head bowed, then he walked to the chair in front of my desk and slouched into it.

"If we find Cassidy, I'll tell her my name," he said simply.

Nobody said anything else. I couldn't say thanks. I didn't know that I felt any. It was then I knew how much Schroeder cared for Cassidy. I didn't ask what his first name was. To me he was just Schroeder. We sat quietly for a long time, no work getting done. When we'd both had enough silence he quietly got up and went back to his office.

Landon Wilson had mixed feelings about reading Cassidy's story. It was no secret. If I hadn't threatened him repeatedly he would have made a move on my girl. Cassidy and Landon were frequently search partners and Cassidy had developed a deep respect for Wilson, but encouraged him to find a girlfriend. He respected her tracking ability. He'd follow her to the ends of the earth, but he only playfully flirted with her when he knew it didn't matter. On the other hand, he kept her out of a lot of trouble and he patched her up when he couldn't. I owed him a lot. I didn't push the books on him. I just let him know he had access to them if he wanted them. He was in most of them, since Cass and Landon had many, many calls together.

"I can't," he finally decided. "I've got to let her go. I can't bring her back."

"I will. I'll find her, no matter what," I said. "The books have helped. When I think there's no hope, I read about Cass' hope and I can cope again. If you change your mind let me know."

"Okay."

Her other search partner, Victor, on the other hand, got a kick out of reading the stories. He talked about them the few times we ran into each other on the job. His normal job didn't cross mine often but his search and rescue work did occasionally. Cassidy liked Victor, but she dreaded going on a call with him because he insisted she carry all the proper gear. He did things by the book and he made sure Cass was well taken care of. So I owed him a lot, too.

I heard back more often from the officers in the station. They would stop by my office when I was there and they had read something that caught their attention. It was almost like having Cass back when the officers talked about her like she was still around. Then I'd go home to my empty house and it hit hard. When it hit I knew time was running out and, I had to find that guy. I had to find Cass. I needed a lead, a clue, a hint, anything.

I replayed the times she tried to contact me. I could hear the tension in her voice. It wasn't the tension that violence caused. Cassidy had a very cool head in the face of danger. This was the voice of someone beaten down, but not ready to give up. It was the voice of hope, but not much.

"Black car," she choked out, "Four doors."

"Cass! What? Where are you? Please, babe, give me more."

There was a noise in the background and the phone was thrown against a hard object.

The next time she called was a few days later. This time there was less tension but less energy.

"Black car. White guy, thumb tack in his shoe. Knife cuts on his soles.

Russ, I need you."

"What else? Where are you?"

But there was no one there.

"I'll find you, babe," I said to the air. "If it takes my last breath, I'll find you."

Replaying the conversation helped. Every time it replayed in my mind I doubled my resolve, though I got so choked up I only got through the first part. The sound of the phone slamming against a wall would slam my brain, too. My determination felt like a lump in the pit of my stomach that wouldn't go away until I found Cassidy, or... Then I had to stop and let the determination permeate my mind. Revenge could not be my motivation, though it tried to take over. To call it revenge seemed to carry with it a negative outcome. Though my detective mind held little hope, I had to remind myself that I was not dealing with a typical case. No matter how great the danger, how beaten she was, or how little she had to work with, Cassidy refused to give up. She wouldn't give up this time either, so this was not a typical case. I repeated that over and over to myself.

Each time she called I called back, of course. We had traced the number. The owner of the phone, Derrick Bellows, cooperated but the phone had been missing for weeks. How was it staying charged if it was missing? Who ended up with it? The phone pinged off the same tower every time, but the area the cell tower covered was huge. I had knocked doors and questioned residents throughout the region. The officers had, too. Nothing.

He's got a thumbtack on the sole of his shoe and his shoes have knife cuts. That was odd. That was something to watch for, but there were fifty thousand men in this city. They all had two feet. Why would a guy have knife cuts on the soles of his shoes? Bored knife collector? Why would he cut up his shoe?

Chapter 3

With the few clues I had I made the rounds. Cassidy knew a lot of people. I went to the gym in the morning when I thought Cassidy would have gone. I talked to many of the people there. The women were more talkative, but the men knew Cass better. None of them had noticed a man with knife cuts on the soles of his shoes.

"Cassidy would be the one to notice a person's shoes. She knew the soles of everybody's shoes," said a man named Denny.

I heard that over and over. She could also identify a person by a partial silhouette or by just a glimpse of the way they walked. Cassidy was, if anything, observant. I wish other people were. I gathered more names. Who did Cassidy talk to? Who did she get along with? Who did she avoid?

One man was particularly protective. He wanted to know who I was and why I was asking questions. But when I explained that Cassidy was my wife and I was a detective he backed off quickly.

"Fred Nichols, narcotics, San Francisco, twenty six years."

A fellow detective.

"Cassidy's very well known here," he said. "You won't find a person here with a bad thing to say about Cass. She took beginners under her wing and taught them how to use the machines. She'd make them think they could succeed. Didn't matter if a person was an Olympian or a four hundred pound doughnut junkie, Cassidy knew they could do better."

"Did she have any new acquaintances?"

"Cassidy always had new acquaintances."

"Can you watch for a man for me?"

"Why sure. But I doubt you find your connection here."

"You must know Cassidy was a tracker. She noticed people's shoes, the way they walked. The only way I have to identify this guy is that he had a thumb tack stuck to the bottom of his shoe and knife cuts on the soles."

"That does indeed sound like a Cassidy description," Fred answered. "If I see a person like that, I'll give you a call."

"Thanks," I said handing him one of my cards.

At the gym I added many more names to the list. I walked the parking lot looking for a black, four-door sedan. No luck.

I used a diagram Cassidy had frequently found useful. I put the names in circles. The gym crowd I put in a circle labeled gym. I added more circles, one for each aspect of Cassidy's life. Cassidy's diagram looked very different from most I'd seen. Very few of the circles overlapped. Each group of people she knew seemed to be totally disconnected from the others. The exception was the search and rescue group who consisted of many officers, EMTs and firemen.

I attended a search and rescue meeting. Having known Lou "Strict" Strickland for many years, he welcomed me. I made the rounds, asking the same questions that I had at the gym. Many of the officers I knew from work. Many were volunteers I seldom saw. Most of them knew Cassidy. Strict allowed me to address the group.

"Does anybody know if Cassidy had any recent acquaintances?"

"We just got a fresh group of academy grads," Strict said. "But none of them fit your description."

"I have two clues to go on: a black, four-door sedan and a man who had a thumbtack in the bottom of his shoe. Cass also said the soles of his shoes have knife cuts in them. If you notice anybody, anywhere who has an affinity for knives, I'd like to talk to them."

Next I tried questioning the forest rangers. Cassidy checked in with the rangers whenever she ventured into the mountains on her own. She stopped at the ranger station and told them her plans, so I could check with them if she didn't show up at home. It was ingrained into us. An unspoken rule we'd formed over time. Tad couldn't remember anybody who drove a black four-door sedan. He admitted there had probably been a car like that up in the mountains many times in the past month but none of them were worth his notice. He could think of many people who carried knives but knives were standard camping gear. Everybody up in the mountains carried them. I talked to Paul. He got out a notebook and looked up the days prior to Cass' disappearance. Nothing stood out. She hadn't checked in for several weeks prior. If she had been in the mountains it had been on official business, with a search partner. I knew that wasn't the case.

I talked to Kelly. He was a forest ranger, too. He was clearing rocks from a piece of road that was notorious for small avalanches. Drivers would try and either weave around the rocks or straddle them. Either way, the cars sometimes lost.

"What are you doing up here?" he asked as he worked.

"Questioning people."

"Yeah?"

"I'm turning into a tracker of sorts. I'm mostly working off of Cassidy's last words. I'm looking for a guy with knife cuts and a thumbtack on the bottom of his shoe."

It sounded like a reasonable Cassidy clue to him, but he didn't know anybody who fit that description. He watched me, taking in his own clues,

clues about what shape I was in, how I was dealing with this. The answer was lousy, but while I was doing something about it I was coping. He knew that. We'd been friends for many years. I couldn't put much of anything past Kelly.

I checked out the library. Cassidy had befriended a homeless woman there and recruited her to baby sit. One more example of Cassidy seeing the good in any person.

The likelihood of finding anything out at the library was remote. Nobody at the library was going to know what the bottoms of some guy's feet looked like. Nobody in their right mind would sit around a library carving up their shoes with a knife. Of course I wasn't sure this guy was in his right mind, either. I walked the building noticing that people did tend to sit in the reading chairs with at least one foot up. I looked at feet. I watched for cut marks. I assumed the thumbtack would drive anybody nuts and they'd take it out. I questioned a few people who looked like regulars. Most didn't even know Cassidy. Nobody was helpful.

The homeless shelter seemed a little more promising. Who knew the number of misfits who had made their way through the shelter? Bertie had always insisted the homeless were simply a subgroup of society, that she met wonderful people there, temporarily fallen on bad times. As a detective, I knew people tended to make their own hard times, sometimes in ways that society didn't permit. When I visited the shelter I saw people on the fence. One hard night could make any one of them one break into an empty house to keep warm, to find food, to steal something to make a buck off of. I saw people who shouldn't be on the streets. Some I'd haul in simply for existing, like the guy who sat in a corner mumbling to himself about government corruption. Nobody at the shelter could afford a four-door sedan. If they had one they probably slept in it.

Zeke's and Trujillo's made the list. Cassidy and I were regular customers and the owners often came to our table to chat. Trujillo's was the local cop hangout and Benny Trujillo knew all of the officers on the force. If the staff at either of those restaurants thought anything would point me in the right direction they would tell me. I ate at both establishments regularly now. Sometimes it brought back too many memories and I'd take the food home in a box and eat where there were even more memories. Sometimes I drove to Kelly's house and knocked on the door, box in hand. It didn't matter what was going on. I could eat in peace there. Kelly understood. He'd do the same thing if he'd lost Rhonda and I'd let him in no questions asked, no matter what. Cass would have, too.

One thing the restaurants did. They gave me more eyes. The girls who worked there thought it was exciting to watch people's shoes for mysterious cut marks.

"If you see anybody like that, just quietly call me. I'll come. I won't cause a scene. I'll wait until he's safely out of your establishment. But I need your eyes. You see a lot of people coming through here."

At least I felt like I'd accomplished something there, even if I didn't learn anything.

I found out where Cass got her hair cut. I even reluctantly let the woman cut my hair and I questioned her while she worked. But Cassidy didn't come in often and the last time she had was over six months ago.

I went to the cop shop, the gun shops, the knife shops. I was drawing a blank.

Cass even had a few untouchable contacts. Movie stars, their bodyguards. People off on location somewhere. People too busy to talk to a detective or too hard to find.

Everywhere I went I asked for more names. The diagram quickly outgrew the papers and began to fill a small notebook.

Chapter 4

"Rusty, you've become obsessed with this. Cass wouldn't let you do this to yourself, so why are you putting yourself through it?"

I ran my hands through my hair. A classic sign I was stressed. Kelly knew it. I hated being so readable.

He continued, "It's been a long time. Do you really think she's still out there?"

"She's out there somewhere."

"Is it Cassidy you're seeking or is it revenge? Cassidy wouldn't take revenge. She would want the guy off the streets. She would want the danger to others removed. But how far are you willing to go?"

"Talk to the guys at the station. If we find this guy, he'll be shot on sight."

"Who got assigned to Cassidy's case? You need help."

"Kel, I've been questioned by so many people. Whoever asks me questions, we just hash it out. Everybody is after this guy. Every detective, every officer. We're going to find her. I search, because I have to. It's what I do and I do have help. Cassidy's writings do wonders for me."

"Do you think she wrote in the days before she went missing?"

"If she did, it's not a filename like the rest of the books."

"Maybe she took notes until a book took form."

Kelly's observation should have been one of the first things I checked, but I had been so stunned at discovering them at all I didn't think to look at smaller files. Then with a shock I realized how many oddly named files I'd been tossing out trying to clean up my hard drive. Cassidy could have written about some trouble I didn't know about and I might have deleted the file. I did stop deleting when I discovered the books, but I'd still cleaned out a lot of seemingly junk files. Could I get them back?

The first thing I did was go back to my desktop. I looked at the little trashcan icon. With a flood of relief I saw there was something in it. I right clicked on it and clicked *explore*. There were six documents in the trashcan. I knew I'd trashed more than six but six was better than nothing. I opened each one, hoping for something Cassidy had written. The first was notes about a murder in 2001. I deleted it for good. The next was an old business letter I'd written for work. Back it went, into cyber oblivion. Another useless file got sent back to the trashcan. But there was one file that, though it didn't contain any useful information, Cassidy had written. How could I get the *really trashed* ones back? Was it possible? Before I called up the cyber detectives I decided to read through each and every file in my Word document folder. I was a time consuming, tedious process. I couldn't do it while I was at work and as I spent hour after hour on the computer I could feel the trail growing cold. When I opened a file and it wasn't my writing my hopes would soar. Then I'd find out it was a recipe for pumpkin bread and they would plummet again.

Then one day I got a call on my cell phone.

"Hello?" I said. There was a day when I could count on a call from Cass. I always prayed she wasn't going on a call. It meant a day or two or three she'd be gone. I knew she was in good hands, but I worried. I would check in with Strict every night that she was gone.

"Rusty Michaels?" a man said.

"Yes, what can I do for you, sir?"

"You can meet me at the medical complex on Thurston Avenue. Now." Something in the man's tone told me I better do it. "And Michaels. If you're at work bring along a man who can take an impression."

"How will I know you?"

"I'm standing in the parking lot, waiting for you. I have an appointment in twenty minutes."

"Would you show up if you had my job and the caller wouldn't identify himself?"

"Fred Nichols. You met me at the gym."

"I'm on my way."

Fred Nichols, the detective from San Fran. I made a dash for the office, grabbed Takeo Fujioka and his gear, then ran for the Explorer.

"Rusty wait. What are we doing, man?" Takeo asked.

"I don't know. But the guy knows his job and he told me to bring you, so I'm bringing you. I only have twenty minutes."

I took the quickest route, speeding, running borderline red lights. I knew I was on the edge, just acting like this. I pulled into the parking lot and found Fred Nichols standing next to his car. He took in the rush, the air of desperation and nodded.

"It isn't much, but it could lead you someplace eventually. Look at this," he said as he bent over the island separating two parking places. A tree grew in the middle and there were shrubs on each side but the soil had been moist when one shoe landed in it. Then it had partially dried. When I looked at the track my heart stopped. "I was just getting out of my car when this track caught my eye. It might not be anything. But yet it might be, too. You see them marks? Looks like knife marks to me. An' see that dot. Could be part of the tread, but could be a thumbtack."

"I see it," I said. My throat had suddenly gone dry. I bent down to examine it closely. I wanted to know this track. I wanted it ingrained in my mind. If I ever saw another one like it I wanted it to leap out at me.

Fred walked off in the direction of the building and I ran after him and pumped his arm up and down, "Thanks," I said. "You don't know how much this means to me."

"Oh, I think I do," he said and walked away.

I went back to the track. Even I could tell it was made by a large, powerful man. The cut marks were plain as day to me. I tried to do what Cassidy would do and imagine the movements that went into marks like that. Obsessive. Compulsive. Bored. The picture in my mind didn't change much on seeing the track. I still pictured a bored individual. A knife collector. Perhaps a hacker, bent over his computer, fiddling with a knife. One shoe up, nothing better to do than carve at the shoe. His hands needed something to do while his mind was elsewhere. I tried to figure out how long the track had been there. Pinpointing the time of events was frequently crucial in my job. There were several facts that could affect the age of the track. It could have been placed recently and dried out. Studying the track, I guessed it had been made the previous day, been soaked by the sprinklers and dried overnight. The knife cuts were no longer crisp, but they were still obvious. I made a point to ask the maintenance man at the building about the sprinkler schedule and intensity of the water flow. I asked to see the tapes from security cameras, but the track was too far out into the parking lot to be considered a threat to the building's security.

Takeo waited patiently while I soaked up all the information I could. He understood what drove me. The whole station knew what drove me. Some walked a wide berth around me. Some slapped me on the back, even gave me a hug, and asked me for an update. Some joined me in the gym and worked on their frustration while I killed an unknown man at the punching bag for the hundredth time.

I stepped back and gave Takeo the go ahead. He knew what he was doing, making the mixture thin enough to flow into all the nooks and crannies, yet thick enough to dry into a durable slab. When he pulled it up, there it was, the track in relief. My first real piece of evidence.

Chapter 5

Seeing the track at the medical complex brought with it a whole new string of questions. Was he just passing through the parking lot?

No, I decided. He was walking toward the building. If he was passing through the parking lot he would have been going an entirely different direction.

Did he have special medical needs? I couldn't imagine Cassidy being taken down easily. The person who took her had tremendous strength.

I remember the call. If Schroder called, I always knew it was serious. "Michaels, you need to get out to Sunset Road. It's Cassidy."

That right there got me moving. Need, Sunset Road, Cassidy. I didn't even bother going to my car. I grabbed the nearest officer, and shoved him toward the lot.

"Michaels! Damn it, man, what's up?"

"Just head for my house," I said as I flipped on the siren. We lived on Lost Hills Road and it intersected Sunset.

Thompson floored it taking the most direct route he knew. People weren't pulling over for the siren. He didn't give them time to. He wove in and out of cars, drove on the wrong side of the street, anything to get there.

We found Cassidy's Jeep off the road. Three squad cars were already there.

"Don't cover the tracks," I warned the officers. "Where is she?" I demanded.

"We don't know. All we know is there was a call-in about an accident and we know Cassidy's Jeep." Mike Townsend said.

"If it was an accident, where's the other car. Where's the damage?"

I heard soft voices behind me.

"How'd she get out without undoing her seatbelt?"

How indeed.

Cassidy must have been rubbing off on me. I looked to the tracks outside her Jeep. They were a confusion of tense scrambling around. A large man. Footprints bit deep, slid. Boot tracks. Clumsy. I had to think. What would Cassidy notice? Pointed toe. Rounded heal. So they weren't cowboy boots. Cowboy boots had a narrower heal. Not work boots. Not enough tread. Not biker boots. Biker boots were rarely pointed. Those boots had moved around a lot of loose sand. When I saw the tracks, for once I could see the urgency in them. Cassidy had told me that tracks reflect feelings. I'd never seen it until that day. Maybe I was reading into them my own sense of urgency. I looked frantically for Cassidy's tracks, but I only saw one. One. How could there just be one?

Takeo had taken impressions from that scene, too. The Jeep had been fingerprinted. The prints hadn't matched anybody on file.

"Tom? We need to look at the track impressions from the scene."

"Okay. Why?"

"I just need to see them. I've got something to add."

"Michaels, leave it alone. You're going to drive yourself crazy if you pursue it."

"I'll drive myself crazy if I *don't* pursue it. I'm looking for one thing. That's all."

When we went through them I felt a stab again as I saw the smooth, clean line of Cassidy's moccasin in with the other prints. One thing leaped out at me on seeing her track.

"This wasn't made while she was standing," I told Tom.

"How can you tell?"

"She's my wife. This shows mostly the side of her foot. Cassidy wouldn't have stood like that. She was very much aware of what her feet were saying. Walking, standing, it didn't matter. She would not have left this track if she was on her feet."

I examined the impressions one by one and I felt a flash of anger. I went through the same thought processes I had at the scene of the abduction but I had a different reason this time.

"This is the guy you're after," I told Tom. "But look at this other one I found."

I looked up the number and the new track was set on the table with the others. Tom looked up, surprised.

"Where'd this come from?" he asked.

"The medical center on Thurston."

"When?"

"Yesterday."

"How?"

"A handy tip."

"Why wasn't I told?"

"You don't have the same connections. And I *am* telling you."

I compared the two again. Probably the same size, though the differences between the boot track and the sneaker track were hard to be sure.

"This," I said as I tapped the sneaker track, "is what Cassidy told me to look for."

"So I see."

"I walked the medical center. Talked to people. I'll go back again. There's a link there somehow."

This added a whole new page to my diagram. I made a circle for each office. It was a big building. Four stories. Probably a hundred different doctors in there. It would take ages. I scrapped the first diagram. I went to the lobby of the building and looked at the names and I grouped the doctors by their types of practice. I ruled out a lot of doctors just from my profiling of the suspect. I was left with about twenty. One by one I questioned the doctors, who were very reluctant to help. Of course, they didn't want to condemn an innocent person. I didn't blame them at all. It went like this:

"I'm detective Rusty Michaels. Do you mind if I ask you a few questions?"

"Not right now. I've got patients waiting."

"When will you have more time?"

"Stop back at eight o'clock. You can catch me between office visits and hospital rounds."

"Do you have any patients that you know are powerfully built, have large feet, an interest in knives, and who have a peculiar habit of constantly doing things with their hands?"

They all admitted to having large, powerfully built patients with large feet. And they would admit they had patients with nervous habits. But they couldn't think of anybody who matched most of those traits who would kidnap somebody. They would admit they had patients capable of it. They would admit they had patients who had records, but they were people that didn't match the description. I felt like I was being led on a wild goose chase, but I was used to that. It was just part of the job.

Every evening I would weed out more documents on my computer. I quit deleting them. I didn't know how computers worked but I imagined all the deleted files marching off the edge of some cyber disc world. And when I deleted another one it got in line, knocking the one on the outer edge off into some black hole of nothingness, from whence it truly could not be retrieved. The files that were there, I wanted to preserve.

"You're not really dissecting every document on your computer for clues about Cass, are you?" Kelly asked.

"When I'm home. It's better than pacing the house. Do you have a better way?"

"Yeah. I thought you knew."

"Knew what?"

"You can do a search of your whole system for key phrases. It'll search all your documents in a matter of minutes. What are you looking for?"

"Mention of a black four-door, a person who plays with knives, I don't have a whole lot to go on."

He showed me how to do a search. I was watching carefully in case I needed this feature for something I discovered later on. We tried a search for *black four-door*.

"Make sure you have it search for the phrase, not the words. I'm sure most of her books have the word black or four or door in them. We need to search for those three words, in that order."

A few clicks and the computer started looking.

"Is it getting any easier?" he asked.

"No, it's getting harder. Every day I think she might be coming home. But she doesn't."

The computer drew a blank on the black four-door.

"How do we word the other search? We can't search for knife. Cass always had a knife on her," I said. "The way Cassidy phrased it was: he had knife cuts on the soles of his shoes."

"This guy sounds like he needs help."

I started typing in a phrase but there were so many ways to order the words.

"Wait," I said. "Let's try thumbtack. He had a thumbtack in his shoe, too."

Thumbtack was much easier so we tried that and came up with one file but it was an early one, and the man wasn't mentioned because Cassidy hadn't met him yet. That document got me to reading the book, though. I read several pages before we went on to search the computer for knife cuts again. Kelly waited patiently, hoping as much as I did that some small clue would be there.

"Sorry, buddy," he said when it was all over. "If the computer didn't find it, it's just not there."

"I have one more option, and it's a slim one. I can take my hard drive in to the station. Maybe they can get back the files I deleted. It might be in there."

I was grateful to Kelly for showing me that process. I may have finished dissecting my system for clues, but now, if I wanted to go back to that sunny day in San Diego I could think of a key phrase and find the document, then find the scene. I walked in Cassidy's shoes on searches. I watched her try to stand on a surfboard for the first time again. I looked up skinny-dipping. I saw her again the way she had been; twenty-five, full of life, scared to death my parents were going to catch us. Oh Cass, we could do it again if you were just here.

Chapter 6

I was at work one day, actually working on real work for a change when there was a knock on my office door. I opened it and in walked an old friend. Farley McGyver.

"I need your help," he said.

"What's the problem?"

"You need help, too. Maybe we can help each other."

"If it's help with the school, the answer is no. I don't know the first thing about horses."

Farley ran a therapeutic riding school for kids. Cassidy had taught many kids at Farley's school. Most of Farley's students were handicapped in some way; they needed an activity that they could succeed in. Any kid could sit a horse and be led in a circle. Some kids that's all they needed. Some kids learned and progressed to competition.

"You spent years with Cassidy. You know more than you think. Just sitting next to her you soaked up a feel for horses. Besides, it's not the horses I need help with. I need a big, strapping guy to help me with a student."

"No. I can't face the horses without memories."

"And what's wrong with memories. You've got them anyway. They aren't going to go away. Some of your fondest memories are of Cassidy and horses. At least you'll be thinking good memories. You can turn me down. But can you turn down Brian?"

"Yes."

"How?"

"Like this. No."

"Fine. I'll turn him away."

"You've got volunteers who are good with the kids. They all know the horses."

"Bailee suggested you. The teachers I have can't work with this guy. He's too big. He's got the mentality of a five year old. He loves the horses but he has little patience. When he loses patience he needs someone who can restrain him until he calms down. Once he calms down he's fine again. He forgets what made him mad, just like a little kid. We think, if he works with the horses he will stabilize and be more even tempered. If we can teach him to focus and think instead of lashing out he'll make a good rider. He just needs a firm hand. Half an hour a week, that's all I'm asking for."

Just like Cassidy, when she got roped into doing something she didn't like, I thought, oh hell.

I didn't answer Farley right away. I went home, got on my computer and searched Cassidy's life for Farley McGyver. I read until I realized I'd read right through dinner. Katie sat on my lap, but when she tried to type on the keyboard Bertie took her away. What I found out was that I owed Farley, big time.

"What time?" I asked Farley the next day.

"I know you got a job. I'll not take you from it. Name a day. Brian thinks better while he's fresh. As he tires he gets short tempered. So mornings would be better."

"I have a kidnapper to track down, too."

He didn't respond to that. I think he disapproved of it but he knew how I felt. Cassidy had been taken from him, too.

"Choose a day," Farley said. "I'll see if Brian can make it. I suspect any morning is fine. He's a full time job for his mother. She'll work with us."

"Saturday? You're sure. I don't have to know horses."

"You'll have everything down pat the first day."

Oh hell.

It wasn't so much that I didn't want to do it. I loved kids. I was just not ready to put my sorrow aside and I knew I'd have to do that for a half hour a week. I refused to burden Brian with my worries.

Tom called me with an update but it didn't amount to much. They had been patrolling the medical complex, watching for black four-door sedans. They had found a few, questioned the owners. Other black four-doors had been pulled over, the owners never coming close to the right description.

"Do you even think the guy's in town any more? He could have skipped town long ago," Tom asked.

"When you give up, let me know. I won't. I have to find this guy. I'll spend the rest of my life at it if I have to. It'll give me something to do in retirement."

My cell phone rang. Like usual, I snatched it up hoping it was Cassidy.

"Hey, big bro. I'll be in town for a week. Do have room for me?"

"Of course, you know you're always welcome. But there's something you should know."

I guess I must have sounded pretty depressed. The line went silent.

"Cassidy's been missing for a month. We don't have much to go on. While you're here, can you help me with something? I need to take my hard drive out of my computer and take it to the station."

"Sure, backup all your files and I'll take it out."

"What do I use to back them up?"

"What have you got?"

"What do I need?"

"Do you have a flash drive? How much do you want to backup?"

"My Word documents."

"That can't be all."

"I need to read my Word documents. That's all I care about right now."

"Why are you taking your hard drive out?"

"I need to retrieve some deleted files. They can do it at the station. It applies to Cass' case so they'll do it. If I find anything I'll share the information with Tom. He's on the case."

"Go get a large flash drive. I'll backup what I can on that."

"Thanks."

When I met Brian Lamb I could see why Farley needed help, and why Brian would benefit from the school. Thirty-one going on five, that was Brian. He was six feet tall, two hundred pounds. He wasn't strong but his size and his inability to control his reactions made him a danger to the mostly female staff at the ranch. He wore a new western shirt and new blue jeans. He probably would have had a cowboy hat, too, but I doubted he could find one that fit. He was closely shaven and his hair was cut in a flat top. His mom took good care of him.

"Brian, this is Rusty Michaels," Farley said. "He's going to be your new teacher. He's going to teach you how to ride a horse. You must listen to him very carefully and do what he says."

"Missur Michaels," Brian said as he extended a meaty hand. His handshake was soft.

"It's good to meet you Brian. Have you ridden before?"

"Ony once. Missur McGyver let me ride once, then I wait for teesher. You good teesher?"

"I hope so. We'll see."

"Missur McGyver say I need big horse!" he said proudly.

"Let's go find you a big horse," Farley said.

Fortunately the biggest horse was also the most gentle. His name was Elmo and he was a rich red color.

I found out I did know more about horses than I thought. I knew the steps to saddling and bridling a horse. I just did it automatically, if tentatively. I'd watched Cassidy do it many, many times, and helped her with it when she was injured. Working with a living, thinking animal felt strange to me, but I followed what I had seen Cassidy do and Elmo was a gentle giant. I even remembered to stick a couple of fingers under the girth to make sure it was not too loose, not too tight.

"Next time, Brian, you're going to saddle your own horse," Farley said.

Brian had a faraway sad look to his eyes, like he was not all there, until he got into the saddle. Then his eyes crinkled and he danced in the saddle.

"Ooh yeah, ooh yeah, I ride! I ride!" he sang. We did a lot of walking around in a circle that first day. As Brian passed the fence where Farley supervised from he called out comments to Farley.

"My mama get me new boots!" he said proudly on one pass. On another he said, "She say I be real cowboy!" He bounced in the saddle accidentally hitting Elmo's sides with his newly booted feet and the horse lurched into a trot. Brian bounced in the saddle.

"Pull on the reins to slow down," I called up to him.

"Aw, no, me go faster!" He kicked the horse again and Elmo bunched his legs ready to canter.

"No! Brian, you're not ready to do fast yet. First we have to go slow."

"Me go fast! Me go fast!" he cried.

"Not yet. You have things you have to learn before you can go fast. Let's work on those."

I had learned the basic commands for horseback riding by watching Cassidy on trail rides. I thought it would be simple to teach Brian how to direct a horse forward, left and right, but I found out Brian didn't know his left hand from his right hand. How was I going to get around that? I decided repetition was the key so we walked up and down the corral with me calling out, "right turn, left turn, left turn, right turn, stop, go..." and guiding Elmo myself from below. I don't know if he picked it up or not. He had only ridden for about twenty minutes when Farley stepped into the corral and led Elmo to the gate.

"No! Me ride!" yelled Brian, "Me ride more!"

Farley remained calm. "When you aren't used to riding you need to start slow. If you ride too long you'll be sore. We don't want that. We have things to learn in the barn. If you're going to ride, you need to learn to take care of a horse, too."

Brian climbed from the saddle and dropped to the ground. He nearly fell over. It was a long ways down. He stood, defiantly facing Farley, and stomped his foot.

"Me ride more!"

He stepped toward Farley, fist raised, and I stayed his hand.

"Brian, if you want to ride, you have to listen to Mister McGyver."

He turned to the fence ready to take out his wrath on the fence post but I didn't release his hand. He stood there glaring, anger in his eyes.

"I'll let you do the saddle," I offered. "If you do a good job I'll let you saddle Elmo up next time."

He calmed at the idea that he got to do something. It didn't matter that he was going to do it anyway. If he got to do it, it was better than if he had to do it. I'd have to remember that.

Farley turned to me as Brian and his mother pulled out of the ranch in an old white station wagon and headed for home.

"Now you see why I need you?"

"Would he really have struck you?"

"I don't know. Thanks for stopping him."

"Do you think he got anything out of it?"

"We don't measure learning by the lesson. We just learn here. Does it matter *what* he learned? Did he learn his left from his right? I don't know. Did he learn he has to go slow? I don't know. Did he learn he's going to be a cowboy some day? I don't know. Did he learn we won't take no nonsense from him? Probably. Will he try it again? Most likely. Will we keep on keeping on? Yes."

"Well, I learned something," I said and Farley just nodded his approval of that, too.

On the way home I bought the biggest flash drive I saw on the shelves. I wasn't sure how big big was, but I bought the one with the biggest number on it.

Chapter 7

The next day I was driving by the medical complex and I noticed an odd number of black cars. I pulled in and cruised the parking lot. A woman came out and got into one of the black cars. I parked and went inside. I walked the building, looking at shoes. The patients grew uneasy. I knew I was tense but I didn't know it showed. I was always tense these days. As I was walking around a waiting room I heard a noise. A typical office building noise but distinctive to me. *Step, click, step, click*, like a person would sound if they had a thumbtack in one shoe. I dashed out into the hall but the noise stopped. The hall had several people in it. Moms with kids. An elderly couple. A nurse. Then the noise started up again. My eyes were drawn to a small man at the drinking fountain. The clicking noise was caused by a rattle in his walker.

I went out front and watched people coming and going. Watched for big men. Watched their shoes.

I drove to the knife shop, knowing I should be at work. My profiling of the man had led me to believe he would be going for the odd shaped knives. Knives with fancy blades and carved handles. I looked over the wares.

"Sold any of these lately?" I asked.

"A few. Lots of people look. Not many buy. They might look pretty but they aren't practical."

"I know what you mean. My wife is a tracker. She camps. She gets along in the outdoors. She's carried the same knife since she was twelve years old. It saved her life a time or two." It bothered me to talk about Cassidy in the present tense but it hurt worse to talk about her in past tense.

"If you're looking for a gift. Those aren't what she'd be interested in."

"Oh, I know. It's not a gift. In fact, I'm looking for the man who took her. She's been missing a month. All I know is whoever took her had knife cuts on his shoes. Doesn't sound like an outdoorsman. Sounds like a bored collector."

"Your wife ran out on you?"

"No. She was taken by force. I know. I saw the scene. Can you watch for a man for me? Big guy. Powerful. Powerful enough to pull an adult out of a car without undoing the seatbelt. Likes knives. Has a nervous habit of carving on his shoes with a knife. Watch people's shoes. Anybody match that description, give me a call." I handed him my card. He probably wouldn't have agreed to it but he saw I was a cop and he nodded assent. "If he also drove a black four-door that would help identify him, too."

I went back to the gym and checked in with Fred. Fred seemed to know everybody. If there was any news, any speculation about Cassidy, Fred would catch it.

When Cody came to town he brought reinforcements. In some ways I was thankful. In other ways it was a burden. I wanted to wallow in my sorrow. I needed time to think, puzzle out what had happened. I didn't need my parents and Chase involved. I had called my parents and bounced some ideas off Chase. Track impressions had been taken at the scene, but nothing else had surfaced since then.

My dad might help. He had been a cop. He had a cop mind.

Mom would take care of Katie.

Cody would help with the computer but he had business in town. A job interview or something.

Chase would be a help if we had to do any tracking.

"Take me to the scene," Chase said.

"There's nothing left. It's been a month."

"That's okay, take me there."

I drove him down there anyway.

"I've been back. There's nothing to see."

"That's what you think."

All that was left was a few very faint car tire prints. Another car had used the pullout but Chase was used to dealing with layers of tracks. It wasn't a high traffic road.

"Think back," he told me. "If the Jeep was parked here, what's this?"

"Squad car. There were four of them once I got here."

"Point out the others."

So I did. The scene was branded into my brain. So was the fact that Cassidy was nowhere to be seen.

"So these are the tracks are from the suspect's car," he said pointing. "And it was gone when the guys arrived."

"Right."

"Signs of force?"

"Yeah...Chase...whoever the guy was just walked up to the Jeep and pulled her out bodily. The seatbelt was still fastened. You know what that would do to a person."

"Any sign of a fight?"

"No. I think that scares me more than anything. That and the time that has gone by."

Chase was measuring tire tread.

"Okay, good," he said as he stood up.

"What's so good about it?"

"The Jeep has wide tires. We knew that. If there is one thing we know about Cassidy, she knew how to outfit a Jeep. The patrol cars all have the same tires. The odd car out has narrower tires. Your team took tire impressions?"

"Tom's team. Yeah."

"We don't need them for this. You know what kind of car it is?"

"No, black four-door. That's all I know."

He stopped. "I thought you said the car was gone when you got here."

"It was. Cass tried to call me twice. First time all she got out was 'black four-door'. Second time she said to look for a big white guy, with knife cuts and a thumbtack on the soles of his shoes. That's all my clues. All I've had to think about for a month."

Chase grinned, "I knew she'd find a way. She hasn't called again?"

"No, when she called I begged her to give me more information but she only had the phone for a second."

"I'm going to read this to you. There's not much but we may be able to pull something out of it. Cassidy was driving home. Do you agree?"

"Yes... but..."

"Hold on. I'm not finished. The black car headed her off. Look. It came around the side of her and just about blocked her in. Now the passenger door is facing the Jeep. I wonder why they didn't pull in all the way and prevent any further movement."

"Cassidy could have just thrown it in reverse to get away."

He scratched his chin, thinking.

I let him ramble on. He might put things together that I hadn't thought about. Then he went on about the angles of the tire tracks.

"If we follow this curve around...." He stood in the street pointing out the direction the car had to have come from. I was glad we lived on a rural road without much traffic I was particularly glad when his observations continued. "We see the black car fell off the other side of the road, to make the arc come out right."

He crossed the road and there it was. He measured it to be sure.

"Walk that side of the road," he instructed. "I'll walk this side. Point out any place a wheel came off the pavement."

I didn't see much point in his little exercise but I was willing to try anything. When I found a wheel off I called Chase over. He measured it but it was so brief.

"Hmm, can't be sure," he said, "but a good catch. Keep going."

Next it was Chase's turn to find a wheel off, then mine, then Chase.

Chase was jazzed, well, for Chase. "Whoever it is can't drive. They are either on something or don't have a license."

My cell phone rang and my heart jumped. Since talking about Cass' calls it revived the hope that it could be her. It wasn't. It was Cody.

"Word documents? That's what you're worried about?"

"Yeah…if you take out the hard drive I won't be able to access the files, will I?"

"They'll still be on the flash drive."

"So I can still read them?"

"Yeah."

"Okay, do it. As long as I can read them. I don't know what I need worse, those deleted files or the ones I've nearly memorized. The ones I know keep me going. But it's the deleted ones that might have clues."

"Gotcha. You can take it to the station in a few hours."

"Thanks."

"No problem."

Chase and I followed the tracks as the car weaved back and forth, and cut corners too close. We followed it until there were paved shoulders, but it pointed us in a direction and it certainly told us a little more about the driver. If the guy was on something, that scared me. Who knew what someone on drugs might do to her. What did it mean if they simply couldn't drive? I wasn't sure if I had more answers or more questions. In this line of work it was hard to tell the difference. They worked on each other, questions providing answers and answers providing questions. I might not know the answers right now but I had more facts rattling around in my brain. I just wished they would rattle faster. Too much time had gone by already.

Chapter 8

Brian came to the school again in new cowboy clothes and his new boots. They weren't cowboy boots but he thought they were. They had big, wide heels because he needed the stability. His balance wasn't the greatest.

This time I held back and let Brian do the saddling, teaching him how to adjust everything.

"We're going to take it slow," I warned him ahead of time. "If you learn how to steer correctly, we'll think about trotting. First you have to prove to me that you know how to steer. Remember, last time we learned left and right. Show me your right hand."

He showed me the left.

"Remember the right hand is the one you shake hands with. If you were going to shake my hand, which hand would you give me?"

He knew that one. He liked to shake hands.

"Okay! Good! That's your right hand. So which one is your left hand?"

He showed me the other one.

"Good!"

"Now we go fast?" he asked.

"No, now you show Elmo you know which way is right and which way is left."

It was a very frustrating day. He'd forget and I'd guard my patience.

"Missur Michaels, I never get it."

"It's okay, it just takes practice. You can't expect to be a cowboy the first day. Everybody starts out slow. I certainly did." I avoided getting on a horse at all costs. The only time I got on one willingly was when it meant a chance to spend time with Cass.

"Missur Michaels? Why you sad?"

"I'm not sad, Brian."

"Yes you are. I made you sad. You think I never learn."

"No, that's not it. I just miss somebody very, very much. I think you're doing great. You'll learn the steering. We just need to go through it one more time."

"Sometimes I sad, too. I sad because my pet die."

"What kind of a pet was it?"

"A small, small pet, a mouse. I try to pet it and it try to get away an' I squeezed him. I didn't know. I didn't know it would hurt him."

"I'm sorry your pet died, Brian. Maybe you need a bigger, sturdier pet. Maybe a dog."

"I got new pet. Still miss small one."

We needed to get back to work and I really needed to lighten the conversation, so I said, "Are you ready? Remember how to tell Elmo to go? One, two, three, go."

He kicked Elmo's sides and the horse sedately ambled along.

"Okay! Right! Turn right! With your hand shake hand! Right!" He extended his hand like a handshake, which was the wrong thing to do. "Pull to the side with your hand shake hand."

"I never do right!" he exploded. "I never do right! First you say right hand, then you say shake hand. So I shake and it's wrong. I never, never!" He slipped off Elmo and threw himself into the dusty corral. He pounded the ground with his fists. Elmo skittered away as the violence of the man/boy was unleashed. I knelt beside him and prevented him from hurting himself on the rocks until the outburst passed. When his frustration was spent he propped himself up on his elbows in the dusty corral.

"Elmo won't do what you say if he's scared of you," I said gently but firmly. "Horses only work with you if they like you. You have to be Elmo's friend or he won't trust you. Look at him. You scared him. Now let's go make friends with your horse again." I wasn't sure where that philosophy came from. It felt like it came from somewhere outside me. It felt like something Cassidy would say.

I knew Elmo was trained to stay close by, but I didn't tell Brian that.

"Come on," I said to Brian, offering him a hand up. "Let's go talk to Elmo."

We approached Elmo with an air of apology. I didn't know if that was the right thing to do as far as horse training went but it felt like the right thing to do for Brian. Elmo wasn't a toy. Elmo was a friend to be treated with respect.

Brian had taken me seriously but I also found out he had other things on his mind. "I'm sorry, Elmo. Don't get sick. Please, don't get sick. My pets is always getting sick. You okay, Elmo."

I wasn't sure what was going on in his head. I didn't know how to deal with it.

"What kind of pet do you have?" I asked.

"Name is Rose. She sick."

"Have your mom call a vet. A vet will make her better."

"Mom doesn' know about Rose. She send her away."

A stray he'd taken in? I figured even half a home was better than no home for a dog so I let it pass.

We didn't get much accomplished at that lesson, but Farley disagreed.

"It's not always riding they're learning. It's life. It all gets translated to life. I see Cassidy has rubbed off on you more than you think. You're not the same man I knew before you met her. You've changed, I think for the better. I haven't known her as long, but I bet she's changed for the better, too."

As I was pulling away from the school with a heavy heart my cell phone rang.

"Hello?" I said.

"Rusty? This is Juana at Trujillo's. I got a customer in here who is really strange. He plays with these sharp star shaped thingies and he's dressed all in black. He gives me the creeps."

A lead? Maybe?

"How long has he been there?"

"Maybe half an hour."

"Keep him there!" I said urgently, "Fake a mistake on his check, anything. I'm on my way."

"Anything?"

"Short of a date. Don't encourage him. Just stall."

I was thankful the call came after Brian's lesson. I wasn't sure what I'd do if it had come during.

I cursed the distance between Farley's school and Trujillo's in town. Why did ranches always have to be so far away from anything useful?

When I got to Trujillo's I drove around the parking lot looking for a black car. Not a one. I entered the restaurant and sat at the bar and watched the crowd.

Benny was bartending.

"Rusty, you're here early. What'll it be?"

"O'Doul's in a glass," I said.

Juana came and sat next to me.

"He's at the end of the table across the room. Look at him. Doesn't he look creepy to you?"

Benny looked over at the table in question.

"He looks different," I said, "but he's trying to. The really creepy ones you'd never guess at. Thanks for the tip."

"Do I get one, too?"

I looked in my wallet. If I paid for my drink I'd have five left. Shoot.

"Here, it's all I got. If I had more it'd be more. Keep that in mind."

After watching the group, I knew none of them were my man. The guy in question was barely bigger than Cassidy. There was no way he could have pulled Cass out of her Jeep. She'd have cleaned his clock. But I still might get some useful information out of him. When the group left I paid for my half a drink and followed them out. I tapped the star guy on the shoulder. He didn't like what he saw.

"It's okay," I said. "I just have a question or two. I have a kid who likes stuff like that. Where do you buy clothes like that?"

"Unh, umm, I don't know. At the mall. My girlfriend likes to hang out there."

"They got the chains and everything? What about the stars?"

He pulled four star shaped throwing knives out of his pocket and shuffled them one handed.

"I got them out of a catalog. I don't remember which. I get lots."

"Knife shops don't have them? Are they legal?"

"I don't know if they're legal. That's why I get them from a catalog. They'll sell them to anybody."

"What do you do with them?"

"Me? I throw 'em. At trees and stuff."

"Do you have friends into stuff like that?"

"Umm, sure, they're just something cool to have. It's something to play with when we don't have nothing better to do. You don't look like you got a kid like me."

"I bet your parents don't look like you either."

He shrugged. "There's lots of places you can get throwing stars. Just look on the internet."

"Thanks, maybe I will. Say, you don't get marked as a gang member if you have those do you?"

"Nah, all the kids got them."

"Thanks."

Okay, so maybe I won't learn much. I went home wishing I could be alone, knowing I wouldn't be. Wishing I'd come home and Cass would be crawling on the floor with Katie. I found I was losing hope. I knew Cass wouldn't be home.

That started the old argument. The one I had nearly every day. Cassidy deserves better than that! I scolded myself. But my detective mind and my experience told me every day that passed the chances were slimmer. If I had to face a family with an update, tell them the likelihood of getting their loved one back, I'd say there was no way. Only by some miracle. Only by some freak quirk that made circumstances different from the norm, would they ever see their loved one again. Then I reminded myself that if there was one thing Cass had going for her it was quirks.

"Rusty, you look all wrung out. It's the weekend. Can't you find a moment to relax on a weekend?"

"Sorry, Mom, I've taken on a student at McGyver's school and he threw me for a loop today. Then I got a tip that could have led to Cassidy but it turned out to be a dud. If Cody finished with my computer I need to take the hard drive to the station."

"He's back there now."

I went back to my office wondering where all these people would sleep. Mom and Dad should have the guest room. Chase would sling his hammock in the gazebo. Cody could tough it out on the couch. Or maybe I'd take the couch. I could feel Cassidy better there. That was our spot, when things got rough, when we needed to catch up on minutes we did it there.

"How's it going?" I asked as I entered my office.

"Well, I got your Word Documents and Word, I'm picking and choosing what you might need."

"I don't care. Long as I have those documents."

"What's so important about that one folder?"

"One time Mom suggested to Cassidy that she write about her adventures. After she went missing I discovered she'd actually done it. They're all there. I need those files. They're like a lifeline for me."

"She did?" Mom said from the doorway.

"Yeah she did," I said and it was all too much. I needed to be alone. My mind was crowded enough without family about. I went into the bedroom and closed the door. I lay on the bed and tried to reach out, to feel Cass somewhere out there. Please, babe, if you can feel me, too, do something.

Nothing.

Chapter 9

When the emotion of the moment had calmed I found Cody, still picking and choosing.

"Forget it. Whatever you've got is fine. I need that hard drive."

"Are you sure? You could lose a lot of programs if they slip up."

"The flash drive files are safe, though, right?"

"Long as you don't break the storage device."

"Okay, remove it. Let's go."

He didn't think it was wise but I wasn't really running off wisdom at the time. I could hear Cass' clock ticking. Every tick made the chances of getting her back slimmer.

When I held the hard drive in my hand it felt like the heart of the computer. And it might just restore mine. I felt foolish pinning my hopes on a chunk of machinery, but then I thought of every officer on the force who counted on a chunk of machinery to carry them through the day.

I picked up Katie as I went by and grabbed the diaper bag.

"You're taking her along?"

"Yeah, the guys at the station can use a break. They haven't seen her in weeks."

Dad and Chase caught up with us before we could get to the Explorer. They had friends at the station so they came, too. Mom was left at home alone.

"I'll cook dinner," she called out forlornly.

"We won't be long," I called back.

"Yeah right, your father will start talking to Schroeder and you'll have to drag him out of there by the ear."

First we dropped off the hard drive.

"We need to know what we're looking for," Trey Morgan said. "Make a list of key phrases."

I sat down and wrote out the obvious ones: black four-door, sedan, thumbtack, cuts on the soles of shoes, anything created between March 1st and April 15th. I'd rather get more information back than I needed. I doubted I'd deleted more than thirty or forty files.

"That's all?"

"Yeah, will the information on it be preserved?"

"No guarantees but we always try."

"Good enough for me."

"You made backups, right?"

"Of course," I semi-lied.

Next was Tom's office.

"I don't know how interesting you will find this," I told him, "but Chase and I followed the path of the car that took Cassidy."

"What? How could you do that? The roads out there are all paved."

"Apparently our kidnapper is either a drug user or can't drive worth shit. They were weaving all over the place."

"Really. Hmm."

We went to a meeting room that had a big area map on the wall. I traced the path the car had taken.

"So, they didn't come from town and when they took her they didn't take her to town either," Tom observed.

I looked at the path. Whoa. He was right. You could get to town from there but it wasn't a natural route to or from town. I couldn't rule out Joshua Hills proper but it sure pointed to a different location.

"If we follow this road in either direction where does it point us?"

I searched the roads in the area. I sure wished I knew what Cassidy had planned for that day. Bertie had said Cassidy went to Farley's school and that made sense. It was getting harder and harder for Cass to teach with Katie around. But I'd been to the school. There was nothing fishy there. If Farley knew anything he would have told me about it.

"Was Bertie babysitting for her this time?"

"Yeah."

"Maybe she met someone when she picked up Bertie."

"Bertie would have said something."

"Not if she didn't suspect anything."

I remembered the people at the homeless shelter. I hadn't found anybody who matched my impression of the suspect but people came and went from the shelter all day. The population there also varied depending on the needs of the community. They could have had a complete turnover of residents since Cassidy disappeared.

Cassidy's Jeep was found in the middle of the day. If she had been picking up Bertie so she could teach at the school she would have been in town about eight o'clock. Things didn't get going at the school until about nine thirty. Cassidy was a morning person so it made sense for her to be there early. I went to the homeless shelter at eight o'clock the next morning. They were in the middle of breakfast.

"What can I do for you Detective?" asked Sam Griffin, the shelter director.

"I'm looking for a man. My wife picked up Bertie from the shelter to baby-sit. She took Bertie and Katie to my house. She left them at the house, went somewhere and never came back. We found her Jeep in a pull-out on the road near my house, no sign of my wife. That day she ran into somebody who meant to do her harm. Do you know if she might have met anybody here? Anybody with wheels who might have followed her?"

"I'm sorry, I didn't know."

"Didn't expect you to. You're just watching out for your people."

I ran through the description for what felt like the thousandth time. I sure was tired of hearing myself say it. He told me about a few questionable people but they would have been camped in town. None of them strayed far from the shelter.

I saw Bertie in line so I joined her, not to eat, but to talk.

"The eggs sure are better at your house," she observed. "None of these runny scrambled eggs."

"Scrambled is just the easiest way to prepare eggs for a lot of people," I said.

"Want me to get you something? Slice of bacon?"

"No thanks. I've already eaten. My parents are staying at the house."

"Bet Katie likes that."

"She'd like Cassidy better."

"Still no word?"

"Not a clue. Okay, well, a few clues but none that lead me anywhere. You said Cassidy was going to the riding school?"

"Yeah, she had a new student who would take some work and concentration."

"New student? Did she describe them to you at all?"

"A boy. She said, as long as she didn't push, it should be fine. She said kids like that learn in itty bitty circles and you have to keep them busy advancing like a snail."

"I've been working out there on Saturday mornings..."

"You too? I never would have thought you to be a horse person."

"I'm not. But Farley has done so much for Cass I thought I ought to help him out when he was having trouble finding a teacher. I'm working with a man who needs a lot of patience and occasionally a little physical restraint. If I were him I'd just quit. He gets so frustrated. He's only had two lessons but I don't see any progress."

"Cassidy would tell you, not all progress is visible."

"Cass, didn't meet anybody new here? Or at the school, except for the boy?" I asked.

"Nope, course we don't know what she did after she left the school."

"Right. You can't think of anything that will help me?"

"I'm sorry, Rusty, I sure wish I could. I've been wracking my brain. I miss that wife of yours, too."

Chapter 10

I thought we could eat a peaceful dinner but with three cops, a dispatcher and a busy body at the table it was no use.

"Any motive?" Dad asked.

"She wasn't robbed. The Jeep was just left running on the side of the road. She didn't even have time to turn it off."

"Where did she go?" Cody, the busy body, asked.

"To Farley McGyver's school."

"Any place else?" Chase put in.

"We don't know. The school was the only plan she left with Bertie."

"No bloodshed?" Dad said.

"None that we could see at the site. I've been through this a thousand times. It's not like it happened yesterday. I've been at this too long. I go through the same thoughts every day and it leads me nowhere every day."

"One of these times, something will click," Mom said.

"But will it click in time? I'd already say it's too late if it was anybody but Cassidy."

"It *is* Cassidy," she reminded me.

"She's never been gone this long before. If she could escape she would have by now. Just the amount of violence it takes to get a person out of a car with the seat belt still buckled.... We have seat belt cutters because it's so difficult without one. Just pulling her out of the Jeep could have broken her back. She'd have been helpless."

"You can't think like that," Mom said uselessly.

"Mom, I need to thank you for something. A long time ago, you asked Cassidy if she ever thought about writing. Since then she has written about many of the searches and bouts of trouble she has run into. I didn't even know she did it until recently. I want you to read some of her stories. They are all true, though she remembers things differently than I do. You'll get to know her better if you do."

"Oh my, I don't think I can take it on top of what is going on now."

"Read the one about when Patrick was at your house for Christmas. You know how that one turns out."

"How is Cassidy's family taking this?"

"Stoically. They've been through these things before. This one is rough because she's been missing so long."

The phone rang and I got up to answer it.

"Hello?"

"Missur Michaels?"

Sigh, "What is it Brian?"

"I'm scared."

"I told you, Brian, you need to call a vet. A vet will make Rose better."

"No! I can'. My mama be angry. She no call vet. She don't unnerstand."

"Rose won't get better without help. It's up to you to help her. If you can't do it, a vet has to be called. That's all there is to it."

"But I'm afraid she die! She die I be so sad. She can't walk."

"Brian, when an animal gets sick enough that it can't walk it needs help. Either to make it better or to end its suffering."

"What you mean?"

"You can't let her suffer. It would be better to kill her than make her suffer. Is she in pain?"

"She was. I don't know now."

"Well, don't be scared. Where are you?"

"I'm outside."

"Where's your mom?"

"She in the house."

"Go in the house. Talk to your mom. You'll feel better."

Now how did *he* get my number?

When I came back to the table Katie held out a bite for me.

"Daddy! Bite!"

I took it from her, "Mmm, yum, yum," I said making a show of eating it.

"What was that all about?" Chase asked.

I explained the situation to them. They'd gotten the gist of it from my end of the conversation.

"What are you going to do?" Mom asked.

"It's their problem. It's not mine. I have enough problems of my own right now."

"You can't let the poor thing suffer," Mom said.

The phone rang again. I was going to be really irritated if this was Brian again.

"Hello?" I said gruffly.

There was nothing there. With a shock I realized it could be Cassidy. I switched the phone to speaker mode.

"Cass? Is that you?"

Nothing. I could hear quiet noises in the background.

"What is that?" Mom asked.

I shushed her.

"Cassidy? Can you tap? Anything!"

The noises continued. Something metal fell over with a clang. *Scrape, soft thud. Scrape, soft thud.* On and on it went.

"Babe, can you talk? I need to hear your voice. I need to know it's you."

A shuddered breath.

We never heard a voice. The scraping and the one breath was the closest to human sounds we heard and then finally steps and the phone disconnected. We all sat in numb silence. I looked on caller ID, jotted it down for the third time, and called it back. Nothing. I got the feeling time was running out.

Chapter 11

Sunday morning I drove to Derrick Bellows' house. Hopes battled with fears. I tried to stick to the job but I pinned so much on this call…

"Mister Bellows?" I called out as I pounded on his door. "It's Rusty Michaels, Joshua Hills Police, open up!"

"Again? What's up, Detective? I told you, that phone was misplaced or stolen several weeks ago."

"I received another call. Last night."

He stared at his shoes and stuffed his hands into his pockets.

We had talked many times. He ran a roofing business. I asked him to check around to see if anybody had found the lost phone. He had contacted his customers. Nobody found a phone.

"Could you tell me where you have had roofing jobs in the past two months?"

"Look, I haven't done anything wrong. I run a tight ship. I have an honest crew."

"I'm sure you do. If you will answer my questions you can help prove that's true."

"We'll have to go down to the office for that. Off the top of my head all I can give you is a bunch of last names."

"Okay we'll start with that."

He scratched his head, thinking. "Well, we just finished one for Knowles. Let's see there's Myers, Slipmannoff. We had fun with that one. Don't want no one slippin' off the roof! Har, har. Then there was Rueben, Swartz, Lamb, Snitzer and Slowden. Sounds like a lawyer firm or something, don't it?"

He had told me most of those names before, but there were a couple of names I didn't remember from last time.

"When will you be at your office?"

"Seven thirty in the morning."

"And when will you have time to go over a few records with me?"

"Now hold on here…"

"Do we really have to go through this again?" I asked. "If I can find that phone, I think I can find the girl. Time's running out."

"It's my turn to ask some questions," he said. "How will my phone help you find her?"

"She tried to call for help. She used your phone to do it. She couldn't even speak this time. I tried calling it back but there was no answer. Names. Addresses. Dates. I'm putting a rush on that search warrant."

"How can that be? That phone should be useless by now."

"That's another reason I'd like to talk to your clients. If the phone is being charged regularly somebody is choosing to do it. Finding that person could be crucial."

I went back to the Explorer, took a deep breath and fell apart. I couldn't make Derrick Bellows work any faster than he wanted to. All I could do was hope he did it. One name I could check up on. Lamb.

I drove by the Lamb house. It was a nicely landscaped rural home, not far from the riding school. No cars were visible but I noted the neat, unblemished roof. Rose bushes stood in a line in front of the house needing trimming. Weeds were making a comeback. The lawn needed mowing but I could tell it did get cut on a regular basis. I wondered if Brian was trusted with a lawnmower.

I reluctantly knocked on the door.

Dolores Lamb opened the door hesitantly. Unexpected company was not normal where she lived. She was in her fifties, slightly bent. She walked stiffly. Her hair was up. I wondered how a woman like her could handle Brian.

"Mrs. Lamb? I'm Detective Michaels. I'm Brian's riding teacher at the school, but I'm afraid I'm here on police business this time. I'm trying to track down a lost cell phone. A construction worker lost it on a roofing job. Did you or Brian happen to find a cell phone when the workers were here replacing your roof?"

"Why, no, I haven't seen a cell phone besides mine and it's right here in my purse. Oh, Brian will be upset to know he missed you."

"Brian's not home?"

"No, he's out. Maybe I better not tell him you were here."

"Where would he go?"

"We have an old barn up the road. He keeps begging for a horse but I tell him he can't have a horse because he can't take care of it. He asked, if he learned how to take care of a horse, if he could have one. He wanted to fix up the barn just in case I change my mind. So he walks out there every three or four days and works on the barn. I don't know what he does out there but I suppose he can't hurt it. The work is good for him. My husband bought the house because he wanted to restore cars in that barn, but he never got to. Now Brian wants a horse."

"You're not worried about him being out there alone?"

"No. He knows the way. It's straight down the road. You can't miss it. He comes home when he gets hungry. I can't walk out there. It's too hard on my back, but he seems to like it out there. Most kids these days don't want to play outdoors. I'm glad to see he's not sitting in front of a TV all day."

"And you haven't run across an odd cell phone?"

"No."

"Will you ask Brian about it when you see him?"

"I sure will."

"Thanks."

I left her with my business card and went on my way.

"Mr. Michaels!" she called as I was getting into my Explorer.

"Yes?"

"*Please* don't teach Brian enough for him to take care of a horse!"

"Okay."

The day at work was torture. I couldn't keep my mind on the job no matter what I did so I looked up Derrick Bellow's roofing business and stopped by there. A young woman sat at a desk.

"May I help you?" she asked, blushing.

"Is Mr. Bellows in?"

"No, he's out on a job. Can I take a message? He'll call you back as soon as he gets a chance."

"Did he come into the office this morning?"

"Yes, in fact he was here longer than usual. You just missed him."

"Tell him Detective Michaels stopped by. He has my card."

"Okay," she said jotting down the message in a spiral notebook.

"Rusty? I got some files for you. I can keep going but this will give you a place to start."

"What is it?"

"It's not much. But it's the files from your hard drive."

"You got them back?"

"Not all of them. It's a long, laborious process. You were lucky you stopped using your computer when you discovered your mistake. Maybe I should explain to you what these files are. That way if they don't make sense to you, you can figure out how it might have been."

"What do you mean?"

"When you delete a file it gets stuck in the recycle bin. When you empty the bin the space on the disk becomes available again to be written over. What we recover from your disk is all the information. The old files, the new things that were written over the old files, everything. So the data is usually somewhat broken up. If it has been written over it is lost forever. So pieces of the deleted files were written over and lost, but this is part of the files we were able to restore. I was really surprised. Many people wait too long and the files are long gone. They can take weeks to decipher. We end up with little bits and pieces that are useless and hard to understand. Since you didn't do a lot of writing over the deleted files you preserved more of the files you deleted. On the other hand we didn't find many of the key words you gave us. We found some files dated in the time frame you mentioned. If this seems disjointed as you read do you understand why that is?"

"Yeah, I think so. You mean that if things seem disjointed it might be because they were put back together in the wrong order?"

"Sort of, yeah. Think of it like trying to piece together the contents of a shredding machine."

He handed me a small sheaf of papers.

"Oh, and Rusty. We had to read it to put it back together."

"Any clues about who could have taken her?"

"You'd know better."

The top two documents were just dated in the right time frame. It seemed none of the files were complete. They had pieces missing, but maybe I could still find something useful in the remnants. The next Cassidy had written, again in the right time frame. It was a letter, to me, unfinished, just like some of the letters to her I'd found. We never sent letters to each other. I guess we only thought about it.

My Dearest Rusty,

Sometimes when I sit down to write to you I only get a few lines in because so many thoughts come to mind all at once I can't unscramble them. I want to tell you how much I love you but it's all too complex. If you were to ask me a question, like what made me love you first, I could answer that. It was your eyes. Your eyes talk. You don't have to say anything and I know you care.

If you were to ask me what I love the most about you. I'd have to say your heart. When we're together I can feel your heart beating for me, dedicated to me, and I feel so inadequate. I don't deserve that kind of love. The things I put you through. If trouble would just stay away maybe I could make it up to you.

I didn't know if part of the letter was missing or whether she hadn't finished it. I was almost glad she quit writing. I couldn't take much more. I found a short piece that looked like it might have eventually worked its way into one of her books:

"Farley McGyver's school is either going to make me or break me. I don't know which. I see the kids dealing with all their various challenges and I wonder at how they do it. How do they cope in a world that looks down on them because they are different? I try to take each kid as an individual but there are so very many problems to try and overcome with these kids. I can deal with limitations. Physical limitations are easy. Find something that works, go slow. Mental limitations I can deal with. I just have to find the niche, the one way that kid learns the easiest and work there. What I am really having trouble with is the kids who don't know right from wrong. One minute they will be easy going, fun overachievers and the next they think it's okay to beat the horse. How do you teach a kid who has no concept of right and wrong? I fear for them. What will they grow into? So I teach them anyway, hoping they can get a grasp. If it's bad to hit a horse, it's bad to hit a person. Hitting is bad."

I was shocked to note that had been written two days before Cassidy disappeared. I looked at the time. I wasn't going to accomplish anything at the station anyway. I locked up my office and left. As I was walking to my car I got a call on my cell. Derrick Bellows.

"Hello Mr. Bellows, I hope you have some good news for me."

"Nobody has seen the missing phone. I'm still waiting on two more calls."

"Are they cooperating or are they giving you the brush off."

"No, for the most part people have been very nice about it. They know what a pain it is to lose a cell phone, have to get a new one, and reprogram everything. They have been glad to look around, and see if they can find it. I just haven't had any luck."

"You might ask if their kids suddenly had a cell phone for no reason. If a kid picked it up they might claim it belonged to a friend so they could use it without getting in trouble."

"Hmm, I hadn't thought of that. I'll remember to ask when people call me back."

"Thanks for the update."

I pulled into Farley McGyver's riding school and parked next to the office. Farley was rarely in the office. He was usually walking the grounds, supervising from one corral to another depending on how much he trusted the teachers. He spent the whole lesson supervising me, but he knew I appreciated it too. I really didn't know what I was doing, just trying to help Brian in some small way. I was growing fond of the boy. He wasn't a boy but I couldn't help but think of him that way. I felt for him losing his pet. Poor guy. He had a heart. If only his hands were as soft as his heart.

I thought about Cassidy and her sheltie. Shadow missed Cass, too. A very real part of his flock had gone astray. I knew how much Cassidy loved that dog. She trained him every day and he showed me every day how much time Cassidy had put into training. He hung on every word, waiting for a command. Sometimes I gave him commands for no reason, just because he looked so intent.

I found Farley leaning against a fence. A young woman was helping a little girl in the ring. The girl's legs were misshapen. Her crutches leaned against the corral fence.

"Can you kick your feet against Brownie?" she asked the girl.

Her feet moved but not in the right direction.

"A little harder," she instructed.

The girl tried ineffectually but the teacher pulled on the horse's bridle enough to get it moving.

"Good girl!" she praised.

"Can I talk to you for a minute?" I asked Farley.

"I got to keep an eye on this but I can talk. What's going on?"

"I'll wait until you're through. You need to read something, then tell me what you think of it."

"How long is it?"

"Less than a page. But I need you to be able to think about what you're reading."

"What's this got to do with?"

"Cassidy."

He left the fence and headed for his office. I followed his familiar limp to the door. He opened the door and motioned me in. His office was more of a tack room. It held horse gear specially designed for a variety of physical disabilities. A dusty desk stood in one corner. Guess he didn't spend much time on paperwork. He lowered himself into his old, wooden, swivel chair.

"Make yourself comfortable," he said. "I just have to be back out there before they finish. That kid isn't going to do much more than a little pony ride at the fair. What have you got?"

"Cassidy did some writing. This was recovered from my hard drive. I don't know if this is all there was or if this is all they could recover. I need to know what kids she's talking about at the end of the paragraph."

He read it through twice. It wasn't critical of his school. Just like everything about Cassidy, it was an honest look at her work and her place in the world.

"Lots of kids have trouble distinguishing right from wrong," he explained.

"Got any extreme cases?"

"Yes, but they'll outgrow it. *Every kid* has to learn right from wrong. Kids with learning disabilities take longer to learn some things. That's what we're here for, to help them work through it."

"Is there anybody at the school Cassidy should have been wary of?"

"No. Nobody."

"I'm glad. I really am. I just have to follow every lead I can."

"I know. I'd be disappointed if you didn't."

"I'll let you get back to work."

"That girl of yours has a good heart."

"I hope so."

I took my stack of files with me. I headed for home but I didn't want to face all the people there. I wanted to read in peace. I drove, debating with myself and ended up on Kelly's doorstep. He and Rhonda weren't home from work yet. Perfect. I felt under the eve of the porch roof until I found the key that hung on a nail there and let myself in. They would see the Explorer in the driveway, and they would understand why I was there.

As usual, Kelly's house bordered on clutter. It was a small house with a lot of activity and it barely managed to contain it all. I looked forward to my own house attaining the status of Kelly's, when the life of the family made a house take on a life of its own. Cassidy was more organized. It might take a while.

Amos greeted me as I came in. Amos was Kelly's old black Labrador retriever. He was graying around his muzzle now. I took off my suit coat and tie and laid them over the back of the couch. I settled into the big, plaid easy chair that faced the fireplace. Amos went back to his usual sleeping spot on the hearth, after I scratched him behind the ears.

I opened the file folder and the documents greeted me in cold, crisp text. I found a document that looked like poetry. Then I realized with a start that Cassidy had been trying to record the songs I sang to Katie. If she caught me at it she asked me to sing it again but I never could. I made them up as I went along and they were never the same twice. I read the words, tried to think what tune I would have used, and couldn't reconstruct it. I had to laugh at the way I stretched the words or timing to make it rhyme. Katie didn't care and apparently Cassidy hadn't either.

I should be home, I thought. Mom has been taking care of Katie all day.

But I needed to at least glance through the rest of the pages. I found a reference to a black four-door but it was old notes I'd made. It included facts that Cassidy wouldn't have known about her captor's car. The page about the school was the only thing even close to a clue and I'd checked that out. Another dead end.

Rhonda came in with a rustle of grocery sacks. I went out to the car and brought the rest of the groceries in.

"Thanks," she said. "What brings you here? Can you stay for dinner?"

"No, thanks anyway. It's tempting. I've got a house full of family and I needed time to think. Mom will have dinner ready at the usual time, so I better be there."

"What are you doing here?"

"Working through some files that I thought might lead me to Cassidy."

"Rusty... it's been too long."

"I don't think so. We got a call just two days ago. It could have been Cass."

"You don't know?"

"I can't think of what else it could be."

"Misplaced hopes?"

"I'll take any hope I can get. Got some to spare?"

"It's been too long, Rusty. She's not coming back. If you need more hope, talk to Kelly. He won't give up on her either."

I went home to my crowded house. Katie was creeping along the couch, one hand on the seat for balance. She had her eye on the chair. No baby, not yet, I thought, wait for Mommy. I couldn't stand the tension waiting to see if she'd do it. I picked her up before she could try.

Dinner brought another heart wrenching. Everybody was talking and eating. I didn't even know what we were eating. It was just food. Mom cooked it so it had to be good, but I was dwelling on Cass, already feeling about as low as could be, when Katie looked at my mom and said, "Mommy! Ba-bite!" Such a simple thing. Nobody else seemed to notice. Katie couldn't help it. Cassidy had been gone a month. But my mother was not her mommy. To think my mom had replaced Cassidy in Katie's eyes hit me like a Mack truck. I couldn't eat. I left the table, left the house, paced up and down the back yard trying to control my emotions. After a few minutes the backdoor opened.

"Rusty, telephone," my mom called out.

Maybe it was Derrick Bellows. I counted to ten, stilled my breathing, calmed my nerves, put on my detective hat and went into the house.

"Hello?"

"Mr. Michaels? I'm so sorry to bother you. I was hoping you could help me with something."

Dolores Lamb.

"What is it, Mrs. Lamb?"

"It's Brian. I haven't seen him *all day*. He's been out at the barn but he hasn't come home to eat. He doesn't have anything out there to keep him busy this long. I can't imagine him purposely missing a meal."

"He wouldn't wander off, would he?"

"I don't think so. He's been very moody. I don't know what's wrong with him. I'd go myself but the walk is too much for me. If he's doing something and doesn't want to come back I can't make him. If I make him angry he…"

"I understand. So you would like me to go make sure he's okay, and bring him back."

"If it's not an imposition."

It was a hell of an imposition but she needed to know he was okay. I needed to know he was okay. I'd have to deal with Rose.

"I'll be right there."

"Thank you, thank you! I worry so much. I know I shouldn't, but I can't help it."

"It's okay."

Public service stinks, I thought.

"Chase, eat up, you're coming along," I said.

"What? Where?"

"It won't take long. The walk is short."

"Then why do you need me?"

"In case it turns out not to be short."

I strapped on my sidearm. He raised an eyebrow.

"Remember the dog? If it's what I think it is, I'll probably have to shoot it."

"No!" my mom cried.

Chase huffed stoically and shoveled in his favorite bites before heading for the door. An officer always had time for that last bite. He might swallow it in his car but he'd always grab one more bite on the way out.

We drove out to the Lamb house. I didn't bother stopping at the house. I parked in the driveway, leaving room for another car. Chase followed me up the road. I broke into a jog. It couldn't be far and I wanted to get this over with.

The road was rough and rutted. I was glad Mrs. Lamb hadn't tried to walk down it. Chase jogged silently beside me. I could tell he was tracking, even at a jog. He wasn't pleased with what he saw in the worn ruts of the road. The further we went the more his face betrayed the fact that he was reading a disturbing story in the dust.

We came to a barn landscaped on one side with rose bushes, just like the house. These were not trimmed, though. They grew with wild abandon, thorny tendrils reaching out from the barn with dark red flowers on the ends. I opened a door that led to a tack room, took a quick glance around and decided Brian wasn't there. We started a methodical search around the outside of the barn. Suddenly Chase put a hand on my shoulder to stop me. His gaze was glued to the earth. His brow was furrowed, his manner tense.

"What?" I asked.

He pointed.

I looked down, not expecting to see anything that meant anything to me, but there was… the track. Oh lord. It was the track. My breath quickened, my mouth went suddenly dry. My hopes did a little flip flop. I could feel them, little stirrings that were afraid to break free. My eyes darted around. My hand went to my gun. The thumbtack. The cut marks. They were all there.

Chase began casting around, looking for signs of Cassidy. He'd recognize Cassidy's tracks anywhere. The size, shape, and mannerisms were permanently logged in his mind, just as his were in Cassidy's.

We found Brian in a big hole just behind the barn. He just sat there cutting at his shoe with a pocketknife, worrying, then he looked up, alarmed.

"Missur Michaels! I can't do it. I can't!"

My mind was going in little circles. I had to quiet it somehow. I reached for the only thing I could come up with.

"You can't do what?"

"She dying, but I can't. Fix her! You make her better. Please! I can't. I try and I try. She can't walk. Can't eat. She on'y sleep."

"Brian, where is she?" I said, every ounce of restraint going into my voice. "If she can't walk and she can't eat it's time to end her suffering."

I pulled my pistol.

"No!" Brian yelled. He staggered out of the hole, tackling me. "No! You can't! I love her. I love her! You can't! Me not let you!"

Chase stepped to the side, drawing his own weapon.

"No! Chase, no. It's not necessary," I said.

Brian was powerful but he had no idea how to use his weight to his advantage. I rolled him over and pinned him to the ground.

The track still haunted my mind.

"Brian, sometimes when you love something you have to love it enough to let it go. Now where is she?"

"My Rose," he cried, "can't kill my Rose. Me love her. She sick. Make her better. She in the barn. Don't kill her. Please make her better. Missur Rusty…" He struggled but I had twenty pounds on him and knew how to use it.

"Can I let you go? You're not going to fight me? I'm only doing what's right. Sometimes what's right and what we want aren't the same. Now," I said backing off a little, "let's go look."

I let him up, ready to restrain him again, if need be. He followed me to the barn wringing his hands all the way, wiping tears from his eyes, sniffling like a big baby. Hell, I wished I could do that, too.

I tried to open the wide barn doors but they were locked. Brian stepped forward and reluctantly unlocked the door with a key he kept in his pocket. He sobbed and stomped his feet in the dust, raising little, depressing clouds. He turned his back on the door as if praying I wouldn't go through the doorway.

I pulled on the heavy wooden door and it slowly swung open wide. I waited for my eyes to adjust, then slowly made my way toward a small lump lying motionless next to the barn wall.

Brian was begging at me, "No, please, Mizzur Michaels, please don't shoot her... I don' know what I do without my Rose. Please..."

I flipped off the safety. Gun in hand I walked over to it, checking the magazine. I was distracted, arguing with myself over how to handle the other half of this situation. How was I going to find out what he knew about Cassidy? It was my best break yet. But how could Brian... one thing at a time. Shoot the dog. Then deal with Brian.

"Please Missur Michaels, you can't hurt her. You said vet make her better...."

Weapon check complete, I looked down into the emaciated form of... Cassidy.

Chapter 12

Fury exploded inside me. At first it was all I could see, pure fury. Panic was just below the surface. My brain kicked in just enough to maintain a sort of physical control. I slowly turned back around, every ounce of control I possessed packed into my actions. If I'd gone with my first reaction, I would have killed him. I would have pulverized him, just like I had the punching bag at the station so many times. So many conflicting feelings battled it out that I couldn't think. There was no procedure for this, at least not in my book. I had to do something… but I couldn't. I couldn't. Sometimes what's right and what we want aren't the same. Walls. Steel walls. I had to focus, while my heart was breaking, splintering into a million tiny pieces and being blown away by the wind. I needed those pieces. I needed control.

"Chase, get him out of here." I said, my voice cold as steel. I'm ashamed to say I wasn't an officer that night. Not an officer, not a cop, not a detective… I was just a man, a broken man. I was afraid of what I might do if given the chance. "Get him out of my sight!" I turned on Brian, gun in one hand, other fist clenched. "Go home!" I yelled. "Go home before I kill you! How could you? People are *not pets*! Brian, people aren't pets. Go home!"

As I yelled I was aware how my voice could frighten Cassidy. She said it sounded like a thunderstorm. I glanced down at her, worried that I had alarmed her, but she hadn't stirred and that scared me more.

Brian cowered in fear. He put his arms over his head, then he ran in an odd shuffling gait toward the house.

Chase knelt beside Cassidy.

"She's alive," he said softly, as if speaking up might shatter her.

Just those few words gave me more relief than I'd felt in a lifetime. I took a deep breath, almost… almost ready to take charge again.

"Take Brian home and call an ambulance. No. Call an airlift."

"Are you going to be okay?"

"No… but do it anyway."

I was crumbling. All the emotion and hopelessness of the past month and a half crumbled away and I couldn't stop it. I sat beside Cassidy fighting the torrent within me until, finally, I couldn't any more. All the worry, all the guilt, all the sorrow, the anger mixed with relief; it fought until the whole mess was too much and I just sat there letting it flow, wracking my body like I'd never felt before. I cried for release, for help, for God to see us there in that cold barn and perform some miracle that would preserve us, to make us… us again.

Please, babe, please be okay. What did he do to you? Cass, what did he do?

I lifted her hand. It was limp and nearly skeletal. Had he even thought to give her food? How long could a person go without food? Six weeks? Could they endure six weeks? Please…

I heard a mechanical click and some sprinklers came on outside. No wonder the roses stayed alive out here. A tiny trickle of water ran down a board and landed on Cassidy's face. Now the spot she laid in made sense. She'd found water. Five minutes of trickle a day. I moved the board so the water stayed outside but I wondered at her ability to make do with so little.

"Babe, can you hear me? It's Rusty. It's going to be okay. You're going to be all right. You just hang on and it'll be okay."

Everything felt so still. All I could do was reach out to her, but I felt nothing come back. Even having her near, I was losing hope. I needed hope. I needed it more than anything. If I could have traded places with her I would have in a heartbeat. Please, babe, just hold on…

Her breathing was shallow, her pulse faint. She was so cold, so still. I couldn't move her. Brian had said Rose couldn't walk, so I shouldn't move her. I wanted to. Oh, how my arms ached. I wanted to pick her up and head for the house, for warmth, for something comforting. I took off my suit coat and laid it over her. It was the tweed one. The one Cassidy always asked me to wear. The coat was old and threadbare but she still insisted she liked it the best. I didn't know why.

I started talking, just talking because I had to get rid of the tension somehow.

"I've been looking… Cass, I've been searching. If only I'd been hearing, too. Babe, I'm sorry. I was so worried about you that I couldn't hear Brian. He told me you were sick. He's been telling me for a week. I let you lay here for a week when I could have found you. Hon… I didn't know. I swear, I didn't know."

I decided I better called home.

"Dad, I'm not going to be back for a while."

"Is everything okay?"

"I don't know… Dad, we found her. I'm sitting here with her."

"Cassidy? Is she okay?"

"No, Dad… she's unresponsive. We're waiting for an airlift."

"What happened?"

"I… I can't talk about that yet."

"We'll hold down the fort."

"Thanks."

"No problem."

"And Dad?"

"Yeah?"

"Cassidy's going to be there to see Katie's first steps."

"We'll be counting on it."

Four EMTs jogged up the road with a backboard. Two officers had blocked off the road so the air ambulance could land on it.

"Mizzur Michaels. She no die," Brian said as we watched the EMTs stabilizing Cass enough for transport. Just the fact that she needed stabilizing told me too much. I willed strength her way knowing all along she was stronger than I. Pound for pound there was nobody stronger than Cassidy. Hold on Cass, fight. Fight it.

I couldn't hate Brian. I tried to, but when I thought about it I couldn't really. I could be plenty angry, but I couldn't bring myself to hate him. He didn't know what he'd done wrong. It's very hard to hate a man who thinks like a kid. The kid part tends to take precedence. I was relieved, in a way. I didn't want to hate him. Cassidy wouldn't want me to hate him.

"Why did you name her Rose?" I asked still holding my emotions in check.

"She beautiful and soft and she… she die when I pick her."

"She won't die. I know her. She'll live."

"You know Rose?"

"Yes. Very well. Do you remember when you asked me why I was sad?" He shook his head but I continued anyway. "It was because I missed Rose. She's my wife. I thought she was dead. When you took her… you took her away from me. Her real name… is Cassidy."

"I didn't know. I on'y know I love her. I thought she stay with me. But she no stay with me. She un'erstand me. She try to talk to me, to let her go. To call for help. She never stay. Then she get real sick. She quit talking. She sleep a lot. I get scared. I stay away. I scared she leave. I lock the barn. She couldn't walk. She couldn't open the door."

"What did you give her to eat?"

"I sneak food every day but Mom start asking questions. So I stop. She not let me go to the barn every day, only sometimes. Every time I see Rose she sicker. Every time I see Rose I get scared. Then I meet you."

"How long has she been sleeping?" I asked using terms he understood.

"Long time."

"Days? Weeks?"

"Two, three days. Before, she sleep a lot, wake up when I come."

"How did you take her?"

"I take Mom's car when she nap. I go school to watch Rose. She no teach me. Make me mad. I want pretty teesher. She nice. She un'erstand me. She no teach me so I find way to keep her. For me."

"So you followed her until you could take her?"

"She fighter! On'y when I take her she hurt. She sleep long time. I take her to the barn. Mom mad I take car. I get big trouble."

Mrs. Lamb was distraught. She waited in the house with a female officer wringing her hands and rambling on about how she should have checked, she should have suspected something...

When I put it all together it made sense. The erratic driving, the thoughtlessness of just dragging her out of her Jeep, the lack of food, the odd track. It all made sense. Now. He was five. With the power of a man.

"Rusty? You coming?" Vance asked.

I climbed into the helicopter and we took off for LA.

Chapter 13

The ride to LA was quick. Time was of the essence. The stats were scary. Cassidy never stirred. I talked to her anyway, desperate to find a connection, needing her to know I was there, needing some kind of response, fearful I was too late.

At ER I got shoved off into a waiting room. A doctor and several nurses converged on her room. All I could do was wait and hope. At one time I would have insisted I had to be there. I wanted to, but I felt such a jumble of fear and hope that I knew I'd just get in the way. I had to stay out, for Cass' sake.

To ease the tension, I used the time to make phone calls.

Kelly:
"Yo, how's it going?"
"Kel... I found her."
"I'm on my way."
"No. We're in LA. It's okay. It's going to be a long night. They're working on her."
"I'm on my way anyway."

Landon:
"Sorry to be calling so late. I thought you would want to know you'll be getting your partner back."
I wondered if he was still there.
"Thanks," he finally said. "When?"
"Long time."
"How bad is it this time?"
"I don't know yet. We just got here."
"You okay?"
"Better than I've been in a long, long time."
"Michaels... you wouldn't tell me this if you didn't have hope."
"Never lose hope."
"At least not where Cassidy is concerned. I'll stop by."
"Thanks."

Schroeder:
"I'm taking a month off. If you don't like it I'll quit."
"What?"

"I have to. Schroeder, I just have to."

"Keep Tom updated."

"I will. Tell him he can quit looking."

"No."

"I found Cassidy." I paused, while he processed what that meant to me, to him. "I went out to find a missing man and shoot his dog and I came back with Cass. The case isn't closed but tell him he can quit looking. The guy isn't going to run. He'll probably show up to see if Cass is okay."

"You're not making sense. Cassidy gets kidnapped, the kidnapper is loose, he knows he's in trouble, he's not going to run, and he's welcome to visit his victim in the hospital."

"Makes sense to me."

"The guy is still alive? Sounds like you need a month off."

Big Wayne Gordon:

"Rusty?"

"Sir."

"Good news or bad?"

"I think it's good. I'll keep you updated."

"Tell her when she gets well I'm going to wring her scrawny neck."

"Yes, sir."

Chase came in and sat with me.

"I went back and tracked the barn."

"And?"

"I'm glad you couldn't read it. Any reports?"

"No."

"It's going to be a rough haul. She's been injured the whole time she's been missing. I only found one spot where she was on her feet and she couldn't put any weight on her legs. Only reason I know that much is because the kid always used the same door and Cassidy went for the other one. Everything was preserved inside the barn. No erosion except where the water came in. Vegetation outside that hole was stripped."

As long as he was talking like that I could take it. It was more like an officer reporting on a crime scene. It wasn't a friend telling me my wife was put through hell.

A doctor flew into the waiting room. The veins on his neck stood out and just the fact that the doctor came to the waiting room himself told me he was serious. There was no nurse to calmly tell me the doctor was ready to see me. He almost chewed me out right there in the waiting room, but he paused, looked around at the nervous faces and led me to the examination room.

"Tell me how this happened. I want the truth and I need it straight up," he said, reminding me a lot of Cassidy's dad.

"She was kidnapped by a mentally disabled man who didn't know his own strength. He didn't know how to care for her. He tried to get food to her but as time went by he was less able to get to where she was being held. He didn't even think about water."

"You expect me to believe that?"

"No, sir, but we'll have a police report to back this up as soon as the guys get them filed."

"How long has she been going through this?"

"Six weeks."

He sat back against an examination table and gawked at me.

"She endured that *for six weeks*?" He paused, thinking. I guess he decided he was on my side because he said, "Let me show you what she's going to be up against after we stabilize her." He pulled out some x-rays. "See this? This line and this line are both fractures. The right side is partially healed. The left side has a lot of displacement," he explained pointing to an x-ray of Cassidy's pelvis. "How did that happen?"

"He pulled her out of her car."

"That wouldn't harm a young, healthy woman to this extent."

"He... he didn't think to undo the seatbelt. He just grabbed her and pulled. I was called to the scene. I saw the car."

"She'll need surgery on her hips. The bones have begun to heal with significant displacement. They need to be rebroken and set properly or she may not walk normally again. She's got three broken ribs. Here, here and here," he said pointing to another set of x-rays, "You can't see them very well because they have healed. I'm sure they caused her terrible pain for weeks. She'll have to watch her movements for a while. They may still bother her. She made it through the concussion. You can see that one in this x-ray here." He pointed out a crack in her forehead, probably from being jerked into the doorframe of her Jeep. That explained why we didn't find any of her tracks at the scene. "The first step is to get her through the night. We may have a few tricky days due to dehydration. She was lucky the weather was mild. Our next step will be getting her healthy enough for surgery."

"When will we know more?"

"When she wakes up. She's being sent to CCU. I don't want to give you any false hopes. She was very lucky. We can only hope we caught her in time. Let's hope that luck of hers holds out.

"I talked to her doctor in Joshua Hills. He told me to put her in a body cast and not let her out until the fractures are healed. I don't know what to tell you right now. It all depends on her. I'm hoping for a quick short term recovery, then a long recovery from surgery. You just can't rush the healing after the surgery she's going to need. If you rush it, you risk even more damage. She's going to have to stay down for three months."

Three months. That was a lifetime to Cassidy. I wasn't sure she could do it.

I fumbled around for words. I didn't know what to say. I wasn't sure I'd get her back at all and now it sounded like she could make a full recovery. My hope was growing. I could see it glimmering, still a bit afraid to break out of the cage I kept it in.

"What about her spine? I was told she couldn't walk."

"All the damage is to the pelvis. With surgery, therapy, and plenty of time, she should recover fully. All this, assuming she makes it through the next couple of days."

When they let me see her in CCU she already looked better than she had in the barn. Her color had returned. She had a difficult night. The alarms on the machines went off a couple of times bringing the nurse running. It made me wonder what another night in the barn would have meant for her. I tried not to think about what it must have been like for her, alone, unable to move, hurt. When I got that far I started kicking myself again for not getting there sooner. I worried and stewed, but I had to smile when she finally woke up. It was just briefly. Just a quick reaction to the unexpected. She felt weakly to her right. From her actions and her expressions I could tell exactly what she was thinking. She was feeling for the board that brought her water and when she didn't feel it she came awake with a jolt. Her water was gone! She was still in survival mode. I took her hand and she pulled back, still in fight mode.

"Cassidy, it's over, babe. Look at me. You'll see. You're back," I told her quietly.

I took her hand and rubbed her arm so she could feel me there.

It took her a moment to figure out her surroundings.

"Rusty?" it was just above a whisper, "it was so long." Her eyes were so sad. I fell into them.

"I know. It was forever. Every day was forever without you."

"Mr. Michaels? You have a visitor," the nurse said.

"Can they come in?"

"Only family can come in."

"Then let them in. We only have family."

"They have to sign in. It asks the relation."

It was Kelly.

"Couldn't sleep," he lied.

"You're Cassidy's brother. Remember that for next time."

"Cassidy needs a big brother," he said as we entered the cubicle. Kelly was about as different from Cassidy as a white guy can get. He was tall, broad, and had dark, curly hair, while Cassidy was petite, blonde, my little Skipper doll. Kelly bent over the bed. "Rusty... she's barely there."

"She's stronger than she looks."

"She needs to go to Vegas. She beats the odds every time."

"I spent two weekends teaching riding lessons to Cassidy's kidnapper. I knew I was looking for a powerful man, one Cassidy had met recently. I looked everywhere except right under my nose. He kept telling me about his sick pet. I could have found Cass two weeks ago if I'd showed a little compassion and helped him with his sick pet. He would have trusted me. He would have led me to her. And when I turned my back on Brian, I turned my back on Cass."

"You didn't know. You had enough on your mind without worrying about other people's problems."

"That's what I thought at the time. But it wasn't true. I could have helped him. In the process I'd have been helping Cassidy. I'd have saved myself two weeks of grief. Cassidy would have been stronger... I put her here. Two weeks ago we would have found her conscious, functioning. Now here we are hoping her organs don't fail from dehydration."

"Take all that and flush it down the toilet. What ifs will get you nowhere."

"I wonder if word has gotten around."

"Nope."

"How do you know?"

"Because I'm the only one here. When word gets around you'll have to fight off the visitors. You just wait until morning. I bet Wilson is the first to show."

Cassidy stirred and I leaned closer.

"It's okay, babe, I'm right here."

She felt for a hand so I took hers in mine. It felt like a child's. Her wedding ring was so loose they took it off in ER. I ran my finger over the white line where it usually rested.

"Can you hear me?" I asked.

She squeezed my hand weakly.

"Thank you for your writing. It got me through when I thought I'd fall apart."

"Russ..."

"What is it?"

"You... you didn't..."

"Didn't what?"

"… arrest him."

"He broke the law. He almost killed you."

She became very agitated. "Russ… you can't… jail's no place for him. Please, let him go!" Her voice was fading even as her pulsed raced. I watched it on the monitor.

"Shh, hush, babe. Don't worry. I could have pounded him. I came so close. I could have arrested him. But he needs help. He can't be trusted, but I know jail isn't the answer."

"He didn't know," she said, as she faded again. "He didn't know what he was doing. He's just a kid…"

"He called you Rose because he thought you were soft and beautiful," I told her, not knowing if she heard me or not.

She said softly, "He didn't think that for long."

Landon did visit the next morning. One advantage to being the boss' kid. His dad ran an ambulance service. Landon was an EMT there. He seemed to be able to get time off whenever he wanted it. He sat with me for an hour or so but Cassidy slept on.

"The only thing that kept me hopeful was knowing Cassidy," Landon said.

"I know what you mean. It was that way for me, too."

"It's hard to believe that much stubbornness lives in someone so… I don't even know how to say it. I can't say delicate, though she seems that way today. I'd say cute but she'd hate it. She's a puzzle. I doubt anybody ever figures her out. Have you?"

"No. At times. I guess I'm getting closer, but… no. I don't think it can be done. She changes. She's not the same girl I met four years ago. She's not as much of a kid now."

"Trouble will do that to anybody," he observed.

"If there was any way, any way in the world to keep her from it, I'd do it, but she won't have it. She won't be held back and I can't force her. It's like caging the wind. It can't be done."

Her other search partner, Victor Gomez, came by. It was harder for him to get to LA. He had a job, a family, but search and rescue was sort of a family, too. Cassidy could track Landon or Victor anywhere, could pick their tracks out of a crowd because she had been on so many calls with them. Their tracks were ingrained into her mind.

"Cassidy certainly has a mixed heritage," the nurse said knowing none of these men were really Cassidy's brothers. Landon Wilson was the closest to looking like Cassidy's brother. Blonde, shorter than the others, he had been mistaken for Cassidy's brother before. Victor was Mexican. He had the classic Mexican features, black hair, brown eyes, quick smile, ten years older than Cassidy. I couldn't have asked for better partners to watch over my wife on the trail.

Victor sat with me while Cassidy slept, but she woke up for a little while.

"Rusty?"

"I'm here. Victor's here, too."

"Vic...feels like I've gotten hold of another scorpion."

When I'd read about the scorpion in her stories I was angry at first. She'd told me what happened. One thing I learned reading her stories was she had never told me everything. She only told me enough to justify what I could see, or would hear at work. I'd have to remember that in the future. I'd never known how much of a setback the scorpion sting had been. She'd been incapacitated for most of a day. Victor took care of Cass. He was always the careful one. So in the end I was just glad he was there.

"What do you mean, Cassidy?" Victor asked.

"Can't feel. Can't think. I'm falling but I never land."

"Babe, you're right here. You're not falling. We've got you," I told her.

"Victor's tracks. Wide. Sandals. Hundred seventy pounds. Wear spots inside on ball of foot. Purposeful. Careful. Always thinking. Short stride. Leans forward 'cause of his pack... purposeful but calm. Used to unexpected little things coming up. Goes with the flow..."

This scared me, the fact that she didn't know she was profiling Victor's tracks. If there was one thing that typified Cassidy, she was aware, so where was she? My girl. She faded out again.

Tom visited. He came in all business, wanting to find his man.

"Michaels."

"Tom, thanks for coming."

"I need some facts."

"Come back later. We're short on facts at the moment."

"Schroeder says this guy isn't going to run. What makes you think so?"

"He isn't capable of running. He doesn't even understand the depth of the trouble he could be in. He's not going anywhere."

Tom stood by Cassidy's side. Often voices would bring her out from wherever she was. Sometimes I sat by her bed wanting to talk to her, just to keep her with me but after a while she would tire and slip away. She opened her eyes.

"Cassidy? Can you talk to me for a few minutes? Who did this to you?"

"Tom," I said. "I know who the guy is. I can take you to him. But I'm not going to yet. Leave Cass alone."

"Cassidy," Tom insisted. "How did you get like this? Tell me what happened."

"No…" she said. She was worried. It was written all over her face. She knew whatever she said would condemn Brian. "Tom, he didn't know. He wasn't intentionally mean to me. He just didn't know. Didn't know he hurt me."

"Oh, come on, how could he not know?" Tom barked. His irritation led to more worry on Cass' part.

Cassidy answered weakly, "When he asked me why I didn't walk I told him that he had hurt my legs. He said he would never hurt me. He didn't understand what he had done."

"He's got the mentality of a five year old," I told Tom. "I've worked with him at McGyver's school. He doesn't even know his right hand from his left. He behaved like a toddler. He threw temper tantrums. He couldn't follow instructions. I can easily believe he had no idea the extent of Cassidy's injuries."

"So, McGyver will tell me where I can find this guy?" Tom asked.

"No. You head for McGyver and I'm on the phone. Drop it for now. If there is one person alive who would want to track down this guy, it would be me. When I saw Cassidy lying there in the barn I could have torn the guy limb from limb, all six foot two hundred pounds of him. But I didn't. He's not going anywhere because he's a big kid. He lives with his mom and the only difference between him and a five year old is a five year old goes to school. Instead of school he shaves. Or maybe he doesn't. Maybe his mom even does that. Drop it. I'll take you to him when the time is right."

"The time is right now."

"No."

"We need to jump on this."

"No. *We don't. We* are going to get out of CCU. *We* are going to stick together and *we are* going to make it through this with as little interference as possible and then we're going to go home and… Tom, I'll take you to him when the time is right. It's not right. It's not. And I can't make it be right. So either sit down and be a friend or go back to the station and do whatever it is you do. This case will be closed soon enough. If you don't want to sit down, then ask Schroeder for a new case. There's nothing more you can do for now."

I don't know what it was, the quiet desperation for things to be right from minute to minute, maybe he could see that I wasn't going to be pushed. Maybe he knew that pushing Cassidy right now could put me over the edge. Whatever it was, he sat down and resigned himself to just being a friend.

"What's next?" he asked.

"We make it through the day."

"And then?"

"We make it through tomorrow."

"How's it going?"

"Good."

"When do I get my next boxing match?"

Tom and Cassidy had an inside joke. Tom was the only guy who would box with Cassidy. He took her on when he was new to the force, and didn't know me yet. When Cassidy would box with Tom it was a sure thing she was well on her way to recovery. She may be working through some limitations but Tom knew his bounds.

"Three months. At least three months."

"A rough one, was it?"

"Yeah, you could say that."

"Tom?" Cassidy said. She had drifted off while we talked but she had something she needed to say. "Thanks. I know you put a lot of time and work into this case. Thanks for giving me that. If you ever need tracking down... I know you put your all into it. You can take a well-earned break now. I'll be after you for that boxing match."

A few days later Tom visited Cassidy again, but he wasn't there to visit Cassidy. He dropped an evidence bag into my hand. Then he handed me the report that went along with the analysis of the evidence. He did this because he knew I couldn't open it up and examine it. Just glancing at the old cell phone in the bag I could see why it had been useless to try to track it down. It had been taken apart and put back together but the report revealed the inner workings of the phone had been heavily damaged.

"He thought he could fix it," Cassidy explained weakly. "I told him it needed charging. I needed him to try to keep it working. It was my only link. I cringed every time he poked the inside with a screw driver."

The case had been clumsily taped. It was a miracle the phone worked at all. Tom seemed to agree.

"Buddy," he said. "My head knows better but I can't help but think God preserved a tiny thread between you two to give you hope."

I didn't think so. I thought if God was out there he could have done a better job than that. But I couldn't help but wonder. The phone looked totally useless, but it had worked whenever Cassidy managed to get her hands on it.

Cass' first meal should have been something to celebrate but she just looked at it.

"What's wrong, babe? You haven't eaten for weeks. I thought you'd make yourself sick the first time you got real food."

"I just got so used to not dwelling on my feelings. I don't know how to feel anymore. I shoved away the hunger. I ignored the cold. The telephone and the water became my priorities. I could do something about the water and the telephone."

"I've never felt hunger like that," I said. "What does it feel like?"

"Never. You'll never feel it if I can help it. I was forgotten." She slumped into the pillows. "I didn't know how long I could last. I yearned for you. I missed you so much. All I could do was think. I couldn't move. I was trapped in my body and my body was failing. I tuned out so many things. I withdrew until I was nobody. Rusty…" She pushed the tray away.

I couldn't hold her. She still hurt to be held. But I hugged her gently. "You were never forgotten. Not for a second. I thought about you every moment of every day."

Once her system was back in working order she was allowed to go home for a week until her scheduled surgery. I knew it would be a battle of wills to keep her down but I wanted her to see Katie. *I* wanted to see Katie. I wanted us to be a family again.

Chapter 14

I had a lump in my throat as I wheeled her out of the hospital and an even bigger one when she didn't want to go home first. She wanted to go to the station. She thought if she went home first she'd be stuck there. She had people to thank. She wouldn't let me push the wheelchair, either. She let me open doors but she wanted to do as much as she could by herself. I could tell the activity was wearing on her but she smiled and spoke to each person she knew. She reached out to each person like long lost family she hadn't seen in years. People recoiled when confronted with her gaunt frame but brightened considerably when they spoke to her and saw the life in her eyes. When an officer meets a person who has been run through the mill they have to do a few thigs. First they wonder how it happened. Then they wonder how to help. This happens in a matter of seconds. It takes an experienced cop to see those thoughts flicker in their eyes. When they get to the stage where they can focus on helping they are ready to talk to the person. I'm sure Cassidy saw this progression over and over during our time at the station, but she didn't let it get to her.

She knocked on Schroeder's office door.

He opened it and had to look around before he saw Cassidy sitting in front of him. He squatted down to her level. "We knew you could do it," he said.

She reached out for her hug. When he put his arms around her we exchanged glances. He could tell what she'd been through. She was all skin and bone. She weighed less than a hundred pounds. Her arms looked like sticks. I was lucky in a way. Though I felt her frailty, it just felt so good to hold her. Just her being there overcame anything else. My heart overrode my brain and I could enjoy her easier than others could.

"I promised Rusty something if you came back. Did he tell you about it?"

"No, but I won't hold you to it, if you don't want to."

"Do you really want to know what my name is?"

"You know I do. You caught me snooping through your Christmas cards looking for it."

"I'll tell you, if it means that much to you."

She thought about it for a second. "What will I do for entertainment if I don't snoop through your Christmas cards?"

"You'll have to pester me to play the piano."

"I can't do both? Schroeder, I'm curious about your name, but I think I'd rather discover it. You don't have to tell it to me."

"Will you stick around until you find out what it is?"

"I'll try."

"Then I'll keep my secret a while longer."

"What's going to happen to Brian?"

"We're still working on that. I don't think you need to worry about him."

"Schroeder, I'm not worried about my safety. I'm worried about *him*, as a person. His situation isn't the same as most of your kidnappers. He…"

"We're on it. And so is social services. It's complicated. But you don't need to worry about Brian."

"There's another stop I'd like to make if we can get there on time," I said. "Are you up to it? When is Fred Nichols usually at the gym?"

"He leaves about eleven thirty. How do you know Fred?"

"Anybody who visits the gym in the morning knows Fred. And… I know just about everybody you do after questioning people for a month straight."

Fred was working out in the weight room when we arrived but many people waved at Cass as she wheeled herself around the gym. Gradually, as they finished a set, or a mile, or burned off an even hundred calories…they would come see her. She greeted them all, most of them by name. When Fred saw a lull in the activity he came over.

"Well, well, if it isn't our little tracker back from the dead. When are you going to do your five mile run again?"

"Not for a while. But I'll be back."

"I know you will. Because you got what it takes. You got to put some meat on them bones. Remember, you need a hand you just call old Fred."

"You're not old. You're in better shape than some of the twenty year olds."

"See?" Fred said to me. "She doesn't let anybody put themself down. She's a picker upper, she is. We need her here. Look. See that heavy, black lady in blue on the treadmill? She huffs and puffs for fifteen minutes. She needs a Cassidy pep talk."

"What's her name?"

"Georgia."

Cassidy wheeled over, "Hi! I'm Cassidy. Fred says you're new here…"

I don't know what they talked about. I was busy filling Fred in on what had happened.

"She'll be back," I said. "But don't push her."

"No one needs to push Cass. She pushes herself. Sometimes I wonder why she's punishing herself but she never seems to overdo it."

"She will at first."

"We'll see. She's got Fred watchin' out for her. Just don't know how I can slow her down. She takes almost anything as a challenge."

"You'll figure something out. Surgery in a week. Then she'll be out until she feels up to coming. No walking for three months."

Cass wheeled back over. "She's going to work on that first mile and I'm going to work on crunches."

"Can you even do crunches? It's likely to be painful with those ribs and you're not going to want to crunch anything after surgery."

"Oh, this is just before surgery. I don't know if I can crunch or not but I've got to start somewhere."

"Are you ready to go? There are people at home waiting to see you, too."

"I'll see you tomorrow," she said to Fred. She wheeled over to Georgia. "One week?" she asked.

"One mile?" Georgia asked.

"Yeah and crunches for me."

"Deal."

Mom was waiting at the window when we pulled into the driveway. She came outside and watched as I lifted Cassidy from the truck to the wheelchair. Cassidy took off pushing herself before I could get a hand on the wheelchair. Mom took her worry and stuffed it away. I watched the transformation as Cassidy wheeled up the walk.

"Cassidy... Cody was coming up for a job interview. He asked Rusty if he could stay here. That's how we found out what happened. I was so worried. As time went by we didn't know what to think... Rusty was not himself. He was... It's so good to have you back. Is the wheelchair..."

"Temporary? Yes. Some dumb bone called an acetabulum seems to have broken. I need a realignment. Unfortunately it's more complicated on people than it is on cars."

"What happened to you? You..."

"Bev, I'll be fine. I need to put on a little weight. I'll need to go back in a week and let them cut me up, but then I'll be back. I'll be fine."

Mom straightened up, put her hands on her hips, glared at Cass and said, "Now look here, young lady, you can make light of this if you want to but you're stuck with me until I'm satisfied you can take care of things yourself."

I laughed to myself and went to Cassidy's rescue. "Mom, I've got a month off. I told Schroeder I was taking a month no questions asked. We figure it will probably take longer than that. You're welcome to stay..."

After a long discussion we could see we needed help.

The first night home I put Cass in bed. We stripped her slowly. I was worried about movements hurting her. When she lay there before me I couldn't believe she was mine again. Nothing looked wrong with her. She just looked frail. I wanted her so bad. I climbed in bed next to her. I took her in my arms, afraid to squeeze, and just breathed in her presence. She still smelled like a hospital.

One of my fondest memories of the week she was home was the showers. I don't know if Cassidy needed help in the shower. It was built for wheelchair access because of the previous owners, so she might have been fine, but since we had live-in babysitters we used the shower as an excuse to play. It was a place where we could be as sexy or funny or loving as we wanted to, or felt up to. Each morning we started out, me worrying about hurting her, her trying to make it into play time. Her mischievous side came out. She didn't feel sexy. She felt beaten but she would quickly decide she wasn't going to let that get in the way and we ended up in a soapy, slithery embrace until we both turned wrinkled from the water.

Another thing that gave me a lot of joy was watching Cassidy on the floor with Katie. They lay on the floor working through the pockets on a quilt Cassidy's mother had made. Katie liked it when Cass lay on her back on the floor and lifted her up over her head to grab things from the floor. Katie was getting big. I wondered how Cass' matchstick arms did it.

Every day she took a "walk" around the block with Katie. At first I paced the house, just waiting for them to get back. A walk around the block was over a mile. Cass said there was no hurry; if she got tired she'd just rest. The first walks took a long time and I wondered if I should drive around and see if she needed a ride. I always talked myself out of it. As the week progressed she made the circle faster. The last time around she came in all scraped up.

"Wheel off the pavement," she explained. I tried not to think of the struggle she'd had, righting the chair, picking up Katie, working her way back into the chair with a kid to deal with.

Every day we went to the gym. I worked out on the machine next to her and we worked our way around the machines that didn't require the use of her lower body. She avoided any twisting motions. Every time we came into the gym Georgia's attitude suddenly took on a determined look and she trudged a little farther. Cass did her crunches. Each day she reported her progress to Georgia.

"Have you lost any weight?" Cassidy would ask her.

"It's hard to tell, it comes off and it comes back, comes off and comes back."

"It'll come off more the farther you can walk. Have you tried the elliptical?"

"No. They look like they're for healthy people."

"Anybody can try. Try all the equipment and find what you enjoy doing.

If you like it you'll be more likely to keep it up."

"How 'bout you? Have you gained any?"

"It's hard to tell, since I'm not supposed to stand."

On Friday Cassidy and Georgia made a deal. Cassidy would make it through a successful surgery and Georgia would be walking a full mile the next time they met.

I dreaded Saturday. I didn't want to take Cassidy back to LA, but it had to be done. Friday night I undressed and got in bed. Cassidy sat in her wheelchair by the bay window. She liked to sit there and watch the deer come down to the yard to graze. I could see the longing in her eyes. She wanted to be out there with them, but the deer were long gone that evening.

She turned her chair to me and began taking her clothes off. I started to get up to help her.

"Don't. Stay there. Please."

I settled back and she slowly undressed in her chair. She struggled with the pants but shot me a warning glare. When she was nude she flipped up the footrests and stood.

"Cass! No," I said, my heart hammering.

"Stay there. I want to show you something."

She slowly took a step. Her left leg jerked oddly when she walked but she didn't show any traces of pain. That didn't mean much though. I knew she was very capable of hiding it.

"I'm stronger now than I will be for three months," she said. "I did this before. It showed me I have to have the surgery to work again. I can't track like this. But there's some things I can do. You're not going to want to do what I'm going to ask." Step after jerky step she crossed the room until she stood at the side of the bed. "I've been a good girl all week. Make love to me. Please. You're afraid of hurting me. I'll tell you what I can do and what I can't. Just make love to me."

"I can't."

"Yes you can. You won't hurt me. You don't have it in you to hurt me."

She was wrong. I did want to make love to her. I did most of the time. But she was right. I was scared. Just imagining my two hundred pounds thrusting into her scared me.

It was like the very first time. She'd written about that in her books, too. It was a night of quiet talk, sensuous touches. Tentative teasing. Patient guiding. It was caring for one another. This time we were comfortable together. Communication was better.

"Ah! No, that won't work," she'd tell me. "Help me flip over. Okay, that's better."

It was hard for me to tell when she'd come. She didn't come with the usual frenzy of action. It was gentle, sensuous, frail and honest. When it was over she lay there exhausted.

"I'll be back," she said curled up against me with her head on my shoulder. "As soon as I can. I'm going to miss you so much."

"I'll be right there. You won't miss me."

"If I could work like this I would skip the surgery. But I'll never build back up like this."

"You'll build back up. I know you. You'll do it. When Georgia is going for a mile and a half you'll be doing two and when she gets to two you'll be jogging again."

She spent as much of Saturday morning as she could with Katie. They read Katie's favorite book, ate breakfast, rolled around on the floor together. Katie was there as she packed a bag of things to do at the hospital. A flash of inspiration hit me and I went to find Cody. I tossed him the keys to Cassidy's Jeep, a credit card and instructed him to go buy a laptop computer small enough to use anywhere, but large enough to have a decent keyboard. Off he went, while I stayed and soaked up minutes.

I felt like I was condemning Cassidy to three months in prison even though we both knew the surgery had to be done. The surgery and recovery was going to be hard for her. I was amazed how easy it had been to keep her in the wheelchair for a week. I worried something deeper was wrong. Was she in more pain than she let on? One reason I took a leave of absence was so I could keep her busy enough to prevent her from getting bored and stir crazy. I wanted to spend some time just being together having fun. I knew that girl of mine could have fun in a wheelchair. If I could keep her active, I was convinced, she would sail through these three months. We'd have some challenging times getting mobile again, but I thought that would be the easy part. After the pain eased she would begin trying too hard, too fast. That's when I'd have to change from quiet supporter to firm disciplinarian. I hoped the detective in me was ready for a rest. She didn't need that kind of help.

When Cody got back we put the computer in the truck, out of sight.

The time came when we couldn't put off the drive any more. Traffic was flowing and we pulled into the hospital parking lot a little early. We sat there in the Explorer, staring at the bleak hospital building, wondering how long we'd be here, missing Katie already. I couldn't think of any good reason to go in, so I started the truck again and we left.

"Where are you going?" Cassidy asked.

"As soon as you get admitted it's going to be clear liquids until after surgery. We're going to find a piece of cheesecake."

We drove around until Cassidy pointed out a restaurant that would have cheesecake. We circled the block a few times before we found a parking place. I got out the wheelchair and she got into it reluctantly. We were shown to a table for two and ordered two desserts. She got her cheesecake and I got a hot fudge brownie ice cream creation. We took two spoons and shared both. We were both feeling rather down, not wanting to continue down the path we were walking.

"After you can get around we're going to go show your family you're alive and well. Then we're going to take our time driving down the coast. We're going to go try on foam alligator hats on the pier and eat Ben and Jerry's on the patio of that little scoop shop."

"Are you going to drip all over me again?" she asked.

"Only if I get to lick it off."

"I doubt I'm going to have a swimsuit body when I'm through with this. It doesn't do much good to drip all over clothes."

"You'll be beautiful no matter how it goes."

"Maybe they'll give me a cute butt so I can wear those tight jeans."

"I thought you didn't like to be cute."

"A cute butt and overall cuteness are different."

"You want guys to notice your butt? Babe, believe me, they notice."

"I'm just joking. Hey, one thing about needing to put on weight, I don't have to count all the calories in this chocolate fudge. There are advantages to being a ninety-nine pound weakling."

"You're not a weakling. You're one of the strongest people I know. The doctor was amazed you survived."

"Me too. I don't even remember some of it."

"Do you remember trying to call me?"

"Two times. Brian would leave the phone on the ground and I'd roll or army crawl to it but he'd remember it and take it away. He'd scold me that it wasn't mine, that I shouldn't touch it."

"You called me three times. The last time you didn't say anything. I could hear Brian in the background digging a hole. Now that I've been there and seen it, I think he was trying to dig your grave. He thought you were dying."

"Don't. Don't start. You'll get yourself all depressed. There's a rule. Let's see. It needs a number. Pick a number."

"Cass…"

"No, come on pick a number."

"Okay, fifteen."

"You don't want a more interesting number? We might have to say it a lot."

"An interesting number?"

"Oh! I've got it! Three point one four one five."

"What?"

"The rule of pi! Rule three point one four one five says you can't eat dessert and be depressed at the same time."

"Babe, where do you come up with these things? How can anybody be depressed with you around?"

"So, we're going to the ranch and then down the coast? How far down the coast? San Diego?"

"If time permits. Speaking of the time, we better get back."

"Oops, I got some fudge on my finger," she said mischievously.

I could take a hint. I licked it off, slowly, with lots of eye contact.

"Oh, now you have a little smudge on your lip."

"Cassidy…"

"These people don't know us and they'll never see us again," she said as she leaned over and kissed me.

Admission was a slow, tedious process. Our patience was stretched by the time we were shown to a room on the surgical floor. After all was said and done, Cassidy was stuck in bed with an IV. It bothered me to eat dinner when she couldn't have anything. I remembered her weeks of starvation and thought it wasn't fair.

"I'm not hungry," she assured me. "They're pumping me full of something. I don't know what it is but I don't feel hungry."

I didn't eat breakfast in front of her. I just couldn't.

She was wheeled into surgery early. I'd just gotten her back. I was still in wonder over it, and seeing her being wheeled away, her life in another man's hands, left me numb. I ate a tasteless breakfast in the cafeteria downstairs, then I checked in with the surgical nurses so they'd know where to find me. Time crawled. Later in the morning Cody and Kelly came over, slapped me on the back, hauled me out of the chair and pointed me at the door.

"Leave your cell number with the nurses, we're not going far."

We went to Cassidy's room and Cody set up Cass' computer, started the battery to charging and made sure everything was in working order. He showed me how to hook it up to the wireless Internet. I was pleased. We put the computer away until Cass was ready to use it. I knew she would be groggy for most of the day.

"How did the job interview go?" I asked Cody.

"It was okay, but I don't want to live in the desert. It's taken Cassidy two years to learn how to surf because she can't get to the water. I've been surfing since I was six. I think I'll stick closer to home."

That was my brother. He'd rather rent kayaks to the tourists than make three times as much in the desert being a "respectable businessman." I couldn't imagine him as a respectable businessman anyway. In a way I'd rather see him renting out kayaks.

When I got a call to go back downstairs Kelly and Cody said they had someplace to go and they'd see me later. I met with the doctor who assured me everything went as planned.

"She's young and strong. If she'll take her time and let the bones knit she should be on her feet again by the end of summer."

I sat with Cassidy in Recovery. She lay so still, so small. I kept thinking if I pulled the covers down there would be nobody in there. The bed seemed to swallow her. I wished I could fix her, like Brian had asked me to, but I knew, too, that she would be back. This bout of trouble hadn't beaten her.

She had a miserable time getting over the anesthesia. The anesthesia made her sick but there was nothing in her stomach to come up. Her head pounded. She tried to shield her eyes from the light, tried to curl into a ball on her side but she couldn't move. Then as the sickness eased the pain grew. She was too miserable to even know who was there. The nurse came and went frequently, checking on things I'd never understand. She must have noted Cassidy's condition because the doctor, at last, prescribed something that sent her into a deep sleep. She slept for a day.

I slept in the chair next to her bed knowing when she came around her days and nights were going to be confused. If Kelly and Cody came back I was either in Recovery or asleep. When I woke up I checked on Cass. I knew medications would hit her hard right now but it seemed like she was taking an awful long time to wake up. I debated trying to talk to her and decided as long as she was asleep she wasn't in pain. I longed to hear her voice. Something to show me we were back on track.

Cody and Kelly burst into the room, loudly joking but their faces quickly fell.

"She's still out?" Kelly asked.

"It's from the medication. She woke up sick and in pain."

Cody and Kelly looked at each other.

"Oh well," Cody said. "I give her five seconds."

"Five seconds for what?"

"I can't tell you. Just tell us how long it takes."

"How am I supposed to know, if you won't tell me anything?"

With voices in the room Cassidy began stirring.

"Hey, Little Sis. It's about time you woke up," Cody said.

Cassidy looked from face to face, puzzled. I wondered why she would be puzzled. Kelly and Cody were often visitors when Cassidy was under the weather.

"Why is there a disco ball in the middle of the room?" she asked.

Huh? I just spent two days in the room without noticing anything odd and Cassidy spotted it in… well, about five seconds.

"Because, we figure you'll be up dancing in a few days. You need a disco ball," Cody said.

"Cody, this is one of your jokes, isn't it?" she asked. "I don't know how to dance. I've never been to a dance in my life."

"Then study break dancing. You're all set up for that."

"Ha, ha, very funny."

I had my girl back.

They turned off the room lights and turned on the disco ball. Cody had just started demonstrating when the doctor walked in.

"Are you single?" the doctor asked Cody.

"Very," Cody answered.

"Go talk to the nurse in the Vegas scrubs. Tell her she owes me."

"I'll be back," Cody said as he walked out the door.

Kelly turned off the disco ball and turned the room lights back on as he went out.

"How do you feel?" the doctor asked.

"I don't know. I'm not quite awake yet. Maybe in your poking around I'll find out."

I was shocked at the sight of the incisions. I knew they would be extensive but it still took me by surprise.

"I've got some good news and some bad news. The good news is the right acetabulum was healed enough that we decided to leave it alone. The bad news is the left side was worse than we expected. The result is that you should be able to move about sooner, but you will have to rest that left side a solid three months."

"That sounds like mostly good news," she said. "The bad news was expected. Being able to put weight on the right side will help a lot getting in and out of the car and gym equipment."

"Gym? What are you doing going to a gym? What do you do there?"

Cassidy rattled off a list of machines she had been using. He scratched a couple off her list.

After the doctor left I brought out the laptop. Cassidy cast me a questioning look.

"I thought you'd be bored. And I wanted you to be able to write."

"You want me to write?"

"I do."

"Why?"

"I told you about it before but you've had a lot coming at you for the past week."

"I was kind of overwhelmed there for a while," she admitted.

"When you'd been gone for weeks and I was facing the fact that I might have lost you, on top of everything else, I ran into computer problems. I was cleaning files off my computer, and I stumbled on your stories. When I wasn't at work or searching any tiny lead, I was reading. It brought you back to life and restored my sense of hope. I hit the search with new determination. As I went along the stories kept me going. Some of the guys have read them, too. Kelly has read about his rescue. Schroeder's read some of them. That's why he offered to tell you his name. He read the story about the Christmas party his wife threw."

"He read about the party?" she said, embarrassed because she had teased me mercilessly until we left the party early and made love in the Explorer on the way home.

"Victor has read many of them. Jacobsen, Thompson, Big John. They've read parts of them."

"Rusty! How could you? If... if I'd known others were going to read them I would have... I would have written them differently. Now they've been passed around the station? Who else has seen them?"

"Don't worry. If I hadn't found those writings I don't think you'd be here today. I wouldn't have met Brian. Farley asked me to teach Brian and I turned him down until I read about Farley in your books. When I saw how much he'd done for you, I thought I owed him a half hour a week, at least. That's how I met Brian. If I hadn't met Brian. If I hadn't gotten ticked off about his sick pet. If his mother hadn't called me to go find him at the barn, I don't think you would have lasted another day. Will you keep writing? For me?"

"It gets harder the older Katie gets."

"I got to see what you were doing while you were at the ranch without me. I found out what really happened when you were carjacked. I got to see what makes you happy and what makes you mad. I felt the hurt you had when you had to shoot a man for the first time. I saw the girl I love so much from the inside out. It was the best gift you could ever give to me."

She was in the hospital for a week because a fever sprang up and they worried about infection. Cassidy had plenty of time to write but she had trouble writing with me in the room. She wrote a lot in the early morning when her thinking was clearer.

We went home with a hefty dose of antibiotics and mild painkillers. We had two very rough days of constant pain and sleepless nights.

Cody took the disco ball home and hung it in our living room, then he moved the furniture against the wall so there would be room for dancing. He asked to borrow the Jeep and drove back to LA for a date with that nurse in Vegas scrubs.

When Mom, Dad, and Cody went back to San Diego and we were alone, I did a lot of the work around the house. I learned how to cook a little. Cassidy helped me and watched Katie. Laundry was a never ending chore with a baby in the house. Cass caught up on her time with Katie and she had time to write as stories came to her.

One last note. After the case was closed I took the cell phone back to Derrick Bellows. He stared at it, still in the evidence bag.

"So it comes full circle," he said. "I'm glad you found your wife, though I am sorry about what happened."

"It was a rough one," I admitted.

"You talk like this isn't anything unusual."

"I… I asked her for any time I could get. I signed up for this."

"I've got no use for this anymore," he said as he took the phone out of the bag. "It's old. Broken. I should replace all the phones the crews carry. Do you want it?"

I stuck my hands in my pockets, thinking, but not. This decision didn't require thinking. It required feeling.

"Yeah, I think I do. I might need a reminder that anything is possible when it comes to Cassidy. If she can make it through this she can make it through anything."

I keep the phone in my desk drawer at work. When I feel like a case is hopeless, when I have a family to talk to and the news is bad, I take out that phone and just hold it. The little bit of hope it contains seeps into my hands. I take a deep breath and do what I have to.

Chapter 1

Cassidy's Story

Brian took me completely by surprise. I had seen him at Farley's school. Just like all the kids, I chatted with him as I moved around the ranch helping the one student assigned to me. He asked me if I could be his teacher and I responded that Mr. McGyver decided who his teacher would be.

"You nice teeshur," he said.

I thanked him and went on my way. I had a thirteen-year-old kid waiting for me. We were going to learn posting that day. It was important that this kid learn to post because he needed to build up strength in his legs. It was an easy lesson. There isn't anything difficult about posting. Anybody who has been bounced on a rough horse figures out how to post on their own. This boy learned to push down with his legs to ease the bouncing but he didn't have the strength to do it for long. It would come with time. If there was anything I learned at Farley McGyver's school it was that most anything will happen given a little determination and time.

Another thing I learned at the school is that age is relative. Farley would introduce me to a new student saying, "This is Aaron, he's thirteen." He never mentioned what the kid's disability was. That I learned when the student was out of ear shot. While we were with the kids they were simply kids. I'd have to work with Aaron and decide for myself how old he really was. In Aaron's case he really was about thirteen. Gangly and shy, he watched the girls at school. He wanted to make advances but was scared to death to. He thought he'd be laughed at because of his awkward stance.

Sometimes I was assigned a thirteen year old and they were more like small children, but some were surprisingly mature. Trials could do that to a kid. Every kid was a new challenge. The only goal was to make their life better. We did that by letting them ride, challenging their current abilities just a bit, and listening. Many kids needed a friend more than anything else. I found the work rewarding. I never intended to keep teaching but when my first student didn't need me anymore I just kept going back.

Brian leaned up against the fence and watched as I worked with Aaron, and then I didn't see him for a long time.

It was a few weeks later that I was driving home from the school and I noticed a black sedan driving erratically behind me. Having close ties with the local police department, I wondered what kind of a driver I was dealing with. I watched in my rearview mirror as the car swerved back and forth. It was odd and stood out in my mind because I couldn't match up the action with something that made sense. This was no drunk driver. Drunk or sleepy drivers have a pattern to their actions. They drift until they realize they are off and then correct suddenly, stay on track for a little while, until senses dull again. This guy was all over the place. There were no sudden corrections. It was just complete inability to drive straight. The driver cranked the wheel hard one direction and when he realized he was headed toward the shoulder he cranked hard the other direction. Micro corrections were a mystery to this person.

I pulled off the road to let the car pass. I wanted it to get well ahead of me so I dug in my pack to find money to pay Bertie for her babysitting. I considered calling an officer to pull the guy over, but I never got a chance to. I stuck a twenty dollar bill into my pocket and closed up the little daypack. I had just set it on the passenger side floorboards when the door of my Jeep was yanked open and a vice like grip encircled me. I fumbled for my gun, but I knew it was well hidden. I kept it locked up so Katie couldn't get it. At least that's what I told myself. The truth was I had an aversion to shooting people. My arms were pinned down and the man just jerked harder and harder, not even thinking about the seat belt. I was more worried about the violence of getting yanked out of the Jeep than I was about the man. A man I could deal with. I pulled on the seatbelt trying to unlatch it so I could run. I didn't unlatch it, but I managed to loosen it. A forceful tug brought my head into the roll bar of the Jeep and I didn't know anything until I woke up in a barn.

My head pounded. My ribs screamed with any movement but what alarmed me was I couldn't do anything with my legs. They would move but just rolling over caused a wave of nausea and I passed out again.

When I woke again Brian was sitting on the floor beside me.

"You sleep a long time," he said.

"What am I doing here?" I asked.

"I'm keeping you. You're nice. You stay with me."

When he spoke I recognized the classic signs of a mental handicap. He certainly wasn't physically handicapped. Six feet tall. A big man. His flat top contrasted with a broad childlike head. He looked like a ten year old schoolyard bully all grown up. Unfortunately, he was still a ten year old. Later I refined my guess about his mental capacity.

"You can't just keep people. It's wrong," I told him.

"Why?"

"Because people are meant to be free."

"I wasn't," he stated. "Mom keep me."

"You have to let me go. I have a family. I need to go home. I have a home, too. If I don't go home my family will start looking for me. If they don't find me they will call the police."

"No. I keep you. You like me someday. Maybe you stay."

"What's your name?" I asked.

"Brian."

He didn't ask for mine and I didn't tell him what mine was. I thought if I did he'd think I liked him. If he thought I liked him he would think I was staying. I had no intention of staying.

When he left he locked the doors. I tried sitting up. My hip wouldn't let me. I tried an army crawl, dragging my useless legs behind me. My ribs wouldn't let me go far but I set my determination to reach the nearest wall. If I had been able bodied I probably could have knocked out a board. I'd learned in police academy how to kick in a door. The same principal would work for a board. I tried but I couldn't even raise a leg to give the board a kick. To use my arms I had to put weight on my ribs. I decided to bide my time. It wasn't as if I was awaiting execution. I thought dealing with Brian would get me further.

At first Brian came to the barn every day. He would bring a packet of fruit chews, a bag of chips, maybe a sandwich if it was right after his lunch. He never thought to bring me something to drink. It was the second day after I'd heard some sprinklers come on outside the barn that I eventually broke off a piece of board. I looked through the hole where the board broke off. I saw scraggly grass, a very sharp, tough looking rose bush, and a sprinkler. At first I twisted off the head of the sprinkler but then the water shot straight up and I had no way to contain it. I ended up putting the head back on the sprinkler and angling the board to make the water run into the barn. I lay at the downhill end of the board twice a day, every day as often as I could. Eventually one of the branches sprouted out sideways and a tiny bud began forming. I was tempted to eat it and I did eat the grass and milkweed beside the hole, but I let the rose live. Sometimes I lay gazing out the hole, that bright red blossom dominating the scene. Nobody came to the barn except Brian.

"Brian," I said. "How often do you eat?"

"Mom good cook. She makes breakfast and lunch and dinner."

"So how often do you think I should eat?"

"I can't come to the barn every time. Mom ask questions."

Good, I thought, maybe she should.

"I get hungry just as often as you do. Everybody needs food."

"I try. Tomorrow I try."

"I'm starving. People need regular meals. It isn't right to keep me here. If you don't let me go the police will come and take you to jail. It's against the law to keep a person against their will. It's called kidnapping. The police take kidnappers very seriously. If they think you will hurt someone they will definitely hurt you."

"Police no catch me. Why they think you here?"

He only stayed briefly. Sometimes when I ate he would sit beside me and stroke my hair. He was very tender in some ways and very hard headed in others.

After several days of only eating a half sandwich or less a day I started getting weak and shaky. I made sure to break off the grass outside the hole in the wall and not pull it up. If I broke it off it would grow back. There wasn't much there but it was better than nothing.

Necessities were a problem. It was sheer torture. Each time I had to go I rolled across the barn, ribs and hips exploding in pain. Getting my pants down was worse. There was no toilet paper. I just had to do my best and live with the consequences. Then I would roll back to be close to my water source. As I grew weaker and weaker I couldn't roll far but as Brian's visits tapered off I didn't have to go as often. I could feel myself slipping away, gradually entering a slow decline.

My thoughts were usually about practical things. I thought of different ways to escape. I tried yelling. There was no one around. I worked on the boards but the barn was good and solid. That one small piece of board was the only one I could budge after hours of excruciating tugging and pushing. When it broke it almost fell out of reach and I had to grope around through the hole to get it back. It took an hour to get that little piece of insurance, that trickle of water each evening that saved my life.

I rolled to the door but I couldn't open it. I managed to pull myself upright one time but it didn't do any good. I couldn't put weight on my hip and I fell, writhing in pain even though I knew I was just making it worse. It wasn't until the pain turned to tears that I lay still enough for the pain to subside. It took me most of the day to make my way back to the water and lay as still as I could.

I scolded myself for letting my guard down. I assumed the erratic driver was just driving in the hills and high on something. If I had just looked up a second or two sooner I could have prevented my situation from happening.

I was convinced that if I could get out of the barn I could army crawl enough to find help. I was willing to endure the pain if I just got a chance to try it, but the barn was stronger than I was.

About this time Brian began wondering if I was sick.

"What's wrong Rose?" he asked.

"I need food and water. Everybody needs food and water, just like you."

"I bring food. I bring you apple. Apple good for you."

"Yes, can you get another one?" I asked.

"Maybe tomorrow. Mom not let me come. She make me stay home."

"You're going to kill me. The way you're treating me is hurting me. Let me call my husband. He'll come get me."

"No, you not go away." His brow furrowed and he glared at me. I counted my lucky stars he was not a violent man.

"Would you rather I be here and dead or someplace else and alive?"

"You no be dead! You my Rose! You my Rose and you no go away."

I never got that other apple.

I had a particularly bad night where temperatures dipped. I shivered and the shivering hurt every broken bone. I worked all night at ignoring the cold, ignoring the hunger.

After a few weeks had gone by and existing had just become a necessity, I noticed with alarm that I couldn't remember long stretches of time. I'd fall asleep at night, barely glimpse daylight and then it would be night again. I lost all track of time. I tried to reconstruct how long I had been in the barn and couldn't do it. I had to do something.

"Rose? Why you sleeping? Always you are sleeping. Are you okay?"

"No. I need help. Please get me help. Bring your mom here. She'll know what to do."

He flew into a rage, very scared of his mother finding out about me.

"Can't!" he yelled, stomping around the barn, "Me can't! Mom find out about you she send you away! You no go away. You're mine! Don't be sick, please, don't be sick. Rose, you get well. I get sick. I get well again. You'll be well." His ranting petered out into a quiet sadness and he paced the barn nervously until he calmed down and then he wandered off.

The request had made one breakthrough though. Brian knew I needed help. Where would he turn to get it?

The next time he visited he had a cell phone in his hand. It was a very old, very battered cell phone. It had been through the wars. He didn't know how to use it but he knew it was useful. He knew help was on the other end. He puzzled over the tiny buttons and his big fingers and lack of coordination were too much for him. He set the phone down and went to work. He often worked in the barn after he visited with me. I never could figure out what he thought he was doing. He would walk around like he was planning something. He mucked out the imaginary stalls, not understanding where the mess came from. When I saw the cell phone on the ground I rolled to it slowly. Fighting tears, watching Brian, and ignoring the pain in my ribs took a lot of will power. At first Brian didn't notice the intentions of my actions.

"Why you no walk, Rose?" he asked.

"I can't. You hurt my legs."

"I not hurt you. I love you," he said and then went back to work.

With my hazy thinking I speed dialed Rusty and a girl answered the phone with the name of a company. I was puzzled. I should have asked her for help but I just got fuddled and hung up. I punched in Rusty's number and Brian walked up. When he did, he accidentally hit my hip with the toe of his shoe. Pain lanced through me as Rusty answered the phone. I couldn't think. It was my one chance and I couldn't think! I weakly said, "Black car. Four doors...Russ..." Brian glared at me, arms crossed over his chest, then he whipped the phone out of my hand and threw it across the barn.

"*My* phone! You don't use it! You no go away!" He bellowed. I thought he was going to pick me up and I cringed away from him but he didn't. He stomped his foot and clenched his fists but he turned away and took out his frustration away from me. "You no go away. Rose, you stay."

I lay back completely spent. I wondered if Brian's reaction and turning his back on the conflict was a coping response he used with his mother. It made sense that he would hesitate to attack her. Maybe when he got in trouble he was used to turning his back on her and separating himself from it. I'd have to remember that.

The next time I woke up I realized I'd missed a watering time. My one chance for water that day and I'd missed it. I rolled back to the hole in the wall and waited and waited, fading.

When my thinking grew hazy I reached out to Rusty, conjuring up pictures of him and Katie. I wondered how Rusty was coping with a baby, work, and his worries about me. When more than two weeks had passed I knew the trail was growing cold. I knew my chances shrunk daily. I knew my body failed a little more with each passing day. And then my mind began failing a little more as time went on until I only existed. I think, therefore I am. But what am I when I cease thinking? I am. What am I when my heart ceases? I am, a little less, but I am. What am I when my body slowly disintegrates? Then... I am... a barn. In and out of my thoughts I drifted.

Water, the water was on. I tilted my head to catch the drips. I coughed and gasped because my throat was so dry it didn't know what to do with water any more. I swallowed as much as I could, hoping it was enough.

"Rose? I bring food. Wake up. Eat."

I pulled myself up out of the depths of semi consciousness. It was chips. Great. Just what I needed, salt. Something to make me thirsty. And a small glass of milk. Milk? Now that I think back about it, the milk might have been what saved me. A whole four ounces of liquid all at once.

Brian sat and watched me eat. He got out the cell phone. He pushed buttons. He brightened, put the phone up to his ear.

"Hello? Hello?...Who is this? My name Brian. Me talk on telephone."

"Help!" I croaked to some unknown person on the other end, "Send help!" Where to? Some barn? Some person named Brian's house? I had no idea where I was. "I'm in a barn. Call the police. Tell them I'm in a barn."

But Brian got irritated and I think he disconnected.

"You no go away. You not try that again! You mine. Mine, Rose!"

The milk made me feel ill. I thought things couldn't get worse and then they did. Abdominal cramps went on for hours. I lay as still as I could, tuning out everything I could, waiting for water. Waiting. Silently I cried out for Rusty, for Katie. Would I ever see them again? There were so many people I wanted to see. If I ever saw them again I'd give them a hug. Even Schroeder. Big, tough Schroeder.

I turned my head to the side and an object on the ground seemed different somehow. I had to think to focus on it. The phone. I dragged myself over to it and collapsed. Had to get back to the water. I picked up the phone and dragged myself back. I collapsed again, crying at the pain in my ribs and hips. I inched my way back into the spot where the water would fall and looked at the phone. My hands wouldn't work right. I'd tried to do too much. I managed to shakily punch in Rusty's number but I could feel myself slipping. I found myself babbling useless information, "Black car. White man. Thumbtack in his shoe. Cuts on the soles of his shoes... Rusty... I'm in... a barn. Help. I need help..."

When I looked at the phone again it was dark. How much had gotten through?

A couple of days passed. I only woke up to catch the water. When I felt it hit my face I woke enough to swallow. I didn't see Brian. I tried to reach out to Rusty but my thoughts would fade. Just existing. Then, nothing.

Chapter 2

I was cold. I was used to being cold, used to tuning it out, but this time when I was cold I felt a movement and someone pulled a blanket up. Brian? Brian wouldn't have brought a blanket to the barn. His mom would ask questions. I thought my mind felt sharper. I wasn't floating in a half dream state. I reached for the hole in the wall. Where was the wall? I thought I had accidentally rolled away from it and lost my water supply. I woke with a start and realized I wasn't in the barn. I blinked at the brightness. I had lived in a very dim world in every sense of the word. The light was dim. My thoughts were dim. My captor was even dimwitted. A touch. I flinched.

"Cassidy, it's over, babe, you're back," I heard. Rusty. Rusty was here. A cry tried to work its way up but I didn't even have the strength to cry.

"Rusty… it was so long."

"I know. It was forever. Every day was forever."

And so I was back in the world of the living, just barely. I don't know how long I just drifted, neither awake nor asleep. I was back to just existing but it had a different feel to it. Rusty was there. It was a more hopeful existence because Rusty was there.

It was a long road back. Recovery from the starvation and dehydration was quick. Recovery from the injuries would take longer. A week down and then a surgery, then three months of restricted movement. After what I'd just been through I was ready for anything. I just wanted to get on with it.

Mentally I rebelled against the wheelchair. I didn't mind the image it conjured up. I think I mostly felt that Rusty would think differently of me. He worried too much and to me the wheelchair was just a constant reminder that things were not made right yet. I did my best to appear able. I was determined to strengthen my arms, even though I couldn't do much with my legs. It hurt to sit in the chair, but if I was careful I preferred it to laying around. Rusty took me to the gym. It was difficult to find machines I could use but just the exertion of moving from the chair to the weight machine gave me a workout. I went for "walks" because I couldn't stand to be indoors for very long and wheeling around the block made me feel semi mobile.

Rusty was so caring to me. Sometimes it touched me deeply and sometimes it irked me. He made sure I ate. He bought me cheesecake. And he caught up on minutes. He tried not to be overbearing, but it wasn't working very well.

I had my surgery. I thought I was ready for the surgery, but I was afraid when I thought about the anesthesia. I'd be gone again. I didn't want to be gone again. I wasn't afraid of dying. I was afraid of nothingness again. I had a moment of terror as I felt myself drift away. I wanted to reach for Rusty but I found I wasn't even capable of that.

He was there when I woke up. Rusty, Cody and Kelly. I had four miserable days where nothing went right. Everything made me sick. Everything hurt. Everything crowded me. I tried to back off and see the sickness was temporary, the pain would ease, the people would back off. And eventually they did.

When we were finally alone again, Rusty tried to settle us into a time of healing. We ate peaceful meals as a family. I spent hours on the floor with Katie. We went to the gym. It took forever to build back up, but over time it got easier. I grew stronger.

Katie gave the babysitters at the gym a workout.

"Cassidy Michaels please come to Play Space."

Rusty would go because he knew it was hard for me to extricate myself from the equipment. If I was in my chair I'd wheel over and find out what went wrong. What was usually wrong was that Katie had climbed to the top of the play place.

"How does she do that? She can't even walk yet!" Yoli said.

It had netting on top to keep kids in and netting around the sides to keep them from getting into the area under the tubes. Katie thought of the netting as a ladder. Rusty would call her to the side of the play place. Katie would crawl to the edge and yell down, "Hi! Dada!" He'd lift her down and put her on the floor and we'd go back to our workouts.

Every day I tried something new, working through the pain, unless it involved my hip. I was gradually getting a grip on a recovery plan. I could do this. Given enough time I could make it through this and come out stronger for it. Time was all it took. Time and determination.

"See you tomorrow!" Georgia called out as we left the gym.

"We won't be here tomorrow," Rusty told her. "We're going to be doing a little travel."

"Oh really? Where are you going?" Georgia asked.

"Yeah, where are we going?" I followed up.

"I promised your family we'd come for a visit as soon as you could travel."

Chapter 3

When we pulled up to the ranch house, my mom, dad and sister lined up on the porch, not knowing what they were going to see this time. The ranch hands were out doing their work. My nephew, Patrick, had no reservations, though. He dashed down the steps and ran around the Explorer until he found Katie's widow.

"Katie! Peek-a-boo!" he said as he popped up in front of the widow by her car seat. Rusty came around to the passenger side. He lifted me and carried me to the porch and set me on the swing then went back for the chair. He unfolded it on the porch and I made my way to it. Everyone was scared to ask. I'd been in a lot of trouble in the past and nothing had landed me in a wheelchair. What had happened this time?

Martha spoke up first. "Young lady, you need some real cooking!"

Mom stammered, "Cassidy… look at you… you've been…"

"Starved," put in Rusty, "but she's doing better. Some rest, some good cooking and we'll be back. There will be no riding, and no walking."

"Do you need a downstairs room? We fixed up your old room but we had no idea!"

"My old room is fine. It's got a bathroom right there; Katie will be on the same floor. I'll just need help on the stairs."

Rusty set Katie in my lap and she sat down gripping the armrests.

"Go! Go!" she said excitedly. I wheeled to the end of the porch and turned around. "Go! Go!"

"We don't have room to go fast, baby. She's used to going on walks with me. She likes me to go as fast as I can. You should see her when we really get going."

"Hey Katie! You want to go to Herschel Hill?" Patrick asked and everybody in unison said, "No!"

"What's Herschel Hill?" asked Rusty.

"It's like Deadman's Curve for skateboarders. It's like landing in Mrs. Rathburn's rosebushes."

"Yeah!" said Patrick, who really had landed in Mrs. Rathburn's rosebushes.

Rusty's parents live on a hill and Mrs. Rathburn lives in the house at the bottom of the hill. Every kid on the street who gets new wheels eventually ends up in Mrs. Rathburn's rosebushes.

"Cassidy, your clothes just hang on you," Mom said, and then the inevitable, "Don't you want to go shopping?"

Katie caught one of her favorite words and brightened. "Go!" she said.

"Shopping will be fun but I don't want to buy new clothes. I'll be back to my old size soon."

"Tell me what you did to lose all that weight!" Jesse said. Jesse was pleasingly plump and didn't like it.

"You don't want to do what I did. How would you like to eat only half a sandwich a day for a week, then half a sandwich every few days, then once a week? Then eat grass and a worm or two until about six weeks go by. A kiddy cup of milk about week five was a bonus."

"No thanks," Jesse said. "I liked it better when you were pregnant and we had that Ben and Jerry's binge."

"Well, look on the bright side, if we go buy some ice cream, we can do it again," I told her.

"Well, don't just stand here," Mom said. "Let's do it!"

But Dad said, "Rusty, I'd like to have a word with you."

Gulp.

Rusty gave me a wink, letting me know he had the situation under control. And he probably did. Rusty seemed to know how to handle my dad better than I did. Maybe it was a guy thing. If my dad asked for "a word" when I was a kid it was like being sent to the principal's office.

All the women went into the house and Rusty followed my dad down the porch.

"So," Mom said, "if you don't want to shop for clothes what do you want to shop for? Does Katie need anything?"

"Mom, Katie won't need any clothes until she's at least two. You bought so many baby clothes right after she was born. She could change clothes three times a day and still not wear them all."

"But babies do need to change clothes three times a day," she said.

"I might look for a swimsuit," I said. "Rusty said we were going to take our time on the way back so that means a night in a hotel. Laying around on a beach sounds wonderful."

"Goodie!" said Mom. "We'll do that then."

Usually I tried not to go shopping with my mom. I'd rather track or ride or help the hands with the horses. But since I was limited in that regard shopping would give me something to do and Mom would feel like she was helping. Mom helped people by shopping.

Dad helped by controlling. He had a hard time controlling me. That's probably why Rusty was getting a grilling. If Dad couldn't control me, maybe Rusty could.

Then there was Jesse who helped people by doing things for them. A side benefit of that was if she couldn't help directly she helped indirectly, usually in the form of making elaborate craft projects.

Martha helped people by cooking.

Steve helped me by putting me to work, and then talking as the work progressed. I'd worked with Steve a lot as a teenager.

Old Frank was gone now, but he had helped people by asking questions. Somehow he always knew just the right question to start me thinking my own way through a problem or situation.

Rusty entered the living room and we finished our welcome. There were hugs all around and then Rusty gave me a lift up the stairs. He set me on the bed and went downstairs for the suitcases.

"What do I have to do to get carried up the stairs?" Jesse asked.

Rusty brought the suitcases in and began unpacking. He put my clothes in the lower dresser drawers and his own clothes in the ones out of wheelchair reach. I could hear Katie laughing at Patrick in the playroom across the hall. It progressed to a crawling race down the hall. Patrick was winning easily. I checked over the contents of the bathroom. Sigh, I sure was going to miss the shower at home. I wasn't even sure how I was going to use this one. I needed a chair.

"Rusty?"

"What?"

"When we get downstairs we need to ask mom for a chair for the shower."

"Are we unpacked? Let's do it while we're thinking about it."

He picked me up to take me back downstairs to the wheelchair. Gee, I hated being carried around like a helpless invalid. Okay, I had to admit, I didn't mind being carried around by Rusty. I just hated the fact that it was necessary. We left the bedroom and stopped while Patrick ran by, flipped a U turn and ran the other way.

Rusty stepped out and I saw Katie walking along step by step using the wall for support. She turned and smiled her big three-toothed smile then let go of the wall. She stood there for a few seconds and then took one wobbly step. It was then I noticed she was at the top of the stairs.

"Rusty! Put me down!"

"What?"

"Put me down! Drop me! I don't care, just get her!"

Two wobbly steps. Three and she got a surprised look on her face, started to tip, started to fall. Rusty set me down and sprinted for the top of the stairs, took a flying leap, grabbed Katie, and went face first down the stairs.

"Rusty!"

I couldn't get to the stairs. There was a tumble, then a moment when the landing was too quiet. I heard footsteps closing in from downstairs. I couldn't get up without using my bad leg so I army crawled to the top stair and looked down.

"Go! Dada Go!" said Katie.

Rusty held her close and looked up the stairs. "Well, we wanted to be together when she took her first steps. Somebody needs to tell her that steps and stairs are not the same thing."

"Katie walked?" my mom asked.

"Three steps," I said.

"We need pictures!" she said running off to find her camera.

Flash! And the results of Katie's first steps were recorded for her baby book. After Rusty dusted himself off and got his whole family downstairs we took some pictures of Katie walking. She managed three or four steps at a time before finding out why diapers have a lot of padding in the bottom.

For some reason Martha thought that if she cooked for twenty I'd eat for two. The ranch hands didn't complain. They dug in hungrily. There were mounds of steaming mashed potatoes, inch-thick steaks, salads, desserts, fruit and wine. Everything got passed to me twice, though I couldn't eat any more than normal. I never was a big eater. I learned to eat frugally on the trail and the habit was hard to beat. When my stomach was full there was no point in eating more.

Martha was tickled by Katie's habit of showing everybody her bites before she ate them.

"Gama! Ba-bite!" she announced over and over.

Martha would name each bite as Katie held it up, "Yes! Meat!" she'd say.

As usual Patrick wanted to hear all the stories I'd accumulated since my last visit. As I related my latest escapade Patrick said, "We knew you'd escape. You escape every time."

"This time I couldn't. I couldn't move enough. I was trapped as trapped could be. Only Rusty's determination got me through."

"You're lucky Uncle Rusty's a detective!" Patrick said.

"No, we're lucky Aunt Cassidy is a writer," Rusty said. "Something she wrote put me on the right track."

I glared at Rusty. I didn't want other people to know about my writing. I wasn't a writer. I only did it because… well, because nobody would believe it anyway. And because Rusty's mom had mentioned that she would like to read about my "adventures." I never expected anybody to know about those stories except me and maybe Rusty and maybe Rusty's mom if I ever got brave enough to let someone else read them. Now I guess many people had and I was embarrassed.

"You write stories?" Patrick asked.

"Yeah, sort of. It's just memories. It's nothing you would want to read. It's not for kids."

"Aw, that's no fair! You know I can read it. I've been reading books for grownups since I was seven. I know the words."

"There's things in them kids wouldn't understand," I said.

"Can I see parts I *would* understand?"

"Let him read the first one," Rusty said. "It isn't very violent, the ranch is in it. He's in it. He'll understand it."

"*I'm* in it?" Pat asked amazed.

I hesitated. My first husband, Jack, was mentioned. Patrick didn't even remember Jack. I wanted Patrick to remember Rusty as his uncle. And I worried about what Patrick would do with the knowledge he gained about my exploits.

"No, you can't read it," I told him. "You'd get too many ideas for trouble. Just because I managed to survive doesn't mean it was a good thing to do."

"Like what?" Patrick asked.

"I'm not saying! I'm not giving you any more ideas. You get into enough trouble on your own."

"Don't leave your computer on the network," Steve warned. "He knows how to hack it."

"It's not hacking," Patrick said. "If it's on the network and there's nothing blocking me then it's not hacking. Just because I know how to use the network doesn't mean I do things I shouldn't."

"If Cassidy doesn't want you to read her stories then you leave them alone," Jesse said.

Pat looked disappointed.

"How did the stories make it so you could find Aunt Cassidy?" Wyatt asked.

"Accidentally. It was just chance. Chance and time," Rusty said glumly.

Chapter 4

After dinner I helped clear dishes. Martha put a big tray across my chair and we piled on the dishes and then I wheeled them to the kitchen. We filled the giant dishwasher that got run every morning and every night. With at least ten people to feed three times a day it amounted to a lot of dishes.

Jesse played with Katie in the living room.

James took the boys outside to do their evening chores.

Rusty was nowhere to be seen. I wheeled out onto the porch. I looked down the road toward Jesse's house. I looked up the road to the barn. I had a feeling something was bothering Rusty. He was different somehow.

I couldn't go down the steps or up the stairs. I could see his tracks at the bottom of the steps, but I wasn't sure from the top if they were put there before or after dinner. I wheeled around to the back of the porch where there were only two steps. I grasped the porch railing and pulled myself up, then one-handed the chair to the bottom step. Holding onto the railing, I used my good leg to make my way back to the chair. The ground behind the house wasn't nicely smoothed like the front was. I had to wrestle the chair over bumps and through grass and softer soil. I was beginning to wish I'd just stayed in the house, but since I was on my way I continued. It was harder to go back so I bumped my way around the house, nearly getting stuck a time or two. When I got to the front of the house I could easily find Rusty's tracks. I knew every pair of shoes he owned and none of them were boots. He'd gone up the road with…Elan. Yes, it was Elan. I ruled out the hands I had grown up with and noted the different attitude of the young Indian man. He wore boots, because boots were needed for the job, but he still walked as if he wore moccasins. I could see the rolling action in the tracks of a man who walked in the woods, feeling with his feet. The other hands always came down with a firm heel print. Whenever I could follow a new pattern I was glad to have the opportunity. I learned something from each person I tracked. That was one of the things I liked best about tracking. It was a continual learning experience.

I followed the two men's tracks to the bunkhouse and wheeled up the ramp that had been built for Old Frank in the months before his passing. There were voices within.

"One cannot pretend to know the workings of the world," Elan said.

Rusty's deep voice said quietly, "I have to know the workings of the world. It's my job. Cassidy doesn't belong in that world. It's too violent. She doesn't see it that way. She sees the good in everybody. When she came to in the hospital she was worried about what had happened to Brian. The guy nearly killed her. My ineptness nearly killed her. But does she look at it like that? She does not."

"Would you change that about her? If you could? I think deep down you would rather she see the good and not the bad."

"There's a balance. But that's not what bothers me. It's me that bothers me. Here I am a detective. My wife goes missing. What does a detective do when they lose someone they love? What would anybody do? Cassidy knows what they would do because she does it for them. They look. I did everything I knew to do. I talked to everybody she knew. I discovered people I didn't know she knew. I talked to those people. I had a month to organize my search and it led nowhere. At the start all we had to go by was the Jeep and Cassidy's morning schedule. Gradually the search evolved but, looking back, it was evolving into a dead end and I'd never have found her in time. It was purely chance that I found her at all. And I almost turned my back on that one break I had. When I think how close I came to just walking away from Brian it gives me chills and then I feel what went through me when I saw her. You couldn't understand. What you see in her today is a miracle. What I saw in that barn was barely there. Cassidy takes nothing and makes something of it. That's what I see in her that keeps me going. However things stand she takes that and works with it and makes it better."

I could hear the clack of a game of pool. Neither man was shooting very well. Rusty had to focus on his shots and he wasn't doing that. I didn't think they cared much about the game. I decided Rusty was better left to Elan and made my way back up the road. I couldn't get back to the ranch house so I kept going until I got to Jesse's house. It was a long push in the wheelchair down a gravel road. I was glad my dad was worried about appearances. He kept the road flat and the gravel neat. When I got to Jesse's house I didn't know what to do. Jesse was at the ranch house, James was doing chores. I was just taking a walk to think and I wasn't thinking much because the wheelchair was fighting me. I decided I needed a quiet place, so I climbed the rope to the tree house. I could do that with my arms but once I got to the top I had to figure out how to get into the tree house without using my legs much. It was a struggle and I had a couple of scary slips but finally I managed enough leverage to drag myself in. I lay on the floor of the tree house and rested. As I settled down, my thoughts returned to the problem at hand. What it boiled down to was that Rusty blamed himself for what happened to me. Well, not really what happened, but the fact that it had such dire consequences. When I thought about it, though, finding me earlier would only have started the recuperation sooner. It would have saved me two weeks of near starvation. But that was the easy part to overcome. They pumped me full of all things nutritious and I came back skinny as a rail but healthy. I think the shock of almost losing me and then the shock of finding me was just battling it out in Rusty. I thought time would heal him but it was weeks later and he was still dealing with it. I had a feeling a month off wasn't going to be enough. I even wondered if he was contemplating changing jobs. It wouldn't help for him to do that. I'd still work search and rescue. I'd still be a trouble magnet. In fact, with Rusty working law enforcement, we had all the backup one could wish for. Rusty couldn't quit. It was his life. It was *our* life. It wasn't just a job. It was his job, my job, our friends, Katie's adopted aunts and uncles, a lifestyle.

I could see the sky gradually darkening and I began to wonder how long I'd been up in the tree house, when my cell phone rang.

"Hey!" I said knowing it was family.

"Cassidy! Where are you? You've been gone for hours!" Jesse said.

"I have? I'm sorry. I'll be back as soon as I can."

"Where are you? We've looked everywhere!"

"Why? You know I can't go far. I'm just in the tree house. I'll climb down and be back in a bit."

"She's in the tree house!" Jesse said to some one behind her.

Rusty was on the phone in an instant. "Don't climb down. I'll be right there."

"Rusty, it's just a tree house. I've climbed up and down from this tree house lots of times."

"Please, just wait for me."

"If I wait for you, can I climb down myself?"

"Just wait. I'm on my way."

It only took him a few minutes to jog down the lane to the big oak tree. He stood next to my chair looking up into the house perched high in the branches.

"Babe, how'd you get way up there?"

"I climbed. Is there another way?"

"Do you know what you could have done if you'd fallen?"

"I wasn't falling. I was climbing. I know how to climb a rope. It's very hard to fall off a rope. If you have trouble on a rope you just slide down it again. Are you alone?"

He just looked around.

"Come up," I said.

He climbed up using the ladder and sat down next to me.

"How did you get all the way down here?" he asked.

"I was worried about you so I tracked you to the bunkhouse. You and Elan were talking so I headed back to the house. I couldn't get up the steps without asking for help, so I just kept going. I climbed up here to think."

"It's a little ironic that you couldn't get up four wooden steps but you can climb into a tree house."

"If the rope was longer I probably couldn't, but I managed it with just my arms. I've had a lot of training climbing things."

"So did you think?"

"Yeah, a little."

"Did you think you were stuck?"

"No, getting down will be easier than getting up."

"So, what were you thinking?"

"I was thinking you need to go back and read about the fire. It was a time when I was in your shoes. The house was on fire. You and Chase were in the basement. I knew I could get Chase out. And I knew I couldn't get you out. I had to make a choice. Save Chase? Run for help? As I dragged Chase out of the building I was counting down your seconds. Then I had to run for help. I didn't know what I would find when I got back. I risked your life and I was numb with guilt for a long, long time. Do you remember?"

"I remember. I also remember spending hours trying to get you to put it behind you."

"We did, eventually, and this time you will, too. Just give it time. We can't change the way things are but we can decide how we're going to deal with it. I think we're doing well. What about you? Do you think we can decide to get on with this in the least painful way possible?"

"We can try. We had to tell your family what happened. Telling it always brings to light what I could have done differently."

"Had you known. But you didn't. You couldn't expect to. We beat trouble again. Now let's beat a path in another direction."

"What direction?"

"We have a few days here. Then we'll head for the coast. I don't know what your plan was for the coast. But that sounds like a good direction to me."

"It's getting late," he said. "We need to give Katie a bath and put her to bed. Are you sure you can get down?"

"I'm sure."

"Let me climb down first, just in case."

He climbed down and moved the chair out of the way in case I needed room to maneuver. He waited as I made my way to the edge of the doorway. I leaned out and grabbed the rope. I dangled above Rusty as he nervously waited to see if I could make it down without injuring myself. He needn't have worried. I slid down the rope, stopping myself just off the ground. I stood on my good leg briefly until Rusty brought the chair within reach. He sat down in it and pulled me into his lap.

"You came out here because you were worried about me?" he asked.

"Yeah."

"Babe, don't worry about me. You have enough to worry about without worrying about me."

"I'm not worried about me. So I'm stuck in a chair for three months. I decided a long time I ago that I could be mad at the situation or be happy with it so I decided to be happy with it. Three months will go by before we know it. If I'm stuck in a chair maybe it'll be three peaceful months."

Bertie had taught me that, to just decide to make the best of things and they would surprisingly turn out better.

"That's my girl," Rusty said. He tried to push the wheelchair with me in his lap but we got nowhere so I let him up so he could push it from behind.

Chapter 5

Shopping with Mom and Jesse the next day was fun but I decided real quick to buy the first useable swimsuit and make do with a tankini. There was no way to struggle into a one-piece swimsuit in the chair and I had too many ugly scars to wear a bikini. I didn't even try on the bottoms. I just tried on the top and imagined how the bottom would look. Then I hoped I could get into it at the hotel.

"That's no fair," Jesse said. "You have a baby and end up a size four. I have a baby and I end up a twelve."

Since I refused to buy any more clothes for me, we looked at baby clothes and toys. At this age Katie did play with toys. Given a choice between a toy and a TV remote she'd go for the remote, but given a room with toys she would play with Patrick and Wyatt for an hour or more. She loved riding toys and would like them even more now that she had begun to walk. She was a bookworm. If she found a book and there was an adult handy she would hold up the book and call out, "Ba-book!" Every word had at least two syllables. If they didn't she added some.

I heard a cell phone ring and Katie put it up to her ear, "Yoyo..." she said, "yoyo?"

All the adults looked at each other with the same question: Is it yours? Sigh, it wasn't any of ours. I took the phone from Katie.

"Hello?" I asked.

"Is, um, Derika there?"

"No, I found this phone at the mall. If you hear from her tell her the phone will be in Lost and Found soon."

"Okay."

I closed the phone and glared at Katie. "No telephones!" I scolded, "No, no telephones." I figured she was old enough to learn that her pick pocketing days were over. She pouted at me. My mom gave her a sympathetic look and I glared at Mom, too. We took the phone to Lost and Found.

A grandmother approached Katie in her stroller. I saw Katie's eyes brighten.

"Oh, look at you, you cutie!" the grandma said. Katie smiled her big three-toothed smile.

"Katie, no purses," I warned her. This was going to be tough. She didn't know what a purse was but she had to learn soon. The scolding accomplished two purposes, though. Katie was learning what a purse was and people guarded their purses closer. Unfortunately this also caused my mom to feel sorry for Katie so when Katie was in the toy store and she correctly identified a stuffed horsy it was just natural for that horsy to end up in our shopping cart. Shopping was getting much more complicated than I ever thought possible.

During the shopping trip Katie learned a couple of new words. Now when I glared at her she glared back and said, "No pho-phones."

"That's so cute," Jesse said.

"It wouldn't be cute if I did it. It would be talking back," Patrick observed.

"That's because you're old enough to know better," Jesse said.

We were sitting on the side of a fountain resting when an elderly woman walked up and looked at Katie. Katie waved a baby wave at her.

"Well aren't you the dickens?" she said.

"She's not the dickens. She's Katie," Wyatt said.

"Katie, you look like a Katie. I remember when my granddaughter Katy was your size. I have seven grandkids and they are all grown up now."

"These are my three," my mom piped up proudly, "Patrick, Wyatt and Kaitlyn."

Katie looked at the woman's purse.

"No purse," I reminded her, then to the woman, "She tends to be a bit of a pick pocket."

Katie pouted and said, "No pho-phones."

"Oh dear, with a pout like that you could get anything," the woman said. Then a distressed look came across her face. Her face turned bright red. She began gasping for breath and she fell over, the contents of her purse scattering all over the walkway. Patrick and Wyatt scrambled to pick up the items as Mom and I looked at each other, alarmed.

"Call 911!" Mom said.

I got out my cell phone but before I could even start pushing buttons a voice from Katie said, "Emergency Medical Response how may I direct your call?... hello?"

Katie looked at me with a guilty face. "No pho-phones," she said and held up a device with a single button.

The device said, "Hello?"

"Hello?" I said uncertainly at the device. I'd been told about these devices in my training but I had never seen one and academy had been years ago.

"What is the nature of your emergency?" the device asked.

"The woman just collapsed, right at our feet!" Mom wailed.

"And what is your location?" the voice asked.

"Oaktree Mall, south entrance," I answered.

"An ambulance has been dispatched. Please stay on the line until help arrives."

"Does something have to happen *every time* you go to the mall?" Jesse asked.

"It appears to be so. Why don't you take the boys to the toy store while I stay and tell them what happened?"

"Because they'll assume you're the patient and haul you away," Jesse said.

"They won't assume that when there's a woman on the floor at my feet."

"Shouldn't we be doing something? CPR or something?" Jesse asked.

"She appears to be breathing. Do you know CPR?" I asked.

"No, do you?" Jesse said.

"Yes, but I'm not sure I can kneel on the floor and as long as she's breathing I think the safest thing to do is keep people away so the EMTs can do their job."

There was a fire station a couple of blocks away, so it wasn't two minutes before help arrived and at first they did look to me, but when they identified their patient they went right to work.

"How did the shopping trip go?" Rusty asked upon our return.

"Katie called in medical help for a woman having a mild heart attack," I reported.

"And how did she do that?"

"Katie is learning *no purses* and *no telephones*. Since we were learning *no telephones* she was particularly interested in cell phones today. When this lady collapsed in front of us Katie grabbed her medical alert device thinking it was a cell phone and pushed the button. We didn't even know she had it until it started talking at us. She also learned how to get anything she wants out of Grandma. All she has to do is get scolded, look a little bit sorry, and then name something."

"I see."

"We now have a stuffed horsy, a stuffed doggy, a ba-book and a half pound of canny. Katie can't even eat more than a few pieces. What are we going to do?"

"Eat the rest?"

"I mean what are we going to do with a shopping crazy grandma who feels sorry for a kid just because they can't filch cell phones anymore?"

"Babe, your mom is your problem. I say there's no harm in it. Did she buy the boys something, too?"

"Of course, but that doesn't make it right. Katie doesn't need anything. I hate to think of what she will be capable of once she starts talking."

Katie was doing very well in the walking department. She could walk halfway across a room but then she would get distracted and look around. Looking around would throw off her balance and then over she went. Now she could play with both her cousins. She played trucks and cars with Wyatt and played tag and chase with Patrick.

"Can I take Katie outside?" Patrick asked.

"Can you keep an eye on her and not let near the horses? She doesn't know how easy it is to get hurt by a big horse."

"Can we just go to Snoopy's paddock and look for rabbits? Snoopy won't hurt anybody."

"Just keep her away from him."

"All right!" he said and then ran home. In about ten minutes he was back.

"Lookie, Katie! What's this?" He opened a small box and took out a tiny pair of moccasins. "For rabbits we have to be sneaky," he said pulling the little moccasins onto Katie's feet. She looked at the shoes wondering what they were. She pulled the laces, untying them.

"No Katie!"

"She's not used to shoes," I explained to him. "She only wears them for pictures and she spends most of the time playing with them."

I tied the laces in double knots. Katie walked with her feet held high. She wiggled her feet around trying to shake off the shoes. She fell over.

"That was so nice of you to get Katie her first moccasins," I told Pat sincerely. When I was still pregnant he was saving his money for moccasins for his new cousin. He was convinced the baby was going to be a girl and she was going to be just like me. He got the girl part right, now he thought it was his duty to teach his little cousin how to be a tracker. "She's still real little for stalking animals. You're going to have to have patience. Keep her away from the horses."

"You said kids learn anything they want to learn. If she has fun she'll want to do it again."

"Don't let her eat the grass."

As Patrick led Katie out the front door Rusty asked, "Do you think that's wise?"

"I suggest giving them a chance. You can walk out there and see how it's going in a few minutes. Don't interrupt them unless it's as frustrating as I think it will be."

Being stuck in the house, I didn't see the kids out "stalking rabbits." I know there were no sirens. No major injuries. And surprisingly Katie did learn a thing or two about stalking. I almost laughed until I fell out of the wheelchair when Katie was making odd squatting motions in the living room.

She kept saying, "Neak, neak." Rusty came into the room and Katie stood up and toddled his direction.

"What's so funny?" he asked.

"I don't know if she'll do it," I said, still laughing. "Katie! Sneak up on the rabbits! Come on, sneak, sneak."

She squatted down, got a crafty expression on her face and said, "Neak, neak."

A quiet smile spread slowly across Rusty's face. "Dangerous tracker baby," he said.

"I wish Chase could see them out there."

"She wouldn't do that out there!" Patrick complained.

"Sometimes a baby needs to think things through for a bit before they try something new."

"Katie! Walk when you sneak," Patrick instructed. "Come on sneak. Like this." He crouched over in a classic stalking crouch.

"You can't expect much at this age," I warned him. "I think you did very well to get her to do what she does."

"But it won't work," Pat said.

"It will someday, just like walking."

"Try combining sneaking with peek-a-boo," Rusty suggested.

"Oh goodness!" Mom said, "I just realized! We need to go shopping again!"

"What for this time?" I asked, though my mom didn't really need an excuse to go shopping.

"You're leaving tomorrow and your birthday is coming up!" she said.

"Mom, there's nothing I want for my birthday. I don't need anything. I don't want anything. All I want is to get rid of this chair and you can't buy that at the store."

"We need to shop for Katie's birthday, too! Hers is next month."

Now that caught me by surprise. Katie was going to be a year old? Already? It seemed impossible.

"Mom, Katie doesn't need anything either."

"But a baby has to have presents to open on their first birthday! Need has nothing to do with it. When you take pictures of her first birthday party there has to be presents. What would you do when she's ten and looking at her baby pictures and there's no presents at her first birthday party? You'd be branded a terrible mother for life! A kid has to have presents. It's a rule."

Chapter 6

"Mom? Do you know how much of a risk this is?" I asked.

"A risk?"

"Normally I can't go to the mall without something bad happening. It's tempting fate for me to go to the mall twice in one week."

"You got your dose of trouble the last trip," she reminded me.

"Trouble doesn't know how to count. I've gotten into trouble more than once in a single trip to the mall, just ask Patrick. He was there."

"Cassidy? How do you do it? Everybody and their cousin can go to the mall without mishap. What is different about you?"

"I don't know, Mom. If I knew I'd sure change it."

The plan was to hit the toy store, the bookstore and a department store. I thought going to just three stores would be safe. How much could Mom find for one kid in three stores? I was mistaken. Everything at the toy store was "just the thing" or "just too cute to pass up" or "something educational" or "looked like fun." Books were "adorable little stories" or about animals and "Katie loves animals" or "fun to read." At the department store she ended up with frilly dresses because Katy looked "so pretty" and jeans so she "could look like a real cowgirl" and play outfits because she "is getting to that active stage."

Since I was on wheels I became the shopping cart. Mom carried Katie. The boys carried their bags. Jesse pushed the wheelchair because I couldn't find the wheels amongst the bags of purchases on my lap.

"I'm tired," complained Wyatt. "Can we stop at the cookie store?"

"Cookie!" said Katie.

"I don't see why not," Mom said.

We found a cookie shop and the kids put in their requests for chocolate chip and a small soda.

"What does Katie want?" Mom asked.

"Cookie!" Katie said.

"I can't see over the bags, just pick something not too sweet. Oatmeal? Do they have oatmeal?"

"What do you want?"

"Nothing, Mom, I can't even find my mouth. I'm lost in the bags."

"Well, we can get rid of the bags long enough to have a cookie."

She took the bag that was blocking my view of the counter. There was a commotion up the mall from us, and lots of yelling. I heard footsteps pounding our direction. I was glad trouble couldn't see me behind all the bags.

"Stop! Stop that man! He's got my bank deposit!" a woman was yelling.

I thought that wasn't a very smart thing to yell but I didn't have to think it long because my chair was jerked around and I found myself being pushed at a fast sprint down the mall. People were scattering. Bags were flying off the wheelchair left and right. At first I was taken aback. Then I started thinking. My first thought was a crash was going to put me back in the hospital. And my second thought was I could catch this guy. If I was going to crash I wanted to hit with my right side down so I pulled the right hand brake quickly and sharply. The wheel stopped and the guy and the chair kept going. I felt the chair lurch and twist. The chair hit the floor with a loud clatter, I slid out and the thief went flying over me coming to a halt when he hit a store window. The window broke and an alarm went off bringing more people running. He started to get up and I grabbed his foot. He twisted and squirmed and made a grab for me. He could do what he wanted. Thieves don't escape on my watch.

"Damn it lady! Just let go!" He raised a fist, ready for the first blow, when a gray uniformed man grabbed his arm and hauled him to his feet.

"Cassidy! Are you okay?" Mom shrieked as she ran toward me.

"Yeah, I think so. It was a planned crash. Give me a hand up."

"No. I'm scared to. You're not allowed to stand."

"Mom, I can stand on my right leg long enough to right the chair. This isn't the first time I've crashed. The first time Katie and I were a mile from the house. Just give me a hand up."

"What on earth were you doing a mile from home in your condition?"

"Taking a walk. Mom, this is embarrassing, just give me a hand up."

A gray, uniformed arm appeared. Attached to the end was a helping hand.

"Thanks," I said as I pulled myself up.

Another security guard righted the chair, dumped the glass out and set it where I could get into it easily. I almost didn't want to use it but I knew I couldn't walk on my left leg. Shoot. I settled into the chair grudgingly.

The thief was struggling against a guard.

"Next time you need a getaway chair," I told him, "remember they have brakes. And don't chairnap a cop. I might be stuck here temporarily but I still think. If I could run, you would have been brought down before you passed the cookie store. Speaking of which, where's my cookie?"

"Cookie!" said Katie.

We headed back up the mall to gather up our bags again but an officer stopped me.

"Miss, could you come to the mall office and answer some questions?"

Sigh, stupid reports.

"Sure, I suppose they need to be filled out in triplicate…"

He laughed, which helped a little. "Probably. It won't take long."

"I know exactly how long it'll take."

Paperwork, the bane of every call.

"Judging by the bags, the shopping trip went well," Rusty said when we got home.

"I'm not going back," I said. "I don't care what's on sale. I'm not going back to that mall."

"What happened this time?"

"I got chairjacked!"

"Aunt Cassidy caught another robber!" Wyatt said excitedly. "I finally got to see one happen! I didn't even know what was going on! It happened so fast! One second Mom handed me a cookie and the next Aunt Cassidy was speeding down the mall with some bad guy pushing her chair! I thought she was a goner!"

"Can you take me upstairs?" I asked not quite able to hide the stress in my voice.

"Looks like that's a good idea," Rusty said.

I didn't know why the incident was hitting me now. It was minor compared to most. But I could feel the tension forming and I didn't want to be down stairs with a bunch of family when it hit full force. Rusty carried me upstairs. I wanted to curl up in bed and I couldn't even lie on my side. My hip was still too painful for that. He laid me on the bed and sat next to me studying my face.

"I don't get it," I said. "A hundred people in that part of the mall. All I'm doing is sitting under a mound of bags and this guy picks me! Why me? He could have made an easier getaway without some woman in a wheelchair. He must have been one of Trouble's hired thugs."

"He probably thought you would be less of a fight than an able bodied person in case he needed a hostage."

"Well, he got that wrong. I think he definitely got the worst of it. If we moved to a deserted island that part of the world would suddenly develop earthquakes or tsunamis or hurricanes or something. Pirates would land there."

"Rest, I'll keep things quiet."

"It's not that kind of quiet I want. I just want to know I'm not going to be knocked off every time I turn around. I wasn't worried while it was happening. I was just analyzing the situation. It's just snowballing on me now, that's all."

"Shh, just rest."

"If you'd been there the guy wouldn't have gotten past us. He wasn't armed, just foolish. You would have stopped him easily. I'm just rambling. I'm sorry."

"It's okay. Next time I'll be there. I should have gone anyway. I have nothing to do here. Did you get anything for your birthday?"

"No, I didn't see anything I really wanted. Don't worry about my birthday. As long as we're together I'll be happy."

A nap worked wonders.

Chapter 7

When I woke up the chair was in the room so I wouldn't be trapped in bed. I pulled myself into the chair, my left hip twinging with the effort. I wheeled out to the hall and stuck my head into the playroom. Everybody seemed to be downstairs. I went back to my room and brushed my hair and my teeth, then went to the rail overlooking the living room down stairs. Where was everybody?

"Martha?" I called quietly. If there was one person who was always around it was Martha.

The front door banged open and Martha hurried across the living room and into the kitchen.

"Martha?" I called again, "Is Rusty around?"

"Of course! He never goes far. Let me get this tray and I'll send him in."

Martha came out of the kitchen with a large tray and hurried out the front door. Pretty soon my mom came in and hurried up the stairs.

"Are you sure you're okay after that crash?" Mom wanted to know.

"I think if I'd broken the hip I'd feel it by now. I'm fine. I told you, it was a planned crash."

"I have something for you. You're leaving tomorrow and we wanted to celebrate your birthday."

She wheeled me to her bedroom and pulled a dress out of the closet.

"I found this while you were shopping with Jesse. I knew you'd have trouble trying it on but I think you'll like it. Let's try it now."

"Mom, to wear a dress I'll have to shower, shave my legs. I don't even know if I can reach my legs. I need to curl my hair and put on some makeup."

"Okay! Let's do it. I'll help."

"Where's Rusty?"

"He's still around if you really want him. I thought you'd want to surprise him. I remember when he was here for your birthday the very first time he visited us. He couldn't take his eyes off you. He was so proud of you."

I showered and did my best at shaving my legs. I couldn't twist and turn much. I dried and curled my hair at the same time with a styling brush.

"What made you choose blue?" I asked my mom.

"Your grandmother. She told me about the dresses you two bought. I know you usually buy earth tone dresses so I was thrilled to find out you'd bought a bright blue dress."

My mom had an eye for dresses. I never could figure out why she insisted on buying dresses when she lived on a ranch where a dress was very impractical, but she did. On the bright side, Rusty loved seeing me in a dress. The first year he knew me I only wore a dress once and then it was because he asked me to. Over the years I'd learned to be more comfortable in a dress and now I actually looked forward to dressing up and surprising him.

I unzipped the back of the dress and put my feet through, then stepped out of the chair so I could pull the dress up and my mom could zip it. It wasn't going to fit when I got back in shape but for now it took advantage of what little figure I had left. When I was in good shape I felt like Skipper meets GI Joe. When I was in Mom mode I was more like Skipper grown up. Ever since the surgery I felt like somebody had left Skipper in the driveway and she'd been backed over by the family van. I had a whole lot of training to do. In the mean time I needed to make this beat up old Skipper into a birthday girl.

I looked at the color of my dress and chose a smoky blue eye shadow. I'd never used this color before so I started light, just playing with amounts and colors. I'd never done this as a kid so I had to proceed with caution now.

"Oo, that's good," my mom coached. "Try some gray, too."

I added a little mascara, some lipstick and stood up for a final inspection.

"Shoes," Mom said.

"I didn't bring any dressy shoes and I'm not going to be walking."

"Good! Then you can wear heels. Try some of mine."

I tried, just to humor her, but it felt like my feet were strapped into torture devices. My feet were not used to being bent like that.

"I think I'm ready for Rusty," I said, so Mom went downstairs to get him. In a few minutes Randy walked in. Randy was a ranch hand a few years younger than I was. He'd worked on the ranch since he was fourteen so we were very well acquainted.

"Your mom said you needed a hand down the stairs," he said.

"Randy, this is embarrassing. I need more than a hand. Please get Rusty."

"What's the matter, Cass? I've helped you out of many a spot. It didn't used to bother you."

"I know. It's just that I'm a mom. I'm a wife. Things have changed."

"Do they have to?"

"Yes, they have to. Randy, you can't be my little brother forever. We both grew up a long time ago."

"So I see."

"That's another reason things have changed."

He stood there leaning against the doorframe enjoying my plight.

"Okay," I announced. "I'll make my own way down."

"Now you're just being stubborn."

"Randy, just get out of my way."

"I'm not going to let you fall down the stairs. Your mom sent me to help you, not watch you do something stupid."

"Then move out of the way."

I wheeled to the top of the stairs, then stood.

"Take the chair to the bottom," I instructed.

He carried the chair down with a smirk. I grabbed the rail and hopped down a step, landing on my right foot. I knew even that was pushing it. The right side had been broken, too. I hopped down another step and Randy took the stairs two at a time and scooped me up. He walked down the stairs and put me in my chair.

"There. That wasn't so bad, was it?" he said.

"Now who's being stubborn?" I asked.

"I come by it honestly. I learned it from you."

"Then you got more than your fair share. Give some to Zack, he can use it."

Nobody was downstairs. Nobody was upstairs. Since Martha had headed out the front door, I headed that way, too. Out on the big wraparound porch I found a social gathering in full swing. There I found family, ranch hands, neighbors, people from town, my fifth grade teacher, the local sheriff. I wheeled through the crowd looking for Rusty.

"Cassidy!" Jesse called.

I looked around. I didn't see Jesse either. She caught up to me through the crowd.

"Come look at this!" she said.

She pushed the chair until we got to the steps, then hesitated.

"Go around back. It's only two steps there," I advised.

We went to the back steps and I hopped down as she wrestled the chair down.

"What's the rush?" I asked.

She fought the uneven ground and brush back there until we came to firm ground again.

"You'll see," she said. "Rusty will help you back up. He's out here with the kids."

She wheeled me to the paddock fence. Inside the paddock were a couple of Dad's bay quarter horse mares, a very young filly, about three rabbits, Patrick and Katie. Katie would toddle off toward the rabbits and Patrick would bring her up short.

"No, Katie. Look, you have to be sneaky. Look… sneak, sneak," he said taking silent steps toward the rabbits.

Katie took his cue and squatted saying, "Neak, neak".

"No, walk when you sneak," Pat said. "Walk and sneak, walk and sneak."

Katie had walking down now and she had "neaking" down but the two didn't quite go together yet.

"Isn't that just darling?" Jesse said.

Patrick took Katie's hand and led her toward the rabbits.

"Come on, Katie, let's try it together. Get the bunny. Let's go get the bunny." They walked hand in hand; Patrick stalking as well as he could towing a baby, Katie toddling off through the grass. The rabbits were pretty tame. They saw the kids coming and hopped out of reach. Patrick wasn't going to tag a rabbit today but I doubt he was really trying. He was just teaching. He seemed to have a heart for it. He'd been asking for a baby cousin for years because he wanted to help teach my baby to track. He was starting a bit early but I didn't see any harm in it. Maybe he was right, the earlier you start the easier they learn. I didn't start stalking rabbits until I was four or five. I didn't have a teacher. I just loved animals and wanted to be closer to them. I developed my own method of sneaking up on them through trial and error.

"I wish I could go out there," I said wistfully. It would be months before I'd be able to stalk anything.

"Mommy!" Katie said when she heard my voice. She toddled back to the fence, losing her balance a few times on the way. Each time she pushed her way up again, took a few seconds to find her balance and set off again. She reached through the fence, saying, "Go, go!" She wanted a ride on my lap.

Mrs. Connor, my fifth grade teacher, stepped up to the fence, "It's hard to believe. Just yesterday you were Patrick's age stalking rabbits and now here you are with a baby of your own. I see Patrick is making sure she follows in your footsteps."

"I think he's jumping the gun," I said. "There's plenty of time to teach her the outdoors."

"No one had to teach you that. Why, I remember you in school. Anything that had to do with animals and local geography and you'd take off running with it. Do you remember when I was explaining to the class how to use a compass?"

"In fifth grade?"

"Yes. Children seldom have use of a compass. Most of them didn't know what a compass was. The boys in scouting surely had, but other than that, I think, only you had. Do you remember?"

I had to think back and then I had a Patrick moment. Oh golly, did she have to bring this up? Patrick always complained that he got further into the subjects at school than the teachers wanted to explain and he was constantly frustrated with teachers who would not go into the nitty gritty details. My look told Rusty he wanted to hear more.

Mrs. Connor continued, "She not only explained what a compass was and how they worked, but she had been playing with a sextant, trying to figure out navigation using that. I think she learned more math trying to figure out sextants than she did from the math book."

"It turned out to be too complicated to be useful on a camping trip," I told him.

"Still, very few kids choose to learn how to use a compass, much less a sextant."

"I thought it might prove useful," I said in my defense.

"That's another thing you did. You saw the usefulness of most things."

"Not grammar."

"No, not grammar so much."

"Literature was okay."

"If it was an adventure story. Except you'd pick it apart and ask why the characters chose to do what they did and you'd figure out how you would do the same thing."

"Same with history. I didn't care what year so and so was president but I wanted to know exactly how Lewis and Clark crossed the continent. I wanted to know everything. I wanted to take the same trip and I wanted to see everything they saw."

"No wonder you spend so much time hiking," Rusty said.

"When the other kids were reading Judy Blume, Cassidy was reading the *Journals of Lewis and Clark* for her book report," Mrs. Connor said.

"Cassidy! You're missing the party!" Mom called from the porch, "Come get some food!"

I'm not missing the party, I thought, the party's out here. We all headed back to the porch where we found tables of finger foods, very picked over. Rusty filled a plate for me and found an out of the way place where I could sit and he could join me later. As soon as he left, though, Hank Lawrence sat down.

"I hope this isn't the result of your little trip down to San Diego," he said indicating the wheelchair.

Hank Lawrence had flown me down to San Diego over Christmas so I could search for a missing Chase Downing.

"No, the trip to San Diego went off without a hitch." Well, not quite, but by Cassidy standards…

"You found your man?"

"Yes sir."

"Tell me about this tracking you do."

"How much time do you have? You know what is involved in tracking. You know it's useful for finding missing people. That's what I do, find missing people. Usually it's lost campers. Once or twice it has been fugitives but I leave that to the real police now."

"I bet your dad is glad."

"Sticking to campers hasn't really kept me out of trouble. It just keeps me from having to shoot people. I don't like to shoot people."

"It's hard to imagine you ever raising a weapon against a person."

"I spend a lot of effort trying not to remember those times. I'd be happy to talk about tracking, stalking, camping, outdoor survival, skydiving... just don't remind me of those times I had to use my weapon against a person."

"Okay... skydiving... it's hard to imagine you skydiving."

"That was in the Marines, oh, and my honeymoon. If you want to know the technical aspects the Marines teach it well. The honeymoon version is the kind to avoid. You fly a lot. You know the kind to avoid."

"I probably do, but what are you referring to?"

"Jumping out of a small plane with a faulty parachute over a large section of country you've never visited before."

"Oh, that kind."

"Finish the story!" Wyatt said.

"You know how this story ends," I reminded him.

"I know but I still like hearing it."

I looked around and four or five people were waiting for me to continue so I started the story from the beginning. When I finished Wyatt asked for another one and more people were waiting. The party turned into story time at the library except it wasn't a bunch of kids. It was everybody my parents knew. One story led to another until Rusty asked, "Cass, do you have Katie?"

Chapter 8

"No, you took her from me so I could eat," I answered.

Word spread through the crowd. Nobody had Katie. By now it was very dark outside and the porch was lit up but beyond the porch the light quickly turned to pitch-blackness.

"Okay, everybody stay put. Stay on the porch while I check for tracks," I said. "Does anybody have a flashlight?"

Tracking at night is rough, but it can be done. I don't have to see the whole track. I just have to get enough of a track to point me in the direction of the next track. A flashlight, pointed the right direction, could actually make a track stand out more at night than it would in broad daylight. But at night it is a track by track operation. How long had Katie been loose? Could she have wandered to the big road? The road and Satan's Paddock were my main worries. Satan was the only horse who would purposely hurt a person.

"Aunt Cassidy? Can I track it?" Patrick piped up.

He was closer to the ground and much more able bodied than I was. If it was daytime I knew he could find Katie. Rusty took matters into his hands and he was thinking along similar lines.

"Steve and I will check the road and Satan's Paddock. Elan and Patrick check the immediate vicinity for baby tracks. Cassidy, show them how to spot tracks with a flashlight. Randy, go check the barns. James check the paddock where Patrick and Katie were stalking rabbits. Don't cover the tracks. Take alternate routes, use a flashlight. Try key phrases and listen. She responds well to the words *go* or *cookie*."

Everybody sprung to work except the guests, who stayed on the porch, some visiting, some watching the bobbing flashlights, most staying quiet so searchers would be able to hear a baby voice. Rusty and Steve lifted me, chair and all, to the bottom of the steps so I could work with Elan and Patrick. Flashlights were passed around.

"Okay, guys, have you ever done this before?" I asked.

"No."

"I've done it but I was just seeing if it could be done. The trick is to find an angle where the edges of the tracks cast a shadow. When you can see a baby track shaped shadow point it out and we'll go from there. The angle changes with each change in the tracks so it's a bit tricky. It's easier the closer to the tracks you can get but first we have to find some to follow."

"I'm checking the house," Jesse called.

"Yes, that's a good idea," Martha said and followed Jesse inside.

We shined the flashlight from different angles until Elan said quickly, "Right there! That's a good angle." They studied the tracks in the circle of light.

"I think these are all big tracks," said Pat. "She can't walk very good yet. Maybe she hung onto the posts."

We shifted to the rail, found a good angle again. Patrick found something. I knew it because he giggled.

"Aunt Cassidy look, she went down the stairs feet first and then scooted her bottom until she slipped down a step. When she got to the bottom she kept scooting looking for the edge."

Sure enough there were baby scoot marks at the bottom of the steps. Two baby handprints showed how she pushed herself up. Then baby footprints led across the yard. It was slow going having to shift the flashlight, search the beam, then Pat or Elan would point out a possible track. Sometimes they talked about the possibilities and sometimes they would consult me.

Everybody was tracking, and searching the dark when suddenly all heads came up when we heard, "Waaaahhhhh! Dada! Waaaaahhhh!"

"Katie! Baby, where are you?" I called out.

We followed the sound to a paddock and James called out, "Got her!"

I couldn't go into the paddock in my chair but Patrick and Elan climbed through the fence and Pat found his dad holding Katie. Elan began searching the ground and burst out laughing.

"What?" Pat asked him.

"Read it," Elan said.

The flashlight shined this way and that, paused while Patrick studied the scene, then I saw the beam bob around as they walked back to the house. Patrick ran ahead.

"Aunt Cassidy! Katie tagged her first filly! She cried because the filly got scared and stood up when she touched it. It knocked her over backwards. Good job Katie! You tagged a horse!"

"Waaahhh horsyyyy…" Katie cried as James carried her back.

"Pat, run up the road and make sure Uncle Rusty and Steve know we found her," I told him. Patrick would stay off the big road. He caught the school bus there every day.

I took Katie from James and he helped me up onto the porch. She was still crying but she was rubbing her eyes. I think she was more tired than frightened. I shared some finger food with her and then Martha came out with a bottle. I switched to the porch swing and rocked her as she drank her warm milk and fell asleep. She'd had enough adventuring for one day.

I'd definitely had enough of her adventuring. I was glad it was all just baby curiosity but I'd gotten a good scare out of it. Rusty found us still rocking in the porch swing. He sat down next to me and put one arm around my shoulders. With his other hand he fingered Katie's hair

"James found her in the paddock. She's fine. Did you hear her?"

"No, I was out on the road."

"The filly startled her and she called for you."

"I'll take her. You have guests to visit with."

"If they want to visit with me they can find me."

"Can I take her anyway?"

I could see the signs. He just needed to hold her. I let him take her and he brought her close. We sat on the porch swing for a long time. He could have put her to bed, but bed was upstairs, across a large house, out of earshot. He held his girls close.

People came up and talked. A woman from my old rodeo days showed up. I didn't remember her. I'd won a few trophies in my rodeo days, mostly in barrel racing, but that was a lifetime ago. The trophies meant nothing to me today. The trophies today you couldn't look at on a shelf. I experienced them most days. Every day that was better than the last one was a trophy day, an accomplishment, something to celebrate.

Chapter 9

Goodbyes were always awkward at the ranch. My parents, especially, had a hard time with it. This last trouble attack had left them wondering how many more visits there would be. If they let me ride away, would they see me again? Last time I drove away they thought so and then it nearly didn't happen. They got me back, for a few days, in a wheelchair.

I was surprised what a toll this was taking on my dad. Was he mellowing a little? I got the feeling that he finally, really cared about me. Growing up, I was a kid he was stuck with raising, due to an unplanned pregnancy. I was treated more like a ranch employee. If I wanted anything in the way of parenting I went to my mom. If I needed a friend I went to the ranch hands. If I needed punishing, I was sent to Dad. No, I was sent to My Father. He wasn't even Dad to me until well into adulthood.

Now here he was hugging me and telling me to stay out of trouble, that they knew I'd be on my feet ready to ride next time we visited.

"Be good, squirt," Dad told Katie.

"Rusty, take care, and…thanks," he said with a rough handshake.

Katie said bye-bye to Gama and Papa, Pat, Waya, the horsies and doggies.

We drove away with a SUV full of Katie's first birthday presents, luggage and the wheelchair. Shadow had stayed at a kennel back home. If we had just been coming to the ranch he would have come, too, but he wouldn't have gotten along well in hotels for the rest of our trip.

When we got to the big road Rusty turned north. Joshua Hills was south.

"Where are we going?" I asked.

"Somewhere we can just be us," he answered.

"And where would that be?"

"The coast. We never seem to have bad luck heading to the coast. And after the struggles with the shower I changed all our reservations to handicapped rooms."

"We have reservations?"

"Hon, you know there isn't a room available between San Francisco and San Diego unless you make reservations."

That was true. Popular hotels were booked up months in advance.

It was hard for Katie and I to sit still in the truck for hours. My hips got stiff and sore. Katie grew bored and impatient. I could be comfortable reclined or lying down or in the chair where I could shift around as needed. A four hour drive turned into a six hour drive with stops to move around. Each stop required a diaper change and snack for Katie and getting out the wheelchair for me. What I really wanted to do was go for a jog but I still wasn't allowed to put weight on my legs. I had two long months to go.

We stopped in Monterey and strolled around Cannery Row. We quickly found out that using my lap as a stroller gave Katie too many shoplifting options. I spent all my time keeping her from grabbing things off of shelves. Putting her on Rusty's shoulders allowed her to grab wind chimes and whirligigs. We frisked her after each shop but a few times we forgot to frisk me and she had dropped little items beside me in the chair. She was still adept at removing people's watches and lifting cell phones from people's purses and pockets. Maybe tourist shops were not the best choice.

We headed for the beach. It was chilly and windy out there but I was still tempted by the wash of the waves. For the wheelchair to have any purchase we had to get right up to the water's edge. The water lapped up around the wheels and pulled the sand from beneath the chair. I knew the salt water was bad for the wheels but I longed for just a touch of the ocean on my feet.

"Rusty, can we go deeper? Just my toes?"

"You're not going out there, even when you're all suited up and it's warm."

"Just my toes?"

He smiled, "We need to take your shoes off."

He laboriously pulled the chair through the sand, removed my shoes, raised the footrest out of the reach of the water, then lowered my feet so they dangled free. He pushed the chair out until my feet dangled in the wash of the ocean. It was icy cold but the water felt good anyway. I was so tired of everything being comfortable. Even remembering the barn was better than everything being even all the time. Comfort was not something I valued. Give me a heavy pack, a rough trail, a cold night, a stubborn stove, a faint track, anything to challenge me and I was happy. Keep me warm, comfortable, keep things easy and straightforward and I quickly grew bored. Katie agreed. She sat on my lap bouncing up and down saying, "Go! Go!"

Going was slow in the sand. Rusty lifted Katie up and lowered her until her toes dipped into the water, too. She jerked her feet up, then lowered them back down. Each time the water touched her toes up came her feet. As the water receded her feet came down again.

"Onward and northward," Rusty said. "We need to get there sometime today."

We finally pulled into the parking lot of a large hotel in San Francisco. One advantage to requesting a handicapped room was we ended up on the ground floor. I opened the curtains and the swimming pool was right outside. The shower had a fold down bench inside. The room was spacious. First I needed to stretch out. Then we needed dinner, but the pool beckoned. As night fell the lights were turned on and it waited out there, sparkling blue, lights reflecting off the constant movement of the water.

"Rusty? Can I swim? Please? I'll be fine in the pool. I can even stand. The water will support me. I can move out there. I won't be stuck in the chair."

"What about dinner?"

"I'll do without dinner just to feel free again. To move any direction I want. Please?"

"You and I can wait. It's a little harder to make Katie wait. Let's go get dinner and we'll all go swimming afterwards. Maybe Katie will wear herself out and sleep good."

I was disappointed but I knew he was right, so we drove around until we found an interesting place to eat. To Katie any place was interesting to eat. If the waitresses had pockets, it was interesting. Unfortunately they rarely even noticed Katie's pick pocketing and it wasn't until they walked away that we discovered what she had stolen. Then next time they checked on us we'd give it back.

"No pockets!" I scolded each time she waved a pen or order book or cell phone that she shouldn't have.

She always pouted and said, "No pho-phones." But how was she supposed to know there was a cell phone in a pocket until she pulled it out? So now we scolded her with, "no pockets" and "no purses."

Our food arrived and Rusty and I automatically started cutting off little bits of our food and putting them in front of Katie. At first she gobbled them down as fast as we could hand them over but when she slowed down we got ahead of her, and then we could eat our own dinners. Katie watched the people around us. She flirted with a man at the next table. She watched a little boy about a year older than she was. Her eyes flicked from table to table coming frequently to the man who was winking and waving at her. She switched her view to the next table and her expression grew stern.

"Nooo, pho-phones," she said. She glared at the other table and said sternly, "No! Pho-phones. No!" She shook her little fist at the table. Her attitude had changed so rapidly that I watched the table she was gesturing at. A woman had left a heavily laden purse next to her booth and the man behind her was sticking his hand into it whenever the women at the table behind him seemed distracted. The women laughed and joked like long lost girlfriends at a reunion. They leaned towards each other talking animatedly, never noticing the theft going on beside them. Katie noticed.

"Um, Rusty? Pick pocket at three o'clock."

"How about if you close your eyes and pretend it doesn't exist?"

"I didn't spot him. Katie did."

Katie was still pointing at the man, giving him a very disapproving look. Rusty watched for a few moments until he was convinced there was really a theft going on. With a big sigh Rusty got up and walked over to the man.

"Let's go have a chat with the police," he said.

"Fuck you!" the guy said.

"We can do this the easy way, or the hard way. The hard way adds about ten years. Make your choice," he said showing him his badge.

Rusty marched him to the front of the building and spoke to the hostess, who went and got the manager, who called the police. The manager approached the woman who owned the purse. She followed him out. Rusty was gone for over an hour. Katie got full. She got bored. The flirt finished his meal, paid his tab and left. I ate my dinner. Rusty's dinner grew cold. Katie got bored and fussy. I ordered a dessert hoping she'd take an interest in that. I ate nine tenths of a piece of cheesecake. I had left my pack in the hotel room so I wouldn't have to juggle the pack, Katie and the wheelchair. I didn't have any way to pay for the meal. Katie grew restless. She needed changing. She was tired. All I had to work with was a wheelchair and a diaper bag. I asked the waiter to box up Rusty's dinner to go. I took Katie to the restroom and changed her awkwardly on a too-high changing table. Then I took her to the bar where a big window overlooked the bay. I sipped on a strawberry daiquiri while we watched the comings and goings in the bay. I was tempted to give Katie some of the drink so she'd sleep. She wanted to run around but I couldn't keep up with her in the wheelchair.

"Mama, go," she whined.

"I'm sorry, baby, if you'd have kept quiet we'd be swimming in the pool by now. Look, see the boat? Can you say boat?"

"No...no boat."

A man sat down across the table from us.

"Looks like you've got your hands full."

"It's okay, my husband will be back any minute. He just had some sudden business come up."

"You folks come here often?"

"No, we're from out of town. We're just here on vacation to put the wheelchair incident behind us. I usually don't even go into bars. I only did this time so my daughter could watch the boats."

"What's wrong with bars?"

"I have a terrible habit..."

"Of drinking too much?"

"No, of attracting felons. Seems like every time I go to a bar I end up talking to some drug dealer or con man. You aren't a drug dealer or a con man, are you? If you are I suggest you make yourself scarce. My husband has had enough of arresting restaurant guests for one day."

"I'm not a drug dealer or a con man. I'm just here on business. I come to San Francisco a lot and I like this place. Are you sure you don't need a hand?"

"I'm sure, I'm just a bit short on baby toys right now and I'm trying to teach her not to steal, so letting her loose is out."

"Your baby steals?"

"She's learning not to, but she doesn't understand why she shouldn't."

"Really. She couldn't possibly get away with it. Don't you end up with irate people cussing you out because you can't control your kid?"

"No. I wish I did. Maybe she'd learn quicker. If they catch her at it, which is rare, they tell her how clever she is. My doctor actually times her. He's never seen a baby with her dexterity before."

"This I've got to see."

"No, it's not fair to the poor kid to set her up and then punish her for it."

"What does she steal?"

"Watches, cell phones, wallets, calculators, whatever people are wearing or keep in purses or pockets. We're trying to teach her to not to."

"No pho-phone," said Katie with her pout.

"She's a smart one," the man said. "So you say she could figure out how to get my watch off?"

"In less than a minute."

"I don't believe you."

"Okay, don't. But don't get your watch within reach, because it'll be gone before you know it."

"I'll bet you a hundred bucks she can't do it."

"I don't want your money."

"It would pay for your dinner. You could get out of here."

"My husband will be back any minute."

"Still...I bet she can't take my watch off in a minute."

"Mister..."

"Is this guy giving you a hard time?" Rusty asked behind me.

"Daddy!" Katie said happily reaching up for him.

The guy backed off immediately.

"No," I answered. "He just wants me to prove Katie can steal his watch."

"Have we started scolding her about watches?" Rusty asked.

"No, I thought we should concentrate on one problem at a time."

"Then let her try it. She needs something to do. She's bored. Give her a little challenge."

"Watches are not a challenge. She's been stealing watches since she was six months old."

Rusty took Katie and handed her to the man.

"No pockets," Rusty warned her.

She pouted.

The guy did have pockets. He was wearing a business suit. At first Katie was a good girl. She sat there puzzling over this new character. It didn't take her long to find his watch. Four quick tugs and the watch was free.

"That's amazing," the man said as Katie put the end of his watchband in her mouth. Rusty took it away, quickly.

In another ten seconds she had his cell phone.

"No pockets," scolded Rusty. "No cell phones."

"No pho-phones," pouted Katie. She put it up to her ear, "Yo-yo?" she asked.

"And you say she'd empty my pockets in a matter of minutes."

"Yeah," I answered.

"Would you consider letting her do that on TV?"

"No," Rusty and I said in unison.

"Most parents would jump at the chance to have their kid on TV."

"Most people don't need to lay low to prevent trouble from taking over their lives. We've had quite enough of being on TV. We would rather avoid it if at all possible. What kind of business did you say you were in?"

"I guess you can say I'm a talent scout. I watch for odd talents to feature on a reality TV show. Katie would fit in perfectly."

"Thanks, but no thanks."

"What if we could do all the filming tonight? Right now. I've been watching you all evening. We've been filming this whole conversation. Add an introduction, find a couple of victims who want to be on TV and we have a fifteen minute spot. What do you say?"

"You're already filming?"

"As we speak. Come on, it'll be fun."

"I just want to eat my dinner," Rusty said.

"I'll pay for dinner," the man said.

We were still skeptical. I didn't see any cameras around. I couldn't imagine somebody walking into a bar, looking for some chance talent to show up and having all the gear ready just in case it happened. No way. That just doesn't happen. The guy stood up, faced the far wall of the bar, took off his suit coat and pants. Yes, pants. Under the suitcoat was a neon orange shirt and a red and blue striped tie. Under the pants were some very distressed jeans. The whole display looked like, well, like one of those corny reality TV shows.

"Hi! I'm Kevin Koukalaka and this is…"

"Cassidy."

"And…"

"Rusty," Rusty said reluctantly.

"Cassidy and Rusty have the most amazing baby I've ever met. You'd never guess by looking at this innocent face but in reality little…"

"Kaitlyn Michaels," added Rusty.

"…is a natural born pick pocket. Now, I didn't believe them… at first… but eventually I was able to see for myself just how good this kid really is."

"Hey!" Said a guy at the bar, "Are you Kevin Koukalaka?"

"I am, and I'm looking for a victim."

"You're kidding? You want me to be on your show? Now?"

"It's now or never."

"Where's the camera? What do I have to do? I'm not eating bugs or jumping off skyscrapers."

"Nah, it's nothing like that. All you have to do is hold this baby for about two minutes."

"That's all? You're not going to make me learn to tap dance in five minutes? You're not going to have me down as many shots as possible and still stand up?"

"No sir, this is Hidden Talent Tuesday. Kaitlyn has a hidden talent that we are going to demonstrate. Tell me what items you have on your person right now."

The man felt in his pockets.

"Car keys, wallet, cell phone, check book, fingernail clippers, change, little black book."

"Let me see that!" Kevin said snatching the book out of his hand. "I bet once this hits the TV screen you get a call from…let's see…Leslie. Yes! Leslie, if you see…"

"Leon Odell."

"If you see Leon on TV we want you to call him right up! We aren't just into general silliness. We have a serious side to us as well. We take guys' love lives very seriously. You got that Leslie? Okay…so, Leon, you have all these things on your person. We are going to see how long it takes little Kaitlyn here to find those things. You all saw how fast she took my watch. What kind of watch do you have, Leon?"

It was the metal clasp variation, even easier. I was wishing it was the metal spandex kind. That was always funny. The metal links would grab the hair on the back of the arm and her victims always gave a yelp of surprise when the watch pulled loose a couple of hairs on the way off.

"Are we ready? Leon, do you have kids?"

"No."

"Well, good luck. Here we go."

Kevin handed Katie over. The glasses came off first. Then the cell phone. She flashed her pout, which I'm sure the camera zoomed in on.

"Mama, no pho-phones," she said handing it over.

What was truly amazing is that Katie never appeared to be searching the guy's pockets. She sat in his arms and looked around and her hands would disappear for a second but there was no squirming to get a better angle. No struggling. Things just appeared in her hands. She liked the little black book. She opened it and shook it. Out fell a little packet of white powder. Leon turned as white as the powder but played it cool otherwise.

Unfortunately, the toupee was next. I wondered if Leslie was still calling. Kevin burst into a belly laugh at the toupee theft.

"Aw, that's no fair!" Leon whined. "This kid is killing my coolness factor."

"Leon," Kevin said patting Leon on the shoulder sympathetically, "They have to know eventually. What have we got so far? Let's take an inventory. Glasses, cell phone, toupee, wallet, little black book, loose papers from the little black book, keys. Leon, I'd say this kid has taken you to the cleaners. How are you going to pay your bar tab? You lost your wallet."

"They know me here," he joked.

"Leon, thank you for being a good sport. And Leslie, we're not going to hold you to that phone call."

Leon quickly gathered up his possessions including the items dropped on the floor.

"It's been an honor, Kevin," Leon said pumping Kevin's hand.

Leon handed Katie back to Rusty and offered to shake hands. Rusty shook his hand and Katie held her hand up, "Fi-fives!" she said. Leon gave her a high five.

Leon slapped a twenty onto the bar and almost ran out the door. Rusty didn't pursue it.

Kevin turned to us. "We actually came here to find a guy who plays the guitar with his feet. When I saw the wheelchair I thought we'd heard wrong."

"Har! Har, har," guffawed a man at the bar, "That was Leon! He can play the guitar with his hands or his feet. Leon had his chance for his five minutes of fame and he gave it to a one year old kid."

Chapter 10

Rusty got his warm dinner but we ended up taking it back to the hotel. Katie fell asleep on the way back. He ate a too peaceful dinner in a too quiet room.

"Maybe we should have eaten in the room to begin with. How do you get me into these things?"

"Katie saw it first. She was scolding the guy for getting things out of that lady's purse."

"Well, at least she recognized the fact that he was breaking a rule. Do you think she'll stay away from purses now that she knows it's off limits?"

"No, she didn't stay out of Leon's pockets."

"And how did you run into that Kevin character?"

"I just sat in the bar to watch boats. I didn't do anything but talk to him. I didn't know what he was doing there until you showed up."

It was a short night. I never could sleep well in a hotel. I woke up uncomfortable. I couldn't toss and turn much. Each push with my legs made my hip twinge sharply. To roll over I had to grab Rusty's arm and pull myself over. I didn't want to wake Rusty so I lay there awake until dawn started lightening the sky a pretty pink color. I stepped over to the chair and sat down. After a stiff motionless night the pool beckoned even louder. I wheeled over to the sliding glass door and peeked out. The pool was steaming slightly in the cold morning air. It had been heating all night. I could go for a swim and be back before breakfast. I struggled into my swimsuit. I cursed the chair and my inability to move without pain. I cursed the fact that I wasn't allowed to work through the pain. If I could, I would just tough it out but I knew the pain was a signal, and if I pushed it the bones would heal wrong, and then I'd be back to square one.

I wriggled and squirmed trying to get the swimsuit bottom on right. The top wasn't as bad. I'd tried that on in the store. I grabbed a towel from the bathroom and made sure I had my cell phone, then I snuck out the sliding glass door to the courtyard outside. The morning was chilly, as it always is near the coast. Goosebumps stood out on my legs and arms by the time I figured out the gate to the pool. I wheeled over to the deep end. I wanted to enter the pool where my legs wouldn't have to support me. I found a metal rail and used that to help lower myself into the water. The water was still cool but it was warmer than the air so I slipped down in and spent a few minutes getting used to the temperature. I swam from the deep end to the shallow end, letting my legs drift behind me. The feeling of the water slipping the whole length of my body was heavenly. I tried kicking as I swam and that worked as long as I was gentle. I dove for the bottom of the pool, not quite making it without the use of my legs. But swimming under water gave me an exercise in holding my breath. I swam laps, one on top of the water, then one under water, back and forth, back and forth, working my arms, giving my legs a chance to stretch, to move without pain. I tried every stroke I could think of that didn't require my legs. The only time I had trouble was when I was swimming a lap and I thought I heard my cell phone. I stopped to tread water and quickly found out I couldn't tread water. It hurt to move my legs like that. Down I went. I didn't have enough air. At first there was an adrenaline rush and I reached for the side of the pool without thinking. After my brain caught up I was fine. I used my arms to swim to the side but the sound had stopped. I took a moment to catch my breath and went back to my laps, this time swimming the short way across the deep end. I wished I could spend all day just swimming. I came up for air and there stood Rusty.

"You sure know how to scare a guy," he said standing there with a still-sleeping Katie in his arms. "And you sure know how to make up for it. Do you know how beautiful you look? Like you belong in there. I'm sorry I kept you from it last night. I should take Katie back inside…I just had to check. When I woke up I called your cell phone to check on you."

"I must have been underwater."

"Then I saw the empty chair. At first it scared me. I didn't know if you could manage alone."

"I'm fine. It feels wonderful. I wish you could join me."

"We'll come back later. Katie loves to swim. We'll all swim when it's warmer. You sure you can get out okay?"

"I think so."

I was probably the only person he'd admit his fear to. And it was probably because he knew I'd be careful of it. It was his way of letting me know he needed me.

He went inside and bundled Katie in a blanket, then came back and sat in a patio chair watching. It was a peaceful time. He knew I was comfortable while I was in the water. That could never be said when I was stuck in the chair. Being seated or lying down all the time was beginning to wear on me. The water eased my aches and I wasn't trapped in one position.

When Katie started waking up I knew we'd have to get ready to eat breakfast so I used the bar to pull myself out of the water and my right leg to make my way to the chair again.

People were starting to stir around a bit. Early risers who needed to hit the road were wheeling suitcases toward the hotel lobby. They were dressed in long pants and sweaters. When I got out of the water I quickly found out why. A chill wind was blowing off the ocean. I wrapped up in the towel as soon as I got settled in the chair and shivered my way back to the hotel room. Rusty turned on the hot water in the shower and helped me dry off so I'd quit shivering. I took a quick shower and dressed for the day. I hung my swimsuit in the shower hoping it would dry before I needed it again.

As we went through the lobby, the room was filled with about fifty good-looking young men and half as many young women. All fit. All checking in at the same time. All trying to check in before guests had checked out.

"Our first class starts in half an hour. We were told we could check in at ten o'clock," one of the men insisted.

"I'm sorry, sir, we're cleaning rooms as quickly as possible."

"I wonder what's going on," I said to Rusty.

"Personal trainer convention?" he offered.

Breakfast was uneventful. Bacon and eggs, pancakes. Katie hadn't discovered syrup yet. As long as she liked pancakes without it I was happy to let her deprive herself.

"Ba-bite!" she announced.

"Eggs!" I said animatedly.

"Ba-bite!"

"Yay, meat! That's meat!"

Everything was a lesson. Sometimes I felt silly identifying everything but I thought it might pay off. She seemed to be talking well for her age so I must be doing something right.

We walked around Pier 39. We found Lombard Street, the crookedest street in the country. We took pictures at the bottom and then walked to the top. It was a quite a climb with the wheelchair, even with the switchbacks. We forgot to set the brake on the chair when we stopped to take a picture and I rolled backwards and crashed into a colorful planter of flowers. My head snapped back with the impact and the chair clattered over on its side, dumping me on the street. Katie tumbled out.

"Waaahhh, Mama!" she cried as she pushed herself up and toddled toward Rusty, who was running down the street to render aid. He scooped up Katie. She was just a little scratched.

I was still trying to figure out if I was all right. I was shaken more than I thought possible from a short coast into a hard object. The wind was still blowing. I was cold and I ached from the jarring.

"Babe, are you okay?" Rusty asked.

"I-I don't know. Help me up." I was shaking like a leaf. "Rusty, I don't know what's wrong with me."

"It's okay. Cops see this a lot after a traffic collision. Does it hurt?"

"Maybe. Not too much."

"Just take a minute to let things settle down."

"I don't think anything is broken."

"That's my girl."

"Why am I shaking so much?"

The shaking eventually stopped but I was rattled and sore. I couldn't think enough to sight see. Rusty took me back to the room and I tried lying down. I couldn't settle down until he lay beside me rubbing my back. Finally the gentle stroking brought with it relaxing. Seems like every time I thought I was nearly normal I got humbled. How could a little tumble hit me this hard? I'd tumbled off mountains. I'd jumped out of a moving car. I little tumble out of a wheelchair shouldn't hit me this hard.

Katie grew impatient, wanting to go someplace. She was really good at going, but she wasn't very good at waiting. Rusty offered her toys but toys were a social thing to her. Toys were what you did with cousins.

"I'm going to take Katie for a walk. Try to take a nap. You'll feel better when you wake up," Rusty said.

I laid on the bed and rested. I tried not to toss and turn because I had to use my legs to do that. I told myself that if I wasn't asleep in fifteen minutes I'd get up and find something to do.

When I woke up Rusty was still gone. I debated and then put on my swimsuit. I almost gave up on trying to tug on the damp bottoms. I was still sore from the crash and wondering how such a little thing could affect me this long. I wheeled out to the pool and lowered myself in. I swam a couple of lazy laps. As I rested I noticed a man on the third floor balcony watching me through a pair of binoculars. It didn't bother me because I thought he'd be watching whoever was at the pool. He was probably surprised there was anybody at all swimming on such a cold, windy day. I must not have been very interesting because a few laps later I noticed he was gone.

I was tiring quickly but the pool still felt better than lying stiffly in bed or sitting stiffly in the chair. I figured I might as well lounge in the pool until Rusty found me.

A man entered the pool area and tossed his towel on a patio chair.

"Is the water warm?" he asked.

"It's warmer in here than it is out there," I answered.

"This yours?" he asked indicating the wheelchair.

"Temporarily."

He entered the pool at the shallow end and gingerly waded deeper. He stopped when he was waist deep.

"What are you doing out here all alone?"

"Trying to work out the kinks. Sitting in a chair all day isn't exactly fun. In the water I can move."

"No, I mean, why are you alone?"

"My husband is taking our daughter for a walk. When he gets back I'll have to get out. I'm sure he'll have thought of something for us to do."

"I never would have guessed you were old enough to be married."

"I get that a lot. Supposedly, I'll appreciate that more as I get older but so far it isn't working."

He finally made the plunge and swam to the deep end.

"So what landed you in the wheelchair, if you don't mind me asking?"

"I do. It's not wise for a woman alone to admit her weaknesses. So I'll keep you guessing."

As he talked, he gradually made his way closer. He seemed nonchalant, in a planned sort of way. I cast off from the side of the pool and swam a lap, landing on the other side of the pool from him.

"What's the matter," he asked when I surfaced across the pool from him, "shy?"

"No, just wary. Everybody should be wary, but especially me."

"And why is that?" he asked.

"Because it pays off too often," I answered.

"You're not afraid of me, are you?" he asked.

"I'm more afraid of what I might have to do to you."

He laughed a fake laugh and swam over to me. I inched away.

"What could you do to me?" he asked, inching closer. Was this the binocular guy? I was starting to get nervous.

"I've had plenty of training."

"Bet it didn't involve wheelchairs or swimming pools," he said following me. I made my way down the side of the pool until the wheel chair was behind me. I debated. I was probably more able to defend myself in the water but I didn't know what kind of a guy I was dealing with here. I didn't know if he was trying to scare me or make advances. Either way I wanted to get out of there. I pushed myself up with my arms until I sat on the side of the pool. He tried to pull me back in.

"Lay off!" I warned him.

"What's the matter? You don't like me? You don't trust me?"

"No. And I don't want to do something about it either. Let go. Now."

He just laughed at me. I always had that effect on guys. They never believed my threats.

"Come on, cutie, I won't hurt you. I just want to have some fun."

"Go find your fun somewhere else. And don't call me cute!" I said. I put my right foot up and pushed him away. I couldn't push hard. It hurt like crazy and he quickly swam back.

He laughed at me, "That's what I like to see. A little fight. I like spunky girls."

"When my husband shows up you'll have more than spunky to deal with."

"I'll risk it."

"Rusty catches you and it's going to be more than a little risk. It'll take you a while to try this again."

"Ha, when a woman brings her husband into the picture it just means she can't handle the situation on her own."

"You have practice at this, do you?"

He tried to pull me back into the pool. I let him. As I came down I boxed his head into the side of the pool and brought my other hand up into his nose. Without any hands to grab the side of the pool I plunged under water. He held me down until he figured some of the fight had gone out of me. I popped back up.

"What are you trying to do!" I gasped. "If you're trying to kill me you picked a bad place. There are security cameras all over the place. If you're trying to rape me, it isn't going to work. This place is too public. If you're trying to scare me, it's not working."

"Everybody's scared to drown," he said matter-of-factly. He reached out and grabbed the wheel of my chair and pulled it into the pool. It quickly sank to the bottom. So did my cell phone. I was stuck until Rusty came looking for me and he wouldn't see the chair by the pool. All I could do was take the situation moment by moment.

He's a bully, I told myself, just a grown up bully. He has to feel superior by shoving down the weak. And what happened to bullies when they didn't come out superior? They slunk off and nursed their wounded pride. Or they got meaner.

"You've crossed the line," I said evenly. "When you get physical and you threaten me I have no choice but to see your actions as an attack. So you can expect a fight out of me."

"Thanks for the warning."

He pinned me up against the side of the pool. He brought his hand up my side going for a feel. His fingers found the hem of the tankini. He watched me for a reaction.

I was having a major fight with myself that went something like this:

"Just cool it. You're in no shape to take this guy on."

"But he's a jerk. He deserves whatever he gets."

"You'll get out of this quietly if you just put up with it."

"Put up with it? Phooey!"

"Let Rusty deal with him."

"And what's Rusty supposed to think when I'm talking to a guy at the pool who has his hands up my shirt?"

"Okay, so the guy's a jerk. What exactly does a jerk deserve?"

"Break his nose and make it so he can't have kids."

"No. They'll have to clean the whole pool if they know he bled in it. You won't get to swim with Rusty."

"So what am I supposed to do? I can't run away. I can't swim away. I don't want him to bleed in the pool…"

"You could make a scene."

"I am NOT going to make a scene. He'd have to do a lot more than this to make me scream. I will *not* scream."

"You are just not being sensible. What's a little embarrassment? You could get rid of the guy, get help, get your chair back, all you have to do is open your mouth and let loose."

"I…don't even know if I CAN scream. It's so…un…Cassidylike."

"Oh hell…"

I broke his nose. I put the ball of my hand up into his face with as much force as I could and when his hands came up I pushed off from the side of the pool and swam as fast as I could to the other side. I pushed myself up onto the side of the pool. Behind me was a small shed that had cleaning supplies in it. A hook on the side held the wand and the tubing for vacuuming the pool. I grabbed the tubing and hauled myself up but the tubing was just plastic and it ripped when it took my weight. I lunged for the rope on the safety ring and kept pulling. I was most of the way up when the shed started tipping. The wall facing me buckled and the top came over, first with a loud crash, then with a mighty splash. It knocked my foe on the head and drove him under water, but it knocked me back into the pool as well. I came up coughing and sputtering into an avalanche of pool chemicals, water testing supplies, skimmers and filters. A small toolbox full of heavy tools sank quickly to the bottom of the pool and little bubbles leaked back up to the surface. As the chemicals dispersed into the water the fumes within the shed were overwhelming so I ducked under the water again and swam out.

My foe was cursing up a storm, treading water just out of reach of the shed. I grabbed the wand from the pool vacuum and prepared to fend off my attacker. People heard the crash and heads began appearing in hotel room windows. I heard running footsteps heading for the pool area. Security came banging through the metal gate.

"Miss, drop the pipe," Security said.

I dropped the vacuum cleaner and it slowly sank into the depths of the pool.

"Both of you climb slowly out of the pool."

"Can someone fish out my wheelchair?" I asked. "I think I can walk, but I'm not supposed to."

I pushed my way out of the pool and sat there waiting while one of the men used the rescue hook to pull the chair up out of the water. It must have been right about then that Rusty arrived back at the room and looked out the sliding glass door to see if I was swimming. He couldn't see me because some shrubs blocked the view, but he could see the shed listing into the pool, a group of security guards standing around and a man pulling my wheelchair out of the deep end of the pool. I heard him approach the man at the gate. They stopped him, but like usual, he managed to talk his way through. There were a few advantages to having someone on my side who knew how security worked. He knelt down beside me. I couldn't tell if I was getting the irritated look or the worried look.

"Cassidy…first of all, are you okay?"

"Yeah, no thanks to *him*," I said.

Rusty looked at the man standing shivering in a towel on the other side of the pool. His nose was still bleeding and he had a gash on his head, but blood in the pool was the least of our worries at the moment. There was a lot more than blood in the pool. It reeked. It didn't take long for the hotel staff to decide the courtyard was too full of noxious gasses to allow guests to enter so all the entrances were blocked off and we took the discussion inside.

As we walked to an office indoors the binocular man shrunk noticeably. One sight of an angry Rusty and he was ready to make a run for the hills. He had made the mistake of bringing the binoculars poolside and I didn't notice until he gathered up his towel afterwards.

Since the shed in the pool was the most visible result of the altercation they started with that.

"I didn't mean to pull the shed over," I explained. "I was just trying to get away from *him*! I couldn't use my legs, so I had to use my arms. How was I to know the shed wasn't stable? Sheds are supposed to stay in one place. I figured I'd be buying a new vacuum hose. It seemed a bargain compared to the alternative."

"A bargain! Do you know what your little fracas has done?"

"Yes," I said. "I am well aware of it. I am also aware that you can't put a price on the next hour."

"What do you mean by that?"

"He threatened me. He held me underwater and threatened to drown me. I was ready to try anything to put an end to the confrontation. I knew I could end up paying damages but it seemed worth it. What do you think I *should* have done?"

"Try *not* shutting down half a hotel," the manager said.

"I think," said Rusty, "that if you were to consult your attorney about this incident they would tell you, you are lucky not to have a lawsuit on your hands. My wife was accosted on your property by another guest. Where was security when this was going on? You have cameras. Was anybody monitoring those cameras? A more observant staff might have prevented the whole incident. You are fortunate that things turned out like they did. There could have been serious legal consequences just from having a large unstable object in a public gathering place."

"Are you threatening me?" The manager asked.

"No, just putting things in perspective."

"Perspective?"

I was thinking that just having a trouble magnet in the hotel was a more unstable object than the shed was. I was thinking I owed him a shed and pool cleaning supplies. I was thinking I ought to pack my bags and get to our next stop before my reputation preceded me. I was thinking this jerk was going to get off too easy.

The police were called. The attorney was called. The surveillance recordings were confiscated. My statement was recorded. After all was said and done we doubted there was a case against the guy but we left it up to the police. The attorney seemed to agree, the hotel could very easily be held liable and so they didn't have a case on me either. The courtyard was closed all the rest of the day and a HAZMAT team walked around out there in their alien looking protective gear as they got rid of all the chemicals that I'd spilled into the pool. As guests became aware of the goings on in the courtyard word spread and in the evening a news crew showed up. When the news crew showed up we beat a hasty retreat. We holed up in the room and called out for dinner. Katie got bored and fussy. She wouldn't watch TV. She only sat through one storybook. Peek-a-boo games lasted about a minute. Some vacation.

In the morning I looked out the sliding glass door and the pool was once again a sparkling aquamarine. The caution tape was down. I had one last chance.

The past few days had left me stiff and sore in spite of my lack of activity. I swam two laps and then hung on the side of the pool, watching the activity around me. The conference rooms were filling up quickly. The personal trainers had a lot of training to do, I thought. Maybe they were psyching themselves up for some big fitness campaign coming up.

I tried just floating on my back and relaxing but that didn't work because I had to hold my legs up and they quickly grew tired. I turned over and floated face down, turning my head occasionally for air and letting my legs and arms relax and dangle in the water. I was resting and relaxing like this when all of a sudden the pool erupted in a frenzy of activity! The water churned around me. Arms grabbed me and turned me over. Everything happened so quickly and I was so used to sudden surprises that I lashed out with a quick right and connected with bone. When I looked around there were six men in the pool with me and about a dozen standing around on the patio. More people rushed out of the conference room.

"What the heck is going on?" I almost yelled.

"Umm, lifeguard convention?" the man with the bruised cheek said.

"You were out here in a dead man's float with a hundred lifeguards in the next room. What did you expect to happen?" another said.

"Where were you *yesterday*?" I asked.

"Doing drills in the Olympic sized indoor pool," someone answered.

I just couldn't win.

A man in tan slacks, a blue dress shirt, red tie, and shiny black shoes stepped out of the crowd. He had an official look and an official name badge. All the lifeguards were wearing jeans and red polo shirts. The conference leader said, "Alright you over-zealous SOBs, how many guys does it take to rescue one swimmer?"

"Depends on how hot she is," one said.

"Bradley, we'll talk about this later. This is part of the lesson, guys. It's like baseball. If you have three guys going after the same ball, only one guy can catch it. If they all try to catch it, nobody catches it. One. It only takes one, if you do it right. There was nothing in this situation that merits six guys being in the pool. One guy with the hook could have accomplished more than one guy nearly getting knocked out by a panicked swimmer."

"I was not panicked," I insisted. "I hit exactly what I aimed for...um... sorry."

"I am not going back out to that pool again!" I said as I wheeled into the hotel room. If I'd been walking I would have stomped in. "And Jesse is never going to hear about this. Do you hear me? Never."

Rusty was towel drying his hair after a shower. He was only wearing boxers. "What happened this time?" he asked.

"It's a lifeguard convention! Leave it to me to be peacefully floating in the water and have six lifeguards try to rescue me for no reason!"

"Why can't Jesse hear about it?"

"Because! She'd *love* to be rescued by six lifeguards. I'll never hear the end of it. 'Why don't lifeguards ever try to rescue me?' she'll ask. And the answer is because nothing *ever* happens to her! Why does everything have to happen to me?"

"I thought you said they rescued you for no reason."

"They did!"

"Then nothing happened, right?"

"Right, well, until all the lifeguards jumped into the pool. I hope that one guy doesn't end up with a black eye. They kind of took me by surprise."

Chapter 11

"Shall we continue south and terrorize another hotel?" Rusty asked.

The next hotel was a little one. No handicapped room here, but it was only one night. The hotel was perched at the top of a cliff in Big Sur. We'd have to keep a very close eye on Katie. We walked along a trail that followed the tops of the cliffs. Rusty tipped the chair back so the little front wheels wouldn't get stuck on the uneven ground and we made our way out to the lookout point. Cliff swallows dove and circled overhead hunting insects on the wind. The rugged coastline begged to be explored. I wanted to walk the shady trails and surf the pounding waves. I knew better than to try that, though, even if I was able bodied. The rocks were treacherous.

We drove down to the elephant seal beach.

"Look, Katie! Seals!" we said.

To her they probably looked a lot like rocks.

"What does a seal say? Ouoo, Ouoo."

It was a refreshing change from the city. Our little room overlooked the ocean and the cliff swallows hunted bugs all day. We explored groves of redwoods and I so wished I could walk. I wanted to get in amongst the trees and feel the earth beneath my feet. I wanted to crawl around and look for evidence of small animals. I wanted to track the tourists and profile their funny little picnics in the woods. Was it a fat and happy American family? A well-ordered military family? Maybe a big boisterous home school family with six kids out for a day of learning. I wanted to read it. I could catch glimpses from the chair but I couldn't follow long enough to piece things together. It was like picking up a story but only being able to read, "The big, clumsy man stumbled over the tree root and kicked at it angrily." I wanted to know where the man came from. How big was he? Did he have an anger management problem? Who was he with? Oh, he was with a teenage boy. The boy didn't have trouble walking in the woods. But who was the boy? A son? I didn't get many questions answered. Mostly I just found new questions on the forest floor.

"Rusty, I want to walk," I said longingly as I gazed into the miles of trees. "I just want to walk. The forest is talking to me and I need to walk to hear what it's saying."

"Where would you like to go?"

"Just walking in the woods."

"Hold onto Katie," he said.

He put his arms under us and lifted the two of us, then walked off into the woods.

"Rusty...I appreciate the thought, but it just isn't the same."

"I know. Now hush."

"If you know, then why do it?"

"Just because it's not the same doesn't mean it isn't worthwhile. Come into the woods with me."

He walked and walked. I didn't see how he could carry both of us that far but it didn't seem to be difficult for him. When we had gotten out of sight of the trail and the wheel chair he said, "Find a spot."

I looked around and pointed the way until I found a place with some signs of life about it. Of course, every place in the forest had some signs of life. A forest is a growing place. But some places have grown to be favorites amongst the animals and those places have telltale signs about them. Little trails or gnawed vegetation or scratch marks. These woods were old and the animals had learned to find food near the campgrounds and towns. All the larger animals would shy away. What drew my attention to that particular spot was some indentations in the sand. Rusty set me down on the ground and sat beside me. I lay back on the ground and felt the earth beneath me, soaking up the nice solid feel to it. I tried to feel the ebb and flow of the wildlife there. It was slower than other forests I'd been to.

"What brought you to this spot? I don't see anything here," Rusty said.

"We won't see much in the way of animals here. See the indentations in the sand? What do you think made those?"

He looked over me and puzzled over the indentations he saw there.

"Horses?" he guessed.

The dents were large enough that he'd never guess. They did in fact look like some horses had stood there bored for a time and then moved on. But horses had not left those marks. When a horse leaves a track it leaves a U shape. These indentations were perfectly round.

"Lay still and quiet and maybe they will stop by and show us."

"Okay, I'm curious. They're too big for deer. Elk?"

"No, think small and be quiet."

Katie didn't want to be still and quiet.

"Babe, this isn't going to work. Let me take Katie where she can run around and I'll be back."

"Sparrows," I said. "Those marks were made my sparrows taking dirt baths."

"We'll be back in a little while."

The sparrows never did come to the little bathing spot. I knew from experience they tended to visit places like this more in the mornings and late afternoons. Being in the forest felt wonderful. The breeze sighed through the treetops. The scent of the soil made me long for a trail to track, and a camp to sleep in. This place ran on a different timetable than most places. It was slow, trouble-free and ancient. I rolled over onto my stomach and looked at the ground around me. I felt like Katie, seeing the ground from close up. I could see why rocks fascinated her. I could see why a stick was a toy. To see the world for the first time again would be precious. I wished I could remember what it was like the first time I really noticed the small life of a forest.

Too soon it was time to go back. Rusty came back walking slowly, helping Katie walk on the uneven ground.

"You doing okay?" he asked.

"Yes, I could stay here all night."

"You need some dinner. Katie, especially, needs some dinner. There were crackers in the diaper bag but she's had enough snacks."

"I got to visit the trees," I said.

"I'm glad. They miss people who take the time to visit with them."

"The sparrows never showed up. Maybe they hang out in the campgrounds to get people food this time of year."

"Shall we go find some people food, too?"

"Maybe we'll see the sparrows if we do," I said, melancholy.

"We see sparrows all over the place," he reminded me needlessly. I noticed them much more often than he did.

"But we don't see these sparrows."

"How do you know? I bet if we go into town and ask the sparrows if they ever visit the redwoods they will all say that they do."

"Rusty? Why are you doing this for me?"

"Because I need to. More than anything. I need to see you through this. I need to see you happy. I've come so close to losing all this. I need this, for me. If it means carrying you into the woods, I'll carry you into the woods. It's a small thing compared to what it would be like otherwise. I think back to one day when I thought you were gone and I fall into an endless emptiness."

"Rusty, I'm sorry… I…"

"If Brian had been any other man, he would have died the day I found you. And I wouldn't have just shot him… Cass, trust me, you can't ask me to do anything that is harder than what I've done the past three months."

"I'm sorry… if I could have prevented it…"

"It wasn't your fault. You did everything you could have. Just let me do this and don't fret over it. If I want to carry you, let me carry you. I can feel you be okay when I carry you. If I can make any of this easier for you, I will. Just let me, for me."

Chapter 12

By the time we got to Santa Barbara the weather was warming up. The sun was shining. The wind had calmed. We built sandcastles on the beach with Katie. I filled a pail with sand and turned it over.

"Katie! Come here, pat the pail. We have to get the sand out, pat the pail."

"Pat?" she asked searching the beach for her cousin.

"No, Patrick isn't here," I told her, surprised that she remembered to connect the name to the person. "Come help Mommy."

Our sandcastles never got very big because Katie got distracted and toddled off down the beach and Rusty spent more time chasing her than playing.

"We're getting so close to home. Can we stop?" I asked.

"You want to go home?" Rusty asked.

"Yes, I mean we can keep going if you want. At home we don't have to wonder how to fill our days. We don't have to search out wheelchair ramps into places. We can eat what we want, when we want."

"Mom and Dad would be disappointed. They were hoping we'd stay there a few days. We were going to stop in Santa Monica for a night and then go to Mom and Dad's house. You can swim there to your heart's content." And I wouldn't have to worry about being attacked or rescued either. We had fond memories of Santa Monica. It was one of the first places Rusty and I visited together. We had a favorite restaurant on the pier.

"Okay," I said. "Let's keep going."

We walked Stern's Wharf. We took Katie to the zoo. She added tigers and elephants to her list of animal sounds.

In Santa Monica we went to Rusty's Surf Ranch. It's a rule. If you're in town and they have a place named after you, you have to eat there. They had a big marlin mounted on the wall.

"Dat!" said Katie pointing.

"Fish!" I answered cheerfully, "Can you say fish?"

Dat was a new word.

As we walked the pier she asked again, "Dat?" as she pointed at the sky.

"Seagull!' I said. "It's a bird."

And so the questions began. Boat. Bus. Girl. Boy. Baby. Sand. Half of me celebrated and after a while half of me wished she'd suddenly develop laryngitis. Babies suddenly fascinated her. She would toddle up to strollers and point asking, "Dat?"

"That's a baby!" we'd say.

"Beebee?"

Then she'd try to pick up a toy from the stroller and we had to pull her back.

"No, don't touch. Say, 'hi! Baby!'"

She'd give a little baby wave and squat down looooking into the stroller.

While we were on the beach a flock of seagulls landed nearby, squawking noisily. Rusty told Katie, "Sneak up on the birds! Get the birds, Katie."

Katie did her little squatting, "neak, neak" act. Rusty took her by the hand and they snuck up on the flock.

"Get the birds!" he said.

She toddled off after the birds and, of course, they all flew away. She watched them circle overhead and promptly fell over backwards.

The family time did wonders for Rusty. I hoped he would be back to his old self by the time we reached his parent's house in San Diego.

During the day, while we were busy sightseeing and shopping and juggling Katie, Rusty was fine. But something deeper was going on. At night he became sad and he frequently had nightmares. These weren't the normal cop dreams where I had to stay an arm's length away or risk a punch. It was just overwhelming sadness. I tried to get him to talk about it. All he said was, "It's okay, you're here, so it's okay."

"It's not okay. Tell me what you're seeing," I finally insisted.

"I can't. It's not usually a seeing."

"Tell me."

It took several tries to get him to talk to me.

"It's just…utter helplessness. It was endless emptiness. I could only barely exist in it but I didn't want to."

"Why won't it go away? Why do you still feel it?"

"It's just… it takes over, it's all I can feel. Babe, it's like… remember when you were trying to feel again. You had food before you but you didn't feel like eating, even though you'd been starved. You fended off the hunger until you didn't know how to enjoy a real meal. I didn't know how to exist in all the emptiness I felt without you. When I dream, it comes back and it takes over."

"We can shrink it. If you will just talk to me it'll get smaller. Don't punish yourself like this every night. I love you too much to let you go on like this. If you love me, talk to me."

"I went into the barn intending to shoot Brian's sick dog. I walked up to you, my sidearm ready. You can't even imagine what went through me when I saw the dog… was… you. Anger at Brian, relief that I finally found you, fear that I wasn't in time, anger at myself, my stupidity that let you lie there broken all that time. Each of those was like a freight train and they all collided on top of me. You were so frail. You were only skin and bone, broken, unconscious."

"It's past. It's gone now and here we are whispering in the night so we don't wake up Katie."

"I came so close. Hours. If I'd finished dinner before I went to look for Brian, I could have lost you forever. It was that close."

"How do you know?"

"The alarms. At the hospital. They went off and the nurses came running. Just think, if you'd been in the barn nobody would come running."

"The machines are programmed to watch for certain things. Just because my pulse rate got slow or my breathing got shallow doesn't mean I was going to die."

"It was too close for me. Cass…"

"I know. It's all right, and it's going to stay all right. I'm right here with you, enjoying every minute."

"When I think how simple the whole situation was, how easily you disappeared so completely, with no clues. It was too close."

Every night that we woke up, we talked. And every night that we talked we had fewer nightmares to face. We shrunk it. And here we were one night away from San Diego.

I couldn't wait to see Bill and Bev's reaction when they saw Katie walk for the first time. I was looking forward to seeing Cody and Chase again. I wanted to show Rusty's family we were back on track. Each night, as I slept tuned to Rusty, I hoped we were. We recreated the whole kidnapping so he could see that he really *didn't* have anything to go on. We recreated all his investigation so he could see that he had done it right and that Brian was just too far out of the loop to be a suspect. We replayed the lessons at the riding school so he could see he had no reason to suspect Brian as being anything other than a mentally disabled man who had taken in a stray dog. While he knew all these things were true, he still blamed himself for allowing me to suffer.

"Rusty, I didn't think of it like that. I missed you terribly. I felt pain when I moved wrong. But suffering is a state of mind. I was not suffering. I was planning. I was watching for breaks. I tuned out the negative and focused on anything the least bit positive. It's just instinctive for me to do that when trouble strikes. No matter what happens to me, I don't dwell on the negative. Let's look at the positive. I've only got two months left in the chair. I feel like I could walk if they would let me. That's one reason I'd like to get home. Maybe, if they x-ray me they'll see I'm progressing enough to give up the chair. Maybe they'd let me use crutches. If I could use crutches I could help with searches."

"Then let's spend plenty of time with Mom and Dad," he said.

Rusty's mom had been watching for us. When we pulled up to the house the front door burst open and Bev met us at the curb.

"Hand over that baby," she said. "I know you have a lot to deal with."

"Go grab your movie camera and wait at the front door," Rusty said.

When she returned, Rusty put Katie on the ground. "Go see Grandma!" he told her. Bill slipped out the door and knelt with his hands outstretched. Katie walked up the sidewalk to her Grandpa's arms.

"Would you look at you!" Bill said, "You're walking and talking!"

"No pockets," Rusty warned.

"No pho-phones," Katie pouted.

"Oh dear," said Bev. "Would you look at that face. Cassidy, how are you doing, dear?"

"I'm fine. Still stuck in the chair, but fine. I can't wait to get in the pool."

"Oh dear, do you think you should?"

"She should," Rusty said. "It's great exercise and the water takes the stress off her joints."

"Good! Well, we'll just have to have a barbecue tonight then!"

Spending time at the Michaels' house turned out to be more difficult than we thought. Even the bathroom was upstairs. We gave up on the idea of sleeping in the attic. It was just too far, up too many stairs. The only rooms downstairs were the living room, dining room and kitchen. Once we got settled into the guest room we developed a system. It left me feeling like a toddler, being asked if I needed to go upstairs every couple of hours, but it worked out. The diaper bag and some toys were brought downstairs. Not that we were short on baby caretakers. Bev spent as much time as she could with Katie. She followed her around with the movie camera. She taught Katie more words.

I was glad when the aromas from the Michael's barbecue wafted all the way over to Chase's house and he showed up, silently, in the middle of cooking time. I don't know how he always sensed when something was going on at the Michaels' house. I suspected somebody called him, but nobody admitted it. Another part of me said he just spent an evening there every once in a while. Cody certainly never seemed surprise when Chase showed up. I was swimming laps in the pool when he quietly slipped into a seat beside Rusty. I was sure he'd already studied the situation and come to his own conclusions about how we were doing before he opened the gate. I continued my laps, one on top of the water, one under water. This pool was small enough that I could swim the length of it in one breath. Each time I got to an end of the pool I had to stop. I couldn't quite bend enough to flip over and I couldn't push off, so I stopped and took a quick look. Surprisingly both men remained cheerful. I was worried about Chase asking about the chair and Rusty having to tell him about the past few months. He must have heard something from Rusty's family. I shrugged it off and kept swimming.

When dinner was ready Rusty handed Katie off to Bill and went to the deep end of the pool. I took his hands and he lifted me out of the water and set me down by my chair. He wrapped a beach towel around me and I sat down and headed for the little tables next to the house.

The pool took up nearly the whole yard. Only a narrow flagstone sidewalk separated the pool from the back wall of the yard. A five foot strip along the other end held two little round tables with umbrellas. The barbecue grill stood next to the back door of the house. Everything about the Michaels' house was snug. The rooms, the dining, the yard…but it was a friendly snug.

"You look well," Chase said. "A lot better than last time I saw you."

"Ha, I must have been awful last time you saw me. Wait a minute, wasn't that right after the Tecate trip? You were the one who came out the worst for wear on that adventure."

"Cass, Chase was with me when I found you," Rusty said. "Brian's mom was worried about him. I brought Chase along in case Brian had wandered off. When we found you in the barn… I couldn't think, I couldn't act. I was just doing my best not to strangle Brian… and Chase checked your pulse."

"Okay, so I look better than three quarters dead. That's good, right?"

"It's amazing," Chase said. "I never expected to see you swimming laps. Even a month later I thought you'd be bed ridden."

"All they said was not to put weight on my legs. I took that to mean no walking. So I don't walk. But I've been going to the gym and swimming and wheeling around. What have you been up to?"

"Fixing my porch. I tore off the patio cover and I've been replacing it with something sturdier. Next time you break into my house I don't want you falling through."

"I have no plans to break into your house again."

"You didn't six months ago either."

"Gama! Bite!" said Katie.

"Yes! Yummy bite!" gushed Bev.

"How long until you're on your feet again?"

"Two more months, unless I can get my doctor to ease up."

"Yeah, right. He suggested a body cast for three months," Rusty said.

"I've been active enough to get into more trouble," I said. "I closed down half a hotel when some creep made advances. Hmmm, I'm still not sure what his intentions were but it kind of started a chain reaction that ended up with the courtyard and pool area being closed all day. And I learned not to rest in a dead man's float during a life guard training convention."

Cody busted out laughing, "I can just imagine that!" he said. "Gave them a surprise drill, did you?"

"It's not funny! I socked one of them because he surprised me."

"If you're well enough to evade one guy and attack another I think you're well on your way to recovery," Cody said.

"Good. I'm glad you think so because I've been dying to go swimming in the ocean."

"I wish you'd rephrase that," said Bev.

Chapter 13

The next day was a glorious day at Mission Beach. The whole family went so we'd have babysitters. Bev slathered sunscreen all over Katie and made sure she wore a hat. Katie hated hats. She tugged it off and Bev put it right back on. Rusty made me use a tether and take a boogie board out with me so I wouldn't have to touch down. He swam with me, keeping an eye out for rogue waves.

I was counting down the last two months. If at all possible, I had a goal to stand on the board by the end of summer.

Rusty carried me out until we got to water deep enough to swim in. He let me go and I grabbed hold of the boogie board. It wasn't the same as swimming in the pool. Just floating around wasn't active enough for me but I couldn't tread water. I didn't have the movement I needed in my legs yet. For a while I was content hanging off the boogie board but I really wanted to just swim so I tried swimming around tugging the boogie board along behind me. After all, Rusty just wanted me to be able to find it if I needed it.

I was beginning to appreciate the nice calm swimming pool back home. I could find an edge and I could open my eyes under water. I could visit with everybody, not be fifty yards off shore with a noisy line of surf between us. I swam up to Rusty and put my arms around his neck.

"Big wave. I can feel it in my feet. You ready?" he asked.

"Ready," I answered, thinking he'd jump and we'd clear the top of it.

The wave broke about two feet behind us, the boogie board perched right on top of it. The board slammed into us about a half second before the wave. We were thrown into the water, churned up, torn apart and it felt like forever before the wave released me and I was able to come up for air. I came up disoriented, coughing and looking for Rusty. I stayed on top of the water until my arms grew tired, then I sank, grabbing a gulp of air on the way down. I swam up again, tried to find a stroke that I could use but my feet just sank. I couldn't touch bottom. I had several smaller waves to work with before another big one came up, but where was Rusty? He should have surfaced long ago. Seconds!

Sinking, swimming up for air, sinking again. I was getting nowhere. I wasn't in danger, but I wasn't bettering my situation at all. I was going to tire soon, but where was Rusty? I sank and swam up again and an arm came around me.

"Babe, this is what the boogie board is for. Just pull it in."

"I wasn't worried about me! I just couldn't find you."

"I'm right here. We were just separated by a wave, that's all. Are you okay? The board didn't get you? The wave didn't turn you into a pretzel?"

"I'm okay, now."

"I could use a sandwich, how about you?"

It wasn't until we were back at the beach blanket that he said, "Mom? Do we have something to make an ice pack out of?"

She took a sandwich out of a sandwich bag and handed it to him, then filled the sandwich bag with ice from the cooler. He put it to the back of his head. The board had hit me, too, but it was just a glancing blow that startled me.

"What do you two do when Katie comes up with these things?" Bev asked holding up a pager, a cell phone and a pair of sunglasses.

"Katie!" I scolded, "No pockets, no purses," then to Bev, "When a person starts getting within pick pocketing range, remind Katie not to touch. She knows what *no pockets* and *no purses* means. Usually, if you remind her, it also tells other people to watch their possessions. Between the two we have headed off a lot of her pick pocketing tendencies."

"But what do you do if she still manages to take something?"

"Then scold her and find the nearest Lost and Found."

"I think this belongs to Sergeant Munson," Bev said of the cell phone.

"Great, a cop's grandkid pickpockets his boss," Rusty said.

"Well, *I think* he'll be impressed," Bev said.

"Daddy! Ba-bite!" Katie said. He held out his sandwich and she took a bite. "Mommy! Dat!" she said with a full mouth, pointing up into the sky.

"Kite!" I said, "Can you say *kite*?"

"Is that was she's asking?" Bev said.

"She's asking, 'what's that?'"

"She's been asking that all afternoon."

"Is she getting tired of it yet?"

"No."

"Rats."

"Mommy! Dat!" she said pointing up at a man.

"Umm, I'm guessing Sergeant Munson. Bev?"

"Carl! I think I have something of yours. You didn't happen to have lost a cell phone did you?"

"How did you know?"

"Just guessing."

"No pho-phones," pouted Katie.

Rusty hid the ice pack under the blanket and stood.

"Carl, it's good to see you again," Rusty said.

"This rug rat yours?"

"She's not a rug rat, she's a pick pocket. Sorry about the phone. And this is my wife, Cassidy. Stay down, Cass."

"Mind if I sit down?" Sergeant Munson said.

"Not at all. It's a bit hard for Cassidy to get up."

Actually I wasn't sure how I'd get up from the blanket without help.

He sat down cross-legged on a corner of the blanket. "I heard you got married to a tracker, and that you were working in Joshua Hills, still on the force. Your wife volunteers for search and rescue."

"That's right," Rusty said.

"It's good to meet you miss," he said to me.

"Sergeant," I said in acknowledgement.

"*You're* a tracker?"

"Yes, sir."

"You can call me Carl. Where did you get your training? How did someone like *you* learn something as obscure as tracking?"

"Tracks have always intrigued me, ever since I noticed them on the ground as a toddler. There was plenty of dirt to learn on, because I grew up on a ranch. First, tracks led me to the ranch hands. Later they led me to deer, rabbits and foxes. Then I began noticing the tracks changed based on what the person or animal was doing. I thought there had to be a story behind the tracks. One thing led to another. I learned what the differences in tracks represent. The movements I read began to make more sense. After a lot of consistent cataloguing, I learned so much from the tracks that whole pictures formed in my mind, of what a person did, what they looked like, how they lived and thought... It's easier to read a trail than talk to a person. A trail doesn't lie. As I progressed, I realized I really could read a person by reading their footprints. I understood the nuances. It made sense to me. At academy I found out I was the only one there, besides Chase, who could follow all the trails easily. After graduation I went to work tracking for Strict Strickland. Now here I am on the beach in San Diego because I got sidelined for a few months."

Munson looked to Rusty.

"So you've had no formal training?"

"When they had the tracking classes at academy they actually had me teach a group."

"Tracking isn't something you just pick up," Munson said.

"It isn't something *most people* just pick up. I never claim to be like most people."

"Where'd you come up with this girl?" he asked Rusty.

"She drove a getaway car for a bank robbery," Rusty replied. "I let her off easy when she tracked down my suspect for me."

"Now you've been married, what, over a year. And you have a baby, also with obscure talents. How'd she get my cell phone?"

"We told you. She's a bit of a pickpocket. We're trying to teach her to leave people's pockets alone but she's still learning. Did you pick her up? If you did you're lucky to still have your watch."

"So, why are you sidelined?"

"Broken hip. I'm not allowed to walk. You kind of need to be able to walk to track. And I need to be able to carry a loaded pack for work as well. I wonder how the team is getting along back home. Tourist season is starting. Spring is the worst time of year for tourists getting lost. They think it's nice and warm and then the weather turns on them. I get a lot of calls in the spring because campers come unprepared for the temperature swings."

"Can you answer a tracking question for me?"

"I can try, but you have plenty of trackers down here."

"Are the wear spots the same from one pair of shoes to the next?"

"Are you asking, if one person changes shoes do they have the same wear spots on both pairs?"

"Yeah, or if I have two pairs of shoes, from the same set of circumstances and they have the same set of wear spots, can I link them to the same suspect?"

"No. Not unless there are plenty of other facts to back it up. Any person will walk differently depending on the type of shoe they are wearing. You can test that just by trying on a pair of shoes at a shoe store. If you pay attention when you try on shoes you will admit that two pairs of shoes make you walk slightly differently. Now, if you had a tracker on the scene who gave you a profile, the profile matched the suspect, and the wear spots were consistent, it might be easier to make a link. But if you have shoes you have DNA, so I don't think tracking applies to this case."

"How many tracks do you need to get a profile?"

"Well, obviously, the more tracks there are the more information you can draw from them. With even one track you can get a feel for the person's weight. Three and you can get a feel for their height, if they were three walking or running tracks. Standing tracks don't reveal much about height, just weight. Given a trail like I am used to tracking through miles of woods, I can get a feel for the person's size, experience, and frame of mind. Eventually the personality type of the individual takes shape. The times I have profiled for Rusty I think things have pretty much worked out the way I thought they would."

"Sometimes unfortunately," added Rusty. "At times Cassidy can even tell if a person is right handed or left handed by tracking them."

"Tell me, how do you do that?"

"Mannerisms. Just telltale signs. If a person rests they will fiddle with things with their hands. They almost always use their dominate hand. Show me a resting place and I can usually figure it out. Give me a kitchen and I can tell you if a woman is right handed or left handed. There are little, subtle signs that guys wouldn't think of looking at. You're right handed."

"Most people are, but what told you that?"

"When you lean back you support yourself on your right hand. When you pick things up you do so with your right hand. But even if I didn't see you do these things I could look at the place that you sat in and come to the same conclusion." I drew a box in the sand. "Just this patch of sand right here tells me you're right handed."

"How so?"

"You picked up a pebble. I can see the tip of your finger pointing to the left. Your thumb also points left. Therefore you picked the pebble up with your right hand. It would be very unusual for you to unconsciously use your left hand."

"Tell me about this kitchen idea. How do you tell if a person is right handed or left handed by looking at their kitchen?"

"Simple. Find a well-used pan. If the cook is right handed they will hold the pan with their left hand and do most of their stirring with their right hand. So, if they do things like knock the spoon on the side of the pan to get loose food off, the right side of the pan will be full of little dents from spoons. If they are left handed, the left side of their pans will be dented. Look at their office. The mouse will be on the dominant side. There must be hundreds of little signs to tell you which hand a person uses. Why the interest?"

"I've got a woman in custody. I'm not sure she belongs there. What about stance? Is there a difference in stance between a left handed person and a right handed person?"

"Of course. But you knew that. If you're at the practice range you can tell the right handed shooters from the left handed ones. You've been around long enough to know all these things."

"Maybe I just needed a refresher course."

"I tend to notice odd things. Most people don't think about how they hold a pot when they cook. Or which foot is out when they shoot, but I do. It's just a habit."

"A handy habit. I'm glad it landed in a place where we can take advantage of it. I think I need to go talk to one of my detectives. Thank you for your help. Sometimes I need to remember that the small things matter, too. Often I can't see the trees for the forest. It's been a pleasure to meet you, Cassidy. Rusty, Bev, Bill, it was good to see you again."

"Are these yours?" Bev said holding up the sunglasses and pager.

"Nope, just the cell phone. You folks have a good day."

When Rusty dug out the ice pack it was mostly water but it was too late for the ice to help anyway. We went out swimming one more time. This time we went out together and we watched the ocean so we wouldn't be surprised. Later, while I rested, Rusty took Katie out for a swim. She loved splashing in the water. It would be a while before she would be swimming out there but I thought it was important to keep her used to the water.

The next day we were getting ready to start our day when there was a knock at the door. Bev answered it. I was upstairs and couldn't get down stairs so I continued getting dressed. I could hear women's voices. Soon Bev knocked on the bedroom door, and I opened it a crack.

"Cassidy, Becca Stephens is at the door. She'd like to talk to you."

"I just need a minute. Is she waiting outside?"

"She's in the living room. Katie's trying to get the patches off her uniform."

"Don't let her do that. It's probably a nuisance."

"It's okay, she loves kids."

When Bev left I hurried to get ready.

"Rusty, who is Becca Stephens? She's a cop. Do you know her?"

"Just a little. I never worked with her. She came on a few months before I moved. She's been around a while. She knows her stuff. Why would she be looking for you?"

"I don't know."

I saved my pants for last since it took some tugging and sometimes I needed some help. At least my pants were loose now. That helped a little. I lay on the bed, tugging and pulling. Rusty laughed at me.

"You remind me of a teenage girl trying to fit into too-tight jeans."

"Gee, thanks."

I had pretty good luck if I just stayed on the bed and pulled on my socks and shoes, too. Rusty tied my moccasins for me so I wouldn't have to struggle to reach my feet lying down. I knew it looked awkward but eventually I got dressed. I slid to the edge of the bed and Rusty buttoned his last two buttons, slipped on his shoes and tied the laces. I wheeled out onto the landing.

"The chair or the couch?" Rusty asked.

"The chair."

"The easy way or the hard way?"

Sigh, "The easy way." I preferred the hard way when appearances mattered but I was willing to endure the embarrassment of the easy way. Rusty carried me downstairs. He set me down on the couch and went back for the chair. When the chair was downstairs I right footed my way over to it.

Becca watched the goings on with interest. She didn't look like she missed much. I couldn't wheel all the way over to her. The coffee table was in the way.

"Becca? I'm Cassidy Michaels. I think you know Rusty."

"We've met. I came by to thank you. I'd like to know what you said to Carl Munson yesterday."

"He just asked me a couple of questions. I answered them as quickly and honestly as I could."

"And what exactly did he ask?"

"He asked me if two different pairs of shoes belonging to one person will have the same wear spots on the bottoms."

"That seems an odd thing for a man to ask a woman he doesn't know."

"Yes, well, it wasn't odd to me. I'm a tracker, so it was a perfectly logical question, to me. I told him the wear spots could be very different and that two pairs of shoes with the same wear spots might belong to two different people."

She sat back, pondering what I had told her. "So, what did you tell him that changed his mind about me?"

"I don't know. You'd know that better than I would."

"But I don't."

"Maybe you should ask Carl."

"I think I'll get further finding out for myself. I think he knows that if I look in that direction I'll find what I need to clear myself."

Now I knew that Becca was the woman Carl Munson released from custody, but I wasn't supposed to know that. So what to do? Feign ignorance? I didn't have to.

"Rusty, what would you do? I had this neighbor. The neighbor from hell. I've been documenting all the things she's done to make my life miserable. I'm not talking about the usual things like turning her music up too loud. I'm talking about breaking and entering, stealing things from me, screaming threats, people coming and going from her apartment at all hours of the day and night. I go over to talk to her and everything appears normal. A mess, but normal. You've seen the houses. I can't pin anything on her so I start documenting. I was going to take the list to the manager like we always advise other people to do. Then one night, there's a scuffle next door. I've got this list and, stupid me, I march over there, mad as hell, ready to break up the fight, list in hand, and I find my neighbor laid out on the living room floor. I don't like the woman but I'm not going to kill her. I don't see another person, then as I'm calling the cops they come rushing in the front door. I'm standing there with a list of motives. There's no weapon, no real evidence, so they haul me in."

"Sounds like you were set up," Rusty said. "The only way the police would have gotten there that fast was if the real killer called them. The scuffle was short?"

"Yeah, only a few minutes. I wasn't even going over there to confront her with the list. I went over to break it up."

"And you were off duty so you weren't in uniform."

"Right."

"The guys all knew you. Why haul you in?"

"One: I had the list. Two: all the fingerprints around the scene were mine or my neighbor's."

"There couldn't have been many of them. Was the door open when you arrived?"

"No, but it was ajar. I rang the bell, didn't get any answer even though I knew someone was there. I pushed the door open and there she was."

"Is there a backdoor?"

"No. A window was open."

"Screen?"

"No screen, but that's not unusual around there."

"Is it still taped off?"

"No."

"Think we could get in?" I asked.

"It's no use. There's people over there clearing the place out."

"Still, do you think we could get in?"

"We could try. I'm more interested in why Sarge was asking you tracking questions, and how that led to him releasing me."

"If it's a tracking question we can look around outside and maybe that will tell us something."

"It's been four days. I doubt there's much left."

"It's been four calm days. I've tracked week old trails before. Let's go look."

Bad news for us, the front door to Becca's neighbor's apartment was wide open and a family was hauling boxes out to a small U Haul trailer. Rusty and Becca went into the apartment and I left them to do their detective work. Me, in my chair, would just bring up questions and I would have a hard time staying out of the way. I wheeled around to the back side of the apartment building. It was a fourplex, two apartments downstairs and two up. The apartment complex consisted of about thirty fourplexes. It was an older complex but it was well maintained. The grass was mowed and sidewalks linked the buildings through an attractive landscape of shrubs and trees. The grass and sidewalks were bad news to me. However, the landscapers sprayed weed killer around the foundations of the buildings, and there was about two feet of bare dirt around each building and large, bare circles of soil under each tree.

I counted the windows as I made my way around the building. These would be Becca's windows, so these further down the wall must be the neighbor's windows. I glanced inside trying not to be too obvious in case people were inside clearing out the room. I found a window with no screen but it had been closed. I pushed the wheelchair as close to the bare dirt as I could without obscuring the trail, not that I could find much of a trail in two feet of dirt. However, I did find what I hoped to find. Someone had climbed out through the window. And I found out why the interest in how to tell whether a person was right or left handed. The person who had crawled through that window had placed their left foot first. A right handed person would use their right foot first. I looked at the window frame. It, too, told me that the real suspect was left handed. There had been a screen on the window before the murder. The screen had been pushed out from the bottom left corner.

I studied the track. Left foot. The ground was pretty solid under the window. Four days had passed. I put the size of the woman at about five seven, a hundred forty pounds. I took note of the tread, the wear spots. They didn't show up well at this point but I could still gain enough of a feel about them that I could recognize it again. I couldn't follow the trail over the grass but I got a direction off the two tracks and headed for the dirt area that was under a tree in that direction. For the most part the trees looked very neat but one tree had little streets plowed and a small lake dug by a child playing with trucks and cars underneath it. A rusty toy dump truck lay on its side beneath the tree. I circled the tree in question but I didn't find a track. I moved to another tree and found four running tracks going underneath it. Whoever this person was they didn't think about their trail. I studied these tracks as well, not getting much of a feel for the person but knowing our suspect left them. I looked to the apartments in the distance. I followed the tracks in the direction they pointed.

A door opened.

"Can I help you?" a woman said.

"No, I'm just waiting for my husband."

"You have an odd way of waiting for a husband."

"Yes, well, I am doing something, too. You didn't happen to hear a commotion about four days ago in the building over there?" I asked.

"I saw all the police activity. Isn't it terrible what that officer did? I think the job gets to them after a while. Nobody liked that Stiles woman but I didn't think it would lead to bloodshed. I'd transfer my lease over to that apartment if she hadn't died there! I don't think I could live in a place where I knew someone had died."

"Word certainly gets around, doesn't it?" I asked.

"It's the laundry room. Everybody talks in the laundry room."

"You haven't heard anything else about it, have you? Because I don't think Becca did it."

"Of course you don't. You're Becca's friend."

"I only met Becca today. But she didn't do it."

"Then you're jumping to conclusions. Of course she did it. She got tired of arguing with her and snapped."

"I've been looking around, doing my own detective work. Even I am convinced Becca didn't do this. The person who did it escaped out the back window and ran this way. That's why I thought you might have seen something."

Call me stupid. Call me naïve. I should have known better. As I wheeled back to see how Rusty and Becca were doing a bullet hit my wheelchair back about two inches beside my left shoulder. Diving for cover is a little difficult from a wheelchair, with a broken hip. I hit the dirt and rolled under a nearby bush. It wasn't too smart of the woman. If she was going to pull something like that she needed a silencer.

Becca and Rusty ran around the side of the building.

"Get back!" I called out from under the bush. "I've got a new suspect for you. I think we lost the deposit on the wheelchair, too."

"What apartment?" Becca asked.

"Apartment 8-A, downstairs left. Are all crooks that stupid?" I asked.

"Unfortunately, no."

"Cassidy, are you okay?" Rusty asked.

"Yeah, I'm just laying low for a bit."

"What happened?" Rusty asked.

"I think Trouble has ESP. We were going to the mall to see Sandy, right? Trouble knows we didn't go to the mall."

"That's not what I meant. What did you do to draw attention to yourself? What made you the target of a bullet?"

"Laundry room gossip."

"Quit dodging the answer."

"I was tracking the suspect and this woman asked if she could help me find somebody and we started talking about the commotion over here and I told her that I didn't think Becca did it. Guess all Becca needed to clear her name was bait."

I knew as long as I was talking Rusty knew I was fine. When the police closed in I figured it was safe to come out.

"Cover around back first," I told them. "That's how she left the first time.

She's armed. I'm guessing 9mm pistol."

They looked at me like I was nuts. Wheelchair victim. What did she know about firearms?

"Cassidy, let's get out of here," Rusty said. "Becca knows where to find us if they need anything."

"How about a description of the suspect?"

Rusty waved over a deputy.

"This is Cassidy. She talked to the shooter. Okay, give him your description."

"White, a hundred forty pounds, bleached blonde in her forties, blue jeans, red blouse, shoes match the tracks under Becca's window. Brown eyes, pierced ears. Three rings on her fingers. Let's see…navy blue socks, smoker. Too much makeup."

"Okay, okay, I think they get the picture," Rusty said.

"There's more tracks under the tree if you need them."

"I'm taking her home. Bill Michaels' house if you're looking for more information."

He stuffed me in the Explorer and loaded up the chair before I could protest.

"Rusty! They were just getting started!" I said.

"And it's their party. Just stay out of it as much as possible. What made you go looking for trouble this time?"

"Nothing. I was just tracking. I verified that…oh yeah! Tell him she's left handed!"

"They'll figure it out."

Bev looked at me with disapproval. "I swear, you're worse than Cody!" she said, "Look at you. How did you get covered in dirt and leaves sitting in a wheel chair?"

"I didn't. It was avoiding the bullet that got me all dirty. Rusty would have done the same thing."

"So…how did it…" Bill stopped when he got a look at us.

"I think Becca's name will be cleared by this afternoon," I said.

We spent a few more days with Rusty's family but home was calling me. I longed to get into a training program and a routine. I wanted to be able to cook if I felt like it. It felt like I had been away forever. It even seemed odd to see Katie walking around the house. She had never walked in her own house before. I helped Rusty unpack and we started a load of laundry. Everything was too high for me. The washer, the stove. I didn't know how I was going to manage taking care of the house.

In the morning Rusty went grocery shopping. I made up a long list of ingredients for basic recipes that I knew I could help him cook. He went to the store. I bathed Katie, gave her what little we had in the house in the way of breakfast food. After breakfast we played on the floor. She could get away from me now, so I had to keep her interested in floor games. If she got bored she would toddle off and then I'd have to find my wheelchair and make my way into it to go find her. She loved playing peek-a-boo. She hid behind the couch and popped up saying, "A-boo!" and I would act all startled. She doubled over in a fit of giggles before she tried it again. She was good enough at walking that she could even bend over laughing and not lose her balance. Katie was hiding behind the couch when Rusty walked in, arms heavily laden with groceries. Katie popped up, "A-boo!" she said and Rusty froze.

"Oh! Katie! You scared Mommy!" I said in mock surprise.

Baby laughter bounced off the walls. Rusty dropped the bags, eggs and all. He sat down on the big brown couch and just stared, big tears threatening. He blinked them back. He swallowed hard. His breathing was quick and shallow. I army crawled over to the couch.

"Rusty! What happened?" I asked. I knew it took a lot to hit him like this.

He picked me up and sat back down in our spot.

"A-boo!" said Katie. "Daddy! A-boo!"

He couldn't play along. Katie toddled around the couch and looked up into his eyes. She laid her head on his knee. He took a deep breath.

"Every day for six weeks I pictured you playing on the floor with Katie when I got home. Every day I came home to a still house. Even when Bertie was taking care of Katie and when the house was full of family. It seemed empty when I came home and the scene I'd been picturing all day didn't happen. Weeks went by and I had to face the fact that it might not ever happen. I might have to face this empty room every day for the rest of my life. I didn't think I could do it. Now, I come home and it's back. You're back. You're home. When I saw it, I almost couldn't believe it. It was too good to be true. It was a miracle. I'm sorry, babe, I just couldn't help it. I wanted it so badly."

Chapter 14

Rusty was right about the gym. I didn't want to crunch anything after the surgery. I couldn't even get my legs up on the posts at first. I was starting from scratch.

Rusty's month off from work passed but he couldn't bring himself to go back to the job. He was bored at home, yet he couldn't turn his back on me, stuck in the chair in a house too tall for me, unable to really cook, crawling out of the chair to change Katie on the floor or trying to stand and do it one-footed at the changing table. He knew he couldn't stay home for three months, but maybe he could long enough. He took us for drives up in the mountains and he helped put together Katie's first birthday party. We decorated up the backyard, bought a bunch of different things to barbecue, got a cake, ice cream, balloons, then invited everyone we knew, since Katie didn't know any kids.

Rusty picked out Katie's first birthday cake. It was shaped like a princess castle. Rusty was determined, even though he never voiced it, that his little girl was going to know she was really a princess. He never could convince his wife, but maybe little Kaitlyn would see the princess in her if Daddy tried hard enough to show it to her.

Katie had a blast. The guys were disappointed when she pretty much left their radios alone. They laughed at her pouted, "no pho-phones." The officers came and went as duty called. We made sure they got a good dinner and some cake and ice cream while they were here. Presents were definitely optional. After all the gifts the grandparents sent home, Katie didn't need any more. In a way it was more a celebration that things were back on track, and that the future looked bright again.

Rusty, Kelly, Landon and I were gathered around the barbecue when two ravens landed in the yard looking for accidentally dropped food. Katie spotted them.

"Mommy! Dat!" she asked.

"Birds!" I said enthusiastically. "Watch this, guys, it's funny. Katie, sneak up on the birds. Get the birdies!"

She gave them her sneaky look and did her little knee bend, "neak, neak" routine, but when that was out of the way she walked off to sneak up on the birds. Shadow rushed to intercept her. He took his sheepdog responsibilities seriously now that the little sheep was walking. One of the ravens stared her down and cawed at her and she stopped.

"Starting her out early, aren't you?" Strict asked as he joined the group.

"I didn't start her out at all. Patrick did. He took her out stalking rabbits at the ranch," I said.

"She didn't get anywhere with it, did she?" I heard the unspoken, this is Cassidy's kid, there's always a chance...

"No, not really. Pat knew it was a bit early so he was just hoping she'd like it so she'd want to try again."

They seemed a bit relieved. Maybe this kid would turn out normal after all.

"I don't watch TV," Rusty said. "Did anybody see Katie on TV? They never told us when it would air."

All the hopes that Katie would be normal withered with Rusty's question.

"Katie was on TV? What did she do? Track down a kidnapped Cassidy?" Landon asked.

"No, she was taped for some reality TV show. She pick pocketed this guy in two minutes flat. It was for some show, I guess they have different themes for different days of the week and they were going to use her for Hidden Talent Tuesday."

"Oh yeah! Kevin Koukalaka's show. Man, he makes people do some strange stuff! Katie's going to be on his show?" Landon said.

"It was funny. She even stole the poor guy's toupee," I said.

"When are you going to be back on the trail?" Strict asked.

"I have a doctor's appointment in a week. I'll know more then. I think they are going to run x-rays so that should give us a pretty good idea. I'll start training as soon as I get the okay to ditch the chair."

Doctor Ron hadn't seen me since I broke my leg jumping out of a Joshua tree. He'd gotten the call from the doctor in LA, and they had sent my file up to his office so he had an idea what he was working with.

"Cassidy, you've got to slow down. You're beating yourself up and your body can't take much more. You've broken a leg and both hips in the past year. This is the second time you've had broken ribs. You can't take much more of this abuse. I have rodeo stars that come in less frequently than you do."

"When I did rodeo I never got hurt," I said. "Of course they only let women do the safer events. It's hard to get hurt barrel racing. But I saddle broke horses when I was a teenager. Being a trouble magnet is definitely more dangerous than being in rodeos."

"How did you break both hips? You're stronger than that."

"I don't remember."

"What do you mean, you don't remember? Most people would remember something traumatic enough to break both their hips."

"I was unconscious. I can tell you what the police decided happened to me."

And so began another Cassidy tale which he sat through and made him late for all his afternoon appointments. He sent me to x-ray and I brought back the pictures. He looked them over carefully. The right side was healed so he gave me permission to use crutches and he gave me a sheaf of papers outlining the exercises I could do to get the left side mobile again without stressing the joint.

Now when I went to the gym I had a whole new program to follow. Georgia looked through the papers.

"You're going to do all these exercises? Every day?"

"Most days. Maybe in three weeks he'll let me use a walker. If he lets me use a walker I can do the treadmills."

"Girl, you are *nuts*!"

"I know, but I need to get back to work. My brain is going numb sitting at home all the time. I want to get out in the hills and piece a trail of tracks together. I miss the guys' teasing. I want to bake cookies again. When I can hit the trail and bake cookies I'll know I have my life back."

At first the exercises were torture. I tried doing them at the gym, but I had to do them at home where I could be as miserable as I felt. I pushed for sets of ten. Then fifteen. When I could do sets of twenty I started doing them at the gym again. I graduated to a walker, which meant I could now walk the treadmills with Georgia. It was her turn to egg me on. I had to start slow. Two miles an hour at first. Half a mile at two and I was hurting. Then I went for a whole mile, then I upped the speed. The speed and the distance played leapfrog very gradually. Fred was worse than having my mom in the gym.

"You're going to land yourself back in the wheelchair if you keep pushing," he'd nag me. Or, "Cassidy, it's time to ease up. That ol' no pain no gain doesn't apply to you."

Georgia and I were good for each other.

"You can do it girl! You jus' got what it takes. Look a'choo. You work so hard you'll never gain weight. You need to stuff yourself before you work like that. Give you something to work off!"

I was sore most of the time after I graduated to the walker, because I didn't use it. I figured if I could walk with a walker I could just as easily walk without it. Lugging a piece of metal around with me seemed harder than just walking.

Katie was disappointed that the wheelchair was gone. There were no more rides and life slowed down considerably as I worked at walking again.

I was up to a slow, painful mile and a half on the treadmill when my first search came up. When it came, it didn't come in the normal way, with a phone call from Strict. There was a knock on my door.

Chapter 15

I looked out the peephole. I didn't recognize the face. That was bad news. I thought about who might be after me. Nobody that I knew of. I was very aware of the rifle hidden beside the door as I opened it a little and looked out.

"I was wondering if you could help me. I'm looking for Cassidy Michaels," the man said. He was about five ten, maybe two hundred pounds. His hair was cut short. He wore blue jeans and a Dodgers t-shirt. He took a badge out of his pocket. Okay, so he was an off duty cop. I didn't usually get visits from off duty cops I didn't know.

"I'm Cassidy, how can I help you?"

He paused. Like usual I wasn't what he expected to find. Katie toddled into the room.

"Uh oh, Mommy," she said. What had she gotten into?

"You're the Joshua District tracker?" he asked.

"When I'm able."

"Lou Strickland refused to call you. But I need your help."

"Lou Strickland refused to call me because he knows I'm kind of laid up at the moment. Mr…"

"Bradley Sparks," he said extending his hand. "I know. But I still need your help. I've been on too many searches to send a bunch of guys up there to shake the bushes. Not when I know there's a better way. I can't help it. What would you do when an eight year old kid gets separated on a hike? We've done flyovers. The forest is too thick there. I need a pair of eyes on the ground."

"When this kid is eight years old," I said indicating Katie, "she will have the survival skills to find herself. She'll know how to find water. She'll know how to tell directions by the shadows the trees cast. She'll know what plants are edible and know how to catch and skin a rabbit."

"We aren't talking about some future version of your kid. We're talking about mine. The kid who grew up on a nice, safe cul de sac, who grew up roller blading, bike riding and playing hopscotch, who just thought another part of the forest looked more interesting than the one the group was in. She was just dressed in jeans and a t-shirt. It got down in the thirties last night…"

"Does Strict have a base camp set up yet?"

"No, we got into a big argument about search methods. I insisted on a tracker. I know there are trackers out there. I had to do some research to come up with your name. I've read some of your accomplishments. I know you can find her."

"I know I could, too," I said sadly. "I don't have medical clearance yet. I expect to be able to track again, in maybe a month. It's been slow going. I can walk a mile and a half but I couldn't do it in a pack."

"I'll carry your pack. I'll do anything."

"You can't do that. If you go, you'll have your own gear."

"I'll find a way…"

"How long has she been missing?"

"Overnight… twelve hours."

"How far is it to her last known location?"

"Two miles."

Two miles. Damn, it was more than I'd walked in three months just to *start* the search. But I couldn't turn him down either.

"Where do you think they'll put base camp?"

"Creekside Campground."

That was good news. I knew the trail out of Creekside. Shoot, I was talking myself into it, no doubt about it. I had a camp up that way. Two miles out of Creekside then two miles up a canyon. If she'd taken an interest in the canyon she might be in my old stomping grounds.

"Okay, you've convinced me. There's one more barrier to overcome. My husband. You ready to take that one on?"

"Point the way."

"Let me check my gear."

I led him to the garage, opened the pack and did a quick check, added a change of clothes. Even walking without the pack I had to be careful and walk gently. I put the pack on and tried to walk. There was no way. I felt a deep stab of pain in my left hip with the added weight. I took it off.

"Put this in the car," I instructed.

Next was all the baby gear. I checked the diaper bag, checked Katie, got her car seat from the Jeep.

"What are we doing?" Sparks asked.

"My husband and a babysitter are both in town, just a few blocks apart. You'll work on Rusty. I'll track down Bertie. When I find Bertie have patience. She's not your typical babysitter. I'll ask at the station about her normal hangout for the time of day and day of the week and the officers will know which direction to send me."

"You have close ties with the force down here?"

"My husband is a detective, so… yeah. I've either worked with the guys or been rescued by them, so either way I've got connections. If you get Rusty's okay you'll have to call Strict back. Put a request in for Landon Wilson. He'll be our EMT. He's my usual search partner."

"Why can't I be your search partner?"

"Because you're a cop. What'll you do if we find your daughter and she's dehydrated? What if she fell off a rock or a ledge and needs medical attention? Landon can handle it."

"Where are we going?"

"Joshua Hills station."

"Where's that?"

"Downtown. I'll give you directions. Where are you from?"

"Moorpark. Why don't we just take your car?"

"Because I barely manage to drive to the gym once a day. If you want me to last on the trail I need to rest my leg. That reminds me, I better throw in my crutches."

I directed him to the station and he parked hastily and headed for the door before I could get out of the car. Then I had to get Katie. He was impatient, which didn't bode well for the trail. I set Katie down on the pavement and took her hand. We walked slowly across the parking lot. I carried her as little as possible to avoid putting extra weight on my hip. Sparks walked down the steps and picked Katie up.

"No pockets," I warned Katie.

I led Sparks to Rusty's office and took Katie from him.

"He's not unreasonable, but he's very protective. You'll have better luck with him than I will. I'll introduce you but then I'm going to find Bertie. My advice is to tackle this from a technical perspective. If you make this an emotional appeal it's going to turn into a battle of wills."

I knocked on the door to Rusty's office. He came around the corner as I was peeking in through the little rectangular window.

"Hey princess!" he said as he picked up Katie. Katie handed him a watch.

"I told her no pockets," I said. "I have someone here who wants to meet you. Bradley Sparks, this is my husband, Rusty Michaels. Bradley is an officer based in Moorpark. I'm getting out of the way before the sparks fly."

"Cassidy, no. You get right back here. If you're trying to escape it means it involves you."

"Michaels, I just need a tracker…"

"No."

"I've got a missing kid. I know Cassidy can find her."

"Call Lou Strickland."

"I did. He wouldn't call Cassidy. So I looked her up myself. I need a tracker."

"She's not going. I see you've convinced her already or you wouldn't be here. It's up to me to say no. So…no."

"Rusty," I said, "it's just two miles up Creekside trail. You know what that means. She's probably just up the canyon."

"Then tell Strict that. He can search that canyon easier than you can."

"*If* she's in the canyon, yes. That's what I'm hoping, but if she isn't then I will be able to tell."

"You're in no shape to take this on."

"I'm willing to try. For an eight year old girl, I'm willing to risk it. She's not prepared to spend another night out. Let me go find her."

He stalked off down the hall. He turned left.

"This is not a good sign," I told Sparks.

We followed Rusty to the exercise room. He took a swing at the punching bag, making it lurch violently. The power behind the blow was not lost on Sparks. He knew something deeper was going on.

"Three months and then bam! Right back out on the trail. Only three months. I can't. I can't let you. If he knew what he was asking he wouldn't ask."

"What am I asking?" Sparks said.

"Cassidy, make the rounds with Katie."

The search was too up in the air to go talk to Bertie so I walked the station. It was surprisingly quiet. In a way it was encouraging, but it also meant everybody was out on the streets. I needed to get off my feet so I went to Rusty's office and sat Katie on top of his desk. I got a couple of toy cars out of his desk drawer and let her play with them, rolling them back and forth on top of the desk.

"Mommy! Dat!" she said, holding up a car.

"Car!" I told her.

She held up the other one, too, "Dat!" she said.

"Truck!"

"Dat!"

"Car."

"Dat!"

"Truck."

Could this go on all day?

When the guys came in I knew. Sparks now knew exactly what he was asking. Now even he was uneasy about this search.

It was a solemn beginning to a search. Usually, everybody was anxious, unsure about the outcome but hopeful. Magnify that by ten. I had to pry to get answers because everybody was so quiet.

"I need some sample tracks," I said.

"I'll show you, when we get there," Sparks said.

He carried my pack. I carried my crutches. I walked about a quarter mile and then I crutched a quarter mile. By the time a mile had passed I was ready to chuck the crutches into the forest but I knew my hip wouldn't hold out. A part of me was glorying in the fact that I was back in the mountains. On my feet. Tracking. I wasn't seeing any of Dylan Sparks' tracks but you can't stop a tracker from tracking. I was tracking a couple of young men out for a hike covering up the Sparks family outing with their running shoe tracks. I profiled the trail whenever the talk slowed down. Two men, physically fit, one with new shoes, one with worn shoes, a hundred fifty pounds and a hundred seventy pounds. The smaller man was the more experienced one. He looked ahead and planned his steps. The larger man met surprises and had to correct his gait and foot placement to avoid stumbling. I thought it was odd that a guy who wasn't even present was showing me where I needed to be careful.

Neither Landon nor Bradley was asking for stories, or cookies. When Landon had showed up at base camp he was skeptical and he remained skeptical. Both men knew what had transpired since my last search. The mood was getting dark and each time I shifted from walking to crutches it only reminded them of what I was risking. Landon was wondering how far he should let me go.

"Come on guys, cheer up. The past few months haven't been totally gloomy. Want to hear a funny story?"

They remained silent but I couldn't stand the dark little clouds hovering over their heads so I felt like I had to do something to dispel them. I told them about shutting down the pool at the hotel and getting rescued by a whole lifeguard convention. I told them about my mishaps at the mall up north. Though they laughed in all the right places it did little to lighten the mood.

"You were missing for over a month?" Bradley asked.

"From what I've been told. I lost whole days after a while. I don't remember a lot of it. It was just hunger and pain and waiting for tiny breaks."

"Rusty was right. I didn't know what I was asking."

"It's okay, probably the only thing that made him give in was knowing how you felt with Dylan lost. We'll find her okay. At least she got lost in an area with plenty of water. It's got two creeks, very unusual for these mountains. Almost any other trail and she'd be lucky to find any water. What kind of shoes was she wearing?"

"Just tennis shoes."

"How much tread was left? Do you know?"

"Enough tread to leave a good track. She's outgrowing shoes left and right so her shoes are always relatively new these days."

"So, when she outgrew the left ones you bought her left ones and when she outgrew the right ones…" Landon joked.

"It's just a saying. Okay, she outgrows her shoes *frequently*. There, do you like that better?"

It always amazed me how these guys, complete strangers, acted like they had known each other for years. The common link they shared just put them in a similar frame of mind. Even if they weren't talking about the job there was camaraderie. Even if they didn't call each other by their first names they felt as if they were. Wilson and Sparks were just as friendly as Landon and Bradley would be. They never called me Michaels. Maybe Rusty was Michaels. The only time I had been called by my last name was in the Marines and police academy. Ever since graduation I had been Cassidy, except for a very few close friends who knew it was okay to call me Cass.

I had to rest. Walking a trail and walking a treadmill were two different activities. The trail was harder, even without a pack.

Strict checked in frequently. The calls were rarely in codes as they should have been. This was Lou, checking on his little tracker, not Lou "Strict" Strickland calling for a report on a search and rescue mission. I thought the contrast was funny. He knew I was no cop, and that I was out here because I couldn't ignore a need for help. It bothered him that I'd never be the cookie cutter rescue volunteer, but it endeared me to him, too. I thought the Marines and academy should have hammered a good feeling for procedure into my brain but when procedure seemed to matter the most I relied on instinct and instinct rarely remembered what the book said. I knew Rusty was likely to check in frequently so each time Strict radioed for an update I told him I was fine, no matter how I really felt.

Finally! Two miles. I could tell because the two mile marker was the spot where the two creeks came together. I sat beside the creek and lay back on the bank, needing a few minutes to regroup. Now the real work would begin.

"How did you know where the two mile mark was?" Bradley asked.

"Because my favorite camping spot is two miles up that canyon," I answered. "I used to come here a lot. Before I met Rusty, I practically lived there. I was a young widow, no job, more sorrow than I knew what to do with, so I hiked up that canyon, made a camp there and lived off the land. I haven't been back for a long time. I was kind of hoping Dylan had gone up there so I could see it again."

I lay on the creek bank resting.

"She's your partner. You wake her," Sparks said.

Landon answered, "It's not like Cassidy to fall asleep on the trail. She needs it. Give her a little time to recharge. I've gone on calls where she was so intent on finding her man she forgot to eat. She's not being lazy and she hasn't forgotten about Dylan. I bet she doesn't even know she fell asleep."

"Shoot," I said struggling to sit up. That first bend was always painful.

"Plus, she's a light sleeper. I bet I don't even have to wake her," Landon said.

"Let me get the kinks out and I'll be ready."

Getting the kinks out just involved being straight. I walked around a bit with the crutches. Oh man, the hard ground hadn't helped at all. I was so stiff.

"Okay, show me the tracks," I said to Sparks.

He led us up the creek a little ways to where there was a little clearing.

"We ate lunch here and let the kids play in the water. There are two sets of kids' tracks. I've got a six year old boy, too. It might be a bit confusing because Dustin wears about the same shoe size that Dylan does."

There were tracks everywhere. Bradley's wife wasn't used to being out in the woods. She wore canvas sneakers. The kids wore tennis shoes and he was right, they were almost the same size. Bradley had been wearing hiking boots. New.

"You need to break in your boots before you hit the trail," I told him.

"Now I know. I'm still nursing blisters."

About the only difference between Dustin and Dylan's tracks was the width. I measure them against the width of my hand. These were active kids but I could tell Dustin was the go-getter and Dylan was more thoughtful and careful. The clearing was a mess of tracks. I followed Dylan's tracks this way and that as she explored farther and farther from the group. At first she stayed within sight of the clearing but then one of her forays hit the trail and she followed the trail for a bit, keeping the clearing within sight. Then a rock off the other side of the trail caught her eye. She had worked on climbing the boulder. I couldn't tell if she ever reached the top of it. But then one rock led to another.

It was an interesting looking canyon. There was always something just up the hill to draw the attention, which is how I discovered my camping spot in the first place.

As the terrain became rougher I had to decide between the crutches and walking. The climb was rough for me but the crutches only seemed to get in the way.

"What I'm seeing is good news," I informed Bradley. "She's just exploring. If she was worried I would feel it by now. At first she was concerned about not straying too far. She kept pausing and making sure she could see the group. She's just having fun, now."

"Why'd she take off this way?" he asked.

"Because it's a cool canyon. I know. I spent a few years exploring it."

Dylan's tracks were faint but people rarely came up this canyon so hers were the only tracks around. I went track to track but I didn't take time to analyze unless I was stuck. As long as I was on *a* trail I was confident it was Dylan's trail. Sometimes an interesting rock or a group of trees would distract her. She wandered from one interesting stop to another.

I was flagging. Every step hurt now. The crutches rarely helped. I was winded from the exertion.

"Cassidy, stop," Bradley said.

"There's a place. About a quarter mile. I'll have to stop there. Dylan will have to make a decision when she gets to it. We'll stop there."

"That guy sure does love you a lot. I thought he was going to kill that punching bag," Bradley said of Rusty.

"He counts the peaceful days. This is too soon. He's worried this'll be a setback. And it might be…it just might be. But we'll get through it…And so will Dylan. How'd you get him to let me go?"

"We just reached an understanding. He knew I wasn't going to give up on getting a tracker. I knew I was dead if I let anything happen to you."

"I wouldn't worry about that too much," Landon said. "I'm still alive."

When we reached the waterfall I had to stop. I was counting the steps until we reached it. Just get to the waterfall, Cass. You can make it.

"Dylan climbed it…but I can't…" I said to the guys. "Wait at the bottom. I'll go hike around as soon as I can. Don't worry about the climb. I usually do it, too, in a pack. A kid can handle it. I can tell by the ground that she didn't fall. She's just exploring… It's good to see a kid exploring. But I've got to take the long way… in a minute."

It wasn't a big waterfall, maybe eight feet. Just a small creek taking a tumble, but I couldn't lift my left leg straight up to make the climb.

It was a pretty spot. I was glad Dylan got to see it. I sat down on a rock beside the waterfall to rest. When I got up my leg just plain old went out from under me. I fell to the ground with a clatter of crutches.

"It's okay," I told the guys. "Guess I got up too soon." I tried again. "Okay, the tree first," I said as I took a tentative step. "Now that one."

The incline was pretty steep. By the time I walked up the sloped side of the waterfall I needed to rest again.

"I've found the tracks," I called down. "You can climb up now."

Resting didn't seem to help anymore. When I tested my legs my left leg was useless. I was going to have to use my crutches but I didn't see how I could keep that up in this rough canyon. I was thankful tracking is a slow business. My hip limited my up and down movement so when I got stuck finding the next track it was a major undertaking to get down to ground level to study the placement and figure out the direction.

Landon could tell, I was continuing through pure stubbornness. I was ready to sit under a tree and sleep for a week.

When I got stuck Bradley worried. He didn't seem to know this was just part of the process, but he couldn't have followed her thus far so he didn't have any complaints.

"Don't worry so much. If I know this canyon Dylan is within a couple of miles of us. We just have to traverse the same couple of miles she did to get there."

"A couple of miles covers a lot of ground," he said.

"I know, but we can see where she went. That's why you dragged me out here, remember? This is a fresh trail. We're doing good."

Bradley looked to Landon, who nodded agreement.

"Dylan's light on her feet so she doesn't leave much of a track. I catch a bit of tread here, a turn there. But we're not running into any major setbacks."

"How long does it usually take you to find someone?"

"You knew I couldn't answer that when you asked. There are too many variables to predict, but you called me in as soon as you could. That's an advantage. She's had access to water. She's still doing well on her feet."

"How can you tell?"

"No stumbling. No dragging. She's doing great. Our only worry is how she coped with the nighttime temperatures. As far as how long it'll take… I've had two hour searches and I've had four day searches. It won't be four days. But I can tell you I'm not hiking out of here today, maybe tomorrow. We are stuck up here for one night unless we need to call for a lift. I don't see that happening, though. Landon can tell you about the four day track though. That was a good one. Tell him, Landon."

I focused on my tracking as Landon told Bradley about tracking a rodeo clown over miles of trail, finding his ruined clown shoes…

Dylan climbed a rock, came down the other side and turned. I didn't track her over the rock. I circled it and caught her tracks on the other side. There was no rock climbing for me that day. When she turned she spotted a faint trail and set off down that. The fact that there was still a trail here bothered me a little bit. I checked unobtrusively to see if the guys were armed. The forest should have reclaimed this trail long ago. It was made by crooks hiding out in the mountains. The purpose of them coming had been destroyed so I thought they would stop visiting this place. I didn't see any adult tracks on the trail. That was good. In a way I was glad she was heading this direction. If she followed the trail it led to a sandy place that was easy tracking. It consisted of huge rocks ranging from the size of a van to rocks the size of a house. The problem Dylan ran into in what I called the Boulder Field, was that all the rocks tended to look alike and since they were very tall and haphazardly stacked it was more like wandering in dimly lit caves. It was miserable tracking because Dylan tended to crawl though small spaces where I couldn't use my crutches. In and out of the boulders I followed. Her tracks overlapped and I followed the set that was on top, since they were the most recent. She was really, truly turned around in there. After a while all she saw were her own dusty tracks. It was here that she began to tire. When Dylan stopped to rest, I stopped to rest.

"Cassidy… this isn't the place I think it is. Is it?" Landon asked.

"Yup, it is. You're not superstitious, are you?"

"No. It's just not one of my favorite calls to remember."

"If you're fixing to tell Bradley the story get it out of your system before we find Dylan. She doesn't need to know about that."

"Know about what?"

"This is where Landon got handcuffed to a corpse," I answered.

Landon rolled his eyes, "Do you have to put it like that?"

"Well, you were."

"Now I have to tell it just to save face."

"I don't know if it'll work, but you can try."

It was a modern day pirate tale of hidden treasure and a motley crew of bad guys who led us into a trap. We both made our share of mistakes on that little adventure.

One thing about Dylan's path, though, was that I didn't have to cover all of it. While she spent hours wandering the jumble of boulders, I followed her most recent tracks, so even though I followed through some very odd places, I covered less than half the ground. This shortened our search dramatically. As I approached another small crawl space I groaned. My hip just wouldn't crawl. It complained when I stooped. I handed Landon my crutches and got down on all fours. Hell. What a place. Why would a kid go crawling off through little tunnels in the rock? Because, I told myself, she's like you. You'd have done the same thing when you were a kid. You'd even do it now if you weren't laid up.

"Cassidy, where are you going?" Landon called to me.

"I'm just following the trail. Do you have a flashlight?"

After a moment of digging around in his pack he came up with a flashlight. He crawled into the tunnel and tapped me on the foot with it. I reached back and took it from him.

"You shouldn't go in these places," Landon said. "You're a rattlesnake magnet, too."

"I'm just following Dylan. Meet me on the other side when I tell you where that is."

I turned on the flashlight and found Dylan's knee prints in the sand. Eyes to the ground, lower and ever lower I followed doing an army crawl through the rocks. My hip complained loudly. I was tracking, dragging my legs behind, just following the tracks through an ever smaller tunnel, not looking up, when there was a loud *kaboooom* accompanied by a high-pitched scream. Rocks rained down around my head. *Click, click.* "Stay away! You stay away from me!" *Kaboom!*

"Cassidy!" both men yelled.

"Dylan! Stop! It's just me," I said. I know, dumb thing to say. She didn't know me, but maybe a female voice would be less threatening. "I'm with your daddy. We've been looking for you."

"Come out. Show me. I'm warning you. I'll shoot you if you try to hurt me."

"Dylan?" Bradley shouted from outside.

"Daddy!"

She dropped the gun and ran for the tunnel entrance. I crawled out and painfully stood up and found the tunnel opened up into... Trent's Cave! I snatched up the gun and set the safety. Dylan had really lucked out finding this place. I shined the flashlight around.

"Hey! You did good! You found food," I said.

"I found a pirate's cave! I even found a pirate's gun! Too bad there wasn't a treasure hidden here, too. That would have been, like, so cool!"

"The treasure was found years ago," I told her.

Trent was a man who came up into the mountains to escape a shady past. He holed up in this cave and other men running from the law used the cave as a hiding place, until I had a run in with Trent's son, Tyrone. Word leaked up to the cave and next time I went camping Trent Senior told me exactly how he felt about his son's demise. Since the cave was so close to my camp, Chase was worried I would run into criminals while I was camping, so he blew up the cave entrance. We thought it was closed, lost forever, or at least until archeologists, ten thousand years from now, stumbled on it. It was stockpiled with canned goods and a small amount of ammunition. A creek ran down the canyon nearby. It was ideally situated, until it was blown up. As I was now learning, only the main entrance had been destroyed.

Dylan had tried to open some of the cans with rocks and failed. Dented cans littered the floor. She made do with the pop-top ones. Vienna sausages, condensed soup, little snack containers of fruit cocktail. It was both food and water to her.

"Bradley? Can you make it through?" I called out. "If you can you'll really want to see this."

There were a lot of grunting and scraping noises, a little digging, some rock shoving, but finally he pulled himself through and stood up. After Bradley made it through, Landon shed his pack and made his way in.

"Daddy! Look what I found! Isn't it cool?"

Bradley had that mixed up look I frequently saw on Rusty; relief mixed with worry and amusement. He was still reserving judgment on her actions but the relief was winning at the moment.

"Dylan, why didn't you tell me you were coming all the way up here? We've been looking for you for two days!"

"But I asked first. You said, 'sure, we'll do that next.' I heard you. I thought you and Mom and Dustin would be right behind me. I was going to race you to the big tree and then I got distracted. But I didn't mean to get lost. I wasn't lost at all until I found the rocks. It was so cool being under the rocks, then I couldn't find the way out."

"I didn't hear you ask about the canyon. When I said we'd do that next I was telling Mom she could paint the den. She finally found a color she liked and so I told her we'd do that next."

"Oh," she said. "Am I in trouble?"

"We'll talk to Mom. I don't think so. But I think you owe Mr. Wilson and Mrs. Michaels an apology."

"Me? But I asked you. I asked if we could follow the creek and you said yes."

"Bradley, she still had to be found. The fact that it was all a misunderstanding has little to do with it," I said. "I'm just glad she turned out to be fine. If I wasn't laid up I'd have jumped at the chance to come up here."

"Where did you get a gun?" Bradley asked.

"I found it!" Dylan said excitedly, "in the cave! It looks like a pirate gun! It even shoots like a pirate gun! It isn't nice and smooth shooting like yours."

"You know not to point a gun at a person."

"And I know if I'm in danger, shoot to kill. You said a wounded enemy is worse."

"You need some safety lessons. Cassidy wasn't your enemy! You could have killed her. We have a lot of talking to do, young lady. Now where is the gun?"

I handed over the old-style western revolver. It did sort of look like a pirate gun.

Bradley took the gun so he could turn it in to the police. We led Dylan out of the rocks and stopped to decide what to do next. Landon radioed Strict. We couldn't hike out before nightfall and I couldn't hike very far at all. I was barely walking. I needed an overnight rest.

"I know where we can camp," I told them. "It's a little clearing just a little ways down the canyon. We'll have water close by. We'll just be displacing a few deer."

So we slowly made our way to the little deer meadow near the top of the waterfall. Ordinarily I wouldn't do that but I couldn't hike to the hideout by the big tree, though I wanted to badly. It was calling to me. It was almost like home. But I knew the climb was too much today. A doe trotted off into the brush as we entered the clearing.

"Daddy! Look! A deer!" Dylan exclaimed.

We juggled the chores. The guys did the legwork and I did the cooking.

"That's not the way my mom cooks when she goes camping," Dylan said.

"That's because we were at the campground," Bradley said. "This is what backpackers eat."

"Yup, Landon and I eat a lot of this stuff," I said.

"Is that why you never grew up?" Dylan asked.

Landon busted out laughing. "Yeah," he said, "that's why Cassidy never grew up."

"Actually, I did grow up. I'm married and I have a little girl," I told her.

"What happened to your leg?"

"Dylan, it's not nice to ask personal questions," Bradley said.

"I broke my hip," I answered.

"How come you're up here, then?"

"Your dad needed me to find you. I know how to follow your tracks."

"Mrs. Michaels went to a lot of trouble to find you," Bradley said. "You're lucky she did, too, or you'd have been out here another night."

"This doesn't taste like real lasagna," Dylan said.

"That's because it was freeze dried and reconstituted."

"Do we hafta go home when we get out of here?"

"Of course. You were supposed to be in school this morning."

"Rats. You mean I got to miss a day of school to explore a pirate cave?"

Bradley nodded.

"Wow! It was worth it! Even if I do get in trouble."

The guys slept in one tent, the girls in another. I thought Dylan would ask questions all night.

"How old is your little girl?"

"She just turned one. And she asks as many questions as you. Except they all consist of one word."

"How does she do that?"

"Her only question is, 'dat?'"

Dylan laughed, "Don't you get tired of it? My mom gets tired of questions."

"A little, but I think questions show a kid is thinking. I'm glad to see kids thinking enough to come up with intelligent questions."

"Do you get scared at night?"

"No. Why would I get scared? The same things are out there in the day time."

"I never thought of it that way."

"Dylan, go to sleep," Bradley said from the other tent.

"Do you have to tell your little girl to go to sleep?"

"She's not really old enough to just go to sleep when she's told."

"Me neither. He can tell me to go to sleep but I never can."

"Dylan, go to sleep."

"See? I'll try but it never works."

First light came and I didn't care. I could hardly move. I tossed and turned trying to work my aching joints. They just complained louder. I didn't need to get up until the guys did, so I went back to sleep. Normally, I was up at first light making breakfast, and ready to hit the trail. This time I had the feeling the trail was going to hit me instead. Three miles never looked so long.

I heard camp breaking noises and knew the guys were up. Shoot. I dragged myself out of the tent and fired up the stove.

"Can I fry the eggs?" Dylan asked.

"If you can catch them," I said.

"What do you mean, catch them?"

"The only eggs around here are the ones the birds lay. If you're starving in the woods in the spring you might consider looking for them. Other than that we've got oatmeal and trail mix."

"Oatmeal?" she wailed.

"Or trail mix. The trail mix has M&Ms in it if that helps."

"I'll take trail mix."

"I thought you would."

"It's freezing!"

"That's why we have the oatmeal. It's hot. Would you like some hot chocolate? Hot chocolate and M&Ms sounds like a well-rounded breakfast."

She took a cup of hot chocolate and dropped a bunch of M&Ms into it to melt. I ate my oatmeal and hot chocolate like I usually did. Landon made me into a liar by cooking freeze-dried scrambled eggs.

Bradley took down the tent. I was lucky to be able to sit and cook. When I had the trash gathered, the cups washed and the stove put back together for packing, I did a look-see around camp. It was a rule: pack it in, pack it out. I wasn't leaving anything behind, even if I wasn't carrying it.

The deer clearing was just over the creek from the top of the waterfall so the roughest part of the canyon was behind us after we reached the bottom of the falls. Still, it was a steep descent and one slip could mean real trouble for me. I had to take it very slow. From the very beginning I was just aiming for the next little landmark, a rock, a tree, the trail. Reaching the trail was a milestone. It meant I could use my crutches more. I crutched along until my arms got raw from the rubbing. Then I walked until my hip gave out. I felt useless and drained.

"I'd teach you a marching cadence but we're going too slow to make use of it. And most of them aren't fit for kids to sing."

Dylan ran ahead and explored the area around the trail until we caught up, then ran ahead again. I was like Dylan, when I was in shape. That day I slowed down the whole group. It felt like two steps forward and one step back. The day felt like a week and still the trail went on. I knew every landmark by heart. The distance wasn't far, but the two miles took so many painful steps that they just blurred together in my mind. I was just stumbling forward, step by agonizing step.

"Wilson, I think you better stop her," echoed in my mind. Where did my crutches go? I turned around to look for them and the world spun. Hands reached out to steady me.

"Rest," said Landon but he sounded far away, even though he was standing directly in front of me, hands on my shoulders, pointing me to a sitting spot.

"I don't want to sit. To sit I have to bend."

"Cass, you're going to collapse at the rate you're going. How many times have I told you, if you pass out on me I'm calling for a lift?"

"There's only a mile to go."

"A mile's a long ways when you have nothing to draw on."

"Just go on. Tell Strict he can close down base camp. I'll catch up. Just make sure I have wheels when I get there."

"No way. You haven't convinced me you're even going to make it out yet. I think I should call for a basket but I know how much of a fuss you'd make." He had that right. "I wouldn't even let you drive in the shape you're in right now. Sit. Rest. If you don't want to sit then lay down."

"I just want to be home."

"Now, see? If you're hurting enough to wish yourself off the trail, I know you need to stop."

I lay down on the ground beside the trail and he sat beside me. He talked to me and I lost track of the time as he rambled on. My attention kept switching between what Landon was saying and what Bradley was saying to Dylan.

Bradley: "she shouldn't have come out on the trail, kiddo, but she'll be okay."

Dylan: "Then why did she?"

Bradley: "Because she cares so much about you. And she knows what a Daddy's love feels like."

Landon: "Strict tries to send you out in the next month, I'll shoot him. He should have known it was too early. The only reason I went along with it was because I knew you'd overdo it. I knew you'd push yourself right into the ground. We lucked out that it was an easy call."

Bradley: "Have patience. If you're bored we'll go down to the creek, but Cassidy needs time. She gave us so much. The least we can do is have patience. It could be you who's laid up. If you hurt like that, you wouldn't want people pushing you down the trail."

Landon: "I'm sorry Cassidy. When you went missing, I did it. I finally gave up on you. I thought you were dead. You don't know what it was like. I felt guilty doing it but I couldn't lie to myself forever. When Rusty called I wasn't even sure I heard right. I was too messed up to talk to him. Then after I saw you in the hospital I still wasn't convinced you'd make it back. After Katie's birthday party I was looking forward to your first call. I didn't think it'd be like this. I thought Strict would hold off until you were ready..."

Splashing at the creek...

Landon: "Cassidy? Can you hear me kid?"

I could hear him but I was tired, so tired.

Later: "Cassidy? If you don't answer me I'm going to radio for a basket."

"Can hear you..." I mumbled.

"You need help. Let me call. Two guys and a basket."

"Lan... help me up."

"No. You've done too much."

"I'm not being carried into base camp."

"If you don't let me get you some help you'll be carried in unconscious. You're trying too hard."

"Rusty will ground me for good."

"Okay, just rest."

Gentle hands.

"One, two, three..." a basket. Shoot. I was still too out of it to care. I opened my eyes enough to identify the people. Antonio- fire department, Landon, Bradley, Kelly. Kelly? He must have been at the campground for work when Landon radioed Strict.

"Kel... don't call Rusty..."

"Too late."

Shoot.

Normally just seeing the basket would irritate me enough to make me refuse it. I just didn't have the energy to fight them. I lay back feeling the rhythm of the hike until it faded into my brain and I no longer cared.

Rusty: "What happened?"

Another voice. Landon? Bradley? "Nothing happened. She just over did it."

"Cassidy? Babe... can you hear me?"

"...'s okay," I slurred.

"Take her home. Put her to bed. And don't let her out of the house for a few days," Landon said.

"I want to know what happened," Rusty said and I could hear the storm clouds gathering. Rusty's voice always reminded me of a storm but it really came across when he was angry.

"I made her stop about a mile ago. She fell asleep. She roused just enough to talk to me. She just needs a good long rest... I don't care if it's a life and death situation. Don't let her do this again for at least a few weeks."

Rusty: "Cassidy? What did you do to yourself?"

"I want to go home. Russ, jus' want to go home."

I woke up in my own bed. No hospital. That was good. I could hear Bertie and Katie in the other room. The door was closed. I turned to see what time it was. Ten fifteen. AM or PM? I started to sit up.

"Cassidy?" It was Rusty.

"What happened?"

"That's what I'd like to know."

"It was too far. That's all. I just ran out of stuff to draw on. I'd only trained at a slow mile and a half. It was a good search, but I wasn't ready. How long have I been out?"

"Nearly a day. Sparks has been calling."

"How are you?" I asked.

He didn't answer.

"I'm glad I went even if I'm paying for it. Dylan wasn't where guys out beating the bushes could spot her. She was in Trent's Cave. She'd been turned around in the boulder field for a long time and she got curious about this little tunnel in the rocks. She had food, water, and shelter, but she wouldn't have been spotted, and it would have taken her a long time to find her way out of the boulders."

"I thought Chase blew up the cave."

"He blew up the entrance to it. Only a really curious little kid could have discovered the way in."

I was nearly bedridden for two days. I could walk to another room of the house but I was useless once I'd made my way there.

Bradley called.

"It's good to hear you're up and around."

"I wouldn't exactly call this up and around. Maybe in a day or two."

"Thanks for going out on the call. Dylan is very proud of her little adventure. She's been bragging about the pirate cave to all her friends. We had a long talk about gun safety. She's going to take a class through the rifle club here. She says she thought you were a pirate. One thing the kid has is an imagination."

"I hope they don't need a tracker soon. If they do, I may have to call out my nephew," I joked.

"Really? Your nephew tracks?"

"He's only a little older than Dylan. But he could have found her. He'd jump at the chance to take on a real search."

"Well, I just wanted to check and make sure you were going to be all right and thank you for your help."

"You're welcome, glad I could do it."

Chapter 16

"Where you been girl?" Georgia asked.

"I had a little setback. I got a search and rescue call. Found a little girl lost in the mountains. Only problem was I wasn't ready for the hike. I've been recovering from that. Now I need to build back up again. This rescue showed me how much training I need. I have a hell of a long way to go."

"You forgot something," she said.

"What's that?"

"Where's that hunk of yours?"

"Back at work. Finally."

"Awe, that's too bad. We kind of like having him around. Not that we don't like having you around too…"

"I get the picture. I thought you'd be watching the black guys."

"Oh, I do, but a hot body's a hot body."

"Well, come on. I've got a long ways to go to develop my own hot body."

"Now you're talking. Hey! I lost five pounds since I started here!"

"All right! Now just picture what five pounds looks like."

"Hell, yeah, five pounds of flour is a good size chunk!"

Fred approached me. "So, survived another one, did you?"

"Yup, how did you know?"

"Word gets around."

"How much gets around?"

"That was too close."

"What? The not being able to hike out part or the being shot at by an eight year old part?"

"Looks like I don't need to tell you."

Between Fred and Georgia I had a pretty good balance. Georgia would push me to try harder, and to try new things. Fred would come down on me for doing things that would set me back again.

Then there was Katie.

"Cassidy Michaels could you come to Play Space?"

She was up on top of the playplace again. But I wasn't tall enough to reach her.

"See if Anthony can reach her," I suggested.

"Anthony is working afternoons now."

"Shoot. Okay. Katie! Jump! Jump to Mommy!"

"Yump?"

"Show her how to jump. I can't quite do that yet."

Yoli jumped.

"Jump, Katie! Jump!"

Yoli jumped and jumped.

"Yump!" Katie said with a great baby-sized leap. I caught her but I held my breath while I did it.

"We need to figure out some way to keep that kid's feet on the ground!" Yoli said.

"Give her a picture to color. Teach her how to use crayons. She has pretty good dexterity. She'll just scribble at first but if she likes it I bet she picks it up fast. There's a book in her diaper bag. She likes stories."

Our little lesson at the gym had repercussions. Katie learned how to jump. Jumping was fun. Jumping meant movement. I'd be in the kitchen pondering what to cook for dinner and I'd hear, "Yump! Yump!"

Oh no! What was she jumping off of this time? Usually it was the arm of the couch. And now I was worried she'd jump off the playplace at the gym!

"How was your day?" Rusty asked after being greeted at the door by Katie.

"Katie learned how to jump."

Rusty looked at Katie and smiled, "You did? My princess can jump now?"

"She can say *jump*, too."

"Yump!" said Katie.

"If you hear that word, find her fast."

"So... other than that, how was your day?"

"Better."

"Better as in better than the jumping part? Or better as in better than yesterday?"

"Better than yesterday."

"That's good."

"Yoli, we have a big problem."

"What's that?"

"Katie loves to jump off things now."

"Oh no!"

"Yeah. We have to keep her off the playplace."

"I swear, Cassidy, you're going to give me gray hair and I'm only twenty-three."

"Sorry. I've got an idea how you can teach her not to climb it. As soon as you notice her even looking at the playplace, pick her up and stick her inside it. Then she'll get more interested in the inside of it than the outside and you won't have to worry about her as long as she's inside it. All you have to do is redirect her climbing."

"But she's only one year old."

"If she can climb to the top of the thing she can hold her own inside it."

"Okay, I'll try it."

"Cassidy Michaels to Play Space."

"Oh great, what did she do this time?" I asked Georgia.

I went to the door.

"Any idea how she did *that*?" Yoli said.

"Katie!" Golly, how *did* she do that? This time she *was* inside the playplace. Only problem was she was between the climbing tubes and the netting surrounding them. I went inside and army crawled through all the tubes but I couldn't find a gap anywhere. We had to get a manager to unlock a door in the side of the netting, then Yoli crept in and located Katie, who was having a grand time. She reminded me of Dylan exploring underneath the boulders.

Each day was a little better than the last one until one day I realized I wasn't sore from normal activity. I still did the leg exercises every day. I went to the gym most days. I got called to Play Space most days. I started baking cookies for the guys at the station again. Things were almost normal. I began putting Katie in the backpack again. She had grown a lot since the last time I carried her. I wasn't sure how far I could carry her but if I could pack her around I would be one step closer to carrying a search pack.

Chapter 17

"Cassidy!" my mom exclaimed over the phone, "What are you, Rusty, and Katie doing on TV?"

"We're on TV? What channel? Can you record it?"

"Patrick is working on it now. You didn't tell me you were going to be on TV? Why don't you tell me these things?"

"Um, because I didn't know for sure I was going to be on TV? Because, I didn't *want* to be on TV? How many reasons do I need? I'll keep going."

"If you didn't want to be on TV, how did you get on TV?"

"I waited for Rusty in a bar and this guy came up and started talking to me and before I know it, *boom,* I'm on TV."

"Leave it to you to accidentally be on TV."

"Yeah, almost as bad as the movie."

"You were in a movie? Which movie?"

"Payback."

"Cassidy! Was it good? Is it going to come out on DVD? What kind of character are you?"

"I don't know, I don't know, and I'd have to point me out to you. You'd never recognize me."

"Oh, come now, I'd recognize my own daughter!"

"Well, if you see it, let me know who I am. You might check the dollar theaters. It might still be playing there."

"I got it Grandma!" I heard Patrick say in the background.

I turned on the TV and found the right channel, wondering why we had cable in the first place. The only thing we watched on TV was Dodgers games, or the news when it applied to one of Rusty's cases or a search I'd been on.

Here we were, though, on Kevin Koukalaka's reality TV show on Hidden Talent Tuesday.

"Let me call Rusty!" I said and she hung up.

I speed dialed Rusty's cell phone. He answered on the first ring.

"No," he said.

"No what? Are you near a TV? Mom called to tell me to turn on Kevin Koukalaka's show."

"You're kidding. I don't want to watch it here!"

"Patrick is recording it if you want to wait. I just thought you might want to see it. Then you'll know what to expect at work tomorrow."

"That's why I don't want to watch it here. Half the people at work will know about it. Uh oh, I've got another call coming in. Sounds like I can't avoid it. Okay, I'll see you later this evening. Love you."

"I love you too."

"Bye."

Sigh. I sat down to watch. It started out with Kevin Koukalaka in the studio talking about the real reason for the trip to the bar in San Francisco. He explained about our meeting then it switched to the scene in the bar. He explained how Katie stole his watch and I watched as she did it again. Then he introduced Leon and the rest was just as I remembered it from our trip. When it was over the phone started ringing again.

First was Jesse, "why are you always the one to end up on TV? I never accidentally end up on TV!"

"Because nothing ever happens to you. You're the negative side of the trouble magnet and I'm the positive side."

"Then why don't you attract positive trouble?"

"Because like poles repel. Opposite poles attract. So the positive end attracts negative trouble."

"Then why did you end up on TV?"

"Because I didn't want to, so it *was* negative, right?"

"You're just confusing me."

"Maybe if you don't want to be on TV it's more likely to happen. Like being rescued needlessly by six handsome lifeguards." Oops.

"Now you're really not making sense."

"That's good."

"No it's not!"

Next was Lawanda, the sales clerk at the cop shop.

"Cassidy! That was hilarious! I always turn the TV in the shop to that Dumb Criminals show and you came on right after that ended. That was staged, wasn't it?"

"No. It all happened just like Kevin said it did."

"That poor guy! I wonder if the girl will call him."

"There weren't any cops in the cop shop during the show, were there?"

"Only Ben Tomlin."

"Oh no. Rusty will never hear the end of it."

After that I pretty much quit answering my phone. I ended up with messages ranging from: "That was great! Way to go Katie!" to "A cop's kid on a reality show demonstrating how to pick people's pockets? You should be ashamed of yourselves."

A couple of messages stumped me. One said, "You wouldn't consider renting this kid out, would you? If so, I'd be interested. My number is…"

Another said, "I have a problem I was hoping you could help me with. I saw your daughter on TV and I know she could retrieve a piece of information I need. My uncle keeps it written in a small notebook which he carries in his shirt pocket…"

What were these people thinking?

Rusty came home in a rather stressed out state. He looked like he had about the same day I did, except that he had to deal with the comments face to face.

"How was your day?" he asked.

"I've had better."

"Me, too."

"Once you get calmed down maybe you should listen to the phone messages."

"Are you sure? Maybe I should listen to them and then calm down. Then I can do all my calming down at once."

"Okay, I'll finish up dinner."

He went to the bedroom and changed from his brown suit into jeans and a t-shirt.

"Thirty-three messages?" he asked. "If you listened to them, why do I need to, too?"

"There are a few I wasn't sure how to take."

"Like what?"

"You'll recognize them when you hear them."

"Great."

The phone rang again. The machine clicked on and the message came through. This time it was from my neighbor, Hazel Mireau.

"Cassidy, Katie was just adorable on TV. Where in the world did she learn that charming little pout? I'll be over tomorrow. I want to see it for myself. I can't wait to hear all about meeting Kevin Koukalaka in person! I'll let you get back to whatever you were doing. See you tomorrow. Oh, this is Hazel, but you already guessed that."

Rusty pulled a barstool over to the answering machine and settled in. From the kitchen I listened to all the messages again. Being a trouble magnet I worried a little. People actually wanted Katie to filch things for them? What kind of people were they?

We sat down to a somber dinner.

"Stick close to home for a few days. Let people forget what we look like."

"If they can find our phone number they can find our address. How did they find our phone number anyway? It's unlisted."

"Most of the messages were from people we knew. Only three of them were from people we don't know."

"I didn't even know we knew thirty people."

"Of course we do. Just look at our Christmas card list. How many people do you send a Christmas card to?"

"Okay, we do know thirty people. But that's including relatives in other states."

The phone rang. The machine got it.

"Hello, Cassidy... I know you're there. You're just not answering your phone because it's been ringing off the hook all afternoon. This is Grandma Gordon. You didn't tell me you knew Kevin Koukalaka! Katie is getting so big! Give me a call when you get through all the messages."

Grandma Gordon lived in the middle of nowhere, in Montana.

"It's a nationwide program," Rusty informed me.

"It didn't help at all that we were on after the Dumb Criminals show. Cops everywhere watch that."

"Yeah, they had it on in the break room. I didn't even have to change channels."

"What did the guys think of it?"

"I just blamed the whole thing on you and they understood completely."

"It wasn't my fault. That Kevin guy just knows how to work his way with people. That's all."

Katie and I laid low for a few days. That meant baking a couple of batches of cookies and many, many peek-a-boo games around the couch. It meant walks up into the hills directly behind our house. It meant going stir crazy. Neither of us liked to stay home.

"Where you been this time?" Georgia asked when I finally ventured out.

"Laying low."

"Girl! What'd you do this time?"

"You don't know?"

"No."

"Whew!"

"Why what have you been up to?"

Fred walked up.

"What's the big idea putting pick pocketing demonstrations up on public TV?"

"I didn't mean to!" I told him. "I walked into a trap and didn't even see it until it was too late. I didn't see any cameras. I was just sitting there talking to this guy while I waited for Rusty and the next thing I know we're on TV!"

"That doesn't happen."

"It doesn't happen to most people. Unfortunately, it does happen to me. Believe me, I wouldn't have done it if I'd seen it coming. We've been getting calls from people wanting us to loan out Katie for pick pocketing jobs! That's why I've been laying low."

"*Tsk, tsk,*" said Georgia. "The things you get yourself into."

"On the bright side, my weight is starting to even out. I'm over a hundred again. Time to put my time in at the gym."

I was able to do the leg press now, working my way up to a hundred pounds. I had a ways to go to catch up to my usual one fifty. I made the rounds of a variety of machines and then Georgia and I put in our time on the treadmills. She talked about school. It sure made the time go by faster with someone to talk to.

Chapter 18

"Does Katie have an Uncle Darryl?" Yoli asked.

"No. Why?"

"Somebody came to the door and asked for Katie. He said he was Katie's uncle."

"Even if Katie's real uncle showed up you wouldn't let him take her, would you?"

"No. Not unless they were listed on the form."

"No. Nobody can pick up Katie except Rusty and me. Even if her real uncles were to show up, which I doubt they would, don't let anybody take her."

"So… does Katie have any good looking, single uncles?"

"Yes, but they live out of town so you're not likely to meet them."

"Rats."

I changed clothes after my workout and headed for the station. After laying low, I had an oversupply of cookies. I didn't want to eat them and I didn't want Katie to eat them, so a trip to the station was in order. As I pulled out of the gym parking lot I noticed a blue Acura behind me. It followed me through several turns, but since I was going to the police station, I didn't worry too much about being followed. If the same car was there when I left the station I might have something to worry about.

I glanced in my rear view mirror. It was still there. The driver wasn't being very careful. When I got to the station I circled the block, watching the blue Acura the whole time. I pulled into the staff parking lot because it felt safer.

"Let's go see Daddy," I said as I pulled Katie out of her car seat. I picked up the diaper bag and found the sack of cookies. I brought a gallon Ziploc bag for each area of the station. When I laid low, I had to do something. Cookie baking had just become a tradition. Katie and I made the rounds but Rusty was nowhere to be seen. I fielded comments about the TV show and Katie got a crash course in leaving pockets alone. The guys seemed oddly disappointed.

I was disappointed, too. I left a Ziploc bag of cookies in Rusty's mailbox, since his office was locked, and Katie and I went on our way.

"Kent, are you fixing to hit the streets again?" I asked on my way out.

"Yeah, why?"

"Could you follow me for a few miles and watch for a blue Acura?"

"You want me to follow you? Most people hate to be followed by a patrol car."

"That's what I'm counting on."

"I think I should know what's going on first."

"You heard about the TV show, right?"

"Yeah…"

"One of the things that resulted from that is a couple of people asking if Katie's services could be bought. Then while I was at the gym an 'Uncle Darryl' tried to pick her up from the babysitters there. When I left, a blue Acura followed me here. So… I'd just feel better with a little visual deterrent."

"Does Rusty know about this?"

"No, he's out. Just a few miles. If we see the Acura, we can decide what to do about it. I doubt they are serious enough about this to risk a confrontation."

He followed me out of the parking lot. I headed for home. I didn't see the blue Acura but if the guy was smart he would hang way back and wait for Kent to go elsewhere. I noticed when Kent peeled off he hung back a few cars and then pulled out again. He followed at a distance for another few miles and then pulled forward and pulled me over.

"No sight of him. Are you good to go?"

"Yeah, thanks."

"I'll let you off with a warning, *this time*. Be careful. If you see him give me a ring."

"Okay."

A few blocks later the Acura was back. I scrolled down to Kent Jacobsen's cell phone number.

"You're kidding," he said.

"Nope, he's back. I have an idea, though. Can you get me an undercover cop? I could pretend to be picking up a friend. We can go to lunch and, if my usual bad luck holds up, this guy will approach us, ask me to rent out Katie for a pick pocketing and we can nab him."

"No."

"What do you mean, no? It could work. I bet, if I drove to a restaurant and sat down to order something, he would do it. Crooks have a bad habit of doing that around me. Rusty's tired of arresting them."

"Then have Rusty do it."

"I can't. The guy will recognize Rusty from the TV show."

"I'm not going along with your cockamamie scheme. You want an undercover cop, ask Rusty."

"But he's busy."

"And what am I?"

"You won't help me?"

"Not in the way you want me to. I'll pull the guy over. I'll ask him why he's following you. I won't find you an undercover cop. That isn't even something I'm authorized to do."

"Pulling him over would just give me a chance to get away. But if he followed me from the gym, he might have followed me from my house. I don't think he just recognized me while I was driving around town. No. He tried to pick up Katie from the gym. You could pull him over, listen to him deny he was following me and then I'd drive home and find him sitting in my driveway. So what should I do? I can't drive around town aimlessly forever or he's going to get suspicious. If he goes away I just have to worry about him showing up unexpectedly."

"You sure have a way of complicating things."

"Okay, I'll quit thinking and do what you say. So, what should I do?"

"I don't know. All your points are valid."

"Cops are supposed to be prepared to make instant decisions."

"I don't usually have to deal with people who take a simple situation, turn it inside out, upside down and then throw it back in my face."

"Sorry, so you want me to just do what any normal person should do when they find themselves being followed?"

"Tell me what that is first."

"Drive to a public place, like the police station. Stay in my car and honk the horn three times in a row in a pattern until somebody comes out."

"That doesn't solve the big problem."

"Now who's turning it inside out?"

"Cassidy, I don't know how Rusty does it. How does he deal with your thinking things through until there is no real solution?"

"He stops me before I get there and says *no*."

"Why don't you call Rusty and let him stop you before you turn the problem inside out and then he can say no and you can just do whatever he says."

"Okay, I'll try but he wasn't in his office earlier, which could mean he's on stakeout, or talking to witnesses or following somebody. Keep your phone handy."

I hung up and speed dialed Rusty.

"No," he said.

"You haven't heard the problem yet."

"Do I want to?"

"No, but you should anyway. I drove to the gym. While I was there a guy tried to pick up Katie from Play Space. They didn't release her. When I left the gym I noticed a car following me but I was going to the station so I didn't worry about it. I handed out cookies at the station, but I didn't see you there so I left."

"You handed out cookies?"

"I left some in your mailbox. Anyway, when I left the station I had Jacobsen follow me. The car stayed out of sight until he quit following me. Now it's back. Jacobsen and I have turned the problem every which way and I don't know what to do. Jacobsen didn't like the most practical solution which was to pick up an undercover cop and go to Trujillos and let the guy following me, spill the beans, and then have the guy arrested for... oh... I don't know, conspiracy to commit a robbery?"

"Cassidy, you're not making sense."

"I'm worried that he's one of those people who wanted Katie to perform a pick pocketing for them. If Jacobsen pulls the guy over he'll just deny he was following me and turn up later. No matter what we do, aside from arresting him, he can turn up later when we aren't expecting him. But we need a reason to arrest him. So... any suggestions?"

I hadn't exactly made his day. I could feel the tension seeping through the phone.

"Okay, make a show of hanging up your phone and setting it on the seat and then drive to Trujillo's."

"You're kidding. You really want to try it?"

"No, but I'm hungry. At least if he tries anything I'll be there."

"Can Jacobsen come, too? He's never seen a felon walk up to me at Trujillo's and practically turn himself in."

"The guy is not going to walk up to a uniform and ask Katie to pick pocket for him."

"Okay, I'll see you there."

I called Jacobsen back to let him know he was off the hook.

"We're having lunch at Trujillo's," I told him. "I won't stop unless the Explorer is there."

"I'll be sure and watch the news tonight."

I made a show of closing up my phone and laying it on the seat, and then I drove to Trujillo's. I noticed wherever I went there was a patrol car. Hmm, same number, too. Jacobsen was taking his responsibility seriously. He wasn't letting me off until he knew I was turned over to Rusty.

I drove up and down the parking lot until I found the Explorer, then I parked as close to it as I could.

"Let's go see Daddy!" I said to Katie as I pulled her out of her car seat.

Benny Trujillo was at the bar when we walked in. The place was busy for lunchtime. Trujillo's was a popular hangout for the officers and firefighters in the area but I didn't see any uniforms. I found Rusty waiting in a booth with a clear view of the door. He stood and took Katie from me while I slid into the booth.

"I don't know what this guy has in mind but I wish he would just go away," I said.

"What guy?"

"The guy in the blue Acura. Maybe I'm just being paranoid but I drove all the way around the block a couple of times just to see if he was really following me. He didn't approach me when I got out at the station or here. Why follow me if he's not going to try anything?"

"Maybe he's just curious. Maybe he's gathering information."

"Can't he just ask? After being carjacked and kidnapped I don't take kindly to being followed."

"Lunch. Why don't you just eat lunch and let me worry about you being followed."

"It's not me I'm worried about. Katie would go with anybody. Every man is her uncle and every woman is her aunt. She's so used to being passed from person to person that she likes *everybody*. If a person wanted her to pick pocket somebody it would be the simplest thing in the world to do, if they could just get the kid."

"In a way, it's good to see you being careful for a change."

"I'm always careful, I'm just careful in the wrong direction sometimes. When Brian took me I was being careful of an erratic driver. When I pulled the shed into the pool I was being careful of a creep. When the lifeguards rescued me I was being careful not to overdo it."

"Well, there's an easy way to find out if they were following you or Katie. I'll take Katie when we leave. We can make a show of switching her car seat from the Jeep to the Explorer. If I get followed instead of you, we'll know."

"What are you going to do with her? You're at work."

"I've got a dealer downtown. Maybe Katie can help me catch him."

"Very funny."

Benny came to the table to take our order.

"It's good to see you two back together again," he said.

"It's good to *be* back together," I said.

"You gave us all quite a scare. I hear it all here, with the officers coming in here all afternoon. I heard the goings on from every viewpoint. I'm telling you, it looked grim there for a while."

"It did from my point of view, too," I admitted.

"I heard some of the weirdest stories about you."

"Any true ones?"

"Who knows?"

"As long as they were clean they were probably true."

"I don't know… some of these stories are really farfetched."

"I'll have the combination plate with a chile rellano and a chicken enchilada."

Rusty ordered Carne Asada.

"What story are you two living right now?" Benny asked.

"We're wondering if there's a guy looking for Katie, thinking she'll pick somebody's pocket for them," I answered.

"Okay, maybe the stories aren't so farfetched."

Benny took our orders to the kitchen but each time he came by the table he asked a question.

"Did you really shoot a tiger?" Unfortunately.

"Did you really eat a snake?" I was really hungry.

"Did you really spend a week in the mountains with only a pocket knife?"

"No, I had a hunting knife and a fire starter."

"Oh, that's much more realistic," he said sarcastically.

"Your writing must have started the stories circulating again," Rusty observed.

"Did you really read them?"

"Most of them. Pieces of them I have memorized. There were favorite parts I went back to again and again."

"What parts did you like?"

"It depended on what I needed at the time. Sometimes I needed to laugh with you and so I had funny stories picked out and knew where to find them. Sometimes I needed to know that you still had a chance so I went back to some of those rough times and told myself, 'if she can make it through that, she can make it through anything'. I learned a lot that I didn't know. I got to see the past four years condensed. Do you know how much you've changed since we met?"

"I don't think that's possible. But I know I *have* changed. So have you. We're familiar with each other now. Even at the wedding I wasn't sure you really wanted to marry me. I was still tiptoeing around trying to be something I wasn't. It was like wearing a dress all the time. I had to learn to be comfortable in our life."

"That's an odd way to put it."

"Well, can you think of a better way?"

"No, but I'm glad you're comfortable in our life."

Katie was standing in the booth breaking up tortilla chips and eating them. I didn't know how she did it with only three teeth but it didn't seem to bother her.

I watched the restaurant for people who might be following me. There were other people just watching the crowd, but no one stood out as being particularly focused. I could usually spot the odd man out. Maybe he hadn't followed me in.

A man and woman walked in, were shown to a booth, and ordered drinks. Big John walked in, noticed us and walked over.

"Any sign of a blue Acura out there?" I asked.

"I didn't think to pay attention," he said. "Guess I ought to pay closer attention if I notice your Jeep out there. No telling who might be after you. Black four-door. Yellow van. Big white monster truck. So… it's a blue Acura this time? I forgot my wallet."

He disappeared out the front door was gone for a minute and then came back in.

"You're right, but they aren't parked in the lot. They are half a block down parked in a line of cars on the street. Who's after you this time?"

"I don't think they are after me. I think they are after Katie."

He held out his hands and Katie walked across the seat to him.

"Katie? Why would anybody be after Katie? Hey Katiekins! What's up kiddo?"

"No pho-phones," she reminded herself as he lifted her off the seat. She went after his patches instead. Maybe she was learning.

"Come on, say BIG John," John said.

She wasn't interested in talking. She wanted his patches. When the patches wouldn't come off she tried his hat. He took it off and put it on her head.

"How could anybody be after a little angel like this?" Big John asked.

"They would like her to turn pro," Rusty answered.

"But she hasn't even stolen my watch. She's being real good."

"Yeah, but the people who saw her on TV don't know that. I'm sure if you held her long enough she would get bored and start looking for pockets. But that's not the point. Whether she will pick pockets or not, I'm worried this person in the blue Acura doesn't have the best intentions."

The waitress walked up with two steamy plates. "Combo plate?"

I claimed my meal and she set the other one in front of Rusty.

"Can I have my usual?" John asked her.

"Sure, six tacos with the works. What table?"

"Sit down, John," said Rusty.

"Right here," John told the waitress.

"Coming up."

"Ba-bites!" said Katie enthusiastically.

"What's this?" Rusty asked holding up a bite of Carne Asada.

"Ma-mea'!"

"That's right! Meat!"

"Mexican food is a little hard to identify," I said.

Rusty and I started filling a saucer with little bites for Katie. She held up each bite, like usual, and showed it to us. She was beginning to identify the bites for herself. She had baby words for most things. Popoes were apples, dot-dog was hot dog, yoyo was cereal. Ba-bite was the miscellaneous category of food. Or if something was really puzzling she would hold it up and ask, "Dat?"

John settled into the booth and watched the food quiz with amusement.

"Cha-cheese, rice, ba-beans..." She didn't try to say *enchilada* or *rellano*.

"Does she say anything besides food names?" John asked.

"A little, she says, book, candy, hi, daddy, mommy, go..."

"Go!" Katie said.

"She likes to go. She learned that while I was in the wheelchair. Let's see... horsy, doggy, grandma, papa. She knows a few names. She knows lots of animal noises. Here's one you'll get a kick out of. Katie, what does a rabbit say?"

"Neak, neak."

"No, what does a rabbit *say*? Come on, what does a rabbit say?"

"What's she doing?" John asked.

"She's trying to wiggle her nose. That's what a rabbit says."

John busted out laughing. "Why'd she say neak, neak?"

"She's saying 'sneak' because she associates rabbits with sneaking up on them."

"Only your kid."

"Katie, what does Big John say?" Rusty asked.

Katie looked at Big John. She looked guilty. Rusty asked again.

"Nodoido," Katie said quietly.

"What did she say?" Big John asked, "Katie, what does Big John say?"

"Nodoido," she repeated.

We all looked at each other puzzled. What did it mean and how did she associate that with Big John? She wasn't eager to say it, whatever it was. We finished our meal wondering what *nodoido* meant. It was the longest word I'd ever heard from Katie, and she sure knew what she was talking about, but nobody else did.

I watched the crowd as I ate, categorizing everybody in it. Each person was a piece. Each had a place and purpose. I studied the pieces noting which interlocked and which stood alone. If anybody tried anything I wanted to see it coming. I wasn't going to be surprised this time.

Big John got his tacos halfway through our meal. He heaped them high with salsa, guacamole and sour cream and downed them all as we were finishing up. I could have lived for six weeks just on Big John's lunch.

We all sat back with a contented sigh until John said he better get back to work.

Rusty paid for our meals and we waved to Benny on the way out. I scrutinized the room as we left, watching to see if anybody seemed overly eager to leave at the same time. I was thinking I'd read too many Louis L'Amour books as a kid. But, I reminded myself, those that were alert survived.

"What are you two up to next?" Big John asked.

"We're switching off Katie and then we're seeing who gets followed."

"What are you doing?" Rusty asked John.

"Guess."

"Thanks."

"Meet me at the city park in an hour unless I call sooner," Rusty told me.

"Why the city park?" I asked.

"It's a place where I can spot a follower. If I let Katie play it'll tempt him to come closer, if he needs to make a positive identification."

I didn't like it. It felt too much like they were using Katie for bait. I knew Rusty better than that, though. If there was one thing I did, it was trust Rusty with Katie's safety. We switched the car seat from the Jeep to the Explorer and Rusty tossed Katie up in the air in plain sight so any observers would see he had the kid. Then he put Katie in the car seat gave me a kiss and asked, "You know what to do?"

"Meet you in the park in an hour."

"And?"

"And…if I'm followed just be glad he's not following Katie."

"Cassidy…"

"If he follows me I'll call and we can figure out what to do next."

I got in the Jeep. What to do for an hour? Especially since I might have Big John on my tail. Well, first things first. I had to find out if I had Big John on my tail, the blue Acura, or both. I assumed if the Acura followed me, so would Big John.

I started the engine. For once I was hoping trouble would follow me. I was tempted to drive right by the blue Acura to get a good look at the driver and tempt him, but I knew I was supposed to just take off like I was on my way somewhere else. I watched the Explorer drive away and then I turned out of the parking lot in a different direction. Big John hung back waiting to see what would unfold. I drove away and made a few turns to find a main road. I still hadn't decided where I was going. Why would we trade off the kid if I was just going to drive around? So I decided to head for a doctor's office. That made sense. Dad had to watch the kid so Mom could go to a doctor's appointment. A half mile down Thurston Avenue I knew I was not being followed. Rats. I looked around for John. I didn't see him and I hoped he was helping Rusty. I knew not to call. They had their hands full. All I could do was find something to do for an hour. I always had things I could do in town. There were always groceries to buy and errands to run, but I felt guilty doing everyday things when Rusty could need help.

Who are you kidding? I thought. If he needed help he'd call anybody but you.

I debated going to the park but tossed out the idea. I might be able to learn a thing or two but I risked ruining Rusty's plan and tipping off our follower that we had moved on to stage two of the game. I wanted to keep this as low key as possible. So I had to stay away.

I filled up the Jeep with gas. I checked the oil while I was at it. I washed the windows. How could I kill an hour without going nuts counting off the seconds? I couldn't visit anybody. That would be too hard to extricate myself from. I decided that I shouldn't go shopping. I'd probably run into trouble and get tied up in police reports. I decided to go tracking. I could do that almost anywhere there was dirt so I headed for a little desert picnic ground just outside town. The place was usually empty except on weekends and I couldn't figure out what drew people there on the weekends either. It was just desert and scrub and picnic tables. A dirt road wound around through it and parking places were marked. I watched for recent car tread and pulled into a parking place that had seen some action within the past week.

I got out of the Jeep and found a set of tracks. They were old and wind worn, so they would make a good test trail. I started with the age and size of the tracks, and as I went along I started gathering information. Adult, male, weight was harder to gauge because of the age of the tracks. He wasn't a big man, though. If he were fit he'd be about a hundred seventy pounds. Was this guy fit? I followed along, seeing if he walked like a fat man, a thin man, a man with a disability. The outside of this right shoe was worn more than the rest. He made numerous trips between the car and picnic table. He was with three kids. When I found a family I always found the most distinctive member of the family first. Then I looked to see who they were with. A man, three kids. Where was the mother? It always disappointed me when a family member was missing. Families belonged together. There was no mother on this outing, just a man and three kids, ages about ten, seven, and five. The kids ran around obliterating their dad's tracks but it was good to see it. It was a happy mess of tracks. One set in particular ran up to the dad's tracks and stood there frequently. I imagined a kid with lots of questions. Maybe I just thought that because I was an inquisitive child. Often, though, I was left to find my own answers and I didn't hesitate to search them out. That was where part of my troubles came from, curiosity. Curiosity led to many adventures and many a mishap. I tracked the family through an ordinary picnic. They didn't go out for a hike. They just came, ate lunch and left. While the dad was getting things ready the kids wandered around. The older kid poked around the other picnic sites and climbed up on the tables, walked the benches, found interesting rocks and stuck his hand down a gopher hole. A ground squirrel had ventured to the site after they left to check for food dropped. It found a couple of tidbits under the picnic table.

It was a rather satisfying and disappointing tracking day. Though I had no trouble reading the tracks, they didn't lead me anywhere interesting. That was part of my problem. I didn't go anywhere interesting these days. I needed to go on my own picnic, wander out into the hills and follow a set of tracks until I came to the animal that left them. I needed to stalk it until I got as close as I could. I needed a call, a challenge. I needed to work.

On my way back to the park I assessed my ability to take a call. I needed more physical training but I was ready to tackle the serious part of it now. Training with a pack on seemed to be the next logical step. But first, the park.

When I pulled up to the park it was uncomfortably empty. No dark blue Explorer. No squad cars, no lighter blue Acura. A couple lay on a blanket under a tree kissing. A mom sat on a bench watching two kids play on the playground. I sat in the Jeep and waited. And waited. The mom gathered up her kids and went home. A couple of teenagers walked through the park on their way somewhere else. A kid rode by on a bike and popped a wheelie. A couple of kids went by on skateboards. They practiced hopping their skateboards up onto the curb. A couple of them took tumbles but they all got back up and kept going. The everyday life of a city park.

Now, what was going on in the not so ordinary life of a certain detective? I decided to get out and track the sandbox. Sandboxes were not the best tracking ground. The sand was too loose, like much of the sand on the beach. Once a track was left, the loose sand tended to flow in and cover it back up. Kid's footprints were fun to read. Their personalities came out much easier than adult's. They had a freedom of expression that adults seemed to lack. Adults had a purpose, usually something mundane, like watching their kids at the park. The kids, though, had other plans. They had things to do. They had a flight to catch on the swing set. They had dizzy circles to turn on the merry-go-round. The pole was a firemen's pole and the platforms transformed into a house, a fort, a fairy castle. I couldn't tell what the kids were playing, but it was always entertaining. Here was a girl, quiet, a dancer. Here was a boy, a big boy. He was a rough and tumble kid. He went down the slide head first. He ran everywhere. Another girl, this one more outgoing. She liked to climb. She moved from one set of monkey bars to another. Another kid liked to hop, skip and jump. All kinds of kids. While they were little their personalities came out. As they got older they conformed more and more with their peers until they became a segment of society. I thought it was too bad that people couldn't spend their whole life hopping, skipping and jumping if they wanted to. Would the dancer grow up to be a dancer? I doubted it. She'd work a take-out window at McDonald's until she graduated and then she'd look for full time work, maybe go to college. Hopefully, she'd graduate. Even that was iffy these days. I was tracking myself into a funk. I was glad when, at last, a patrol car pulled up. John sat there for a moment as I finished up my profile of a boy who seemed to be sneaking up on another kid. The kid turned on him and pushed him over. I walked over to the patrol car to get any news John had.

"Rusty's at the station. Nothing happened. Rusty drove away. You took off and the guy waited to see what I was going to do. I waited to see what he was going to do. I got a plate number. I finally figured he wasn't taking any chances so I left and stayed in the area. I stayed in contact with Rusty but the guy never showed. I circled back looking for the Acura, but it was gone. I never ran across it. The police activity must have scared the guy off."

"So he was just observing."

"Could be. Hopefully he's through observing."

"Why didn't Rusty meet me here then?"

"He went to the station to look up the driver."

"It doesn't take an hour and a half to look up one driver. You could run the plates and give him a name from your car."

"It takes an hour and a half to cruise a neighborhood, talk about the situation, and puzzle over what it means that the guy didn't follow. Rusty's more worried than he's letting on."

That's why it took an hour and a half.

"Okay, I'll go to the station and take Katie off his hands. I'm sure he has work to do."

I found Rusty in his office sharing a cookie with Katie. I thought I brought the cookies to the station to prevent her from eating too many of them.

"Sorry to leave you waiting," Rusty said.

"It's okay. Sorry the whole afternoon was a bust."

"You mean it wasn't a bust."

"Yeah, I guess."

"You really think this guy was following you?"

"I'm sure he was. I took weird routes. I circled the block. He followed me wherever I went, even if it didn't make sense. When I went around the block, he followed me all the way around. He wasn't even careful to stay out of sight."

"Does he worry you?"

"If it was just me, no."

"It's not just you. Are you worried?"

"Not yet. Should I be?"

"Have you gotten a good look at him?"

"No, just a rear view mirror image, why?"

"Is this him?"

He brought up a picture on his computer screen. It showed a very normal looking man. Thirtyish, dark wavy hair, hazel eyes. In the picture he had a two day old scruff. Clean shaven the man would be good looking.

"I wouldn't swear to it, but at first glance it does resemble him. Is his name Darryl?"

"Darryl's his middle name. Why?"

"The guy who tried to pick up Katie from Play Space said he was her Uncle Darryl."

He did not look pleased. "Do you want to know more?"

"Should I?"

Katie reached for me and I picked her up.

"Well, he isn't wanted for anything at the moment. He's been clean for several years."

"But…"

"But he has a way of taking advantage of… opportunities that come up."

"Opportunities?"

"Yeah, I have no way of knowing what it might be this time. He's got a long list of failed attempts at getting something for nothing. Forgery, robbery, identity theft. He doesn't seem to be a violent criminal but he's willing to do almost anything for a buck."

"We don't *know* this is the guy."

"This is the man who owns the blue Acura. You say it looks like him. Lots of people go by their middle name."

"There's one way to find out. Take the picture to Yoli at the gym. See if he's the guy that tried to pick up Katie from Play Space. Or check their surveillance tapes. That would tell you more about him."

I took Katie home and Rusty went back to work. Since detective work involves asking people questions, he added a trip to the gym into his early afternoon. He barely caught Yoli and confirmed that Uncle Darryl was indeed Keenan Darryl Duval. So, we had a name. We had a car. We had no idea what the guy was up to.

Chapter 19

The next day Katie had a doctor's appointment. It was one of those things that all parents dread. The booster shot. Shots always made Katie cranky and she was perpetually teething anyway. One of those necessary evils that babies have to go through. Fortunately, visiting Doctor Tiberius was at least entertaining.

"I always get the feeling, when I talk to Katie, that there's an adult in there struggling to get out."

"She's just a normal kid," I said.

"Is she talking?"

"Yes, though she hasn't said a whole sentence yet. She knows lots of words."

"How long has she been walking?"

"Since she was about eleven months. She chose to take her first steps at the top of the stairs. Rusty almost broke his neck catching her."

He nodded at each answer, satisfied that Katie was on track.

"Does she still pick pockets?"

"Not as much. We've been teaching her to leave people's pockets and purses alone."

"No pho-phones," said Katie.

"She means no cell phones," I translated.

"Got any mystery phrases? I always get a charge out of the things parents get hung up on."

"As a matter of fact there is. Well, I don't know if it's a phrase or a word. I don't know if she'll say it. Katie, what does Big John say?"

The question was out of context.

"What does Big John say? Come on, baby, what does BIG John say?"

Nothing.

"What does a doggy say?"

"Woof! Woof!"

"Good girl! What does a cat say?"

"Meow," she answered.

"What does Big John say?"

"Nodoido," she said, again in a quiet, guilty voice.

"Any ideas?" I asked Doctor Tiberius.

"Nodoido. That's a good one. What's the context?"

"Big John is one of Rusty's coworkers. He's a police officer."

"That's a new one to me," he admitted. "She hasn't been scolded about anything. That would account for the *no* part."

"We've been teaching her no pockets and no purses. But what's a doido?"

"I have no idea. Are there any problems I should be aware of?"

"If I ever need to take her in to Emergency it's going to be with a broken leg. She loves to jump off of things."

"Yump!" said Katie.

"She can jump?"

"Yes, most definitely."

"Well, everything looks good. She's been eating well? She's growing well. She seems bright, intelligent. It's a little disappointing that I don't have to guard my pockets anymore. How long did it take her to learn to leave pockets alone?"

"We're still working on it. If she gets bored we still have problems with it."

"She was real good this time. Okay. Melissa will be in in a minute with the immunizations. I hope they don't affect her like they usually do."

"Me, too."

Katie always got cranky and feverish after her shots. She was uncomfortable and wanted to be held a lot. I knew we better go home after the appointment was over, and then I was going to have to spend a couple of days babying the baby. Ironically, she was very grown up about getting the shots. As an infant she wailed loudly. Now she saw it coming and recognized it for what it was. She just cringed and took it. It saddened me in a way. It reminded me of me when I saw trouble coming and it hurt that she was learning to see trouble coming and reacting to it already. I had to remind myself that it was just baby-sized trouble. It would hurt and it would make her miserable for a day or two but it was still baby-sized trouble.

She saw the needle coming and cringed away from it.

"No, no owie," she whined. I hugged her close as Melissa quickly gave her the shots and Katie just burrowed in closer. I think it hurt me as much as it hurt her. I knew what hurt felt like. For some reason this time it hit me particularly sharply.

"I'm sorry baby, now it's snuggle time. Let's go home."

I don't know what it is about doctor's offices and vet's offices. They always expect you to pay for your visit, get receipts and instructions, and make sure you have the right little date and the right little vaccination code written in the right little box on a little card at the same time that you have a cranky baby, a diaper bag, and a stroller to deal with. Melissa called me back. Katie struggled on the way out. I set her down and tried to grab her hand but she was too fast for me. Melissa was writing the dates and shots down. Katie was at the door waiting for me to catch up. I had one eye on Melissa and one eye on Katie and suddenly the door opened from the outside and Katie was gone.

"Shoot!" I said and dashed into a packed waiting room. A man was leaving with a small child. I circled the room quickly.

"Don't worry, Mom," a mother said. "Her daddy's got her."

"Her daddy's not here!" I said.

I dashed out into the hallway and the man was sprinting down the corridor shouldering people out of the way. I ran after him. He ducked into a room and I followed. It was a stairway. Round and round we went. I took the stairs two at a time, my hip complaining loudly. He reached the ground floor and ran out the exit.

"Darryl! Stop!" I yelled. "Put that kid down! She won't do it! We've been breaking her of that. She won't do it!"

He didn't slow down. I saw him heading for the blue Acura. What to do? I needed my Jeep to follow him onto the streets. I had to catch him before he got to his car. He reached the car, unlocked the door and stuffed Katie in. He'd just gotten in when I came slamming into his door, ready to haul him back. How could I stop him now? I grabbed the windshield wiper and pulled it backwards with a loud snap.

"Hey! What are you doing?" he yelled as he rolled down his window.

I swung the wiper baseball bat style and laid open a cut right across his forehead.

"Give me my kid!" I yelled at him.

"You're crazy lady!"

He reached for the ignition.

"You start this car and the whole Joshua Hills Police Force is going to be on you before you can think about what to do next. When I get back to my car I'm going to be armed. You start this car and it's war, mister!"

He turned the key.

The door was locked so I stuck my hand through the open window and pulled on the handle. It opened awkwardly with me pulling it open but squished against it at the same time. I grabbed the door with my other hand and hauled it open. A crowd had started gathering but nobody was making a move. Darryl just wanted to make a clean getaway. He stepped out of the car, grabbed me by my shirt front and gave me a great big shove. I hit the pavement and he jumped back in, threw the car into gear and screeched out of the parking place. I ran after the car pulling out my cell phone. When it was obvious I wasn't catching the car on foot I made a run for the Jeep. I felt through the keys until I came to the little one that unlocked the gun box. I hated to take the time to fiddle with the box.

"Hello?" Said the voice on the other end of my phone.

"Damn! Who did I call?" I said desperate.

"Cassidy?"

"I've got to go. I thought I was calling the police."

"Stop. You're not even thinking. What's going on?"

It was Jacobsen.

"I took Katie to the doctor and some guy made off with her in one of those split second lapses. South end of the Joshua General parking lot. A blue Acura! Can you spread the word?"

The lock popped open. I flipped the box open one handed and the gun tumbled out. A woman whacked me upside the head with her purse.

"What are you doing?" I yelled at her.

"I saw you! You're after that poor man."

"That poor man just kidnapped my baby!"

I picked myself up off the pavement again and grabbed my gun. The woman's face turned white and she backed off, clearly shaken.

"If the police show up tell them Cassidy is after a white guy in a blue Acura and point them in the right direction!"

"Cassidy? Are you there?" Jacobsen said.

"Yeah, I just got side lined by a woman protecting Katie's kidnapper. She must have had a brick in her purse!"

I started the Jeep and put it into gear.

"You're not going to help the guys by getting more involved. Just stay put."

"Have I ever stayed put? I can't talk and drive. I'm putting the phone on the seat. If you want to stay on line you can but I'm finding me a blue car. I can ID it. So can Big John. Where did he go? He couldn't have gotten far."

I pulled out of the parking lot, my heart hammering a mile a minute. My Katie. He had my baby! I had to remind myself that he didn't mean her any harm. He probably just wanted her to steal something for him, but what would he do when confronted with an armed and dangerous, irate mother? Something in me just would not let this drop. Call it mother-bear instinct. Call it trouble. I didn't care what it was. This guy had my baby and he wasn't getting away! I hit the gas and turned right because turning left was difficult and I thought Darryl would take the easiest escape route possible. How many side streets could he have turned off onto? I didn't want to think about it. I was supposed to have learned how to canvass a neighborhood but I was just one person. There were dozens of streets, too many directions, too many cars. After about ten minutes it was obvious I couldn't do this on my own.

"Kent. I can't do it," I said to the air, wondering if he was still there. "There are too many variables. I can't track them all down without losing him and I don't see him. I lost him. I lost him. He's gone." My phone was making noises so I picked it up. "I couldn't hear you," I said.

"Pull over. You can ride with me. Hearing the progress over the radio will help."

"Okay, meet me at the…"

"I think I can find you."

I looked in my rear view mirror and there was a patrol car behind me. I pulled into the first public parking lot I could find. I parked and stumbled out of my Jeep. I must have looked as haggard as I felt because he took in the gun, the look, and put an arm around my shoulders.

"We'll get her back. We've got the information we need. We've got the guys out. We'll find her. There's an Amber Alert out. There are eyes all over town."

"It only took half a second. How could it happen in half a second? She was standing by a closed door. It opened and she was gone!"

"Don't dwell on it. Just keep your eyes open. Come on, let's hit the street."

The guys had a system down. Jacobsen was right; they had eyes all over town. I rode shotgun watching each and every car that went by. I didn't need to do that, but I felt compelled. I knew that Acura from a mile away.

I kept thinking about the last moments I was with her. All she wanted was hugs and right then all I wanted to give her was hugs.

"Kent, where's Rusty? Does he know?"

"I don't know. Maybe you should call him."

I didn't want to call him. I didn't want to force more trouble on him. I didn't want him to worry. And it was my fault. All this was my fault. It was my fault we ended up on TV in the first place. It was my fault the guy had a chance to take her. I didn't want to call in front of Jacobsen. But I didn't want to be dropped off and be out of the action. I had a job to do, too. I hoped Jacobsen knew it when he picked me up, that he became my senior officer. As a reserve deputy I could only act as an officer if I had a senior officer in charge of me, so by taking me in he became responsible for my actions. I wasn't sure that was a wise move on his part.

I picked up my cell phone. Rusty answered on the second ring.

"Hey, babe, how'd the doctor's visit go?"

"Rusty, I'm sorry…"

"What's wrong?"

"He…he took her. He just snatched Katie up! It happened so fast!"

"Where are you?"

"Riding shotgun with Jacobsen. We've got a grid set up. We're looking."

"No. You're not pursuing this."

"Change the description of the car and the guy a bit. The car is missing a

windshield wiper and the guy has a long cut across his forehead. I tried. I tried
to stop him. I might have done it but I got clobbered by a lady who took the
wrong side."

"Let me talk to Jacobsen."

I handed the phone to Kent and braced myself for a fight.

"She's going to look no matter what we do. I figured she was better off
supervised than running off on her own," Kent said. Then, "If you want her
off the streets you're going to have to come get her. If I drop her off at her
Jeep she'll just go after the guy herself."… "Sure, I can do that, but it won't
help. It'll just take two sets of eyes out of commission. I think we need to
keep on. We need Cassidy's eyes. She can ID the car and the driver. The other
guys are just looking for a blue Acura. Cass is looking for *the* blue Acura. If
we see it we'll call in backup." He hung up. "I'm supposed to handcuff you to
the car," he said. "Can I trust you to stay put?"

"No. But you're not handcuffing me to anything without a fight."

"I think I can take you on."

We drove up and down widening our search pattern. We'd been at it for
an hour when the worry settled in and I couldn't even think about what we
were doing. Katie would be hungry and wet and feeling really, truly rotten by
now. Where were they? They had no diaper bag, no nice soothing bottles.

"Kent, drop me off at my Jeep. I can't stand this anymore," I said.

"No. What are you going to do?"

"I don't know, but I can't just sit here."

"You're not just sitting here. You're watching for a car."

"No, I'm worrying. I can't stop thinking about Katie, I need to either do
something, or I need to see Rusty. But I can't just sit here."

The guys didn't trust me on my own.

Jacobsen radioed for Rusty's twenty and got a location. Ten minutes later
they met in a parking lot. Rusty was driving around in an unmarked car. We
stopped and everybody got out. Rusty and I stood, staring at each other, the
obvious lack of a baby hanging in the air between us. I swallowed a big lump
in my throat but it didn't go away. I tried to stuff my feelings away. I really
tried, at least while Jacobsen was there, but it didn't work. I wanted to run. I
wanted to hide and let the bad things go away while I wasn't looking, but I
couldn't. I'd helped them along. I needed to face up to them. And it saddened
me right down to my toes. The sadness weighed me down until I couldn't
think anymore.

Ironically, Rusty seemed relieved. I know I hadn't wanted to be a mother,
but now that I was, I found this little combo kid I was allotted to in life had
worked her way so deeply into my heart that I thought it was going to break. I
thought I wouldn't make it through the day. I thought…I thought Rusty felt

the same way…and I felt guilty for it. The weight of the whole world was on my shoulders and I was too small to hold it up.

Jacobsen took note of the exchange. He looked to Rusty who nodded and Jacobsen nodded back. Another one of those male communications that didn't require words but relayed plenty of information. And even though guys professed to be tough and macho and to have everything under control, I always got the feeling that the reason there were no words was because, if there were, the whole tough guy image would break down. If they had to voice what the look got across they'd be doomed.

So I was doomed. I had to use words. And the words tumbled out and flopped around like a fish out of water, just as desperate for life and hope as a dying fish. Jacobsen took off before it could hit him. Rusty didn't have a chance. He was married. He was stuck.

"Rusty… I'm sorry. I was being careful! I really was. She was only three feet away, behind a closed door! I didn't see a tail. I… I just didn't see it coming. I didn't see it…" and then I lost it. Hell, what kind of a mom are you? I was falling… falling. I was a Marine. I went through police academy. I was supposed to be able to separate what needed to be done from anything I might be feeling. Yeah, right. Then I was a failure at that, too. I didn't care. I was a mom without a baby. I was a wife standing in front of her husband, childless. I was useless. And I was falling. And Rusty… was relieved.

"It'll be okay," he was saying. "Hon, it'll be okay."

"I tried. I ran him down. I ripped up his car…"

"Shhh, we'll get him."

"Maybe you better handcuff me to the car… the way I'm feeling right now, he better not show himself. She's just a baby. She feels rotten. I know she feels rotten. She always feels rotten after she gets shots. And she's teething. She just wants a warm bottle and a rocking. We were going home to spend some quiet time just to feel better. We were going to stay home. In our nice quiet house…"

"Okay, babe, it's okay, we'll find her."

"I don't think he'll hurt her… but… I just need to be sure… I need her back. I need to know."

He held me and let me go on. The guys were out there. They knew what to watch for. Eventually we picked up the pieces and got in the unmarked car. Rusty continued his part of the patrol. I watched for the car. But my thoughts were not on the search. My thoughts were on what Darryl might be doing and they started with the messages. We'd erased them as we listened to them but there was one particular message that bothered me, that might tell us something. Something about an uncle.

"Rusty, stop when you come to a phone booth."

"Why?"

"I've got an idea that I just need to check out."

"Guess it can't hurt to stop at a phone booth," he mused aloud.

When we found one I looked up Duval. Only half the book was still there and even the phone was missing. The phone book was three years old and the pages were water damaged. There were four Duvals listed. None of them were Keenan Darryl Duval.

"What are you looking for?" Rusty said over my shoulder.

"Darryl's uncle. One of the messages on our machine mentioned someone wanting Katie to steal something from their uncle. I don't remember the voice enough to know if it was Darryl. It can't hurt to drive by these places and look for the car."

Three of them had street addresses so I wrote them down. Driving to the houses took us out of the grid but I had a feeling Darryl had a purpose in mind. He didn't just want to baby-sit, so once he had Katie he'd go about his business as soon as was reasonably possible. I didn't think he'd be just driving around with a kid loose in his car.

The first house was just a typical middle class home. There was no blue Acura out front but there was an attached two car garage. Rusty parked.

"Wait here," he told me. He went up to the front door and rang the doorbell. A woman answered the door. He spoke to her for a minute and came back to the car.

"He's not here but if we see him he owes his brother two hundred bucks and he better pay up or else."

"I think he has more important or elses to worry about than her."

"Still, it might explain why he needs Katie to filch something for him."

We went on to the next house. This one was a monstrous estate bordered by a tall, stone wall and an iron gate controlled by a remote. Rusty got out of the car and approached the gate. He pushed a button, spoke into the intercom. A man walked out to the gate. I saw Rusty reach into his coat pocket and pull out his badge. He talked to the man for some time.

"I think we just threw a kink into Darryl's plans. They haven't seen him but they thanked me for the warning. They said they would call if he showed up. Looks like Darryl isn't too popular amongst his family members."

"Are you sure it's a good idea to ruin his plan? If he's successful he might just hand Katie back over and go on his way. If he runs into opposition he might have reason to hang onto her."

We were headed for the third house when the call came across the radio. They had the location of the blue Acura. Rusty hurried to the address we heard on the radio and we found a residential block cordoned off by squad cars. Two cars blocked in the Acura so it couldn't move. Uniforms peeked in the windows of the car, two officers were at the door of the residence. Rusty took it all in. Having been an officer for years, and then a detective, it looked like normal police routine to him. I didn't like it. I didn't want Duvall to feel cornered. In my eyes a show of force would do more harm than good.

The house was in an older, rundown neighborhood of two story houses. It was the middle of the day and there were a couple of cars in front of each house. There didn't seem to be garages except for a few of the larger homes that had a dirt driveway leading to a separate garage out back. Even those houses had a car or two parked out front.

The two officers were shown into the house. It took them maybe ten minutes to search the house. I waited and watched. The only hint that they were in there was when they checked behind curtains and checked for open windows a man could have escaped from.

They came back out and filled in the others.

"The place is clean but there are three houses on the block that let out rooms. The woman we talked to thought Duval was renting a room temporarily in the house next door. She doesn't like the boarding house being next door. Says there's no telling what kind people are going to be living there. She said there are six small rooms on each floor. Tenants share a bathroom on each floor. I asked about a baby. She said there were a couple of families in the house."

"Let's go!" I said, but I was quickly brought up short by a couple of strong hands on my shoulders.

"No way. You're not getting near that house."

"I need to return something I borrowed," I said.

"And what's that?"

"A windshield wiper."

They all looked at one another wondering if I was really that blond. I didn't even have the windshield wiper on me anymore. I was guessing it was in the parking lot at the doctor's office. I just wanted to be in that house. I wanted to find Katie. I knew they wouldn't let me go. I wasn't in uniform. Today I had to be a civilian and a civilian didn't get involved in police work. Even if I did happen to wear it I'd more likely be stuck in a car or relegated to crowd control just to keep me as far from trouble as possible. These guys were not taking any chances after what I'd just put them through.

They began planning. Jacobsen was senior officer. Rusty was out of the loop just like I was just because he was Katie's dad, but they knew he had seniority over Jacobsen. He'd go by the book so he was allowed to stay. It was Jacobsen's show until a higher ranking officer showed up. We had four cars lining the street, four cops on site, two stationed at each end of the block, keeping civilians out. They called in more crowd control. They called in the swat team. They needed a sharp shooter in case this turned into a standoff. Being shoved out of the picture was just what I wanted. As long as they were in their macho cop huddle they weren't watching me.

I slipped away. I wasn't convinced we had the right house yet, but I couldn't just walk up and ask. That was the guys' job.

I was glad these old houses had plenty of shrubbery around the outside. I slipped between the bushes and the house. It was a tight squeeze in spots. Spiders roamed the branches looking for lunch. I frightened a neighborhood cat and it shot out of the bushes and crossed the street. I was glad there were no cars coming.

The first window I came to showed me a large room. A TV blared and kids quarreled. A mother stepped in and roughly settled the argument. She jerked the kids apart and sent them in different directions.

"I'm sick of all this fighting. If you can't get along stay away from each other," she yelled.

I went on to the next window. It was a smaller room. The window was open and the flimsy curtains wafted out the opening. I sat under the window, listening for people inside. I couldn't imagine anybody just leaving a window open in this neighborhood and walking off leaving the place empty. I couldn't pick out any voices that came from the open window. The woman in the first room could still be heard. I took a quick peek. Boxes of clothes. A mattress on the floor. Fast food boxes scattered about. No one was home. I took note of the open window and went on.

The third window was around the back of the house. I had to stay in the bushes because there were cops on the street behind the house, too. This was another larger room with a family living in it. I wondered how all these people got along in such close quarters. How could the single person stand to be sandwiched in between two families? I wondered if the kids ever got to play outside. The second big room had small children. There was a crib against one wall, then a twin bed, then a double. A dresser, overflowing with clothes stood against one wall adding very little organization to the mess. A preschooler jumped on the bed and the mother stood in the doorway talking.

"What do you mean, you're babysitting and you don't have any diapers? What fool takes on a kid and doesn't take the diaper bag?"

"Just until I can get to the store. Just one or two. I've never taken care of a kid before. My sister had an emergency come up."

I froze. I couldn't see the person behind the door.

"I knew you had little kids," he continued. "I thought you might have some to spare."

"Yeah, but diapers don't grow on trees you know. They're expensive. And money don't grow on trees either. If it did I sure wouldn't be living *here*.

Here… two. Now get yourself to a grocery store because two might last you ten minutes or a two hours."

"I don't know how to change diapers."

"Hell, you take off the dirty one. Clean 'em up and then you put the clean one on, same way as the dirty one came off."

I could sympathize with him. I had to change a diaper for the first time just a few years ago.

Come on, show yourself, I thought. I was ninety nine percent sure this was Darryl but I couldn't see him. Then the little girl cinched it for me.

"What did you do to your head?" she asked.

"I hit it on something sharp," he lied.

"I bet that hurt," she said. "Can I play with your baby?"

"No. We need to go somewhere soon."

"Yeah," said the mom. "To the grocery store, pronto!"

I heard him walk down the hall, turn and go up the stairs. I thanked God for hardwood floors. I wondered how far along the guys were getting. They probably had their backup by now. I was guessing, they were ready to question the downstairs tenants about Darryl.

Thunk, thunk, thunk. The woman knocked against the ceiling with a broom handle. "If you're wanting to go to the grocery store you better get with it!" the woman yelled up the stairs, "The whole street is lined with cops!"

"Oh, fuck!" Darryl said.

I heard running steps to the front of the house.

"Aw shit!"

"They better not be lookin' for you! Andrea don't take too kindly to the cops busting up her house! If they're after you, you're outa here!"

There was a mad scrambling noise. I ran back to the open window and squeezed my way in. The room was still empty. I ran across the room and unlocked the door. I threw the door open and dashed into the hall running smack dab into Big John. He spun around warily, side arm ready.

"Cassidy?"

He turned me around and marched me toward the front door.

"John! Stop! Katie's upstairs! Evacuate the down stairs."

"Not until you're behind those lines out there."

He pushed me to the door.

"You can send me away but I know how to get back and they won't see me. I know something you don't know and you need a heads up. Darryl knows you're out there. We need to get up there and we need to do it now."

He pointed me to the line of cars outside and said, "Git."

So I got. I got myself up the stairs as quick as a wink. Rusty almost came over the hood of the squad car as I turned around. John radioed for the guys to take care of the downstairs as he followed me up.

He approached the first door, ready to bang on it and announce his presence to those inside. I put up a hand to stop him.

"I'll know it when we get to it," I told him.

I stood quietly outside the door listening, but all the noise was coming from across the hall. I crossed to the noisy door. A TV was on and a telephone conversation was in progress. I shook my head no. A woman lived here. The next two rooms were as silent as the first. Then we came to a room with quiet voices. John's radio came on. The guys asking a question. He reached up to turn it down but I heard faintly inside the room, "Nodoido." I motioned for John to turn it up. He turned it up and he was going to answer but I motioned for him to hold off. The guys by the cars repeated the transmission and it came through loud and strong.

"No! Doido," Katie whined louder.

"It means *no radio*," we whispered to each other.

"He's not armed," I whispered back.

"You sure?"

"Almost. Enough to risk it."

Big John fired off some commands. It involved getting two more guys upstairs and two guys outside downstairs.

"Nodoido!" Katie said inside the room.

"What the hell are you talking about?" Darryl asked. "If this is what having kids is like I'll skip it. Never! Never will I have kids. I'll wait until they have evolved to be born potty trained. Diapers to change. Cops surrounding my car. It's not worth it. Now I'm on the run with a kid. How was I supposed to know to grab the diaper bag? All I wanted was a pickpocket. And she hasn't picked my pockets yet! Damn. Maybe I got the wrong kid..." He mumbled on and on as he struggled to hold Katie still and change her diaper.

Two cops ran up the stairs. Radios announced the presence of the guys in the back.

"Nodoido," Katie whined again losing patience. She was tired. She felt lousy. I could hear it in her voice.

I listened to make sure they were well away from the door. The guys nodded a go ahead. I nodded a go ahead, even though they wouldn't listen to me. Big John always got picked to knock the door down. He could usually do it in one well-aimed kick. This was an interior door, even easier. The door crashed open and Jacobsen and Thompson rushed past, weapons poised for action. John followed. Darryl looked to the window, nixed the idea, and put his hands up.

"Ja-John!" said Katie enthusiastically.

As the two other officers wrestled Darryl to the floor and frisked him, Big John picked up Katie. She looked like a doll when he held her.

"She said my name!" he bragged to the other guys.

John brought Katie out to the hall and handed her over to me. She handed John a plastic card holder and it unfolded until we could see Keenan Darryl Duval looking at us from the front of his driver's license. John took it from her.

"Say BIG John," he said.

"Bee-bee-bee John," she said and rubbed her eyes.

He gave Rusty the all clear.

I had her back. We were us again. I sat on the floor in the hallway, just soaking up the reality of it. She was here. She was okay. I was so thankful she was too young to know what had really happened to her.

"Mama, bee-bee-bee John."

Thompson escorted Darryl down the hall as Rusty reached the top of the stairs. He brushed past. I sat there on the floor, just holding my baby. Katie pushed around looking for a comfortable position. She put one arm around me and lay her head against my chest. She contemplated sucking her thumb but I'd managed to stop her from that habit long ago. Rusty squatted down.

"Are we okay?" he asked.

I nodded, still just relieved, needing a minute.

"Daddy!" Katie said.

"How did you get in here?" Rusty asked me accusingly.

"I followed my curiosity."

"You disobeyed orders."

"I didn't hear any direct orders."

He thought a moment and made a mental note. From now on I could expect some direct orders.

"You're sure you're okay?"

"I'm sure. I was just scouting. I was just listening while the guys got organized but the more I listened the more I knew until I knew enough to do something."

"You should have come and told us."

"But he knew the police were outside. I had to do something before he tried to get away. That's when the guys caught up with me. They took it from there. This is as far as I got. Did you hear Katie say Big John's name?"

"No," he said half smiling. That was better.

"He was so proud of that. You should have seen him. Katie, say Big John."

She rubbed her eyes again and snuggled deeper.

"She had her shots. I think it's finally hitting her. Maybe she'll say it later."

Rusty dropped me off at my Jeep and then we went to the doctor's office. It was embarrassing going back to the doctor's office for the diaper bag, stroller and shot record. They had no idea why I just took off, leaving everything behind.

"A guy in the waiting room took off with Katie," I explained.

"*Our* waiting room?" they asked incredulously.

"Yeah, he wasn't a patient. Well, we knew that because all your patients are kids, but... you know. He followed me here and waited for a chance to take her."

"Did Katie get your trouble gene?" Arleta, the receptionist, asked.

"We're still waiting to find out. This might have just been my trouble rubbing off on her."

Katie and I finally got to go home for our snuggle time. She had a fever, and once things settled down to normal she got very cranky. All I could do was keep her as comfortable as possible. We walked. We rocked. We talked. We tried reading books. A warm bottle helped and we both fell asleep on the big brown couch. Rusty came home and found us sacked out. No dinner. He went back to town for pizza.

Some husbands would be angry to have a rough day, and then come home to a lazy wife who hadn't lifted a finger to prepare a meal. Rusty is different. Our lives are different. As long as the house was in a semi peaceful state, all was well. Going to town for pizza was a small inconvenience compared to how the day could have ended.

Chapter 20

It was the end of summer. We'd lucked out. For the most part the tourists had stayed on the trails. Only a few minor searches came up. There were several medical calls; cars off the road, kids taking a tumble off rocks, but the rangers had managed to find the few lost campers. It gave me time to train, and once Katie was back to normal I hit the gym with new determination. Georgia thought I was nuts walking with a weighted pack on. I upped the weights on the machines. I added repetitions to my workout with a vengeance.

"Girl, you gonna be buff the way you going," she'd say.

"When I figure I can pass the academy physical requirements I'll ease up. I did it once. I'll do it again."

Fred would come down on me, "It's a good goal, but you're tracking. You're not trying to get through academy again. Why push that hard when you got what it takes to do your job?"

"I never know when I'm going to have to chase down a car on foot. I need to be prepared for anything with this life I lead."

"I don't care who you are. You're not going to chase down a car on foot," Fred said.

"I know, but it would be nice to feel capable again. That's what I'm aiming for. I just want to be useful again."

"You're getting there," he said. "You just wait until you get that first call. You'll see. You're more ready than you think."

"How do you expect to gain weight when you build up like that?" Georgia asked.

"I'm gaining. As long as it's healthy weight I don't care about gaining. I'm over a hundred. As long as I stay under a hundred and thirty I'll be happy."

"You're a pipsqueak, that's what you are."

"Tom's the one who gets to call me a pipsqueak. If he calls me a pipsqueak I know to come back and work some more."

"Who's Tom?"

"He's a detective. He's the only guy on the force that will box with me. If I can give Tom a run for his money, I'm ready for a call. He finds my weak spots. He shows me where I need to work."

Fred said, "Then go pay Tom a visit."

"Are you sure you're ready for this?" Tom asked.

"I'm a lot more ready for it than the first time we boxed."

He smiled faintly. "I didn't know any better then. I didn't know what it would mean. Rusty doesn't like me to box with you. If I win, you go train yourself into the ground. If you win, you go back to work."

"And what's wrong with that?"

"Guess I should go find out whether he'd prefer you to go to the gym or the trail before we start."

"That's no fair. I expect you to try and beat me. I'd be disappointed if you didn't."

"You really think you've seen me in a serious fight with you? Cassidy, I can't hurt you. None of these guys could."

"Any of you guys can beat me if you can corner me, but I need to test myself occasionally."

"Okay, same rules as usual? Hands or feet, stay in the circle. If one goes down we wait for them to get up before commencing."

I had to hand it to Tom. At least he would hit me hard enough to knock me down. And he did, right off the bat, but I got up quickly and went at him. He fended off my blows but nodded his approval.

"You've been working your arms."

"I just spent three months in a wheel chair. All I could work was my arms."

"Then try your legs."

"I doubt kick boxing is on my list of approved activities."

"If you're going to have trouble after you, you're going to have to be ready to kick it in the ass. By the way, what did you clobber Duval with?"

"His wind shield wiper."

"Well, I've got to give you a few points for creativity. I've never heard that one before."

We circled, going for hits or kicks when an opportunity presented itself.

"Cassidy, a fight doesn't work on a points system. What would you do if you were backed up against a wall?"

"There isn't a wall, this is a circle."

"Okay, then let's change things around a bit." He pointed me to the corner of the room and put me in it. "Okay, you're cornered. Uncorner yourself."

I went for the uncovered side. He blocked it easily. I went for the other, and he stepped lithely across the box to block me again, letting me know I had to get through him to get out. He walked toward me, letting me know I was fixing to get really trapped unless I made a quick decision. I feinted to the right and when he went after me I tore into him to with my left side so I could bring in my right hand from further away and put some power into it. He pushed, pushed me closer into the corner and then I changed. I saw Teague Stern. I heard dogs baying, growling, tearing at each other. My anger flared and he kept coming. I cursed the stupid gloves and changed to my feet. My blocks turned into ways to work my way in. I ducked under a blow, brought my foot around, tripped him up and followed it with a punch that brought him down. It was then I saw Rusty standing there.

"Don't let yourself go that far," he said.

"What do you mean?" Tom asked. "That was the first decent hit she got in."

"Ask her who she saw when she landed that hit," Rusty said. The storm clouds gathered. "Ask her!" His voice was hard as granite.

"Rusty, it's okay. I asked him to box. I told him I would when I was ready. Okay, so I wasn't ready. I'm ready to go back to work. I don't have to know how to box to follow tracks. I've been working out. Fred thought I was going too far. He sent me to Tom. Now I can tell Fred I've got a ways to go. But I can track. Don't be mad."

"Who was it? Dirk? Trent? Who was it, Cassidy?" Rusty asked.

"It doesn't matter."

"It does matter. When you let that happen you lose focus. If it comes down to a fight on the job you have to be able to recall what happened. When you're like that, you're not remembering anything. You're only reacting to memories and that won't cut it. Now, who was it?"

"Teague Stern," I said. I should have made up a different name. I knew what that one did to him. These names brought up memories for Rusty, too, but he remembered the result. I remembered the fight. Usually the result was worse. In Teague Stern's case the result was much worse.

"Not yet," he said flatly.

"Rusty, just getting back on the call list doesn't mean somebody is going to get lost. They don't look for my name and say, 'oh good, I can go hiking now, there's a tracker on board again.'"

Rusty must have run into Strict at the station because he showed up at my door. I invited him in.

"Rusty says you're ready to track again," he said as I poured him a soda.

"Did he say how much he's not ready for me to track again?" I asked.

"Mommy, dink!" Katie said.

I poured a tiny bit of water in a plastic cup and handed it to her.

"He's never ready for you to go back on the trail. He knows it's inevitable, but he's never ready. He's never going to be ready. What I want to know is, are *you* ready?"

"Honestly?"

"Of course."

"Physically I can keep up. You're not going to have to carry me out. I can follow a trail. I can do all the things I need to do. I still like to be out in the hills. Realistically, my determination has taken a hit. The trail's going to feel rougher. The nights are going to feel colder. The work is going to be harder. But I'm willing. And I'm able to give it a try."

"What's changed?"

"Four months of ease. I need to be put through boot camp again, toughen me up. I used to be a tracker with a kid. Now I'm a mom who can track. I'm becoming a very odd person. Memories haunt me that no one should ever experience. I fight to be tough. Then I see Katie and I want to curl up on the couch and read stories."

"Nobody wants you to change. We just hope you'll still give your talents when they are needed. The fact is they are needed in some rough country by some very needy people. You think none of the guys that go out have a conflict of interest?"

"I know they have families, too. But search and rescue gets in the blood. Their families know, if needed they will go. This family is still struggling in that regard. If Rusty knew it only involved following tracks, camping in the woods, it would be easier. Circumstances have turned on me too many times for Rusty to trust them. When it happens, I'm busy just dealing with it. He's the one that gets the brunt of it."

"Have you ever considered finding an officer to mentor?"

"If someone seemed interested I'd certainly teach them as much as they wanted to know."

"Good, I'll have Chase watch for someone for you."

Wow, that visit sure took a turn I hadn't expected.

Chapter 21

When Strict came up with a search call for me it was a rough one. It was in a waterless area of the mountains known for the rocky terrain. I was tempted to call in Chase right from the start.

"Strict, this is a monster search. This might be impossible. Do you really think I can do it? This looks more like a team effort."

"If you can't do it, I don't know who can."

"We'd have better luck with two sets of eyes. Two sets of tracker eyes could scout ahead when we get stuck, maybe pick something up while the other puzzles out the last track. I know I don't usually like working like that, but this mountain is the worst we've run up against so far."

"I can call Chase but it'll mean delays. We need to get started."

It wasn't that I didn't want to try it. I did. But I thought it would take both of us to figure it out. We had a few things going for us. We were dealing with a man experienced in the mountains. He knew what he was up against. He wore good, thick boots with a readable tread. He was dressed for the hike. The downside of the tracking was that he was an experienced outdoorsman, which meant he thought he could go almost anywhere and do almost anything. I sincerely hoped he didn't try to scale any of the mountains in this part of the range. He and his hiking partner had set a goal to hike to the top of every mountain in the state over six thousand feet. There are a lot of them. Some of them are pleasant, touristy hikes. Some of them are peaks in the middle of nowhere with very few trails. The reason there are few trails is because the terrain is so challenging and dry that nobody wants to go there. If people liked the place they made it accessible. This hostile peak had nothing to offer, except that it was over six thousand feet tall. And now we had a man missing on it somewhere.

Rusty had a hard time with this call. I couldn't guarantee how soon I'd be home. I showed him on a map where we were going. He could see that it would be difficult. Experienced hikers usually gave us a run for our money, not that we got paid anything. We didn't. He knew it would be stressful both for him tending to Katie in an empty house and for me on a very tough hike with a very heavy pack after a rough recovery. It was just rough all around, but he knew that wouldn't stop me.

Due to the ruggedness of the search, Strict added two rock climbing specialists to the team. Their names, in search and rescue circles, were Rocky and Cliff. They had never worked with me before, but they had heard the stories, and were not exactly pleased with their assignment. I felt silly calling them Rocky and Cliff. Cliff's real name was Edward Heathcliff. But Rocky's nickname was more complex. What was it? I gave up and decided I'd just avoid calling Rocky by name unless I had to.

Landon was assigned to the group, too. He demanded to go and Strict knew he'd add to the team. He was an experienced and knowledgeable EMT, and he had experience with ropes, so he was valuable to us.

Landon wanted to go to watch over me. I knew it. He knew it. It hung in the air between us but it didn't get in the way. Over all of this hung the huge form of the mountain we needed to search.

Strict had done his homework. He showed me the two men's tracks.

"And why is Scott up there alone?"

"They were taking different routes back to the truck and scouting out good camping spots."

"And they were…?"

"Nonexistent as far as Mark is concerned."

"Great. So we've talked to Mark?"

"Yes, he called the rangers. They drove the few roads around the mountain. They called in a fly over. Nothing."

"Can I talk to him?"

"Sure. In fact I think he wants to go back out to look some more."

"So he can take us to a good starting point?"

"Probably."

Mark Howitzer was going to grate on my nerves. I could tell within a few minutes of meeting him. He was a scoffer.

"No way," he said. "You're not climbing that mountain."

"I have to. I get a call. I follow the tracks. If the tracks lead up the mountain, I climb the mountain," I said.

"You follow the tracks." He said sarcastically.

"Mister Howitzer," Strict said. "Cassidy is our tracker, the best one we've got."

"Then go look again. I'm not going up that mountain with a woman in tow."

"I doubt you'll be towing her," Landon said. "She usually tows me. You don't have to go. We'll track down Scott without you. You'd just save us some time by not having to track the first miles."

"And it would help," I added, "if you'd take us the same way you went with Scott. The more of the tracks I can see the easier it'll be to spot them when the going gets tough, and by tough I don't mean the hiking; I mean the reading."

He looked offended, turned to Strict, "Strickland, is there any other way?"

"No, the only other option is to call a guy up from San Diego and he'll likely turn us down. He's probably crawling through the desert hunting illegal aliens or drug runners. If it would make you feel better you're welcome to call him."

Ha! I thought, this ought to be good. Mark was just the type to take him up on it and Chase would make him a believer. Even if he didn't convince Mark to trust me, he'd make Mark wonder if all us trackers were just an odd lot. Strict wrote down Chase's name and number on a piece of paper and handed it to Mark.

"Chase Downing. Is this a joke? You've got a tracker named Chase Downing?"

"No. San Diego does. We just wish we did."

I could only imagine Chase's side of the conversation. It usually started with, "yo," or maybe a quick, quiet, "yeah?"

"Is this Chase Downing?...This is Mark Howitzer I'm looking for a friend...What do you mean you don't do friends?...I'm in the Angeles Forest...Yes, I know...that's what I've been told...but..." he looked at me askance, "you're kidding...okay. Hold on. He wants to talk to you."

"Hey kid," Chase said.

"Hi! How are you?"

"Okay. Are you?"

"Yeah, if I could just ditch Mister Skeptic here, I'd be gone by now."

"Lost camper?"

"Yeah, experienced though."

"If he gives you a hard time just lose the group in the trees and do it on your own."

"Landon's got the radio."

"You're going out with Wilson?"

"Landon, Rocky and Cliff."

"Damn. You sure you're up to this?"

He knew what the addition of Rocky and Cliff meant.

"Guess I'll see, won't I?" I said.

"You'll do it."

"If I can just get going."

"Bye."

"Is he coming?" said Mark.

"What did he tell you?" I asked.

"He didn't say," Mark answered.

"Then I guess we don't know, do we?" I said, "Strict, I'm going out for a little hike. I'm going to follow these tracks. I'll see you in a few days."

"Wait!" Mark said. "You can't just take off. You don't know where you're going."

"Yes I do. If you want to hurry things along you'll come. If you want to extend this search by at least a day, stay."

"But you don't have any tracks, yet."

"Yes, I do."

I pulled my pack up onto my bent leg and slipped my arm behind the strap. Mark didn't believe I was really just hitting the trail, just like that.

Landon grinned, glad to see some spunk in me again. "That's more like it," he said.

I walked over to the spot I had found Mark and Scott's tracks and picked out Scott's. Mark's tread was more angular. His stride cocky. Scott's tread was rounded and his steps were sure, but in a quiet way. They were comfortable. I had a feeling I'd get along better with Scott than I did with Mark. Many people I track with wonder how footprints can be cocky. I'd met Mark, so I expected them to be. But even if I hadn't, they...well, they looked like the footprints of a clown in a big holiday parade. I was thankful they were not careful where they walked. They had no reason or desire to hide their tracks so they just forged ahead. Small plants lay broken; tracks were readable, at least for now. I started the search optimistic.

The guys had quickly pulled on their packs and lined up behind me. I felt like a mother duck with her little brood of ducklings but I really wanted Mark to lead.

"We'd get there faster if we had a guide," I said. "Do you remember the route you took?"

"I think so," Mark said. "I can at least get us to the camp."

"Can you follow the same route? I'd like to read the ground as I go and I need the tracks to do that."

Mark took the lead and I let the guys pass me. Landon stayed behind.

"Landon, I'm fine. I just want to stay on the tracks."

"Just doing my job. They don't need me up there."

Mark hiked off in the direction of the first camp. It didn't take him long to depart from his original trail. I stayed on the tracks and kept the guys in view. Landon stayed with me. I think he could tell I was ready for this search but there was always that little bit of lingering doubt.

If it was just Landon and me on the trail I would be having a great time. Mark kind of put a damper on things. And Bob and Ed...Bob! That was his name. How did they get Rocky out of Bob?

"Landon? What's Rocky's real name?"

"Robert MacKay, why?"

"I've been wracking my brain for an hour trying to remember where the name Rocky came from. I remembered Cliff came from Heathcliff, but I forgot Bob's name."

Bob and Ed were all business. They were model search and rescue guys. My sister, Jesse, would get lost just to be found by them. They were kind, strong, broad shouldered, and technical. They could figure out how to go anywhere as long as they had a rope.

The guys were getting farther and farther ahead as I paused to puzzle out the tracks. Landon radioed for them to wait up a bit.

"What's wrong? Trail too hard for you?" Mark asked.

"No. Not at all. Sorry I'm slow. I am trying to get as much as I can out of the tracks."

"What can you possibly get out a bunch of footprints?"

"I learn a lot about Scott from them," I said. And Mark, too.

"Yeah, like what?"

"Scott's been backpacking all his life. You're newer to it. To Scott this hike is a stroll in the park. To you it's more like a diversion from your real life. I'm guessing you don't get out much. Taking one of these trips is a novelty to you. Not so with Scott. He rests with his pack on. You don't. Scott packs his pack for the trail. Water, snacks, maps, anything he needs while he's on his feet he can reach easily in an outside pocket. You tend to stuff things in the main pocket. You carry your canteen handy but everything else is stuffed in the main compartment."

"How do you know?"

"I've just tracked you. I can tell. When you stop, you take off your pack and rummage around in it. Scott never does. He rests in his pack and, if he needs anything, he reaches up to an outside pocket and there it is, nice and handy."

"But, how do you know?"

"Your trail tells on you."

"That's impossible."

"It is? Are my observations correct?"

"Yeah, I guess so. But you can't guess things like that from tracking."

"Then how do I know?"

"...I...don't know, but I'd have to see it to believe it."

"Stay on your original trail and if I find a good example of what I'm talking about I'll show you."

"I *am* sticking to the original trail."

"Then why are the footprints so far away from where you're walking?"

"They aren't."

"At least you're not obscuring your trail. I can be thankful for that."

"Are you goading me?"

"No, I'm just trying to stay on task here. Believe me, if I were goading you, you'd know it. Now let's find Scott."

He wasn't sure about me not provoking him. Maybe I was just a little. It irked me that he didn't trust me even when presented with facts. If he wanted facts I'd show him facts. The earth did not lie.

About half an hour later I called him over.

"Mark, come here," I said.

"Yeah, what is it?" he answered.

"I'll show you what I was talking about."

I waited until he came over. He'd gotten off track again. I broke off a stick to point and draw with. I knew this was going to be hard for him to see and I didn't want to take all day. We were on a search, not a tracking lesson.

"You and Scott stopped here for a rest," I said.

"How do you know?" Mark asked.

"There's sign all over the place."

He glanced around and took off his pack. He leaned against a tree and looked skeptically at me. I was liking Chase's idea about just tracking it myself more and more except I needed to be able to call them in and Landon had the radio. It was standard procedure with Landon and I. He knew I didn't like dealing with it. So I gathered up what patience I had and pointed to the ground.

"These are Scott's footprints. These are yours." I drew a line next to the tracks as I spoke. "Scott stopped. He just stood there. You can see the patient waiting in this little area here. Small shifting of the feet. You walked off to the side. Here are your footprints leading to the tree you stopped under. You leaned back against the tree. These little mounds of dirt show your feet scooting forward as you slid down the tree. This bark was marred because part of your pack caught on it and pulled a piece off. You sat for a bit, took off your pack. You left it leaning against the tree." I picked up the piece of bark and tossed it to him. "You got up and paced around a bit, here, then over here. You went back to your pack and dug around in it. You can see where the bottom of your pack shifted in your searching." I followed his tracks until I spotted a wrapper in the bushes. "Chocolate makes a mess on the trail. Why do you carry Snickers bars?"

"You can't know what I ate. I don't care what you say."

I picked up the wrapper, crumpled it up and handed it to him.

"Pack it in, pack it out," I said as I handed it to him.

He scowled and threw it back at me. I picked it up and, without taking my pack off, slipped it into a side pocket of my pack. I'd pack it out.

"You and Scott were talking. He took a few steps toward you but for the most part he stood waiting and resting and you walked around glad to have the pack off. I bet getting going again was harder for you than it was for

Scott."

I wasn't making friends. He took all my reading as criticism of how he did things. Guess I couldn't help it. I could identify with Scott. I thought a lot of people grated on Mark.

"Are you through?" he asked.

"I'll quit if you like. You stopped here for a while so there's more sign but you get the picture. Ready to hit the trail?"

He had to put his pack on again. Everybody else was ready to go.

"The guys don't trust you with a gun?" he asked desperate to one up me somehow.

"Look mister, I just want to find your friend. Hell…you don't even deserve an answer. Landon, tell him why I choose to be unarmed. Tell him about the canyon. I don't care what you tell him. I'm tracking."

I found the tracks again and followed them up the mountain as quickly as I could. Bob and Ed were amused. They were used to seeing women stand up for themselves in a mostly male profession. I didn't think of it like that. I didn't care what he thought about me as long as he left me alone to do my job.

I was used to keeping up with the guys. I could rope and tie a calf as fast as Steve when I was a teenager. I would take on any rowdy horse my father's ranch dished out. I'd out hike all the soldiers in my troop. I could shoot better than most on the force. But trouble had beaten me. Trouble had put me in my place. Once or twice trouble had required a sure shot. Trouble got that sure shot and left me with scars that would never heal.

Landon hung back with the other guys. I bet Mark got an earful. I hoped Landon told him the pink bear story but I doubted he would. It wasn't a story Landon was particularly proud of.

I glued my eyes to the ground and kept my feet moving. Mark didn't question the route when he was through getting his earful. He got very quiet. But he didn't take the lead either so I just kept following the tracks until the way got so rocky I had to slow down to puzzle it out. When we were down to a crawl I called Mark back.

"How far to the first camp?" I asked.

"Couple more miles, why?"

"I'm just trying to judge how far we can get today. The farther we get the fewer days Scott has to be on his own out here. I can track our way there but the guys will tell you things are going to be really slow in the rocks. I want to get to my real starting point. The real starting point is the last place you saw Scott. Do you know where that is?"

"I can find it from the top of the mountain."

"Okay, go for it."

"You want to head straight for the top?"

"Show me the last place you saw Scott."

The search took a turn for the better as we left the tracks behind. I was able to just follow along and watch the woods for animals and soak up the fact that I was back in the mountains again. The driest, most barren mountain in the range to be sure, but I was still out and about with the sun shining down on me, my pack on my back, and nice firm ground beneath my feet. Landon took note of the change and the whole group relaxed a bit. Mark cut up into the rocks and we started climbing. As a tracker I felt uneasy leaving the known trail but the known trail was going to take days.

I thought it was funny that no matter what we did Landon was just behind me. Habit? I didn't think so. Though that might have been part of it. I was sure he'd rather be up there with the guys talking shop. He used to joke that he couldn't watch me walk if he was in front. I didn't think that was it either. I think it was an overdeveloped sense of responsibility. He could gauge me if he was behind me and I couldn't fall behind. I was doing well, though. I was glad to be on the trail again.

"What did you say to Mark that made him back off so quick?" I asked.

"You said to tell him about the canyon," Landon replied.

"Now he's probably wondering if I'm mentally stable."

"Nah, though I wonder that most of the time."

"Gee, thanks."

Mark led us almost to the top of the mountain. As the climb got steeper the rocks got looser and Mark was not careful. He just kept climbing. When rocks tumbled off the mountain onto climbers below he hardly noticed. Ed received a lump on the head from a stone that fell off the mountain due to Mark's careless scrambling. Mark never called out a warning to those below him. Bob and Ed began to lose patience. They were by-the-book guys. There were procedures to follow. There was such a thing as climbing etiquette. Bob separated us from Mark and he called out a warning when the rocks tumbled too close. I was relieved when the ground evened out and we could hike again.

For the most part our party was too noisy to observe much wildlife. Mark moved through the forest like a rhinoceros. I could imagine the deer ahead moving out of the way as he hiked along. The guys just didn't have an appreciation for the quiet life of a forest. They spoke in loud voices and they didn't watch their steps as they tromped along. Landon was the exception. I think being partners with me had rubbed off on him a little bit. Though he wasn't particularly careful about his feet, he had quieted his hiking a lot over the years. When just the two of us worked together we maintained a low profile and disturbed little in our passing. With these guys, all I could think was at least we weren't going to be surprised by a bear.

When we reached the summit it was late in the day and everybody's legs were burning. Mark dropped his pack and paced around trying to catch his breath.

"Can you guys kind of stay together so you don't cover the tracks?" I asked as I cast about for sign.

"Does…she ever stop?" Mark gasped.

"Yeah," Landon said. "I have to call a halt to the day and find a campsite, but she does stop."

"Quick, find… a campsite," Mark said.

I headed to the very top of the mountain since Mark and Scott were trying to summit all the peaks. I thought I could pick up Scott's trail there. I located the summit cache hidden under a pile of rocks, and found Scott's and Mark's signatures in the log book. I found the spot where Mark had dropped his pack. He had been exhausted and excited about reaching the top of the mountain and signing the book. Scott's tracks were calmer. Signing the log and summiting the mountain was just part of a day's outing for him. Scott had watched Mark's short outburst and then the two had talked. They appeared to have reached a decision because Mark went back to his pack, found something in it, put the pack back on and rejoined Scott. In all the search for the summit cache Scott had carried his pack.

"What's she doing?" Mark asked in the background.

"We don't usually ask," Landon said. "If you ask, she'll say she's reading."

"Now what's she doing?" Mark asked.

"She has to file a report telling about each stage of the search. She's probably just taking notes."

"Really? You have to file reports about all this?" Mark asked.

"Oh, yeah. We even have to file reports about our reports. Everything we do gets recorded. Cassidy is very detail oriented. She will tell about each piece of trash she finds on a search."

"You're kidding," Mark said.

"It's not trash," I called out. "It's secondary sign. Like the candy bar wrapper. That was not trash. It was evidence."

Bob and Ed shrugged. Mark looked disgusted and I felt a little bit like Warren Randolph, one of the local forest rangers who had nothing better to do than watch for any tiny infraction of the code and hand out tickets to anybody who was careless enough to break one of them with him around. Warren had to be respected because of his title, but most of us had argued with him at one time or another. We could never win, though, because Randolph was always right. Unforgiving, but technically right. I didn't want to be that guy.

I wasn't exactly taking notes when Ed said I was. I was looking at the map, trying to guess where Scott and Mark had gone next. I folded the map back up and slid it into my pack, then followed the tracks downhill. The guys took note of my movement and Ed, Bob and Landon scurried to see where I was leading them.

"Hey, where are you going?" Mark called. "I thought I was taking you to the camp."

"How far is it?" I asked.

"Not far."

"Then I think I'll stick to the tracks. We have until night fall to get there. We should make it no problem."

"It's just this way," Mark said.

"I know. I found it on the map. I just need to read the trail to keep track of Scott's frame of mind."

"I can tell you that," Mark said.

I trusted the tracks more than I trusted Mark to give me an accurate picture so I kept my eyes to the ground and kept tracking.

"How could you find our camp on the map? We could have camped anyplace."

"True. But good camping spots have a few requirements. One of those is flat ground. There's not much of that around."

Mark seemed insulted that I wouldn't just follow him to the camp, but as I followed the trail of the two men it became obvious things were not going as smoothly as it could have gone. Scott stopped repeatedly, turned around and spoke to Mark. Mark's tracks were not physically aggressive, but they revealed an agitated state. When he stopped to make his point to Scott he leaned forward, indicating a belligerent attitude.

"It's none of my business," I said after a few of these altercations. "But what were you two arguing about?"

"We were not arguing," Mark snapped. "I thought we were going the wrong direction to reach the first camp."

"What made you think camp was the other direction?"

"I saw a spot from the top of the mountain."

I hadn't taken the time to look for attractive camping spots while I was up there, but I thought all that could be seen from up there was tree tops.

"And Scott wanted to go this direction instead? Was this a friendly discussion? The tracks…"

"Pshaw, the tracks? The tracks cannot tell you…"

"What was said? No. The attitude they were said in, yes. And I can tell you that you had a quicker temper and more to say than Scott did."

"He was headed to a 'dry camp.' The camp I saw had plenty of trees. It looked more pleasant than where we were going."

"Mark, a dry camp is just a campground with no running water. It's not barren. It just means you have to bring your own drinking and cooking water. Did you and Scott find that?"

"Yeah, we did. But I still think the camp I saw looked better."

"Ahh, so that's why you ended up circling back while Scott continued along the planned route."

Mark kicked a rock. It was all the answer I needed.

I followed the trail into a scrappy, little, abandoned campground. It even had a rough dirt road leading into it. There were no tables, no outhouses, no running water. Camps consisted of a charcoal grill with a couple of rocks in front of them, and a flat spot for a tent. A typical Angeles Forest dry camp.

"Have a seat, guys, while I scope the place out and find the spaces we can use."

"What do mean the ones we can use? It's a campground!" Mark said.

"We need to preserve the tracks that remain, so we avoid the spaces that have tracks at them. I'll let you know when I'm through."

I heard more scoffing noises coming from Mark as I went to read the goings on at the campground.

My first question as I walked the campground was, why didn't I know about this place? I thought I had driven every road in the mountain range and camped at every campground. This wasn't a particularly attractive campground but it would make a good base camp for hiking trips to more interesting places.

There were lots of tracks at three camping spaces. I found plenty of Scott's and Mark's tracks. They camped in two spaces close together and shared Scott's campfire ring for meals. Mark's tracks were always the closest ones to the fire. He was not comfortable in the woods at night. I found their trail out of camp until I had a reliable landmark to help me find it again in the morning. Then I went to find the campsite of the other person who had been in the campground recently. It was a woman. That much I had decided from my first cursory glance at a few tracks. I followed her tracks to her campsite, which was tucked away, out of sight of Scott and Mark's campsites. Was she hiding from them? When I found her campsite I was surprised it was mostly intact, including a once shiny four door sedan. I stood there trying to put two and two together. Nothing was adding up so I ventured into her camp to get a better feel for who this woman might be. Her car was a newer model and I could tell she liked the car. It was spotless inside and had matching accessories. A single flower was bent around the rear view mirror and beads dangled, framing the mirror nicely. A travel mug coordinated with the interior of the car and had the same flowers on it as the one wrapped around her mirror. This woman was not in her element out here in the mountains. Her tracks around camp backed that up. She didn't know how to use a camp stove or peg a tent. It was like she borrowed all her gear and then tried to figure out how to use it after she got there. The ice chest was full of sandwich stuff floating around in the melted ice water. Ick. I wondered how she drove the car over that rough dirt road. If there wasn't a camp I'd think she got lost, but the camp made it obvious she came here intentionally. Now where was she? I was a little self-conscious examining her camp, but I always had the excuse that I was there on police business. The woman never showed up so I didn't need to worry about being confronted.

I located the guys again and gave them an update.

"Stay away from camp sites number six, seven and twenty-two," I said. "That ought to leave plenty of space for us to set up in one through five, or there is a group site that will hold all of us at space number twenty five."

"I didn't see any numbers," Mark said.

"They are stenciled on rocks," I answered. "You'll see them if you watch for them."

We set up in individual camps. I was glad because it meant Mark was less likely to stumble on the woman's camp. Mark didn't have matches for cooking. We managed to get through meal time with minimal fuss but then he wanted to build a campfire.

"No way," Bob said. "For one thing it's against forest regulations. Fire danger was high today. No fire. Secondly, you'd be up all night trying to get the stupid thing out enough to go to bed. You can't find wood without risking your neck. You didn't even bring matches. No fire."

"But it's #$&@!# cold," Mark said.

"Put on a coat."

"I don't have one."

"Then get in your sleeping bag. You'll want a good night's rest anyway. With Cassidy here we'll be up at first light."

"I'm not sleepy."

It sounded like we were babysitting a toddler and that reminded me of Katie. What were Katie and Rusty doing? They had probably gone to town for dinner and Rusty was trying to get Katie settled down for the night. During a lull in the activities he would call Strict to see how the search was progressing.

Whenever I was away from Katie for more than a day I could picture her out there growing without me, learning new words. I did that for over a month in the barn, thinking about life going on in my family's world without me, wondering if it was a permanent thing. I went to bed feeling down in the dumps.

Chapter 22

I wasn't ready for first light when I felt it creeping over the mountaintop. I knew I'd have a battle on my hands just getting Mark to move. It was cold. He'd complain. I didn't want to hear it. I shook Landon's tent first. I heard a groan inside. He knew that sound. He'd be up in a few minutes, reluctantly maybe, but then our talk would wake up the others.

As I was taking my tent down I heard the zipper on Landon's tent and he poked his head out. He still had bed hair. I thought it was cute. All the calls we'd been on he'd never stuck out his head until he was ready for work. Now I wondered how he got it to stay down all those other times.

"How do you feel?" he asked.

"Fine. I want to get to my real trail. I marked it yesterday so we'd be ready for an early start."

"Yesterday didn't wear on you?"

"Some, but I feel fine. Hiking will work the kinks out."

"How much training did you do while you were recuperating?"

"A lot. As much as I could. I went to the gym almost every day. Bet you haven't heard about Katie's adventures at the gym."

"No, why?"

"She's been a real handful." I went on to tell him about it and he just sat back listening. I began to hear stirrings in the other tents. We were right on schedule.

"Does it bother you that she gets into more trouble than other kids her age?"

"Not yet. She's just adventurous."

"Just like someone else I know."

"As long as it's good old fashioned curiosity I approve of it. We've had to teach her to quit pick-pocketing people but she's catching on. She knows pockets and purses are off limits. Now we need to add watches to the list of things she shouldn't touch."

"It doesn't worry you that she likes to jump off things?"

"I have to keep a careful eye on her," I admitted as I fired up my stove. "But I was jumping off the barn roof when I was seven. I thought it was fun. I climbed up the meters on the side of the office and jumped into the hay. One time, when I was maybe nine, I got up there and found out the hay was gone, so I jumped onto the back of a horse. I couldn't see his markings from on top of the barn and mistook him for a gentle mare we had at the time. Turned out it was a two year old racing prospect. He was only recently saddle broke and when he felt a sudden thump on his back he went berserk, bucking and running around his paddock. I got taken by surprise, too. I had no idea he'd react like that and he bashed me against the side of the barn. After that I looked for the hay pile before I climbed up on the roof."

"Were you okay?" Landon asked.

"Oh, yeah, I was always okay. I might need an ice pack or a wet rag. I might have a black eye or a knot on my head, but I was always okay. I walked to the house and inspected my wounds, washed off the scratches, wiggled my nose wondering if it was broken and what one did with a broken nose. I didn't want to find out so I dressed in fresh clothes, pretended nothing had happened and went to apologize to the horse."

"What are you going to do if Katie turns out to be like you?"

"Stay alert and teach her the proper way to jump off barns. So far she is just jumping off the arm of the couch. We made sure there was nothing hard near the couch. We tried getting her a baby slide thinking she'd rather slide down than jump off. She climbs up the slide and jumps off the top."

The camp was full of activity now. Guys took down tents as stoves heated up water for breakfast. Mark was borrowing matches again. I handed him my magnesium stick.

"What the hell's this?" he asked.

"You use it to start fire," I told him.

"Give me a real match."

I handed him my small lighter, more reliable than matches. Actually I relied more on the magnesium stick in a survival situation, but I admit getting a piece of magnesium in the right position to light a camp stove was tricky.

"Okay, I'm curious. How does that thing start a fire?"

"The magnesium is highly flammable. The flint rod, along with a pocketknife, creates a spark. Shave off some magnesium. Get a spark to land on it and you get fire. It's windproof, waterproof, even a rock can help make a spark if you don't have a knife. This thing has saved my life a time or two."

"Why don't the others carry them?"

"Guess they didn't grow up investigating every piece of survival equipment known to man. Not many people carry a magnesium stick. I'm just weird, and still alive because of it. Time to pack up."

"We barely got up," Mark complained.

"Every minute we sit here is a minute Scott is stuck in whatever situation prevented him from meeting you at the cars. For calling us out so urgently, you don't seem too concerned."

He cocked his head at me. "I don't know what happened to Scott. He can usually cope on his own. He also tends to stray out of bounds. Just because he knows what to do if he's lost doesn't mean he wouldn't appreciate a point in the right direction. I think he'll like you. He might be mad at me for calling in search and rescue, but he'll forgive me when he sees you."

"Gee, thanks. It makes me feel so special," I said sarcastically. "I'm ready to hit the trail. I'd appreciate it if you could be ready at oh seven hundred."

I doubted he knew what oh seven hundred was, but I didn't care. I pulled on my pack and walked off into the woods to find the start of the trail I had mapped out the previous day.

"Cassidy?" Landon called out.

"She sure has an attitude, doesn't she?" said Mark behind me.

"She doesn't unless you push her," Landon answered in my defense. Landon should know, he'd pushed the wrong buttons on me a time or two. Enough to get slugged for it.

"Cassidy, wait, you can't just take off by yourself."

"I'm not going far. I won't get out of sight of camp."

I thought the search was going well. We had reached the top of the mountain. I had a clear trail leading in a predictable direction. I was confident we could catch up to Scott. I just hoped he hadn't done anything foolish. I squatted next to the tracks I was going to follow, willing them to speak to me. It was strange, the feeling I got from the two trails. Mark's tracks were a lot easier to read. But even his tracks irritated me. Scott's trail felt like an easy chair compared to Mark's. I'd change my mind about that later, but my opinion of Scott never wavered even when he gave me a run for my money.

I hadn't intended to start the search back up, but tracks are like potato chips, or like cliff hangers in a book. Once I saw the tracks, I wanted to find another one, and another. They told a story and I wanted to find out what came next. So one after another I unconsciously read the morning's news. Mark and Scott's disagreement of the previous day was not ended. They hiked, talking animatedly as they wound around the mountain to the south. I was standing next to a crooked, lightning struck tree reading the sign left by a particularly heated disagreement when the guys caught up.

"You made Scott really mad," I said. "It's not like him to get right in your face."

"Yeah, well he made me mad too," Mark snapped.

"One iffy camping spot seems a small thing to have this much tension built up over it. There are hundreds of places a person could camp between here and your cars."

"He was provoking me," Mark said.

"Over a camping spot?" Ed said.

Mark just folded his arms over his chest and stuck to his story. That wasn't an easy thing for him to do with the straps of his pack in the way.

"I think he was trying to get rid of me," Mark said.

It was Bob and Ed's turn to cross their arms except they just looked at Mark as if he was pulling a fast one on us.

There was no use antagonizing Mark further so I continued down the trail. It hadn't taken long for their disagreement to escalate to the point where they parted ways.

"You went north, presumably to check out that camping spot? And Scott continued south according to the original plan?" Ed asked Mark.

Mark looked like he knew the basis of his argument was not holding up under scrutiny but he nodded assent.

"Not a smart thing to do, dude," Bob said. "You were lucky you aren't the one lost in the mountains."

"The reason why Scott ended up on his own doesn't matter," I said. "I still have a job ahead of me. Let's just hope Scott stays on task. If he shows up at the cars we'll hear from Strict via radio."

I stood behind where Scott had stood and counted the number of times his feet changed position before he went on his way. He must have waited a few minutes before continuing on his own.

"Were you two still friends when you split up?" I asked Mark.

"Oh, sure. I can't say I was anxious to meet up with him for a while, but then when he didn't show up I had to worry a bit. I mean... I thought the tension might carry over into work. I wasn't looking forward to that."

Neither was Scott, I thought.

I followed Scott's trail but it had changed after the two men split up. At first Scott's mannerisms were the same but after a while his tracks revealed a new twist to the camping trip. There was a slight leaning motion involved, like Scott was watching his back trail. Did he expect Mark to come back? At first it was subtle, but as Scott progressed it became more obvious until he began stopping and actually turning around to watch. After three of these stops, I stopped too.

"Wait here, guys. I'll be right back," I said. I took note of the direction Scott was facing and zig zagged, crossing that line of sight into the woods.

What I found in the woods was very interesting. The woman from the campground had followed the men. Was she worried about her safety? Was she afraid of them? Why would she follow them? Did they know they were being followed? Did she need help? Her camp and her tracks both revealed to me that she was not experienced in the outdoors, but then what was she doing here?

I took time to quickly back track the woman to camp. I discovered she was definitely following Mark and Scott. She watched from behind trees and brush and tried to keep out of sight. She didn't usually actually hide. I saw no evidence that she crouched behind things, but she did pause and observe, and keep something between herself and the men.

"Why's she going that way?" Mark asked.

"We'll find out, if Cassidy thinks we should know. In the mean time we leave her alone. She'll get what she needs from the tracks and if we need to know something she will tell us," Bob said.

Mark scowled.

Unfortunately following the woman's tracks gave me more questions than answers, but I filed it all away and went back to Scott's trail.

At first Scott hiked toward his goal of circling the mountain and finding the parking lot, but he didn't seem to be in any hurry. He became distracted by things and his trail wandered. I enjoyed trying to guess what had attracted Scott's attention. He seemed drawn to unusual trees. He stopped to take pictures of a few twisted pine and oak trees. He liked gnarly, old trees. He still watched his back trail and I began to think his frequent stops were an effort to catch his follower in the act. The route became rocky and when it did my tracking slowed to a crawl.

Mark had a hard time containing his impatience. He sighed and scoffed and generally acted like a bored kid.

"Look, there's tracks right over here!" Mark said.

"They aren't Scott's," I answered.

"How do you know?"

"Look at the track," I called over. "See the tread?"

"No," he answered.

"Those tracks belong to a woman. She camped at the little campground, too."

You could have heard a baby bird chirp a mile away. Mark's mouth hung open.

"What?" He gasped.

I repeated what I had told him.

"What can you tell me about this woman?" he asked.

I was uneasy. I didn't want to stir up trouble.

"She's about five eight. A hundred forty pounds. She isn't used to camping. She wore cross trainers. Size eight. She's just a camper out of her element. Ignore the tracks. We're looking for Scott."

A string of expletives filled the space between us. Mark stalked over to me. His eyes narrowed. "What else do you know about this woman?"

I decided to leave the car out of this. Leave it uncertain. If I identified the car he'd just jump to more conclusions. Part of me was wondering how a guy could spend a night in a campground without knowing other people were there. But some people don't get curious enough to investigate their surroundings. Mark could easily be one of those people. The woman had chosen her camping spot to hide her presence. I only discovered it because I was one of those people who did have to investigate my surroundings.

"She's probably just a tourist from LA off the beaten track. She should have stayed closer to the highway. I bet she missed not having an outhouse and running water," I said lamely.

"Find him," he sneered. "Find him so I can knock his block off."

"You're jumping to conclusions," I said, still studying the ground.

"Don't worry about me," he said flatly. "Just find that son of a bitch."

Mark began pacing around nervously. You just can't rush tracking and he was a major distraction to me. He wasn't helping the process at all. After being pulled away from the tracks for the fourth time in a row I called Landon over.

"I don't know what his problem is, but get him out of here. I'm stuck and I can't think. Can't you take him for a walk? We're going to be here for a while. I'm going to have to mark this spot and try looking ahead. Buy me some time. Bob will radio if we need you back here."

"Why me?"

"Get one of the other guys to do it if you can. I don't care. I just need space to think."

Okay, I thought with a determined huff, the trail, just study the trail. Forget Mark. I looked at the last known sign. Guessed a direction based on it, looked for the next step and it didn't exist. I tried different directions, no luck. I tried different angles, no luck. Okay, time for plan B. I got out a marker and placed it next to the track, then stood back. If I was walking across this rock where would I go? I walked that direction looking for sign. Nothing.

Bob and Ed sat cross-legged on the rocks playing poker with an old deck of cards. Apparently they had been in this situation before. Many of the volunteers who went on long searches brought cards along. We had played many a game by flashlight using sticks and rocks for money, never knowing who really won. Were sticks dollars and rocks quarters? Then what was that leaf doing in there? If I asked them to help they would jump to my aid, but I really just had to work this out myself. Adding their tracks to the problem didn't help me at all.

There were a finite number of places Scott would go to from the last track. I walked each of them that looked like it made sense. None of them panned out. Unfortunately, I thought of something else. The woman. Did she play a part in this like Mark thought she might?

If Scott was standing right here, where would the woman choose to observe from? I had never tracked this way before, but the prospect of using another person's tracks to track my missing person intrigued me. I was excited at the new twist this added to the puzzle. I knew this woman was no rock climber. If she was watching Scott she would do it from nice, familiar ground. I went back and found her tracks. It was like tracking a mouse through open ground. Mice don't like open ground. They worry about predators swooping out of the sky and snatching them up. What was this woman worried about? Mark? Or Scott? People who aren't used to the outdoors worry about some of the oddest things. For women it seemed creepy crawlies topped the list. Rattlesnakes. Tarantulas. Scorpions. I'd had my share of trouble with all of those and they weren't nearly as bad as some people I'd met. Still, this woman timidly followed behind Scott. Watching, waiting for something. Her footsteps were stop and go, stop and go. I could tell by the way they shifted when she stopped.

"Cassidy? What are you doing?" Bob asked.

"Primary sign vanished. I'm working off secondary sign."

He nodded and watched as I pieced together the puzzle of the woman involved in all this.

The woman's tracks led past the rocks where I'd lost Scott. Each time she stopped I put myself in her shoes and pointed myself in the same direction and tried to see what she saw. Then I went to the spot I thought she was focused on and looked for Scott's tracks. Hell, this was getting nowhere.

"I've never seen you this stuck," Landon said.

"You've never seen me trying to work two trails to figure out one."

"What do you mean?"

"This woman has been following Scott. At least I think she is following Scott. It makes sense based on her movements. I just can't find Scott's trail. I'm hoping hers will lead me to his."

I went back to Scott's last known track and surveyed what I knew of the woman's trail. I walked to the place I figured the woman was watching and looked for sign there. Rock. I was beginning to hate rock. It was unforgiving. It was secretive. Nothing marred it.

Chase? What would you do? Old Frank? Send me in the right direction.

Strict checked in over the radio. Bob gave him an update. He asked to talk to me.

"Cassidy?"

"Yeah."

"Are you okay?"

"Yeah."

"What's the problem?"

"Rock. Don't worry. I haven't given up yet. I still have a few tricks up my sleeve."

"How are you holding up?"

"Mentally, I'd like to send Mark packing. Can't Bob and Ed escort him back? I may have a situation brewing. Physically..."

"What kind of a situation?"

"One I can't broadcast over the radio."

He paused, thinking of what I might be not talking about.

"Should I know about this?"

"Don't worry about it for now. I'm sure with two cops, an EMT and a chicken tracker we can handle it."

"Can you call me on your cell phone?"

"No reception."

"I don't want you walking into anything that is going to turn on you."

"Okay, I'll see you in a few days."

"Cassidy..."

"Lou, just let me track. I've been on this same spot for half an hour. I need to get us past these rocks."

"You'll do it. You can see the invisible."

"Yeah, right. Over."

I'm afraid I left him with more questions than answers. Welcome to the club, Lou. I had plenty of questions of my own. Like how did this woman fit into the picture and why was Mark so angry about it? I had the feeling I was walking into a triangle that I didn't belong in. I gave myself a good scolding and gave myself direct orders to just stick to the task at hand. I had one job and that was to find Scott.

Scott doesn't need any help, I thought. Now where did that come from? But I was pretty sure Scott was fine. I thought it was Mark who needed rescuing. Shit. I wanted to feed Mark to the coyotes and bears he kept scaring off. I was actually looking forward to meeting Scott and I was wondering how the woman fit in. I dumped all my thoughts into a big vat, took a deep breath and looked for the invisible clue that would lead me to my goal. Scott. Whether he needed help or not, he still needed finding.

Okay, rocks, I need a clue here. I alternated between the woman's path and what I imagined Scott's path to be based on the woman's tracks but I could only hope the two were really connected. Alternating from one to the other I worked my way about a quarter of a mile over the rocks. I took a lot of flack from Mark. He didn't know what I was doing and I wasn't telling him anything. I knew the possibility of Scott having anything to do with a woman up here would set off Mark immediately so I kept my thoughts to myself, took his abuse, and kept to the task at hand.

Ironically, my big break came when the woman ventured up into the rocks, too. With her inexperience she left all kinds of clues along her trail. I found scratch marks where little pebbles had slid underfoot, scuffmarks, places where she had loosened rocks when she leaned against unstable hillsides. I knew I was making a little progress when I realized I better go back for my pack. I marked my stopping point and jogged back. When I strapped into my pack all the guys figured we were back in business again. Maybe we were but it was a very slow business. I might know where I was going, now, but I could still only progress one track, sign or clue at a time.

I didn't know whether to shout for joy or back out of the search completely when the woman at last joined Scott. After he left the rocks she ventured closer and then Scott decided he needed to find out what was going on along his back trail. He turned frequently and stood watching and waiting. When she finally appeared his stance was assured, calm. I thought he was pleased with this little turn of events. I didn't tell Mark what had happened. I didn't tell him how close they stood or how long they stood there like that. I took note of it and kept tracking, wondering what finding Scott would mean. I thought it was odd that Mark seemed to blame Scott, when it was obvious from the tracks that Scott hadn't known the woman was around until after the two men had parted ways. It was hard for me to believe they had just happened to stumble on a campsite in the middle of nowhere where a woman both men knew was camped, a woman who wouldn't ordinarily be caught dead camping. The whole situation just seemed odd to me and I wasn't sure I wanted to walk into it. I also felt like the officers needed a heads up. I wasn't sure how I was going to tell them what was going on without tipping off Mark but I watched for a chance.

We only got a few miles in that day but I called a halt as soon as dusk settled and we had a campsite handy. Mark's temperament had not improved. He was bitter and he wanted to find Scott. I watched him and ignored him at the same time. I ignored his barbs and took in all the hints he was emitting about what the end of this search might entail. I ate dinner as early as I could, got my camp set up promptly and nearly yanked Landon out of camp.

"We need to talk," I told him.

"Why? I mean, not that I don't want to talk. But…the guys are going to wonder."

"I don't care. They won't wonder after you relay the information they need."

I dragged him out of camp and walked swiftly away and as I got out of hearing distance I began warning him, "We're walking into the Bermuda Triangle. I haven't just been tracking Scott. There's a woman with him. A woman Mark knows. And Mark isn't too happy with his buddy, Scott. Bob and Ed need to know what they are walking into. Is Mark armed?"

"I don't think so, although he did make fun of you for *not* being armed."

"Scott and this woman are…rather close, at least closer than Mark wants them to be. You get the picture?"

"Yeah."

"She followed Scott out of the campground. I don't think either man knew she was there…things are not making a lot of sense to me. Something is not right. Something is going to go wrong when we find Scott. Mark is like a time bomb and he's going to go off when he catches sight of those two together."

Landon leaned back against a tree, thinking.

"Thanks for the heads up. I'll see what I can do. You got all that out of the tracks?"

"Mostly. Mark tipped me off a little, too."

"Okay, well, we gotta do what we gotta do."

We'd been on the trail two days. Looking at the big picture, we were doing okay. I wasn't worried about Scott. Scott was having the time of his life. If we were tracking the woman or a kid I'd have pressed on as long as possible, but in our case I thought getting information to the guys was more important than a little distance between us and Scott.

I didn't want to examine the small picture too closely. If I did I might come to some unwelcome conclusions. I just wanted to do my job. I hoped doing it was the right thing in this case, but I was beginning to have my doubts.

Chapter 23

I had an uneasy night. Nightmares woke me up and when I woke up I debated the sanity of finishing this search. I kept picturing what could happen if Trouble raised its ugly head. It would hurt. Me. Rusty. The officers involved. Was I really willing to let them be hit when Trouble came after me? Domestic disputes were one of the most dangerous calls the officers took. People did unpredictable things when tempers flared. But I couldn't call it off. The search was still valid. Only my own tracker's instincts told me Scott was in no danger. If I called it off and then Scott didn't show up I'd be in trouble in more ways than one. First of all, I'd lose credibility in the eyes of the guys. Secondly, I'd fall into a lifelong guilt trip. I'd blame myself for what happened to Scott forever. I had to finish the search, but I didn't think it was wise to drag the guys into a potentially volatile situation. I hoped Landon managed to tell Bob and Ed what they might be getting into. At least they were used to dealing with domestic disputes. That was one thing I lacked.

The only way to end this thing was to find Scott. I should track him as quickly as I could. It would be a lot easier since he was traveling with the woman now. If they would just stay away from the rocks I was confident we could catch up. She would slow him down considerably, though Scott was not a fast hiker. He seemed to enjoy taking his time. And he would enjoy the companionship of a woman. I thought, given a little motivation, I could catch up to him and I was developing motivation as I lay there. The sooner we found Scott the less time Mark had to stew. Yup, the sooner we caught up with Scott the better. We'd all be fresher, better prepared for a confrontation. I only hoped Landon had time to talk to Bob and Ed.

Then there was the matter of supplies. We all went out prepared for a three-day search. I packed for four days, since it sounded like the first day would be wasted. I hoped the guys had brought extra, too. I fell asleep pondering the next two days and the sky was bright when I woke up. Shoot.

I jumped out of my sleeping bag and started shaking tents.

"It's late. Come on guys, time to hit the trail."

Landon poked his head out, looked at the sky and grinned because we were back in our proper roles. It was funny the little things that clicked between the guys and me. For Rusty it had been finding me crawling on the floor playing Peek-a-boo with Katie. For Landon it was waking the guys up at the crack of dawn and an eagerness to hit the trail.

I admit, deciding to hit the trail and finish it got me in gear. I could focus on my task easier, having decided it needed to be done as quickly as possible.

I'd profiled Scott and the woman. I knew what I was dealing with. All I had to do was follow the tracks and make sure to notice if the feeling I got from the trail changed at all. I ate breakfast quickly and packed everything up hastily. I paced, waiting for the guys to catch up to me.

"What got into you last night?" Mark asked.

"I have a better handle on the tracking now. I know I can make good time today."

"Finally."

"Hey, it wasn't Cassidy's fault Scott decided to hike in rocks yesterday. If you think it's easy I suggest you go back and try to find a footprint on rock," Ed said in my defense.

My eagerness seemed to be contagious. The guys seemed more inclined to hit the trail as well. All right! We were set. We could do this today!

It felt good to be on the trail again, different from the previous days. I let the ground talk to me. I gave Landon a questioning glance and he gave me an answering glance. I didn't know if he'd talked to Bob and Ed or he was assuring me he'd take care of it but I took it as a positive sign.

Even speedy tracking requires time and patience. The tracks have to be verified. To be verified they have to be seen. If I don't see tracks within about eight feet I have to go back and search for them.

When the sun was high overhead Landon reminded me, "Cassidy, lunchtime. Eat something, kid." Another thing that tipped him off that I was back to my old self. I could get into the trail enough to forget about less important things, like eating. Even with the uncertainty ahead of us we rejoiced that things were normal again. We could work together. The team was complete again with all its little quirks.

Scott did give Bob and Ed a reason for coming along. He had helped the woman climb a steep wall. Bob climbed up first, since the wall was tall enough that a fall could injure someone. He laid out ropes and the rest of us climbed in safety to the top. I had examined the bottom of the cliff before I decided Scott had climbed it. I sent Bob up with instructions not to disturb the tracks up top. I went up second so I could get a start on the tracking. The day just felt right. We were working well together. Too bad we had to find Scott and put a damper on the day's success.

Chapter 24

After we all made it to the top of the cliff the guys followed me as I followed Scott's tracks. It was early afternoon and I was tracking along when we heard laughter.

Mark tensed.

We all stopped. I looked to Landon. Landon looked to me. I hoped the other guys were prepared for what we might be facing.

"It's just a little one. It's harmless," Scott said.

"Maybe, but it scared me," the woman said.

"I'll turn it loose and it'll slither as fast as it can in another direction," he assured her.

We couldn't see them yet. Even then I could identify with Scott a lot easier than I could Mark.

"How can you pick those things up?" the woman asked.

"It's just like a pet one. If it would bite, I wouldn't pick it up," Scott said.

"How can you live like this? Just hiking the mountains. No trail. No route."

"I have a route. We're headed for my car, then we'll drive back around and pick up your car."

"Do we have to?"

Mark was tensing with every question from the woman. He was a coiled spring and each time someone spoke we pinpointed their whereabouts a little more accurately until Mark started forward, fists clenched at this sides. I moved to block him off.

"Scott has every right to hike with whomever he wishes," I almost whispered at him.

He shoved me aside. I bounced back.

"Stuff that anger aside until you get back to town," I hissed at him.

He stalked off through the trees. We all followed him.

Scott appeared around the side of a tent and released a small brown snake into the brush and glanced up to see his camp being invaded by the police. Then he saw Mark. His look of shock melted into, "Oh, come on. You've got to be kidding." But what came out of his mouth was, "Mark, I told you I'd see you at work in a few days and we'd compare notes."

"It's been a few days," Mark answered, biting back what he really wanted to say.

"You dragged these guys up into the mountains because of two days? You were the one who was ready to leave. I wasn't."

"I wonder why?" Mark said sarcastically. "How was I supposed to know you were going to stay up here? I found the cars and waited. I knew I might have to wait most of the day but I didn't think I'd still be waiting. What the hell are you doing?"

"Camping."

"You SOB, you know what I'm talking about!"

"If you remember back to a certain restaurant and a certain business meeting, you'll also remember a certain girl who you somehow managed to annoy, yet you picked her up anyway."

"Serena, yes."

"Excuse me guys," Scott said to the officers, "this is kind of between me and Mark."

"You might want us handy," Bob said calmly.

"Okay... so what it boils down to is Mark and I have both been dating Serena and Mark has been a little impatient about getting me to quit. Serena sat us down and said she wasn't going to be stuck in the middle anymore, that she would move on. Neither one of us wanted her to do that and it was Mark's big idea that Serena could choose one of us. Mark tried to pin her down. Exactly how were we supposed to know if we'd been chosen or dumped? And Serena said it would be something totally unexpected and we'd know."

I was putting a few pieces together and I really didn't want to be noticed, but I was curious and my curiosity led to nosiness.

"How in the world did a city slicker like her know to go to a scruffy little campground in the middle of the worst part of the Angeles Forest?" I asked.

Scott just stared at me. Guess he hadn't noticed me there. He took in the khaki clothes, the moccasins, the very used backpack and gave me an appraising look.

"I always leave a flight plan with the main office. Serena's the main office. I drew our tentative route on the map with guesses as to where we'd camp. We didn't end up camping in exactly the same spots, but close enough to be found if help needed to find us. I'm still following the plan, just a little slower than I expected."

Mark was building up steam and it was going to be released somehow.

"So she just appears on the trail and you take that to mean she's chosen *you*," Mark said bitterly.

"What would you have done if she'd appeared on *your* trail?"

"You *slept* with her, didn't you?" Mark spit out, "Admit it."

"I didn't have much choice. She just appeared on the trail, no gear, what were we supposed to do?"

Serena had two days worth of camping gear back at the campground, but I decided I better stay out of it.

Mark snatched a stone off the ground and launched himself at Scott. Bob and Ed interceded, but when they flung Mark to the ground the rock went flying and hit me right in the forehead.

"You guys are supposed to be on my side!" Mark yelled as he flopped onto his back. He reminded me of a turtle with the big backpack under him and his arms and legs waving around uselessly.

"We're cops. We try not to pick sides until we have to," Bob said.

A mischievous woman's voice came from the tent. "Scott? What's going on out there? Why do I hear voices? How long does it take to turn loose a little snake?" We heard a rustling as she crawled out of the tent. She stood and took in the scene. Her eyes told me it took about as long to turn loose a little snake as it was going to take *her* to turn loose a big snake. Mark.

I stood there rubbing the lump on my head.

Bob and Ed were pinning down Mark.

Landon was rolling his eyes.

Scott was shaking his head at his former friend.

And Serena just stared at the whole mess of people who had invaded her little patch of heaven.

Mark struggled against the guys. When they didn't turn him loose he yelled at her, "You could have just said something!"

She walked over to us, looked down at Mark, pinned to the ground, and said calmly, "No, I couldn't. I tried that. You wouldn't listen."

"Turn me loose!" Mark yelled.

"Not until we're convinced you're not going to hurt someone," Bob said. Mark still wasn't convinced he wasn't going to hurt someone so he shut up. Even with the growing lump, I felt sorry for the guy. Dumped, with a crowd of people to watch. How was he going to get out of this as gracefully as possible?

"Put your hands on top of your head," Bob instructed.

Mark knew he was stuck doing what he was told so he complied. Bob flipped him over and frisked what he could reach.

"Undo your hip belt," he instructed.

When the belt was unbuckled he helped Mark out of the pack and stood him up spread-eagled. He did a proper frisking, then he grabbed Mark by the arm and marched him off into the brush away from the group. While Bob was gone Ed quickly searched the pack for firearms. The group relaxed a bit with Mark out of the picture, even if it was temporary.

"So, you don't look like you need rescuing," Ed said to Scott.

"Is that what he said?" Scott said.

"He said you'd agreed to meet at the cars two days ago and he didn't know what had happened."

"He assumed that was the plan. He tends to do that...Oh shit, don't tell me they sent out the troops."

"Just us, we're all the troops today."

"The four of you just walked up like you knew where we were."

"We tracked you."

Landon glared at Ed.

"Okay, Cassidy tracked you. Rocky and I were here for technical support and Wilson is our medical support."

"Some medical support. You've got a girl with a shiner and you're standing around like this is a normal thing."

"Let me see," Landon said. "Aw, Cassidy, can't you do one search without something going wrong?"

"It's okay, a rock to the face is nothing compared to usual. It doesn't feel like it would give me a black eye. Did it?"

"A little bit. Every time this happens I get a call from Rusty."

Serena wasn't sure what to think of all this. She looked at me like I was an alien from space. She was wearing brand new camping clothes and her idea of camping clothes was something from the LL Bean catalog. She was cute, in an LL Bean sort of way, but it was obvious she was more comfortable in spike heels and a business suit. Her hair, once fluffed and curled, had fallen. She looked like she battled it every morning she had been camping, trying to get it back to business casual again. She scratched at mosquito bites and I was guessing from the bites that she was wearing perfume and makeup.

"Let's get some of this paperwork settled, since I doubt you want to hike out with us," Ed said. He dug out some tattered papers from his pack and he and Scott went into camp where they ran through the usual list of questions. I got out the map and found the quickest way back to base camp or a ride.

Bob came back. I looked for Mark and he stood sullenly at a distance.

"What's the plan?" I asked.

"We'll wait for Cliff and then decide."

"Okay."

When we all got back together again we decided Scott and Serena were fine. They were free to camp in peace. Mark was hiking out with us, though he didn't want to.

"Cassidy? Do you have a route for us? How long will it take?"

I showed them a route on the map. It was about five miles.

"We can make it today if we keep up a good steady pace," I told them. "What did Strict say?"

"You don't want to hear what Strict said. Okay...he was glad you found your ten sixty-five and he was glad everybody was all right. After that, you don't want to know what he said."

"And he wants us back as soon as possible. I don't blame him. He wants to close down base camp."

Mark hiked like he was on his way to his own hanging. I pushed myself. I wanted to be home. I thought that was odd because at one time it had been the exact opposite. I used to spend uncomfortable time at home while the trail called. It was the mountains where I knew my place and I was comfortable. A tent, a cold night, seeing a hawk overhead was like a welcome home hug. Stalking deer was like visiting family. Though I still longed for the sight of a soaring hawk and I still stalked the deer, my real home was…home. Maybe trouble would have a harder time finding me if I stuck closer to home. Maybe peace could be given a chance, at home.

I hiked and hiked, checking the map occasionally. I hadn't spent much time in this part of the mountains because there were so many more interesting places to choose. I could feel Landon behind me like always, then there was Mark. I could feel his dread all the way at the front of the group. Bob walked behind Mark. I noticed his weapon was no longer clipped down. Ed brought up the rear. I wondered why the cops were so set on keeping Mark in line. Mile after mile passed beneath my moccasins.

I was happy. I was glad I'd found my man. I was glad nobody got hurt. The sun was shining and the day was bright. I got to practice tracking. Life was good.

As the big green and tan RV appeared in the distance I picked up my pace even more. Base camp, yes! Strict gave me the grandfatherly look when he caught sight of my face. He put an arm around my shoulders.

"You done good, kid," Lou said.

"Thanks."

"Wilson, thanks for going out."

Landon nodded acknowledgment of the praise.

"Rocky, Cliff, what are we going to do with this guy?" Strict said to the officers.

"Cass, Rusty should be home. Let me give you a ride home," Landon said.

"My Jeep is at the compound."

"You can get it tomorrow. I want to talk to Rusty."

"Before he calls you?"

"Because I know he's been worrying."

"He always worries."

"Do you mind?"

"No, I don't mind. Let's go."

The Explorer was in the driveway. I knew Rusty would be home because he always wanted to be home when I arrived. He'd checked in with Strict after work so he expected me some time that evening. Bertie would be helping with Katie, maybe cooking dinner. Rusty was in his office when we came in with a clatter and rustle of gear. I set my pack down beside the front door, knowing I had to put it in the garage before Katie emptied the pockets.

"Mommy!" Katie said as she toddled into the living room. I picked her up and she looked at the bump on my head. She poked it to see what would happen.

Rusty walked out of his office and stood at the end of the hall. I set Katie down and dashed down the hall to get my hug.

"I missed you," I told him as he wrapped his arms around me.

"Welcome home," he said, then noticed Landon standing there in the living room. "What happened?"

"Nothing. Just a little mishap."

"Why's Wilson here?"

"He said he wanted to talk to you."

He let me loose and walked grimly into the living room.

"Wilson?"

"Michaels." Landon said, then he grinned broadly, "We've got our Cassidy back. She did great."

Rusty just stood there looking at the floor, hands in pockets. "The black eye?"

"Just a little mishap. No trouble. She stuck it out over a very tough trail. She saw potential trouble coming and gave us all proper warning. With a heads up, we had minimal problems. She kept up. She gave our guide a bit of attitude. She found her man... She's back. Just thought you'd want to know."

Rusty paused, not really knowing what to say. He finally extended his hand to Landon with a "Thanks."

Landon shook Rusty's hand, went to the kitchen and raided the cookie jar, then took off with a "See you next time. Take care, pardner."

Bertie rounded the corner, "You're back!"

Rusty said, "Yup, my girl's really back."

Chapter 25

"This is most unusual," said Rita Ortega. Rita was a social worker assigned to Brian Lamb.

"I know, but please let him do it. He loves the horses."

"Yes, he does. And Farley McGyver has said he would take Brian back. I'm just puzzled why you would want to be his teacher."

"Because someone needs to teach him who will listen to him."

"Have you seen what it takes to work with a man his size?"

"Yes, but I think I can manage. Farley will supervise and my husband might help me if I need it."

It was an overcast day when I stood at the fence waiting for Brian to arrive. When he stepped out of the old white station wagon he didn't know who his new teacher was going to be. Farley walked out to the car and shook hands with Brian and his mom. Dolores Lamb looked worried. I saw Farley nod in my direction and they walked over.

"Brian, this is…"

"Rose!" Brian said. "I on'y hear one time you still sick. Long, long time. I think I never see you again."

"Brian, this is Cassidy. She wants to be your teacher. You must listen to her and obey every word she says. She is a real cowgirl. If you pay close attention, you will be a cowboy someday."

"Rose? My teeshur?"

"Only if you listen carefully, and obey what she says," Farley said. "You give her a hard time and you will have to quit."

"Me ride Elmo again?"

"Elmo's a good choice. Do you remember how to saddle him up?"

Brian had to start from scratch. It took me a month to teach him which hand was which. He got frustrated. He threw tantrums. I let him and I made friends all over again when he was finished. I'll never forget watching him bounce in the saddle the first time I let him ride at a trot. I thought he'd be miserable trotting, but he laughed out loud, "Yeehaw! Elmo he buck! I be real rodeo cowboy!"

I doubt if Elmo remembered how to buck.

Every week Brian relearned how to saddle a horse. There were too many steps for him to remember from one week to the next. But we don't count learning by the lesson. We just learn. Brian and I had some memorable times. And, no, I never did teach him enough to take care of his own horse.